# THE WHIMS OF FATE

## MICHAEL E. THIES

 Writer's Block Press

WRITER'S BLOCK PRESS

For information please contact: Writer's Block Press, 4266 Bonmaur Terrace, Slinger, WI 53086


Michaelethies@michaelethies.com

The Whims of Fate is a work of fiction. Names, characters, places and incidents originate from the author's imagination and are used fictitiously. Any resemblance to actual persons, living or dead, events, or locales is entirely coincidental.

Printed and bound in PRC and the United States of America. Published by Writer's Block Press. All rights reserved.


Family Crests and Badges by Melissa Thies

Maps by Ben Hying

Cover by Christian Bentulan


ISBN: 978-0-9895668-5-8

Library of Congress Control Number: 2023901377


www.michaelethies.com

# CONTENTS

# PROLOGUE

"**B**reathe." Eska sliced down.

With both hands on the hilt, Eirek raised his sword above him.

The force of the blow sent Eirek to his knees. Eska stopped, allowing his apprentice time to recover. "That is why you must breathe. Breathe, brace, and blow."

Eirek shook his fatigue away and nodded. He stood, ready for another round. Apprentice and Guardian touched sword tips, signaling the start of another session.

For a little while, Eska let Eirek take the offensive in order to judge his footwork and the rotation of his torso. His apprentice sliced at him, but the Guardian rolled out of the way, countering with a swipe of his own at the legs. His apprentice jumped over the blade and continued his assault immediately. Still kneeling, Eska blocked and pushed Eirek's sword out of the way, allowing time to stand. The fluidity of Eirek's movements assuaged a portion of Eska's concerns. *He certainly doesn't stand still anymore. But is he ready?*

Eska then began his offensive. With only one or two movement combinations, Eirek performed well and kept good form. As Eska increased the number of combinations, Eirek's posture and focus became sloppy, his breathing sporadic. Noticing this, Eska slowed down his pace. He didn't want to overwhelm Eirek's reflexes; they had already improved so much. But if his apprentice were to ever actually enter a battle with Ether Weapons, it would be a duel for life and death. And in that battle, everything mattered. Eirek didn't have to be as competent as Eska, just lethal enough to survive the changing winds threatening to overrun this system of Gladonus.

Slash. Swipe. Stab. Swipe. Slash. Arm extended, he paused after his follow through. Eirek held his sword with two hands to his left, torso turned forty-five degrees, left foot slightly out with the knee bent for better bracing, and his face full of sweat and determination.

"Good." Eska sheathed his sword. "Your movements are becoming much better, Eirek. And you braced and breathed this time."

Eirek smiled. "I have good teachers." He nodded towards Eska and Ethen who sat on the bench close to the stone court.

"You learn just as quick as—"

"Edwyrd."

"—we teach." Eska turned his head. Tundra stalked towards him. *She's back.* Her pace signaled something amiss. Eska furrowed his brows and cleared his throat. "I am glad to see you have—"

"There is a problem."

Eska clicked his lips. "What kind of problem? I am in the middle of training. Can it wait?"

Ethen joined him, expression pensive.

Tundra took the stone steps leading to the court two at a time. "No. It cannot." She flicked her eyes towards Eirek as she came to stand before Eska.

Eska pursed his lips.

"Do you want me to go, my Guardian?"

Eyes locked on Tundra, Eska said, "No, Eirek. Stay here. This must be important, and you will have to learn how to deal with this kind of news. Tundra, what is it?"

"Hown is gone."

Eska's eyes bulged. "What do you mean, *gone?*"

"All the Hown are dead. Hown is gone."

Eska momentarily regretted having Eirek privy to this conversation, but he was showing truly remarkable progress. Ever since that day he had confronted Eska about the True Kings and Eska had told him how they used to rule over each domain. Not the Twelve. Not the lords or ladies. True Kings. Now, however, they were all but a myth, lost to the fathoms of time, almost as mysterious as the Ancients. Eirek, it seemed, picked up that mantle of his heritage, knowing the trace of blood that he carried with him and had trained as if everything depended upon it.

Ethen crossed his arms over his chest. "But 'ow?"

"Doctor Cere. I think. I'm not sure."

Tundra explained what she had found in Sereya, telling of her execution of Astor Grime and Doctor Cere. When she described her encounter with Doctor Cere, though, Eska noticed that his heart pumped a little irregularly. When she mentioned that Thane had dropped dead in front of her, his stomach churned. If this virus had killed Thane, had it also...

Eska blinked, aware his mouth hung a little agape. *All of it. Planned. But how?* A hand brushed his shoulder.

"Edwyrd?"

Eska shook his head to dispel his dark thoughts. Hopefully his apprentice hadn't seen his confusion; Eska needed to set a precedent of confidence in front of him. . "We have to check something. Follow me."

Eska led them back into the estate and to the telecommunication chamber, not bothering to engage in the conversation that occurred behind him. He needed to check on General Satorus and Captain Arwayn.

"You checked Hown?" Ethen asked.

"Yes, before landing here, I spent a few moments there. Bodies. All bodies. I didn't leave the ship, I didn't need to. I figured if there were any survivors, they would have noticed my approach."

"Edwyrd, do you think it was Luvan?"

Before he said anything, Ethen spoke. "No. Why would 'e betray us like tat?"

Eska thought about the scenario. Someone must have informed Victor Zigarda that they were about to leave for Acquava to attend the Paen funeral. Sure, Eska had dismissed Luvan, but he had remained adamant about his duties until the end. None of the staff had any access to communicators or could use telepathy. It wasn't like Eska to question any of his conseleigh. That left only...

"Cronos? The Sages?" Eska spilled the possibility from his lips as he put his hand on the scanning device.

*Scan complete. Guardian Edwyrd Eska, you may enter.*

The telecommunication door opened in front of him,

the mechanical voice bringing him back again from the thoughts catapulting across his mind. "But why?"

Eska didn't know the answer to Ethen's question. Nor could he ask the Sages why, short of visiting them on Epoch. In truth, though, he didn't need to. The more he thought about it, the more it made sense. A sickening sense, but dark to light all the same.

"Gladima," Eska muttered. "The prophecy."

"The prophecy? Edwyrd, what are you talking about?"

As Eska was about to speak, his apprentice's voice drifted over them all. A soft voice, but with overwhelming authority given to him by the words that had become so hollow and haunted.

"Chosen will be blood from all five domains.

Hope they will bring through chaos, anger, and pain.

Twelve will lose favor, four will regain form.

Bringing with them more death than the Great War."

He turned on the telecommunication machine and, while it was powering up, explained to everyone the meaning that he and his apprentice had derived upon its true interpretation.

"*Chosen* never meant for the Trials. It meant chosen as in who will be responsible for reopening Gladima."

"But what is tere endgame if tey are te ones?"

Eirek offered, "Perhaps they want to get back to the Core themselves? That is what the Twelve wanted."

Eska turned away from the control panel. He waved his hand, dismissing his apprentice's idea. "The Twelve wanted to return because of their deformities. The Sages have always been old. That is how Bane created them."

"Why don't the others talk then?"

Eska glanced at him, encouraging him to keep going.

"During my training with them in the Valley of Power, only Cronos ever spoke. Why is that? Is that how Bane created them?"

Eska's mouth once again hung slack. He covered it quickly. "What exactly happened at the summit? Lead me through it one more time."

Ethen recapped the event, ending with how he and Luvan managed to escape while Cronos fended off the rest of the Twelve.

Eska put his hands on top of the reimaje on his head, opening his chest, and paced the chamber. His eyes widened in lucidity. He spun towards Eirek and his conseleigh. "The staff that Cronos has. It has been him all along!"

"What does the staff have to do with anything?" Tundra asked.

"It's called Foresight. The name inclines one to believe that the possessor can see the future. As to the limitations or the actual functionality of the Ether Weapon, I am unsure."

"Are you suggesting that the Ether Weapons may have an additional function?"

"I..." Eska looked at Eirek. "Apprentice Mourse mentioned the idea to me when we were practicing one day." Eska unsheathed his sword, revealing the smoky gray and amethyst lines that ran up and down its body. "Eirek, could you?"

Before Eska had even finished his question, Eirek had unsheathed his sword and handed it to Eska. He showcased both of them.

"Do you see how Eirek's hilt is different?" Eska waited for their acknowledgement. "Eirek noted that it looks more like a zircha hilt than the hilt of an Ether Weapon."

"So Apprentice Mourse's blade can change?"

Eska shook his head. "No. At least, if it can, we haven't found a way to activate it yet."

"And yours?"

"I do not know, Tundra."

Eska handed back Eirek's sword and looked at his blade. He caressed it with his fingers, sliding them over the fuller. *Is there a secret in you that even I haven't yet discovered? Did the Twelve even know?*

"Edwyrd, if it is Cronos, it would make sense given what Cere told me. He said that Zigarda wasn't the only one who wanted to see you overthrown."

Although he wasn't sure of what they wanted, he was sure now of the Sage's transgression. With such a weapon at Cronos's disposal, however, it made solving the problem much more difficult, as its limitations weren't fully known. If it could predict the future, as its name suggested, then it would make sense how Zigarda's envoy came to Hown at exactly the right time to deliver his gift. If it could predict the future, then it would make sense that Eirek would suggest to Eska that the Twelve be sealed inside and that he would oblige. But the question that gnawed at Eska was if those premonitions were separate or linked. The latter made it seem as though there were limitations to how much one could see in advance, but the former suggested that at any time the user could glimpse what was ahead. Both proved problematic. And with what scope could Foresight see? So far, it had seemed that it had only been his actions, but could it foresee the actions of others like his conseleigh? Or Eirek? All of it made one thing certain to Eska—the prophecy seemed determined to run its course.

Eska tapped his foot and ruminated for a while. Everyone did. Only the hum of the server and monitor behind him brought Eska back to what he had originally wanted to check in the first place. He turned back to the telecommunication screen and dialed General Satorus's number immediately. It rang, but no one answered.

He tried again to the same effect.

Eska sighed. "The general's not answering."

"Tat means…"

"The Hown are gone."

"Yes, the Hown are truly gone," Eska conceded. "And it seems that likely means one more thing." Eska crossed his arms over his chest.

"What's that?"

Before he answered Tundra, he massaged his forehead with one hand. Exhaling deeply, he looked up again at the others. "It means Hydro Paen is still on the loose."

# PART 1 - PLAN A

CHAPTER 1

# BLOODLINE

For over a day, Cain had walked through Kane. The notorious heat of the firelands never dissipated, as if beneath the black that covered the land, magma boiled, keeping it warm to the touch. With each clacking of hooves, Cain expected to see someone from his father's company in pursuit, but it was always just a firehorse. They galloped freely, manes and tails of fire flowing behind them in the wind like ribbons.

The freedom of his disappearance, or the apparently inconsequential nature of it, stirred Cain. *Why hasn't Father sent anyone to take me yet? Surely he must know about my absence by now.* Cain kept his thoughts to himself, hoping they would remain only thoughts, but the more time he spent with Stannon, the more Cain recognized how akin they were. The height, the hair. A similar lanky body type told Cain that he was muscular underneath the fiery shirt that made him look more like a walking flame than a mere guide. Cain supposed a flame and a guide were also akin; both lit the way for those in darkness, and perhaps following him would answer some of Cain's questions.

"How much farther?"

"Brother, we are almost there."

Cain stopped. That word. It annoyed him more than it should. It called back memories he didn't want. The weight of his father's axe in his hand. The voice of pleading leniency that he couldn't oblige. The gust of wind that struck him as he brought down the axe upon the man's neck. The blood that abraded his face afterwards.

Cain crumbled to his knees. "No. I cannot do this. I cannot. I need to leave."

"Brother..."

Cain whipped out his baton and axe, chest heaving. "I *am not* your brother." He stared at Stannon's face, trying his best to ignore the similarities. He pushed himself up and turned around to leave.

He took a few steps.

No one followed him.

Then he took a few more, expecting Stannon to plead with him, but the other man remained silent. Cain continued walking until he stopped on his own volition. Emptiness lay before him. Complete darkness engulfed him now. No one was coming to his rescue. And with dusk fast approaching, he knew another dawn would rise before there was any hope of finding him.

Defeated and alone, Cain looked back over his shoulder. His guide still waited where Cain had left him, his outfit a lantern in this overwhelming abyss of blackness. With a heavy breath, Cain turned around and went back to him.

"There is nothing back there for you, brother."

"I will come with you, but please do not call me brother."

Stannon silently acquiesced and continued forward. Cain trudged on, following the man to whatever destiny the Ancients would submit him to, not bothering to count hours, not bothering to feel emotions. What did it matter? By the time anyone found him, it wouldn't make much difference. The feelings he thought in Lorian fell like rain into a chasm so deep that Cain couldn't care to try to find it.

At the first glimpse of firelight and the sound of chants and murmurs of unrecognizable voices, his senses awakened.

Stannon led Cain through a village made of red clay houses and roofs of black straw. Cain couldn't help but wonder if the straw had been formed from the leftover branches of the Yggdrasil tree when it fell on their land and if perhaps the red clay was the earth made permanently red by the fires of that infamous day. He also couldn't help but notice how very similar it looked to Blen when he had visited the town during the fourth trial. But that couldn't be possible, could it?

Paraded in front of them, Cain fell prey to whispers and watchful, orange eyes burning with intrigue. The fiery eyes matched their hair. Most of the men were tall, some even taller than Cain. Even the shortest, though, stood taller than Cain's father. Hundreds came to see him, lined up in families with the shortest child in front and the tallest man or woman in back, each positioned in a way that none missed the opportunity to observe this foreigner.

At the end of the village stood a man, perhaps half a hand taller than Cain. Like Cain, his lanky body was corded in columns of lean muscle. Like Cain, there was no stubble on his clean-shaven face. Like Cain, glasses sat at the brim of his nose.

Five paces away, Stannon stopped, and so Cain did. The elder in front of him, arms crossed over his chest, surveyed Cain, orange eyes scrutinizing him, meticulously dissecting his physicality, and even piercing him on a deeper level, as if determining his worth. They were the eyes of a leader, and a passion sat inside them that could not be easily extinguished.

For the first time in this valley of fire, Cain felt chills run up his arms.

Arms still crossed, the man looked at Stannon. "Thank you for bringing my son home, Stannon."

A shiver passed over Cain. *Son?*

The man turned his attention back to Cain. "Come inside, Cain, there is much we need to talk about." He turned to enter a house, similar in material to the others but larger.

Cain's eyes widened, and he pushed Stannon aside. "How do you know my name?"

The man bent low at the threshold of the house. "If you want to know, come inside."

Cain eyed the man as he disappeared within, but a gentle shove from Stannon beside him pushed him to the doorstep. He looked inside, cautious of stepping over the threshold, as if doing so would propel Cain into the unknown. Sweat dampened his hands, and he tried to rub it off on his tunic and pants.

"Cain, come." A voice beckoned to him.

Cain obliged. Bowing his head, he ducked and entered. "Why did you say that?"

"Please, the door. Then come and sit here across from me. We have much to discuss." The man stared at him. His hands were folded together nicely on the table. On his left arm, a scar ran across the entire length of his forearm.

Hesitant, Cain searched for any traps or signs of anyone else.

"No one else is here. And I'm not armed."

A sconce aglow helped Cain realize the man spoke the truth. Well, almost. While Cain knew the man carried no weapons, he observed a long spear that hung on the wall, placed upon two skulls. Keeping one arm on the baton to his left hip, he closed the door and took a seat in front of the older man.

"How do you know my name?"

"Your mother told me about you."

"My mother? How do you know her?"

"Dawn came to me twenty-five years ago."

His mother's name sent tingles up Cain's arm and neck. He rolled his shoulders, trying to relieve himself of the sensation. "My mom has never been to Kane."

The man smirked. "As far as you know, Son. But she has. She came alone and afraid. Why? Well, only the winds of fate know that, but perhaps she did not want to be found, and so she thought Kane would be the best place for her."

Cain took a deep breath. Could this be the story his mom had alluded to but never explained? "Go on."

"When three men came to collect her, I protected her. Not one of them survived."

Cain focused on the hanging lance more. His eyes widened. *An Ether Weapon!* The skin of the lance held the signature amethyst coloring coated with swirls of gray clouds.

"What is its name?"

"*Protector.* It has been passed down in my family since the Smiths forged the weapons when Gladonus was created. Did you know that each planet had a native king chosen for it, back before the Great War?"

Instinctively, Cain shook his head. But then he bit his lower lip. Did he know this? It sounded familiar, but where had he heard it?

"Each king had the skill, the stamina, and the strength to rival that of anyone in any of the Ancients' cabinet. And the only reason they were never included is because they lacked First Blood. In fact, because of their lack of First Blood, they were not ever acknowledged by the Ancients Lyoen or Bane. They became powerful, however, after receiving a necklace that granted them the ability to bond with mighty creatures, the Four Creatures of Legend. When the Smiths were banished from Gladima, they stole some of the Ether Weapons and knew that nothing would upset those of Gladima more than giving them to those kings and teaching them the words of Power. So they did, and almost overnight, the four kings became more powerful than even the Twelve. In fact, with the ability to bond, they rivaled the lineage of the Ancients."

More shivers crept into Cain. This was too much to process and digest. Where to start? Fumbling for something, anything, Cain massaged his temples. "Are you telling me that the Ancients had offspring?"

"They most certainly did. One of them helped the people of the first king of Pyre escape death. That is a story for a different day, however. What is important is that because of the actions of that man, a group of Pyre's people ended up here, in Kane. And for more than seven hundred and fifty years now, we have kept the lineage of that first king alive. The True Kings."

Cain gulped. His breathing intensified. His posture straightened. That is what Eirek had told him about before the stump. Before his feet had carried them there, as if fate was guiding him all along. "Did you say True Kings?"

The man's eyes widened. "So you know?"

"I..." Cain shook his head again. "No, not really. I only heard it in passing. In books that I used to read," Cain lied.

"You and I are what remains of that bloodline."

## CHAPTER 2

# SEASICKNESS

Zain wanted to lurch overboard, his stomach churning as if he had drunk spoiled milk. The waves were heavy, sure; they had been for a few days, but there hadn't been a storm. If anything, it seemed the waves were pushing them closer to Ka'Che in a conspiracy of fate with the eastward winds.

Zain opened his mouth and yakked. Nothing came out. *What did I eat?*

He thought back to the fish and potatoes that had been his lunch. There was nothing odd about it. Many others had eaten them as well. They weren't sick. With one arm draped around the side of the ship, he spied Nyrin going about his daily training with Issac. Neither of them seemed impeded by stomach pains. Normally, Zain faced the winner of their duel, but unless the pain vanished soon, Zain wouldn't be partaking in any of those activities today.

Once more, he tried to puke his guts overboard. Unsuccessful, he held onto the ship with one hand and clutched his stomach with the other, hoping the pain would subside momentarily.

Using the least amount of energy possible, Zain turned around, wanting to gauge the fight of his comrades. Perhaps it would get better if he stared at something other than the sea. Something he enjoyed.

Issac's boot heaved towards Nyrin, but the young boy was fast. He dodged the kick with a side-step and caught Issac's leg with his hands, hoping to capitalize on the failure. If Nyrin had more muscle on him, the tactic would have worked. In theory, it still should have. But Issac must have planned for Nyrin to dodge and try something because he continued forward with his follow-through, not letting Nyrin throw him off-balance. With weight and momentum on his side,

Issac pushed his body forward and down and brought a fist to connect to the left side of Nyrin's face. The match finished.

Issac looked over to Zain. "I'm feeling good today. You ready to give it a go?"

Zain's stomach grumbled. He covered it meagerly with his arm. "No. I'm not. Go get Garie."

"What's wrong?" Issac helped Nyrin up, and they both walked over to Zain. "You have the face of a man about to be hanged."

"Is it really that bad?" Zain touched his face and felt sweat.

"You look as if you belong on death's door."

Zain blinked, speechless at both comments. "Argh." Stomach pain lanced through him again.

"I will go get Garie," Issac said. "I suggest you go get Gabrielle or another Gracie's student. They should be able to help."

Why hadn't Zain thought of that? Surely one of their potions could help him with this. "Thanks." Zain pushed himself off of the railing.

"You need help?" Nyrin asked.

Zain shook his head. "I think I can manage."

Zain half-walked, half-hobbled to the other side of the ship and then went below deck. While Gabrielle may not be able to help him due to her impaired vision, he knew that Carla Sonetta may be with her, as she almost always was, so he went to Gabrielle's room and rapped his knuckles on the door. Sure enough, Carla Sonetta answered.

"Gabrielle, Mr. Berrese is here to see you."

"Zain?"

With as much of a smile as he could muster, Zain asked. "Can I come in?"

"Of course, Mr. Berrese." Carla opened the door and ushered him inside. "You look awful. Is something the matter?"

With one arm still over his stomach, Zain plopped down onto a bench next to a large chest. He groaned faintly. "My stomach. It hurts."

To his left, Gabrielle sat on a wooden stool in front of a mirror. She was looking at it and playing with her hair as if she could see what she was doing, but Zain knew that couldn't be true. Zakk had robbed Gabrielle of her vision in her last duel, and all the apothecaries thus far had told her that nothing could be done for her eyes. Forever in darkness she would live.

"Did someone forget to say their prayers this morning?" Carla asked.

Zain had forgotten; that was true, but he couldn't let them know that. Nor did he see why it was relevant. "No."

"Well, then perhaps it is just seasickness."

"And if I hadn't said my prayers?" Zain arched his eyebrow at the head-mistress.

"Guilt. Regret. Shame. Loss. Loneli—"

Zain waved his hand. "I get your point. I guess it's seasickness."

"Well then, Gabrielle can help you with that. Fare—"

"Wait!" Zain raised up his hand.

"Yes, Mr. Berrese?"

"I think it's better if you stay."

"And why is that?"

"I feel queasy."

"You feel *queasy*?" She repeated, unimpressed. "I already told you—"

"Listen, for the last thirty minutes or so, my stomach has been in knots. I've wanted to throw up but can't. I've never felt like this before."

Carla Sonetta laughed. "Such a trivial thing Gabrielle can take care of."

Zain stammered. "No offense. Isn't mixing potions ... uhmm ... complicated?"

"It is as complicated as you want it to be. Alleviating a simple stomachache, that is child's play. I have full faith in Gabrielle, even with her condition. Turning someone invisible, now that is a whole different process."

Zain blinked. "Wait. There are potions to turn someone invisible but not one to heal the blind?"

Carla Sonetta laughed. "In theory, Mr. Berrese. Myths mention Galan making something invisible long ago, but it has never been replicated because the ingredients are next to impossible to acquire. And eyesight is particularly troubling due to the condition of each eye, the nerves, cornea ... I'm sure you understand. Invisibility is a whole-body process."

Zain righted himself. Suddenly, his stomachache didn't seem so bad. Intrigue was besting it. "What do you need?"

"A blind person's tears. A dead person's blood. And a shapeshifter's skin. And then a matching bond to tie the ingredients together. I suppose we could get one of the ingredients here, hmm." Carla Sonetta smirked. "Anyway, luckily the only thing you need to make invisible is your stomach pain. Gabrielle can help you with that. I am positive. Gabrielle?"

"It shouldn't be so difficult, Lady Sonetta."

"Good. Then I'll leave you two alone. Have more faith, Mr. Berrese. Often times those who seem the weakest are actually the strongest." She left, closing the door behind her.

Gabrielle scooted closer to Zain on her wooden stool. She unlatched the chest next to Zain and began blindly feeling the vials and concoctions that lined the multi-fold chest. Her fingertips strummed against them, as if she were running them across a piano keyboard. Watching her work so deftly mesmerized Zain.

"How can you know what you are looking for?"

"Every student receives a chest upon a formal acceptance into za academy. I am sure Gazo's gives you somezing as well."

"A sword," Zain admitted. "And books."

Gabrielle giggled. "Consider potions our sword, Zain. And each chest has za same dimensions as every ozer chest. Inside, za potions are arranged in za exact same way according to za table chart of elements. Part of our training process is to know zis chest by heart. What you are looking for is here." She plucked out a tube that was five columns in and two from the top. She handed it to Zain.

Zain rotated the container of yellow powder in front of him. "What is it?"

"Turmeric root. Mix it wiz hot water and it will make a tea zat should take away your stomach pain."

He took off the cap and sniffed it. Slight notes of ginger and orange came into his nose. "It smells great. Is it really that easy?"

"For zis, yes." She giggled. "Not everyzing is so simple. Women get stomach pains all za time. Zis is our lifeline."

"Thank you." Zain stood up, but then he realized his stomach didn't feel any pain. He sat back down and stood up again. Nothing. He patted his tummy. "That's odd."

"What is?"

"My pain. It's gone." Zain rubbed his stomach now, making sure no pain still existed. He sat back down. "Maybe when I smelled it?"

Gabrielle hummed. "Possibly, but doubtful."

"Then how?" He gave the vial of powder to Gabrielle.

After doing a quick calculation with her fingertips, she put it away. "My guess is zat you were so distracted wiz me zat you forgot all about your pain." She turned back to Zain and felt for his hand.

Zain gripped hers and felt her squeeze. "You took away my pain?"

"Women can do many zings, Zain Berrese." She smirked and leaned in closer, her lips pursed.

Zain accepted her invitation and kissed her, their lips meeting as his arms reached around her in a passionate embrace. They were alone, together, safe. At least, for the moment. She closed the chest with one hand, locking it, her lips and focus never leaving him all the while.

Gabrielle bit Zain's lower lip and pulled back. "Do you feel better?"

Zain floundered at his words. "Uh huh." He could feel his heart racing. "What else can women do?"

Gabrielle tucked a strand of hair behind her ear. She smirked and put her lips against his ear. "I'm about to show you."

## CHAPTER 3

# THE WOMAN OF THE WIND

"Approaching atmospheric controls."

Woken by the mechanical voice of C-Bot, Hydro blinked, regaining consciousness. His eyes widened. Dumbfounded, his lips trembled, and his breathing intensified. Deep space. Dark and vast and empty. *How did I....*

*I took you here.*

"You *took* me," Hydro muttered. He looked around the ship as if expecting to see Anne, but she never appeared.

*You passed out in that Twelve-forsaken crystal palace, and I did what needed to be done.*

Hydro gulped. Slowly, he felt the darkness come back into that crystal room, how Anne wasn't actually Anne, but Desmós, and how the black serpent suffocated him into submission. How Hydro had passed out there. Cold and alone. And now he was here. Wherever that was.

Hydro didn't want to think about the implications of that. His face flushed, the area around his neck now burning a little hotter. "Where are we headed?" Hydro glanced at the control panel. Veins ran through it from when the Hown had fought his ship, but it seemed to be functioning in the necessary capacity. "Agrost?"

"Approaching atmospheric controls."

Hydro noticed the control station only minutes away. If they hadn't already scanned his ship yet, they would soon. Hydro bolted from his seat and stood in front of the scanner. He had no idea if the device still worked or not after the fight with the Hown, but he could only hope. Otherwise, this visit would be much shorter than necessary.

"Mr. Dorian Gallahan, where are you flying in from today?"

Hydro looked at the monitor in front of him, which displayed the identity the control center saw. "Onkh," he said.

"And which nation do you have business with?"

"Mistral."

"What business do you have in Mistral?"

Hydro read his job description. Dorian Gallahan had been a collector of minerals. Not too far off from the truth. "Excavation. Mining."

"Very well. Follow one of the Atmos down to Briseas. You'll dock there."

The connection cut.

Hydro exhaled.

He returned to his pilot seat and let C-Bot follow the ship in front of him to Briseas. For the first time in months, awe overtook Hydro as the floating isles of Mistral came into view, allowing him to forget about his current predicament for a stint. Sky traffic that looked like tiny birds fluttered around the islands in flocks, driving in and out of the clouds that hung about the air. Most clouds swirled below them, though, shielding them from the view of those on the mainland.

After docking the main vehicle in Briseas's spaceport, Hydro moved to the left leg of the polymorphous machine, making sure to bring along his portable radar. With a push of a few buttons, Hydro ejected a hovercraft equipped with credentials for Agrost. He drove out of the main docking station with no time caught floundering around on cameras. Truly, Dr. Cere had thought of everything when he put together this machine, and he wondered how the doctor fared now. How did Zigarda fare? He knew Zigarda was on Mistral for the time being. Well, at least, he should still be on Mistral according to their last conversation, but finding him in this nation would be troublesome and risky. He didn't know how many Hown were after him, and he considered it a lucky stroke of fate that he had managed to escape the first encounter with the hunters. He couldn't count on luck in a second rendezvous. Plus, Zigarda had the crystal scry. If he wanted to learn of Hydro's location, all he would have to do was use some of the blood he had collected.

After syncing the radar with the hovercraft's control panel, the hovercraft put itself into auto-pilot mode. It flew away from the capital, off into the seamless sea of sky. Hydro was uncharacteristically grateful. Not having to pilot the craft allowed him to forget about the situation that had been incessantly itching at him ever since waking up in deep space. It freed his mind and allowed him to take in the beauty of where he was. The birds flying in the sky. The clouds. Off in the distance, he even saw a great waterfall spilling down to the lands that lay below. This nation was more majestic than he could have imagined. Hydro drank it all in, intoxicated by the moment of peace and serenity. He was sure that it wouldn't last. He was hunting down jewels, and each jewel had been more difficult than the last. He wondered if he would even survive long enough to see them all gathered or if his quest would come to an end before then. His close calls attested to the possibility of that. And his gut told him that this, this adventure, this folly of his, as Len would have said, would come to an end. All good things did. But the birds floating freely in the sky, gliding on the drafts and currents, no real goal or location in mind, made him believe, even if just for a second, that he, too, could escape his own predicament.

That vision vanished, though, when a family of clouds engulfed Hydro's hovercraft. With nothing else to see, Hydro closed his eyes and focused on his breath until the bleeping of the radar stopped.

*Jewel detected.*

The mechanical voice woke Hydro.

In front of him, a small island floated. Tall and thick clouds of white surrounded it from all angles, making it invisible to anyone who didn't dare to brave the cluster of clouds. A cave mouth opened wide in the vertical face of the island, but there was no place to land his hovercraft. Once again, he would have to disembark and face this jewel alone.

He steered the ship to the mouth of the cave, pushed a button to keep it in hover mode, and then opened the dome to the hovercraft. Instantly, he noticed the difference in air quality. Oxygen levels were low. And it was cold. But not as cold as Crestal's Palace. It was a different cold, one from being so high up in the atmosphere. He jumped off the ship and made it inside the cavern, feeling a little warmer after escaping the buffeting winds.

Within the first few steps, he already felt winded. Even on Mount Volan there had been air, but here it was scarce. Hydro staggered his breaths in cadence to his paces.

Tiled moss-green aventurine floors were an odd sight to him, almost as odd as the jade pillars that helped support the midsize cavity he was in. Blue moss that hung from above cast a glow, acting like torches, showing him his surroundings. A hallway twisted deeper into the cave. To his left, he saw an onyx desk with thick emerald vines sprouting from the floor to wrap their way around its legs. Hydro walked towards the desk and noticed something even more peculiar—a pen.

Hydro's hand went to his hilt. *Who's here?*

*Hydro Paen, I sense a presence here. A presence I have not felt for quite some time. You should be careful.*

Hydro stopped. He bit his lip and surveyed the lobby. Was someone waiting for him? Did someone live here? Was this a trap? He unsheathed his sword and, while holding it out in front of him, advanced down the hallway.

With every step he took, he could feel the air growing scarcer. Soon, it would be a luxury that Hydro may not even be able to afford. Hydro coughed. *Damn—*

A squall lifted Hydro from the ground. It pushed him down the hallway until he came to a stop in a large, circular blue room. The walls seemed alive in five places, like paints continually mixing on a mural. And although that was quite an astonishing sight, Hydro couldn't look away from the woman that stood before him.

Her eyes, a mixture of purple and blue, glowed. Hair as lush and blue as her lips flowed down past her neck. A transparent gown barely covered her exposed body, pale like moonlight. Wind swirled around her, ravishing her hair and gown, but it never got out of control.

Had he seen her before? No. Impossible. But why then did she look familiar? Hydro choked. Her winds held him aloft, and a tendril coiled around his neck, cutting off his air. He put a hand to his neck, fingers useless against her.

She waved a hand and let him down.

He collapsed, sucking in air, hoarding it for the precious moments he could. With one hand on his knee, he got to his feet. "Who are you?"

"I may ask you the same thing." She floated several paces away from him, surveying him and his weapon.

*It is her. Zeph.*

Hydro tilted his neck when he heard Desmós's voice.

"Who are you with?"

He turned his attention back to her. "I am alone."

"You lie." She waved her hand, and a wave of paralysis swept over Hydro. "You are the one, are you not?"

No longer able to speak, only think, Hydro stiffened his neck, cowering his head as far back as he could as she walked towards him. His movements were futile. Her Power was too great; he had never felt a spell like this in his life. How could she do it? How could she freeze him in place like this?

"My daughter told me about you." She circled him once and then stared at him.

The spell intensified. Hydro coughed and choked on his own saliva. Button by button, she pried apart his tunic, and as she did so, she kept her eyes of blue and purple locked with his. Now he knew who she reminded him of—the three-eyed prophetess.

A pain erupted in his chest. Power coursed through his veins. Something from inside of him forced its way into his consciousness. No longer could he act on his own, only watch as his body acted for him—for Desmós.

"*Maa*," he pushed out.

Head still locked forward, he noticed the aventurine walls shifting inwards towards the woman. It formed a barrier between Hydro and her. Still, he suffocated. Air was precious now. "*Vesi. Salama. Palo.*" He could no longer see. Even though his head felt ready to explode, his mind continued thinking, and his lips continued repeating the four words of Power continuously. "*Maa. Vesi. Salama. Palo. Maa. Vesi. Salama. Palo. Maa. Vesi. Salama...*"

His body collapsed on the ground, but Desmós gave him no time for rest. Forced to stand, now unencumbered by whatever spell had held him, he lunged forward, blade in hand. The green walls of the cavern split, and he saw a flash of a void he couldn't fathom. Complete blackness, as if no life lived there or no life had ever lived there, so pure, like the ever-expanding continuum of deep space.

As soon as he invaded the blackness, however, it returned to the room he knew. Centipedes of electricity crawled around the walls. Fireflies lit with life for a brief second, only to die a moment later. Clouds of blue rain burst and regurgitated their contents on the floor, only to evaporate. In the middle of it all stood the woman with blue hair.

The sword slashed its way down to meet her. Something caught him and held his sword an arm's length above her body. He was close enough to see the light of her glowing eyes reflecting on his skin, and he could now make out little sparks of a light blue color, countless in number, all of them fluttering around him. They flew into his mouth, choking him once more. Try as he might, he couldn't move his body, even with Desmós commanding him. Instead, he thought spells once more.

"*Palo.*" All around Hydro, a blue flame erupted as if he burned himself alive, and he heard the shrill cries of the creatures plaguing him. "*Vesi.*" Almost instantaneously, the room filled with water. "*Salama.*" Bolts of lightning coursed through the water and all around the lady. She seemed unaffected. "*Maa.*" The walls closed, and once again Hydro's vision died.

He dropped to his knees, panting and gasping as if he were foolish enough to try to find oxygen in space. Beads of sweat ran down his face. Forced to his feet once more, he jumped and spun his sword at the same time. Midair, the blockade of rock vanished. His eyes closed. There was a faint clack. He landed and opened his eyes. Blood flowed from the woman's side, and a piece of her gown fluttered to the floor.

The woman punched the air in front of her. "*Voima!*"

An invisible force surged against Hydro, and he flew backwards, slamming against the wall. No pain entered his body, for Desmós was his adrenaline now. And there. On the floor. *A jewel.*

The woman bent down to grab it.

*"Maa."*

Spires flew out of the ground to meet her. She floated backwards, avoiding being impaled, and lifted her hand up to the sky. The jewel floated. Hydro's hand raised, and the spires instantaneously became a wall. The jewel was trapped on his side.

*"Palo. Salama. Vesi. Maa."* His lips said the spells in rapid succession. His fingers shook. The jewel collided against the wall, trying to get back to its owner. The spells were held even as his vision blurred. When the jewel clanked to the floor and rolled backwards, Hydro released his Power.

The earthy wall disappeared. Behind it now, he saw no woman, just spinning sections of a blue wall. He gasped again. His accelerated heart rate began to slow. As it slowed, pain coursed through him, and he screamed in agony. Spasms controlled him, bringing him crashing to the cold, aventurine floor. Trying his best, he pushed himself to his knees, only to collapse again. The jewel was a hundred paces away. He tried standing again but couldn't. Resigning himself to the floor, he crawled towards it with his elbows, thoughts controlling him all the while, hoping to get answers from his necklace.

*Who was that woman?*

*Her name is Zeph.*

*What Power did she have? I have never...* Only twenty paces in, Hydro collapsed and waited for energy to come back to him. He breathed and breathed some more. With the woman no longer there, he could actually breathe again. *I have never seen or felt such a—*

*She controlled the wind. Even the air in some regards.*

*How...* Continuing to crawl on his elbows and forearms, Hydro thought back to the elements. *There are only four elements: earth, water, fire, and electricity.*

*Apparently, that is a lie.*

Hydro crawled forward. *What... what did you do? How did you beat it? What did I see beyond the wall?*

*Blackness, Hydro Paen. Pure blackness. Wind is everywhere that the air is. I created an environment where it could not be present. With all the spells combined together, I created darkness like space, and air cannot survive in space.*

*How did you know it would work?*

*I didn't. I felt that it was my only option.*

Hydro dragged his body forward on his left forearm. Then he did the same with his right. Then, using his left again, he reached out, now within range of the jewel. He felt it on his fingertips and stretched a little more. Once under his palm, he secured it and brought it to his chest.

*My body. I... I have never felt this before.* Hydro turned around on his stomach now. He looked at the spinning sections on the walls. *What are those?*

*Portals. I did not know some of them yet existed.*

*What do they do?*

*They can transfer you onto any domain in this system.*

*What? How?*

*Through Power. Ancient Power.*

Using his measure of renewed strength, Hydro pushed himself to all fours and then to one knee. He noticed a trail of blood leading into one of the portals. Hydro managed to stand and walked along the wall, standing in front of each portal for a few moments, finally ending in front of the one where the trail of blood had led.

*So the Ancients created them?*

*No. The Smiths did, out of revenge.*

*Revenge? For what?*

*The Smiths were Lyoen's first four creations, just as the Sages were Bane's first four. Besides the Ancients themselves, these were skilled and powerful people of the highest order. After the Smiths were finished forging the Ether Weapons, Lyoen heard that Bane, along with his Sages, were creating something even more powerful. They were creating something to bring death in spite of Lyoen. Lyoen ordered her Smiths to learn what Bane planned on creating, and they did learn. When they were caught in the act, Bane wished to kill them all, but Lyoen said it was upon her orders and fought for their safety. Bane demanded that two of them be killed and the rest banished, otherwise he would bring his newly found weapon, Power, onto her and her tribe. For the good of her tribe, she obeyed and turned her back on the Smiths. Bane even forced her to pick which two would die. She killed two in hopes of saving thousands. But war was destined anyway. The Smiths created these to whisper the words they had learned from Bane to the other planets and make Gladima no longer special.*

Hydro gulped and continued to stare into the spinning portal of blue. It succeeded in hypnotizing him to the extent where he reached out his hand and took a step forward, wanting to feel it for himself. An invisible force, however, held him in place.

*You cannot go through there. She will kill us if you do.*

*But she is weakened.*

*If you could not beat her here, Hydro Paen, you will not beat her outside. Here we had the advantage of an enclosed space.*

*Why does that matter?*

*It takes less time for me to envelope her in my Power, thus canceling her spell. It limits the amount of Power that she can use. Out there, wherever she went, only a few could stand to her might.*

*Like who?*

*My brother.*

*Brother?*

*Yes. Now, let's go.*

Hydro's heart burned. A storm of Power washed over him. It pulled his arm back from the winding portal. Forced to retreat, he left the cave, the newly acquired jewel in his satchel. Weighing more heavily than it, though, was the knowledge that he couldn't have fought Desmós's Power. And while Desmós had kept him alive, the imbalance in their connection was a significant conundrum Hydro would have to deal with. Or die trying.

## CHAPTER 4

# SUBPOENA

A slow smile spread over Luvan's face as he looked down at the envelope. A heavy hand came to his shoulder.

"It truly is magnificent, isn't it?"

Before answering Senator Numos's question, Luvan let his finger trace over all twelve sigils crested in wax that sealed the subpoena for Guardian Eska to appear before the families in power and face trial. The signatures and wax sealings were collected in the week following the initial meeting, after the document had been drafted, reviewed, revised, and then reviewed again. Every single nation had voted for the impeachment process to continue, and Luvan would be the one responsible for handing over the subpoena to the Guardian of the Core.

"Edwyrd will not know what to think."

Behind him, Numos chuckled. "Do you ever think he imagined having to face another trial? I imagine this next one will not be as favorable as the first."

Luvan brushed his fingers over the wax sealings once more, feeling all twelve of them, and then flipping the envelope over, revealing Guardian Eska's full name. "Do you believe we can actually impeach him?"

"We have made it this far, have we not? We have laid the seeds of dissent and planted them firmly in the ground. During Eska's trial, they will be sown. I am sure."

Luvan sighed. He stood up. "It will be my pleasure to deliver this to him today."

"There is nothing quite like revenge, is there?"

Luvan furrowed his brows. "This isn't so much about revenge, senator. This is about propriety, as I've told you before."

Numos laughed off the tension and waved an arm at Luvan. "Call it what you will, but it's change nonetheless, as I told you that first afternoon we discussed this plan of ours. And Gladonus needs it more than ever now."

"Yes. Change." He barely managed to speak the word. He looked at the letter once more and bit his lower lip.

"What is wrong? Is your interest in this waning?" Numos placed a hand on Luvan's shoulder to bring him back to attention.

"No. But I do need to get answers from you before I deliver this to Guardian Eska."

Numos stepped back, eyebrows arched. "Oh? What words can I speak to you?"

"True ones. This plan of yours was conducted by Victor Zigarda, was it not?" Luvan didn't look away from Numos's eyes.

Numos kept his face stoic but didn't respond for a few moments. "Yes. It was. What of it?"

*Good. He didn't lie.* "Because I am wondering how Victor knew about the meeting in the first place. I never told him."

"You didn't visit him in Mendeck?"

Luvan shook his head. "I did. He wasn't there. The entirety of his Web had been vacated. Scrolling through his telecommunication chamber logs, I noticed he had made a recent call to you. Is he staying at your dwelling?"

Numos set down his cane. He massaged his left hand with his right one. "And if he is, what difference does it make? He had to come to Mistral regardless, correct?"

"Correct. It makes no difference, but letting him stay at your place suggests further collusion."

"I don't understand your meaning."

"We've portrayed the apprentice to be inadequate. His conseleigh to be out of line. But have you ever stopped to consider what change you are bringing about? Who will take over Guardian Eska's mantle? Or is this about getting Victor Zigarda to become Guardian of the Core?"

"Victor and I have discussed that possibility, yes. Would he be such a bad Guardian? He was selected for his own Trials once upon a time."

Luvan circumvented the question. "So, the evidence shown in the meeting is all real? Zain. Gabrielle. Everything?"

"What makes you believe it isn't?"

"You didn't answer the question."

"You saw it for yourself. Didn't you? Unless my own eyes deceived me, I would say for certain that was Zain and Gabrielle."

"But this talk of shapeshifters from Lord Vangle. It concerns me. Just as much as his sudden disappearance."

Numos harrumphed. "He probably just had a stomachache. We are only human, after all. These things happen."

"A stomachache? You expect me to believe that? He still has yet to come back."

"A stomachache, business to attend to, what does it really matter?"

"It may weaken our actual leverage against Guardian Eska."

"We still got the advisor to stamp his approval, did we not? He will be the voice of Ka'Che now. Or, perhaps, Lord Vangle will join us for the actual hearing. Who is to know such things? But, at the end of the day, what does it really matter? It is still a voice of democracy speaking up against an unfit Guardian."

"If he is truly unfit, that is one thing, Senator. The evidence I have provided I know is true."

"And mine?" Senator Numos's mouth hung agape. "You don't believe mine? Come now, Luvan, don't tell me you are starting to believe in such eccentricities."

"I was there on the Core when Zain Berrese had his own hearing for his actions during the second trial. I do not find him to be a liar. Much less the kind of person to lie to his uncle."

Numos guffawed. "And that is exactly my point, dear old Luvan." The senator clapped his shoulder. "The Zain you saw from the Trials has changed. He went from being that man to being the one you saw on the screen. And that is why we are now doing what we are doing. Clearly, something changed in Zain to cause him to reject Guardian Eska's offer. Only a fool would turn down being the Guardian of the Core, am I right?"

Luvan pushed his tongue to his upper lip. He waited for the senator to stop laughing. "But I do not think it from any injury. He suffered the blow to the head before his hearing, and while at his hearing, he spoke competently."

"Well then, there was the shame in losing to Gabrielle during the weapons tournament. Imagine training your whole life for something, only to be outdone by a superior. That coupled with the fact that his chances were sabotaged by a scoundrel of a prince? Surely, that would affect anyone. Or perhaps he didn't take to the heat on Pyre as well as the others. I, myself, found it quite intolerable, even with a cooling ring."

"While still a part of Edwyrd's conseleigh, I do know that there was an attempt to sabotage the Trials. That is why Zain Berrese didn't accept. I saw the footage myself."

"I don't know what you're speaking of. I merely thought it was Zain's own prerogative not to accept."

"I tell you now that it certainly wasn't. Something happened on that volcano during the fourth trial, and I know Conseleigh Iycel was meant to investigate it. My intuition tells me she completed her job as Lord Grime is now deceased."

"I still do not see your point."

"On that call log in Victor Zigarda's Web, I noticed he had made a call to Sereya. It makes sense to me then that this plan to overthrow Edwyrd was originally conceived even before the Trials began."

"And you think I have some part to play?"

"He called you, did he not?"

Numos massaged his hands and the top of his cane again. He bobbed his head. "He did call me to tell me what you witnessed during the meeting, that Zain Berrese and Gabrielle killed some of his men while leaving the city. Tell me, did you see the call to Gracie's Academy while you were scrolling through his log as well?"

"I did," Luvan conceded.

"Then your concern about that footage being doctored should be quelled."

"It makes sense, yes. What doesn't, though, is why he chose to call you?"

Numos shook himself off and pushed out his chest. "He called me after the incident to try and make sense of it. He knew I had been elected to survey the contestants during the Trials and wondered if perhaps this was some unfortunate traumatic aftermath of such an event. I told him I had no idea and then told him what actions could be taken and that I would seek out answers. And that is when I came to you."

Luvan spun around and paced to and fro, his head down, hand underneath his chin.

"Does that help?"

Luvan continued pacing about Senator Numos's office.

Senator Numos cleared his throat and checked the telecommunicator on his wrist. He straightened his vest over his silk white tunic. "I am afraid that I have to be off to another meeting now." Numos picked up the envelope and put himself in front of Luvan, stopping his pacing. "I believe you know where this goes."

Luvan looked down and took the proffered envelope. "I do."

"Again, excellent work. Your speech was quite the stem-winder, if I do say so myself. It has been a pleasure to work alongside you, and it will be an even greater honor seeing this to its conclusion. Shall we?" Numos turned Luvan by his shoulder and held his arm up to the door. Numos opened the door and ushered Luvan out. "Please do tell me how the Guardian of the Core's face looks when you had him his subpoena." Numos chuckled.

Luvan didn't say anything. He exited the office and walked with the senator outside of the parliament, each getting into their own hovercrafts before going their separate paths. Not departing right away, Luvan watched the senator fly off to another area of Briseas. He flipped the envelope multiple times in his hand and ran his fingers over the twelve wax seals once more, closing his eyes and inhaling deeply as he did so. *It's time.*

Luvan laid the envelope on the seat next to him, activated the anitron, and flew off to the docking port where his spaceship was docked. After lines and clearing safety protocols and inputting his destination, Luvan left Briseas's spaceport and the comfort of Agrost's atmosphere. Not even one parsec from the atmosphere, Luvan flew towards the wormhole that would take him to the Central Core. No one else was in line to use the wormhole, but he saw one interstellar cargo ship waiting to transfer to Pyre and other private ships waiting in line for the other wormholes. At this level of the process, there was hardly any security, just one ship at each wormhole to promulgate wait times, but any real threats or security issues were handled while in jurisdiction of the nation in question's spaceport and atmosphere patrol, the Atmos. Once cleared by them, a ship would then be able to leave the planet's atmosphere peacefully. The Atmos ran the spaceship's identification plate through a database to see if there were any warrants or outstanding tickets on the vehicle; rarely did they take the extra step to match owner with registration number.

After jumping through the wormhole, Luvan arrived right outside of Hown a few hours later. As usual, he expected General Satorus to come meet him personally, but to Luvan's surprise, the approach was quiet. Too quiet. He even noticed that the shield that usually covered the wormhole that led directly to the Central Core wasn't enacted. It was left open.

Curiosity getting the better of him, he landed on the asteroid.

He wished he hadn't.

Death sucked the wind out of him. He choked, looking at the bodies that lay shriveling and decomposing as if the asteroid had been home to some massacre. *So it's true. The Hown are gone...* Luvan's hand hovered over the button to release him to the asteroid's surface, but in the end he pulled it back, not needing nor wanting to examine the bodies closer. The graveyard already made it clear enough; something was amiss.

Taking off from the asteroid, he piloted himself through the wormhole, arriving at the Central Core. Evening was descending upon the Core, and the silver skies were turning purple as they usually did. This period of dusk had always impressed Luvan when he stayed on the Core as a conseleigh. Even before landing, he noticed that Guardian Eska stood outside his estate, Tundra to one side of him and Apprentice Mourse to the other. Vesel flapped his wings, flying in the sky.

Luvan put the envelope at the back of his waist and walked out to stand before the trio.

Guardian Eska crossed his arms over his chest and cleared his throat. "Luvan Katore, what are you doing here?"

Luvan ignored the Guardian's question and asked his own. "What happened to Hown?"

"We've solved the issue, Luvan," Tundra said.

"We will start recruiting for new Hown forces during Eirek's training. It will be beneficial for him to see."

Luvan balked. "You're trying to turn this into a positive?"

"Every cloud has a silver lining. Isn't that what they say in Mistral? Now, why are you here?" Eska repeated the question.

Luvan scoffed and shook his head. *Stubborn as ever.* He walked forward, hand going behind his waist, causing Tundra to shift a hand to her hilt. Luvan stopped. He scoffed again and shook his head. "I'm glad you rate me so highly, Tundra."

She blushed and lowered her head. "Sorry, Luvan. It has been a rough past few weeks. Many strange things occurring."

"Humph." Luvan pushed air out through his nose. "Change is always strange." He redirected his attention to Guardian Eska. "This is for you." Luvan proffered the envelope in his hand, revealing the Guardian's full name on the top side.

Guardian Eska eyed it cautiously, glanced at Luvan, and then looked back down at the envelope. He took it and flipped it over. Tundra closed the distance between her and Guardian Eska and looked at it alongside of him, as did his apprentice. The Guardian ran his fingers over all twelve seals. "What is this?"

"A subpoena. You are to appear in the Hall of Voices in Mistral before all twelve families in power. Your actions, and those of your constituents," Luvan spared a glance at Tundra, "have been called into question as of late. As well as the inadequacies of your apprentice." Luvan looked at Eirek, who stared blankly in return, then looked down and kicked the dirt with his feet. Luvan turned his attention back to Eska. "You are to defend yourself at your impeachment hearing."

Tundra gasped. "Impeachment!"

Eska didn't open the letter. He remained silent for a time, staring at Luvan. "I don't know how you managed to convince all twelve nations to agree to this."

"You should know that I have a silver-tongue. I give advice and make arguments. It's foolish of those who don't take it."

Tundra took the letter from Guardian Eska and ran her fingers along the wax seals. "Impeachment, Luvan? How could you do such a thing to Edwyrd?"

Luvan cocked his head to Tundra. "Propriety."

Upon the word, she looked up, brows furrowed. "This is nothing more than an attempt to hurt Edwyrd after your dismissal. It won't succeed."

"It is not your decision whether it succeeds. Regardless, you helped make this possible, Tundra."

"What do you mean?"

"Do you really think it is wise going around lopping off the heads of lords?"

Tundra's eyes bulged; she moved forward. Eska put an arm in front of her. "Lord Grime disobeyed direct commands and threatened the lives of his superiors. As you mentioned, propriety."

"Yes, well, it is clear that you and I have certainly different viewpoints on propriety. I will see you at the trial." Luvan turned on his heel to leave.

"Luvan."

He stopped and spun back around. "Yes, my Guardian?"

"Does this impeachment concern the others?"

"You mean Conseleigh Iycel and Apprentice Mourse?"

"Yes."

"No. Not directly, but I do imagine you will have to answer for their actions or inactions and inadequacies at the trial."

"And can they speak for themselves if they so choose?"

"If you feel it wise for them to do so."

Eska remained stoic to Luvan's words. "Eirek and I will see you on Mistral then."

Eirek's eyes widened.

Tundra gasped again. "Edwyrd, I can—"

"Stay here." He looked at Luvan all the while. "The apprentice is more than capable of defending his *inadequacies.*"

"My... my Guardian...," Eirek bumbled.

Luvan scoffed at the scene. "Do what you think is best. You never listened to my advice, anyway." He turned around to leave.

"May the winds blow the way you want to go."

Luvan ignored the Mistralian adage, figuring Eska said it out of the duty of his position. He couldn't actually mean to send good tidings. Entering his ship, he pushed on the anitron and left the atmosphere, noticing the silver had fully turned to dark, and the silver bands of the Core were present through the clouds. Truly, every cloud did have a silver lining, and the flux in Power that would occur after Eska's removal from office would serve to prove that adage even more.

CHAPTER 5

# TRUTHS

Tension filled the air in Luvan's absence. Eirek expected Guardian Eska to say something, to curse Luvan under his breath, to show some sort of emotion, but he saw only apathy on the Guardian's face as they watched Luvan's spaceship fly away into the purple skies.

"My Guardian, was tat Luvan?"

"Yes, it was, Ethen." Guardian Eska turned to face his conseleigh who proceeded down the steps of the estate.

"Why did 'e fly off all te sudden? Will 'e be back?"

Guardian Eska shook his head. "No. I'm afraid the next time I see him, it will be under less favorable conditions." Eska handed out the letter for his other conseleigh to see.

Ethen's gaze took in all twelve wax sigils and then looked around the party. "Is tis?"

Eska nodded. "It is. It came from Luvan and Senator Numos."

"Senator Numos was 'ere?" Ethen raised an eyebrow.

Eska shook his head. "No, but I have a feeling they conspired against me. Both of them." Eska turned to Ethen, who still held the envelope in his hand.

Ethen looked up from the envelope. "How do you know?"

"I merely speculate for now, but I recall what you told me when you visited Mistral. You mentioned Luvan and Numos had been spending time together."

"Tat is wat Luvan's wife told me, yes."

"Then I expect them to be together in this front." Eska sighed. "How bad company corrupts good morals. You can open it if you like, but I do not need to see it. I already know what is inside."

"Edwyrd, it isn't fair what he is doing. They," Tundra spat, "if that fat senator is truly involved as well."

"Not everything in life is fair, Tundra." Eska smiled. Whether it was forced or not, Eirek couldn't tell. "Who are we to judge their actions?"

"Because we are the ones involved." She pointed to herself.

Ethen had pried about the envelope and had taken to reading out the charges against Eska. With each charge, his voice escalated, and Tundra's voice echoed in fury. Together, they continued lambasting the situation. Eska bore them both, heard their wailing advice as apathetic as a man at the end of his life. Almost as if he had the prescience to see his fate before him, to see how the situation would unfold. Like a man already resigned to his defeat. Or was his stoicism an act of confidence? Perhaps he had accepted what fate had given him once again, but this time chose not to be bedeviled by it, but instead amused by it. Eirek wished he could read the visage of his mentor better.

Eska must have sensed Eirek's confusion, for his mentor locked his gaze on him, ignoring the conseleigh on either side of him. "Do you understand what has happened, Eirek?"

The conseleigh grew quiet, obviously having forgotten about his presence in their diatribes. Eirek's cheeks grew hot. He nodded. "You have to appear somewhere?"

"*We* have to appear somewhere," Eska corrected.

"I will go with you, Edwyrd," Tundra interjected.

"And I as well. Tese charges against you are ridiculous."

Eska shook his head. "Neither of you will attend. I only want Eirek by my side."

"But, Edwyrd—"

"Tundra, I already can guess what Luvan will be talking about at this hearing. I must defend your actions, but your actions were my own actions. I gave you those commands, and you followed them, as you were supposed to. Propriety. I will handle it myself." For the first time, Eska's voice had risen. "Your presence there may give stronger testimony to the other claim I will have to answer for."

Ethen read through the list of charges. "Which one is tat, my Guardian? May I be of service tere?"

For some reason, Eska looked to the sky, as if he searched for some sort of advice the stars might give him. A heavy sigh brought his head back down, and he looked at Ethen first, then Eirek, and then finally to Tundra. He nodded. And in that moment, she nodded too, and they brought their hands together, fingers interlocked. Eska's arm swooped around Tundra's waist, and he pulled her next to him, brought his hand to her cheek, and kissed her.

Eirek's eyes widened.

"My Guardian...," Ethen stammered.

"Tundra and I are intimate. We have been intimate now for years." Eska looked back and forth from Ethen to Eirek.

"Thirty years," Tundra confirmed. She rested her head on Eska's shoulder.

Ethen choked. "Tirty years?"

Eska nodded. "Luvan, I feel, has noted this intimacy. And he will try to use it against me in the hearing." Eska kissed the top of Tundra's head and then locked eyes with Eirek. "You realize, Eirek, what is wrong with this, don't you?"

Eirek gulped and nodded. "The vows."

"You are correct. Luvan will try to use this to undermine my propriety."

"And you are not afraid?"

Eska chuckled. He let go of Tundra's waist but continued holding her hand. "What is done is done. I cannot change the past, but I can look to the future. And when I understand exactly how Luvan is going to formulate his case against me, I can prepare, for that is the key to any true leader, Eirek. Understanding. When you understand someone and their motives, you are able to predict their movements. You become proactive, not reactive to the situation. When you understand your own weaknesses, you take steps to correct them. To make them your strengths. And this is something that I know you already know."

Eirek stumbled. His mouth hung slack. When had he picked up such understanding?

"When you couldn't beat Ethen in battle, you practiced." Eska beamed. "I saw your hours logged into the habitat arena. And when I still didn't let you leave for the second part of your apprenticeship due to your lack of knowledge of the cultures, customs, and traditions of the nations, you began reading more in the library. You came to me with questions upon questions. And now you are ready."

"Ready for what?"

"To show to all the lords and ladies in attendance how competent you truly are, Eirek, for that will be their claim against you. Senator Numos will showcase your ineptitude during the Trials, and Luvan will aim to further accentuate your shortcomings in the months he observed after the Trials. But you will prove them wrong."

"My Guardian, I can help as well. I 'ave been training 'im."

Guardian Eska shook his head, not looking at his conseleigh. Still holding Tundra's hand, he kept his gaze on Eirek all the while. "No. This is Eirek's hearing as much as it is mine. After all, he wasn't my original choice, and it's time he answers the doubts of others for himself." Eska smirked. "It's time he shows them why he truly has the right to be my apprentice and the next Guardian of the Core. It's time for the truth to come out."

"Then what shall you have me do, Edwyrd?"

"And me, my Guardian?"

"With Hown no longer around, one of you must stay on the Core. Ethen, as my weapons master, that will be you. I can imagine no one better suited to defend this place other than you and Vesel."

"Aye, my Guardian." Ethen bowed.

Eska turned towards Tundra. "You will return to Onkh."

"Onkh, my Guardian?"

"Before you returned here, I received word from General Satorus and Chase Arwayn that they had located and captured Hydro outside of the Sacred Passage."

"Why was he there?"

"I think I know, but I am not positive yet. There is something else that needs to be done, regardless. Since the Hown are no more, I hope you can find their last location and properly take care of the bodies. They deserve more than what they received." Tundra nodded her head at Eska's words. "Then, I need you to make amends with Lady Aprah. I am positive she will be against me at this meeting, and this step of meeting her will prove an act of good faith."

"But she will be at the hearing. How am I supposed to—"

"That's because there is something I need you to check before you visit her."

"What is it?"

"I hid a jewel somewhere. And I need you to check upon its status. It will help me confirm my suspicion about Hydro's appearance at the Sacred Passage."

Eirek never knew Eska to circumvent subjects, but it was clear he wasn't saying everything. Even Tundra seemed annoyed by the tangential tone Eska had taken. With an arched eyebrow and a piqued voice, she asked, "And where is it you wish me to go?"

Eska sighed and bit his lip. He looked at her but didn't say anything. He remained mute for the longest time, as if he had almost forgotten what his other request was going to be.

"Edwyrd, what is it?"

He took both of her hands in his own. "I need you to return to Crestal's Palace."

CHAPTER 6

# BACKROOM PROPOSITIONS

"So it's done then?" Lord Victor Zigarda asked, not even giving Senator Numos a breath as he walked back into his own living quarters.

"The subpoena is in the hands of Luvan Katore, and he is delivering it to Guardian Eska as we speak." The senator took off a white glove, hung his cane off the back of a chair, and laid the glove over it. Then he sat down on a couch, filling the space of two seats, leaving only one for Lord Zalos Kapache of Chaon. The man who had introduced himself as Longwei, a member of Lord Kapache's council, stood behind the lord, hands folded behind his back, as silent as Zakk. Every once in a while, Zakk felt Longwei's attention, but when Zakk would look across the room, the other man's gaze would already be averted. To cover his own movement, Zakk would shift his gaze throughout the room, ending on the three mute Sages who stood behind Cronos. Did they remember him?

He had only met them one other time in his life—they were the ones, rather Cronos was the one, who told him he was Denied. Zakk didn't care about that anymore; he had gotten along fine in life without being able to use Power. People relied too much on it in duels anyway when it was really only weapons and skills that mattered. And that is what now drew Zakk's gaze towards the Ether Weapon on the Sage's lap. How had such a weapon got into the hands of someone like him? Could he even wield it properly? Was he worthy of its mettle, or if it was merely just another sad show of superiority that those with Power liked to display.

"Now, when am I going to receive my end of the bargain?" Senator Numos looked from Zigarda to Kapache.

"We do not want to cause a disruption right now with the vote to impeach Eska so close," Zigarda said. "Her assassination will come after the meeting. Is that doable, Zalos?"

"It will be done."

"When?"

"Do not be so impatient," Zigarda said. "I have waited..." He coughed. "Two-hundred—" He coughed again, into his hand this time, instead of his shoulder. He pulled it back, red. He crumpled his fist. "Two-hundred years."

"Yes, and you may not even get to see your own plan succeed. Tell me, how is collecting the jewels going?"

Zigarda cleared his throat. "It's going."

"That doesn't sound reassuring."

"I lost contact with Hydro a week ago."

Cronos's head shifted. "Did you say Hydro? As in Hydro Paen of Acquava?"

"Yes, Cronos."

"Why didn't you tell me *he* was the one securing the jewels?"

"Why does it matter?"

"Do you have any idea how valuable that man is? What he carries!" It was Cronos who coughed this time. The other three Sages behind him put their hands on his shoulder. Just as soon as the fit started, it ended.

Zakk cocked his head, and his eyes widened. *What was—*

"And what exactly *does* Hydro carry?"

Cronos composed himself. "The jewels. Those godstones are invaluable for overthrowing Eska."

Zakk scrutinized the Sage. Was he lying? Did Hydro Paen carry something more than jewels on his person? Zakk chewed on his lower lip. He hadn't had enough time with the Sages to gauge their veracity or not, but something was off about the way Cronos handled himself.

"Well then, there is no one better for that part of the plan should we need him to level the playing field. Hydro Paen is competent and untraceable. He has an Ether Weapon by his side. Who better to send?"

Cronos glared at Zigarda. "Remember, Victor, some of us have been waiting even longer for our dreams to bear fruit. The whims of fate cannot go awry now. Not when we are so close. Not when we have been so patient." Cronos pet his Ether Staff, almost purring the last words as if the staff gave him unparalleled comfort.

Silence added to the tension building in the room. Tension that was cut by a casual interjection from Senator Numos.

"And didn't you say that you've lost contact with him?" His left leg crossed over his right. One arm draped over the top of the couch, he took a sip from his wineglass and continued swirling it again. "Perhaps something has finally gotten the better of him?"

Zakk shifted his focus to the insouciant senator. What was his game? To show Zigarda's further incompetence? For once, Zakk was glad to be an outsider in this arena. He had no love of politics, and he knew the Mistralians fought their battles with words. Zakk much preferred to let his sword do the talking for him.

"The Hown are no longer a factor. You already know—"

"I said *something*. Not someone." He put his left leg on the ground and leaned forward. "Perhaps there are factors beyond our control."

"Like what?"

"The system is quite big. Use your imagination. What could possibly go wrong in this binary star system of ours?" Senator Numos chuckled and took a swig of wine. "But I will give you credit for neutralizing Hown so effectively. Tell me, what has become of Doctor Cere? I see he isn't here."

"Conseleigh Iycel killed him."

"How do you know?"

"Because he isn't here. And he should have been. Jazar returned."

"The shapeshifter with the slew of bodies now in my basement?"

"Yes."

"Do you know how precarious that is, by the way? Luvan Katore asked me if you were staying at my abode. He suspects something."

Zigarda frowned. "And what did you tell him?"

"I am Mistralian. I am good with my words. I told him enough to satiate him. I cannot continue keeping you here. I've already noted Conseleigh Rorum wandering around my premises in my absence."

"He did not find anything."

"No. He didn't. Lucky for us."

"Luck has nothing to do with it," Cronos said. "This plan will work in removing Eska from power."

Senator Numos furrowed his brows towards Cronos. "And what makes you so certain?"

"I have already seen it." Cronos caressed his staff.

Senator Numos scoffed.

"Fool of little faith. If Sage Cronos says it will happen, it will." Lord Kapache spoke again, taking his attention away from the chameleon on his shoulder.

"Well, excuse me if I need more faith than words," Numos shot back at Lord Kapache. "Everyone here seems to be getting everything they desire, except me."

"Your career has literally been built upon words, Senator. And you need more than that?" Zigarda chuckled now.

"I told you Lady Liliana will be terminated." Lord Kapache scratched underneath his chameleon's chin.

"How soon, though?"

"Not before the hearing concludes. You cannot expedite such things."

For the first time in the meeting, the man standing behind Lord Kapache spoke.

Such fervor imbued his voice that he leaned forward as he spoke, hands gripping the back of the couch, almost shouting at Senator Numos by the end. Immediately, Zakk's eyes were drawn to the crippled hand of the man, skin loose and misshapen, similar to that of a shapeshifter's skin.

"Longwei." Lord Kapache raised his hand, silencing the man behind him. "Calm yourself. Some people just need more convincing than others. Senator Numos, I tell you that you will get what you desire. All of us will. Sage Cronos has never steered us wrong. That is how Chaon now controls Callumbra. How it took Verimas in earlier times."

"I gave Verimas to you. Before your family even reigned. It was a blood debt."

"No need to bring up the past, Victor. We are here to look towards the future."

"Of course, Cronos."

"My prescience will make you the next Guardian of the Core."

"Then everything will go according to plans. Fate cannot defeat us again."

Numos scoffed. "Victor, you are so cruel and savage. It is inspiring. Tell me, do you not feel the slightest remorse for your doctor?" Numos lowered his chin.

"Sometimes things do not go as planned. Sometimes sacrifices need to be made. Sometimes things need to change. You know this better than others, do you not?" Zigarda glared back at the pompous senator.

Numos retracted his position. He cleared his throat. "Plans. Sacrifice. And change. Oh my, what a delightful conversation we are having here." Numos rubbed his hands together. "Speaking of change, what do you plan on doing with the apprentice's blood?"

Zigarda withdrew the vial and swirled it in its little test tube. "A shapeshifter will meet Eska and throw him—"

"A shapeshifter will do no such thing with that blood," Cronos cut in. "That is the most valuable blood we have."

Zigarda clutched it and put it back somewhere underneath his robe. "Why is that?"

"That blood may unlock the Core."

"May?"

"May." Cronos nodded.

"Can't you see everything with that staff of yours?"

"No. Not everything."

The room sat in silence. Zigarda tapped his foot. As did others. Until finally Zigarda asked, "Would you care to expound upon that, my Sage?"

Cronos shifted his gaze to Zigarda. "No. I do not. Knowledge is Power after all, correct?" Cronos smirked.

Zakk couldn't help but smirk as well as the old man used Zigarda's words against him. His vicarious victory was cut short when Cronos flicked his gaze to Zakk.

"Boy, you look familiar. Have I tested you for Power before?"

"You have," Zakk nodded. "When I was sixteen, at Gazo's."

"And what did I label you as?"

Zakk's face flushed with the extra eyes surveying him. As if the Chaon man's sporadic gazes hadn't been enough attention on him already, this callout by Cronos allowed Longwei and Lord Kapache to dissect Zakk from afar. He ignored them as best as he could, trying to focus on Cronos and deliver him the proper respect he deserved. He was, after all, the mastermind behind the entire plot, Zakk had come to find out.

"You labeled me Denied," Zakk conceded.

"A pity," Lord Kapache said. "You could have trained at Voima in Kuyan after Gazo's, if you had been Blessed. Longwei here runs the program."

Zakk's eyes flicked to the man behind Lord Kapache. *So he's not an advisor? He runs Voima... Interesting.*

"Thank you, my lord." Longwei squeezed Lord Kapache's shoulder, then looked over to Zakk. "But Gazo's in itself is still as prestigious as it gets. And now you're here." Longwei waved his good hand around the room. "In a room full of powerful people."

Cronos spoke. "Denied? Hmmm, that's a shame. You remind me of someone."

Zakk twisted his head back to the Sage. "Probably Zain."

"Zain Berrese? The original winner of the Trials?"

"Yes. People say we often look alike. And we have similar names, so it's even more confusing. I grew out my hair and got this tattoo so that people wouldn't mistake us for brothers."

"Are you?"

"Only by law. My family died years before Zain's family adopted me."

"And when his adopted family abandoned him, mine took the boy in. He has made a few mistakes like any child would, but he's learned from them." Zigarda shifted in his chair, his unblinking gaze boring into Zakk. "Hopefully."

Of course, Zigarda would try to portray himself as benevolent, but in reality, everything Zakk did had never been good enough. It made him wonder at times why he was even here. Zigarda was capable of protecting himself. He had already seen glimpses of the man's Power and cunning.

Zakk stayed out of necessity. He had a score to settle with Zain, and if that meant continuing to be Zigarda's dog for a little while longer, then so be it. The Castle of Pelopon was already overthrown, and Zain would return soon enough. Then he would understand Zakk's pain. Then he would understand what it was like to lose family. Then they would be equals. Until then, he would swallow his pride, drown his irritation, and stroke Zigarda's ego.

"Yes, my lord." Zakk bowed his head.

"Orphaned twice," said Senator Numos. "How tragic. You never told me this while you stayed on the Core with me."

"You never asked. I wasn't allowed to speak, remember?"

Numos fidgeted in his chair. "That's because voices draw attention, and you weren't supposed to be there in the first place."

"Yes. Well, the past is the past."

"Do you remember much of your past?" Numos asked.

"Not before the Killings."

Numos cleared his throat. "Excuse me, did you say the Killings?"

"The Konmer Killings. I don't remember anything before that."

"And the Killings, do you remember those?"

Zakk turned his head to take in Lord Kapache and Longwei. When he didn't respond, Longwei continued. "I heard about them all the way to Chaon. Infamous they were."

Zakk held Longwei's stare. He pushed his tongue into his cheek. "No. I've learned to forget that memory." He clicked his tongue.

"And some memories are better forgotten," Zigarda said. "I believe we are just prattling about now. So we all are clear on our roles in the upcoming meeting and after?"

"We are."

"Yes. I still do not understand why you cannot be there to attest to Apprentice Mourse's ineptitude, Cronos."

"Sage Cronos," Zigarda corrected Senator Numos.

"My apologies, Sage Cronos."

Cronos waved the senator off with his hand. "My words will mean nothing there."

"But you trained Apprentice Mourse firsthand. You told us of his inadequacies."

"Apprentice Mourse will most likely not be the incompetent apprentice you painted him to be in the initial meeting. Guardian Eska will be sure to highlight that and most likely has expedited his training since I last saw the man."

"So then how will the apprenticeship pass into Victor's hands?"

"Experience," Cronos explained. "There is more to being a Guardian than Power and the ability to handle a weapon. He has to know how to lead, and that is something in which he has only the slightest aptitude. When he was voted apprentice, he only succeeded by one vote. Lord Evber will not be present at this meeting, and I foresee Epoch not voting for Apprentice Mourse's confidence again. Not at such a young age. Look at what is happening to Acquava."

"That reminds me," Zigarda said, "if Hydro still has yet to check in by the time Edwyrd's trial concludes, or this crystal scry of mine continues to not allow me to see his location, my plan will continue for Acquava."

"Plan?" Cronos looked at him.

"Sow discord. That is our goal, right?"

"Yes. The more nations unable to act, the more successful the war will be."

"The war?" Zakk bit his lower lip.

Cronos looked at him, one eye of blue and one of amber fixated on him. "Yes, war."

"On what?"

"Why, on the Core, of course."

Zakk continued staring into the eyes of the old sage, allured by the bi-color. They held a certain knowing about them, similar to Dr. Cere's or Victor Zigarda's. Wisdom dwelled in them, the kind of wisdom only old age and experience could bring.

Zakk gulped, aware of all the others looking at him now. Trying to eradicate his sense of unease, he broadened his shoulders and puffed out his chest. In as confident as a voice as he could muster, he said, "Sounds great."

Cronos's amber eye twinkled, and he massaged the Ether Staff laying on his lap once more. "Yes. It certainly will be."

CHAPTER 7

# TALES AROUND A FIRE

Cain's lips trembled. He blinked and shook his head, trying to rid himself of the ridiculousness of such a comment. "What?"

"You and I, son, we are the descendants of the True King of Pyre."

"Impossible. My father is..." Cain stopped speaking. He didn't want to continue. He didn't trust his lips to finish that sentence. Instead, he said, "Prove it."

"After protecting your mother, I took her back to the village. She was famished. I gave her food. She told me her troubles, of how the man you presume to be your father was sterile, and that no matter how many times they had intercourse, she would not become pregnant. She was worried for her life."

Cain looked on, but he remained silent, locked in the throes of an untold story.

"She told me of this family's reputation, and it became clear to me that this man expected an heir and would take no blame in not being able to produce one, not after all of his family before had been able to. Hearing my own story and who I was, she asked me to give her a child. A strong child. You."

"And who are you exactly? I do not even have your name yet."

"My name is Brenton. And it is a pleasure to finally have you in front of me, Cain."

Cain chewed on his lower lip, eyebrows furrowing as he tried to recall interactions with his mother. She had given him the necklace he now wore. This man had known her name even without Cain giving it to her. His own name, too. As each new strand of story was spun, Cain's heartbeat intensified. "Go on. With your story, that is."

"If it were any other, I do not think I would have done anything. My father and his father and his father's father all married and gave seed to only those from Pyre to keep the lineage as pure as possible. The reputation of the *Evber* household intrigued me, though, and I saw a way out of our current predicament."

"What predicament?"

"We live off the land. That is what we have always done. But the world has changed much in the years since the Great War, and if we were ever going to reclaim our rightful throne on Pyre, we would need to leave this place somehow, by any means necessary. We could no longer return to our homeland the way we got here."

"And how was that?"

Brenton chuckled to himself. "It's a story even I have a hard time believing. We were dropped into a volcano and spat out underneath the boughs of a giant tree."

"The Yggdrasil tree," Cain muttered. "So it was your clan who burned it down?"

Brenton's smile flattened. "We never intended to burn it down. It just happened. At least, so the story goes. And it fell on its own accord. You listen to too many stories told by your father's fathers. And they all paint this land, *us*," he emphasized, "in a bad way. But none of them know the truth. The truth, for most, is too hard to swallow. The truth, for most, is too hard to believe." He took a clay teapot and poured a red liquid into a clay chalice that looked small in his hands. After taking a sip, he set it back down. "Your father could not handle that truth. That is why I am sure he has paraded you as his son for twenty-four years. That's why he surely says you take after your mother. He denies himself the truth. If you only opened your eyes, son, you wouldn't be as blind as him. You would see who you truly are."

"My father... You *used* him." Cain's stomach twisted.

"We are all human, Cain. We all use each other. It is the nature of things."

"You exploited my family for your own personal gains." Cain stood up and turned to leave.

Cain didn't even make it to the threshold before Brenton called to him, halting him in his tracks. "If you walk out that door, you are not the man, the son, I would want my lineage to be passed down to."

Hunched low, his chest heaving, one arm on a wall for support, Cain looked back. "And you think I would want your lineage? My family's lineage is the longest in the history of Epoch. We have been ruling for over six-hundred years."

"And *that* is only a big fish in the pond of history. If you hear me out, I am offering you the chance for so much more."

Cain gulped. His breathing slower now, he turned around. "What then? To be a shark in the sea of stories?"

Brenton smirked but shook his head. "I'm offering you the chance to rewrite history. To be the author of your own destiny. A King in the deep oceans of the universe."

Cain came back to the table. He sat down. "Go on. About my father... why?"

Brenton nodded. "As you say, I did exploit your father without him knowing. Your father had prestige, resources, and coin. But I also knew you would have been raised properly there, and safely, too. My concern is that you would forget who you truly were, so I gave two conditions to your mother before giving her my seed. First, that she would give you the necklace passed down from my family since before the Great War, the very same necklace that you wear around your neck."

Cain reached underneath his shirt and pulled out the necklace. The glow of the room turned the feather to pure fire, red and orange and hot.

Brenton leaned forward and lifted it in front of his face. "It has been many years since I've seen this. You wear it well." He let it go and sat back.

Cain twirled the feather in between his thumb and index finger. "And the second?"

"I told her to name you Cain after the place where you were conceived."

"But why?"

"So you would never forget who you truly were. Has there not been a tugging in your heart and mind, pulling you here? Is it not the reason you let Stannon guide you here when you could have gone back to your camp? I wanted your name to be a constant reminder of us, so that you would, one day, find us and learn the truth."

"But... how did you know I would come back? Kane is so far away from Thoth. No one travels here."

"And that is why we had to lure you and your father here."

Cain tilted his head. "What?"

"Despite what stories may say about us, we are not savages. We quit our ways of being land hungry when we realized that while here on Agrost we are not nearly as powerful as when we were on Pyre. This was proven to us when Syf of Cresica forced us back to our homeland." He paused and folded his hands together. "Those raids on Lorian were to draw your father's attention, to get you to travel to the border and to see your hometown, to interact with one of us."

"But... I... I killed one of your men. It was my first."

"They died for a greater good—to plant a seed so that you would begin to remember who you are. And it worked. You are here in front of me now."

"Why did my mother not say anything about it?"

"Would you have believed her?"

"I... No." Cain shook his head.

"I told her not to tell you but to let you figure it out for yourself."

"Why?"

"Hubris. It is the one thing that kills most great men. If you were told about your bloodline, rather than discovering it for yourself, it could have caused you to do something brash. To avoid this, I needed you to realize who you were by yourself." Brenton put his arms back across his chest, with one arm vertical, hand resting on his chin. "Tell me, when did you start to suspect something?"

"The Trials."

"What are those?"

Cain explained to him the competition on the Core and how it was during the fourth trial when they had gone to the planet Pyre. There he had begun to suspect something when he didn't sweat. Even by the mouth of a volcano, not a drop of moisture escaped his skin, no matter how much the other foreigners around him sweat.

"Fiery blood runs through your veins indeed."

Cain thought back. He remembered something else about that day. "When I was there," he said, "I... I saw something. It... it looked like yellow eyes beneath the lava gurgling in the volcano's mouth."

"You saw her then?"

"Who?"

"That could have only been Chantico."

"Chantico?"

"She is your birthright. She is the Creature of Legend. That necklace you wear; she sensed it. She must have known you had come back to Pyre."

The eruption that day of a volcano that hadn't been active for centuries suddenly made sense. He took another glance at Brenton and saw the facial features his father could have never given him. A burning sensation took hold of his chest. He grabbed the necklace and heard himself yell as his vision faded in and out. Seconds passed, perhaps minutes, and all he heard were shouts and a faint buzzing in his head. All he could feel was the burning sensation in his heart. He found it hard to breathe. A hand came under his chin. Clay touched his lips.

"Here, drink this."

Orange fire danced before him. Before he could object, his head was tilted back and liquid went down his throat. He gulped it, expecting to be burned, but he wasn't. His vision cleared. The chalice he drank from soured his lips with smoky red wine aglow with orange fire.

Cain coughed. His chest no longer burned. "What was that?" The chalice was the same vessel from which the man had drunk.

Brenton put the chalice away. "Fire wine. We produce it and drink it to make us feel stronger."

"Why was it on fire?"

"I added some of my Power to it."

"Why?"

"To give you some more of my strength. Strength that you have been lacking. You will need it for what is ahead."

"And what is that?"

"The initiation into your destiny." He stood and and helped Cain to his feet. He walked around the table and picked up the weapon that hung on the two skulls. "Before you can claim your birthright, son, you must defeat me in combat." He turned around, one arm holding the Ether Spear in the center of the shaft. "Show me the Power of the Evbers, and I'll show you the might of Brenton the Protector, True King of Pyre." Brenton grinned.

CHAPTER 8

# THE HEARING

The room was ripe with tension and awe. Guardian Eska knew he would need to have to speak well in order to overcome the whispers and susurrus that enveloped the entire chamber. While each one fought the next in a domineering cycle of attention, making them impossible to distinguish, he was certain that all of them were directed at him as he sat in the back of the Hall of Voices, next to three other chairs reserved for Senator Numos, Luvan Katore, and Speaker of the Senate, Neil Raiden.

As the senate leader established quorum, Eska didn't speak to the others, yet that did not mean he sat in silence. On the contrary, Eska had closed his eyes to hide the fact that he now communicated telepathically with Tundra. While she had played a part in putting him in this predicament in more ways than one, he preferred her company to the others in the room. He needed her ice now more than ever to keep cool amongst the onslaught of gazes and lights and questions that would shortly be directed his way.

*The hearing is starting.*

*What has been said?*

*Nothing yet. Quorum is being established.*

*Edwyrd, I am sorry for everything.*

*There is nothing to be sorry for. I will come out of this as Guardian.*

*I wish I could be there with you.*

*And you know why you can't. Have you left for Onkh yet?*

*Shortly. How is Eirek fairing?*

*Nervous, but I do think he is ready to defend himself physically and verbally.*

*That is good. Is Cronos there?*

*No. He isn't foolish enough to show himself in such a public hearing.*

*Will you find him afterwards?*

*I may make a trip to his palace in Epoch. There is another place I need to visit, too.*

*How long do you expect the hearing to last?*

*That I do not know. Quorum is established. I should go.*

*Good luck, Edwyrd. May the Ancients be with you.*

*And also with you.*

The connection cut. Eska opened his eyes as Senator Numos approached the podium. "Lords and ladies, I welcome you to the Hall of Voices. The day has finally come for us to hear the Guardian of the Core himself explain the misdoings he has incurred upon us all. As I mentioned in our previous meeting, as an observant of the Trials themselves, I found the outcome of each particular Trial not representative of the aim the Guardian wished to test..."

As the senator went on to explain each of Guardian Eska's wrongdoings in terms of the contestants and the Trials, Eska made mental notes of points he would revisit in his defense.

"My partner Luvan Katore will now outline, once again, the directives Guardian Eska has so blatantly disregarded."

Luvan made a move to stand up. Eska put a hand on his knee. "Are you sure you want to do this, Luvan?" Eska looked his conseleigh in the eye. "It will only end in defeat."

"In your defeat, Edwyrd."

Luvan stood up and exchanged places with Senator Numos. Senator Numos sat back in his chair, an air of confidence radiating from him. With two hands on top of his cane, he turned to Eska. "I am sorry it had to come to this, my Guardian. But Gladonus needs a change. I hope you understand."

"Change it will have, but not the one you are dying for, Nyom."

Eska redirected his attention to Luvan, who had finished warming up the crowd and now was in the midst of talking about Eska's action at the Meeting of the Twelve on Mount Volan.

"...the very people that gave him his Power, he sealed away. They are defenseless now. And can no longer protect any of us. Yes, it is the Guardian of the Core's job to ensure a level of protection, but what happens when he needs help? Let us remember Deimos. It is not Guardian Eska alone that combated the beast, but the Twelve, as well. Without their united strength, this system of Gladonus surely would have seen further ruin.

"His oathbreaking doesn't stop there. He has engaged in intimacy with one of his conseleigh, Tundra Iycel. He used his authority and dominance to cajole her into being more than just someone to lend an ear. Now she lends her whole body. Not only that, but he sends her out on perilous missions that have irrevocable costs. Brothers Grime, please remind everyone here what happened when Tundra visited your father."

"She cut off his head!" they shouted, raising their fists in unison.

*That point I will have to take care of.*

"And Lady Aprah, her demand of your elites—Eska's demand of your elites—puts you on the precipice of war. Every single one of his actions has led to strife and discord amongst the nations, save for the nations on Planet Pyre.

"What favoritism is this? Shouldn't the Guardian of the Core be impartial to favoritism? In fact, his vows dictate that he must remain impartial. Yet, did you know that he rejected a Trial applicant just because she was from Lurid? When asked about this decision to give a man from Mistral such a consideration over her, he mentioned to us, his conseleigh, that he, in fact, *was* doing his duty as Guardian by denying her. But, how? Shouldn't he uphold his duties and responsibilities to the highest caliber? Shouldn't he be the example that everyone, man and woman, boy and girl, in Gladonus aims to follow? Yet, he has failed us in this ideal, and that is why we are here today, and that is why your voice matters. To answer for the claims we have put together against him, I call forward the Guardian of the Core, Edwyrd Eska."

Eska stood and nodded at Luvan as the former conseleigh returned to his chair in the back. As Eska approached the podium, pockets of people in the Hall of Voices stood at attention, which then forced others to stand alongside them in a sense of propriety and duty. Eska motioned with his hands for all of them to be seated once more.

Gripping the podium with both hands, Eska leaned forward into the microphone.

"I am happy to be amongst all of you today. You may think that I find you ill-willed or malicious in subpoenaing me to come before you and answer for everything that has befallen our system as of late, but I assure you that isn't the case. Instead, I applaud your due diligence in upholding the values of your people and putting them first and foremost in your minds, in a time where you thought that I may have forgotten about your nations. We have this system of checks and balances in place for a reason, and so without further ado, let me begin by addressing the charges brought against me by Senator Numos and my former conseleigh. However, I do not want to do so while merely uttering memorized rhetoric. Instead, I want to give you all the opportunity to ask me questions, any questions, ask me to explain any of the allegations against me that you want clarified, and I will do it here, right now, before you."

Not to Eska's surprise, Victor Zigarda stood first. "Why did the Trials you conduct involve such haphazard events and a lack of quality representation?"

Eska held back his scoff. He looked directly at Zigarda. Flashbacks of how the storm of his fire had overwhelmed the man came back to him; tingles shivered through Eska. A part of him had felt sorry for what had transpired that day, but to think a man would keep a grudge after all these years was unfathomable.

"Victor, I am glad you bring up the Trials as you and I both participated in the previous Trials held by Guardian Matthau Crevon. Tell me, do you remember what those Trials tested?"

"He tested our Power. Combat. And intelligence."

"Yes. Do you know what the previous Trials tested before that one?"

"I was not alive. How would I know?"

"Neither was I, but through the reimaje I learned that the previous Trials also tested Power, combat and intelligence."

"Then why break the tradition?"

"Because it is our vow as Guardians to protect Gladonus, and the largest threat that a Guardian has to experience is Pirini Lilapa. In the time that the Trials were first started, there has always been the Curse, and each time it comes, it devastates Gladonus in unforeseen ways. The year of these Trials happened to coincide with the year of Pirini Lilapa, so I changed the Trials to potentially elect a candidate that could bring about an end to the Curse indefinitely and establish a true peace throughout this system. Insanity is doing the same thing over and over again and expecting different results. I changed that formula to produce a different result."

"Is the result so different? Pirini Lilapa still came. The only difference is now you have consolidated your Power, absolved your duties as a Guardian, and put a whole planet into civil wars."

"It is not in me that the system will change, but in my apprentice."

"But he was not truly the winner of the Trials. The true winner of the Trials, Zain Berrese, went on to slay my men leaving my city. We here have all seen the footage."

Eska closed his eyes and breathed out slowly. He would need to speak elegantly about this accusation. When ready, he spoke. "Lords and ladies here, I do not know what you saw, but I assure you that it was doctored. I have first-hand testimonies that Lord Zigarda is using shapeshifters to twist the minds of you and to show you scenarios that could not have occurred."

"And where is your proof of my shapeshifters? Do you claim that the Zain these people saw was an imposter?"

"No." Eska shook his head. "Zain escaped the city where he was being held captive by Victor, being used as a tool to manipulate his father's will into finishing a project for him to witness the whims of fate that has led us here, right now."

"That is a serious allegation, my Guardian." Nathan Alaois stood up from his seat in the Epochian section. "Do you have proof?"

"The only proof I have is the words of Zain Berrese, who saw the shapeshifter transform before his eyes, the woman who you thought to be Gabrielle Ravwey."

"And where is Zain now?" Zigarda called out. "I do not see him at your defense to give veracity to your words. In fact, no one is here to support you. You are alone, just like you have left every single nation in this system. Alone. Ostracized. Alien—"

"Enough of the rhetoric, Victor," Eska cut in. Eska breathed in, reliving his short conversation with Tundra, hoping her ice would still cool him. He needed to appear calm here. And he knew Victor would do his best to show Eska's fire, for Eska was born in fire. Luckily, he didn't have to speak, for a politician in the Mistralian section stood up. It took a moment to recognize the voice and the stature of the man, but Eska saw the resemblance after the outburst.

"My brother wouldn't lie."

Another man stood up from Ka'Che. It wasn't Lord Vangle. In fact, Lord Vangle was nowhere to be seen; instead, it must have been his advisor Errion Vesk, if Eska remembered correctly.

"The boy's mother made claims to have seen a shapeshifter as well. Even claims that she was attacked by one."

"Perhaps she was speaking gibberish? We already know from how the Trials affected the contestants that post-traumatic stress can certainly lead to irrational thinking."

"I saw the scar across her neck, Lord Zigarda."

"And does that make her words any more true? Perhaps she did it to herself."

The advisor scoffed. "And what would drive her to do that? Your logic is ludicrous. If what Guardian Eska says is true, Lord Zigarda, you will have the falcon to deal with. I will make sure Lord Vangle knows."

"The falcon's wings have already been snipped."

"What do you—"

"Conseleigh Iycel also told me to be on the lookout for shapeshifters." Lady Aprah's cool voice broke in.

Zigarda was taken aback. "A change of heart now, my lady? Where was this claim of yours in our initial meeting?"

Lady Aprah stood up. "I was waiting to make sense of it until I heard the Guardian of the Core say it for himself. Shapeshifters *are* a serious thing, and if what Guardian Eska says is true, and you have them in your employment, and you use them to alter the footage we have seen, then I motion to remove Victor Zigarda from office for misinformation."

"With the authority granted to me by Lord Vangle, I second that," Errion Vesk shouted.

"And who is to say the Guardian's words are more truthful than my own? Do you believe him merely because of his title? Have you not forgotten all the other atrocities he has committed?"

Lady Aprah shook her head. "No. I haven't." She stared directly at Guardian Eska with ire in her eyes. She bore into him like a savage about to lead a revolt, as her parents' must have looked when they led the rebellion against Sereya. "And he will answer for those transgressions by the time this hearing is over, but the doctoring of footage to sway lords and ladies over to your cause is not only unethical, it is a serious misfeasance."

Guardian Eska held his tongue. Lady Aprah may have stood up for him here, but he was far from winning her overall support. Movement in the back section of the Hall of Voices caused Eska to tilt his head his former mentor made himself known.

"In my time of mentoring Edwyrd before he became Guardian of the Core, I knew the boy to be smart, intelligent, and truthful. He always had a level head on his shoulder, and that is why I endorsed him for the Trials to begin with. In *this* particular matter, I agree with Lady Aprah." Garrett Omyon gave Eska a furtive glance. "I, too, echo the call to remove Lord Zigarda from his position."

The subtly of the glance made Eska sweat. How he had said it also unnerved him. It was certain Luvan's statements about the absconding of his vows had disembodied any sense of propriety that Guardian Eska may have once had. At the least, it cast doubt in the eyes of those before him. And those shadows of doubt now chilled Eska, but he would answer them in time.

Zigarda laughed hysterically, manically, as if he was possessed by some spirit. When he regained control of himself, he said, "Unfortunately, for all of you, there is no power to remove me directly from my office right here, right now."

Eska's eyes flared. He had had enough of this spider's lies, webs, and vindictiveness. It was time to eliminate the nuisance of Victor Zigarda once and for all.

Eska cleared his throat. "I remove you from your position, Victor, for the collusion against me and the meddling in the affairs of the Trials and the contestants in the aftermath."

As one, the Hall of Voices looked at Eska.

Silence.

Eska bore everyone's gaze, hoisted it upon his shoulders, but would not succumb to the weight of his actions. He understood very well what he had just done and what he had just shown, but he needed to be clear and confident. He needed to act with authority and propriety and utter equality. He had already given too much lenience to Victor's venom over the past years.

"This is another abuse of his Power everyone. Why can you not see that?" Victor Zigarda jabbed the air towards Eska.

No one said anything.

Before he knew it, Senator Numos had approached the right side of the stage. He tapped a button with the end of his cane, manifesting another podium that slowly rose to his height. Waving his cane in the air, he said, "Order. Order. Everyone can take their seats. Victor Zigarda, while it may be unjust, by all means the Guardian of the Core *does* have the authority, and if it has come from his lips, then it will be done. Lords and ladies, let this most recent occurrence not circumvent your conscious. This is another act of Guardian Eska's abuse in Power. There are still other matters that the Guardian has to account for; by no means do these recent utterances absolve the Guardian from all of his misdoings. In light of these developments, there will be a recess for the rest of the day. Tomorrow we will continue the hearing." Senator Numos spared no glance at Eska as he returned to his spot at the back of the stage.

No one moved, still paralyzed by the last acts of the day. Eska turned on his heels and walked out, chest out, proud and confident until he was beyond the stage and out the door. Outside, alone, his shoulders finally slumped, the façade of his fearlessness fading. He had survived the first day of the hearing, but would he be able to survive the rest of the accusations brought before him?

CHAPTER 9

# GAIA

W ith one arm over his body, Hydro tapped his foot and spun his most recent collection in his other hand. *Five more to go. What will be next?* Anxiety gnawed at him as much as his curiosity. If there had been anything this hunt of his had taught him, it was that things would only get more difficult with each jewel he collected. Hydro already supposed that Eska kept one jewel to himself, for he would be a fool not to; the Core was already safe enough as it was. That battle Hydro wasn't looking forward to, especially considering this last one against a woman who held no weapon had almost killed him. Eska, however, had an Ether Weapon, the Power of the other Guardians of the Core, a dragon, and who knows what other secrets.

"Approaching."

Hydro shifted his eyes from the jewel to the partially cracked windshield in front of him. He tucked the jewel away in his satchel and leaned forward onto the ship's control panel, trying to get a better view of what was to come.

Dr. Cere's machine was slowly descending out into the middle of an ocean. A large whirlpool sat in the center of four separate islands, dragging into it the surrounding waters. Three islands were rich in vegetation and forestry, leaving only one island, which looked rather cultivated from above, for landing. The machine touched down on the island amidst an onslaught of attention. Not yet departing the safety of his ship's interior, Hydro hunched over the co-pilot seat to get a look at the dozen or so people who populated this remote island. From a quick survey, Hydro didn't see any weapons about their persons.

"Open up the ship."

With Purge on one hip and the satchel of jewels on the other, Hydro disembarked. Neither side spoke, merely observed the other. For the most part, they all wore threaded robes the same earthen color as their cracked and weathered skin. Brown eyes with no deviation in color looked at him.

One man stepped forward, a clay tunic draped over his shoulders, the collar sitting low enough to expose the upperpart of a well-defined chest and a few quills of a brown feather necklace that hung lower, covered by the clothing. Barefoot, he approached with one hand tucked inside that of a girl older than Aiton but who had yet to see puberty. At a body's length away from Hydro, he began speaking, and to Hydro's surprise, he was able to comprehend the foreign words.

"What is that big device behind you? Why do you come here? Where do you come from?"

*How is this possible?*

*Because I can hear every language perfectly, Hydro Paen, for I am perfection.*

Hydro swallowed. Ignoring Desmós's claim, he said, "It's called a ship. I've come from above."

"What is a ship?" the man asked. He pointed upwards with a finger and arched his back. Shielding his eyes with a forearm, he asked. "Above? The floating isles?"

*He can understand me. Did I just speak in...*

*You can speak in tongues now that you have some of my father's Power within you.*

"Yes. This ship. It lets me travel. See things." Hydro reached into his satchel and pulled out one of his jewels. "I am looking for a jewel." He twirled the topaz in his hand.

The whole village gathered around to see the jewel. Before Hydro knew it, the girl snatched the jewel from Hydro's fingers. She darted away and twirled it around in her hands.

Although tempted to make a move to retrieve the jewel, Hydro stayed in place, his eyes fixed on the little girl.

"The jewel you seek is already gone."

Hydro shook his head. "Impossible. I know it is here."

The man shook his head. "It *was* here. We gave it as an offering to her."

"Her?" Hydro raised an eyebrow. "Who is she?"

"Gaia."

"Where is it?"

"We threw it to her so that she may come up again once more. But she has not. Not yet."

The little girl had disappeared. His neck taut, he searched and saw from over the tops of the villagers that the little girl had dashed out from the protection of the elders and ran towards a long, earthen pier that shot out from the island. On either side of the earthen pier were crude skiffs, but she didn't hop in any of those, instead she went as far as she could.

Hydro moved to go towards her, but the elders stopped him.

"One more offering needs to be made. We are sure. Bonds come in two."

"Let me go."

Hydro struggled against the impeding crowd, but they latched onto him. When he tried to use the Power of the earth to give him space between them, he felt another Power, a united Power pushing back on him, negating his ability. *To Abaddon with this.* Hydro pushed his shoulder into one of the woman holding his right arm and did the same with another villager who took her place. All he needed was a moment's breath.

The girl had stopped on the earthen pier and now retraced her steps. Then she ran forward again and used her momentum to pitch the jewel out into the whirlpool that lay at the doormat to the islands. Hydro skidded to a stop. *What on earth?*

"Papa, I did it!" she yelled, barely audible enough to hear.

The villagers stopped.

"Great job, Bloom."

"Do you have any idea what you've just done?"

Everyone turned to look at him.

Rage ensnared Hydro. He unsheathed Purge and cut through those closest to him. The surrounding villagers drew earthen daggers, but as they approached him, he cut them in two as well, their crude devices being no match for his Ether Weapon. Blood splattered his face and drenched his clothing.

The man who had greeted him lay with a large gash across his stomach, bleeding out. He coughed up blood. "Abaddon take you." He turned his head to the side and reached his arm out for his daughter. "Bloom…" He collapsed.

The others had scurried away from the massacre. They watched him now from the comforts of thatched timber houses. Hydro sheathed Purge and ran towards the earthen pier. When Bloom saw him approaching, she quickly freed a skiff that had been tied around an earthen stump and pushed herself away from shore. Hydro couldn't care less about that. He needed the jewel. At the end of the pier, he stopped, catching his breath, ignoring everything else. Before him was the great whirlpool. *She tossed it in there.*

*Into the Abyss.* Desmós's voice congealed with his own.

*The Abyss?*

*Just like Mount Volan and Mount Klaff extend to the heavens, the Abyss and Abaddon's Towers offer a passage to Abaddon itself.*

Hydro gulped. *What's down there? Does a wish lie down there as well?*

*Flames. Never-ending flames.*

*For who?*

*The dead who never believed.*

*Believed?*

*In us.*

*Who is that?*

Convenient silence gave Hydro his answer. A cold wind dragged around his body, exposed to the open air on the pier. Hydro scanned the waters but knew it was futile. He would have to enter and somehow hope to find the jewel. Two of them, if what the villagers said was true. Hydro peered back over his shoulder; those who had escaped were tending the wounded.

"What did you do? What did you do? You hurt them!"

Hydro's head torqued to the little girl, who rowed in place, undaunted by the force of the whirlpool.

"Why did you do that? I hope Gaia comes and eats you."

Just then a tremor rippled throughout the pier of earth. It brought him to all fours. *What is...*

In the depths of the whirlpool, something darkened, and the rumbling intensified, almost as if the whirlpool was about to erupt or tectonic plates shifted in the deep.

Hydro tensed as a figure sprang forth, an immense creature unlike any he had ever seen, as large as the giants in Volan and nearly as massive as Desmós had appeared to be in the palace of ice. *Could this be...*

*Gaia.*

Hydro blinked. To his right, Bloom still sat in her boat, fixated on the massive being that had emerged from the vortex, from the Abyss, and now hovered over it, casting them all in shadow.

It let loose a roaring caw and flapped its brown and green wings, sending a gust that threatened to push Hydro onto his back. The rushing air carried an earthy smell and dust that Hydro had to blink away. Squinting helped, and when the tremors ceased, Hydro pushed himself onto his feet and stared up at the behemoth glossy black underbelly. A tail as thick as a tree with a green bush at its base swung to and fro. If not for the constant shouting of the girl on the boat, Hydro would have continued staring up at the creature in awe.

"Eat him, Gaia! He is not one of us! He hurt us!"

As if the large earthen bird understood, Gaia turned towards Hydro. A large diadem of diamonds rested upon its brown, feathered face, its features similar to a falcon's. It cawed and twirled in midair. Diving, it hunted Hydro like a falcon would prey.

Hydro could only stare.

Desmós took to the water for him. Focused solely on survival, he was plunged below the surface of the ocean, into the deep and into the unknown.

## CHAPTER 10

# THE HEARING PART II

If whispers filled the Hall of Voices the day before, then today it overflowed with hushed voices. No one had expected Eska to strip Lord Zigarda of his title, especially given the charges laid at Eska's feet. But the move had drawn support, and Eska was more concerned with why his mentor had signed and stamped the subpoena that had called him here.

There were only three people whose opinions mattered to Eska: his mentor, Garrett Omyon; Tundra; and his apprentice. He had told Eirek of his actions after the recess to help prepare him for what lay ahead. Eirek's presence had been kept a secret, though perhaps Luvan guessed at it. Most in attendance, Eska assumed, expected him to defend himself in isolation. Luvan certainly deemed that to be more appropriate, but it was Eirek, Eska hoped, who would be able to sway minds. The last time Eirek had met all of them together it had been at Coronation, and now Eska was sure that he could impress them even more. That is what Eska had trained him for, and the lords and ladies in power would see that. Wouldn't they? While his combat skills still needed honing, he had a way with words; he understood situations and the dynamics involved, and his determination was interminable. Eska suspected Eirek's initial rejection for the role of apprentice had turned Eirek into a more suitable candidate than Zain Berrese would have ever been.

"Order. Order in the Hall." Neil Raiden raised his arms, signaling that the hearing was set to continue. "I will once again call names to establish quorum."

As quorum was established, Eska noted that Victor's voice was replaced with that of his advisor, Edwyn Lyze. Eska was sure not to win his vote, but that didn't matter. As long as two-thirds of the lords and ladies didn't vote against him, he would remain Guardian of the Core. Only five nations needed to see his reasoning.

The only other change in the roster was the presence of Lady Linn Clayse, whose advisor had filled in the first day. Eska was glad to see her. Eirek would help him win Cresica's vote, he was certain. His dismissal of Lord Zigarda the day before would earn him points for Ka'Che and potentially sway the advisor who filled in for Lord Vangle to his side. But who else? If he explained his vows clearly enough, he was hoping that his home nation of Pyre would be one of them. All the nations from his home planet were a fairly sure bet. And there were the Mistralians, who he saved from Deimos during his first Pirini Lilapa. Surely they wouldn't have forgotten the good deed he had done for them all those years ago. That made six votes, and Lady Aprah seemed to have a good head on her shoulders, so if she truly were a pragmatic and a person concerned with propriety, she should understand why those elites had to be taken. She would see his side. That would be seven.

"Quorum is established. We will begin today with the prosecution giving us a summary of what yesterday's session included."

Luvan got up from his seat and began his long-winded, if eloquent, diatribe against Eska's abuse of Power. He concluded with the addendum of Eska's dismissal of Lord Zigarda. When he finished, Eska rose and nodded in Luvan's direction, willing to show respect for his former conseleigh's skills in argument. He had made valid points, and Eska could appreciate that. Doctoring footage and deceiving people to bring Eska before the Hall, as Zigarda had done, was something Eska couldn't tolerate.

Eska raised the podium to his level and began. "Good morning, everyone. Before I begin addressing some of your questions, let's tackle the dragon in the room. Yes, yesterday I used my authority to remove Victor Zigarda from office. While some may think this is yet another abuse of my power, perhaps even an attempt to consolidate it further or to remove a vote against me, I believe I have done the exact opposite of that. Such an action is sure to frighten many of you with what I can do politically to any of you at any time. And while the Guardian of the Core certainly holds this right, it is the only time in the history of my Guardianship that I have done such a thing. I have exercised that right now because I will not abstain from debasement and sabotage and subterfuge when it comes to the veracity of my statements, of my Trials, or of my contestants. There were clear reasons why my contestants were picked, and I do hold myself to the highest fiber of morality. Now are there—"

"Edwyrd…"

Only one person had the temerity to address him by his first name, and only one person in the Hall would be shown respect at such an interruption.

Lord Omyon's voice carried well, despite being the oldest present by hundreds of years. The Power and longevity given to him by his First Blood made him an unmovable force in the room, and his relationship with Eska even begged the Guardian of the Core's respect. Everyone quieted and looked up at the newcomer to the debate.

"I see why you did what you did yesterday. Thank you for addressing that concern, though, for others." He cleared his throat. "However, there are more pressing matters, especially when it comes to your so-called veracity."

Eska tightened. He knew what his mentor would ask about next.

"We need to discuss the larger dragon in the room, the breaking of your vows as Guardian of the Core." Garrett Omyon's gaze came to rest on Eska. "Is it true that you have had an affair with Conseleigh Iycel?"

Not looking away, Eska answered. "Yes. Conseleigh Iycel and I have been intimate."

"Could you please reiterate to everyone here what the vows of a Guardian are?"

Eska resisted the urge to hang his head. Stoic and calculated, he repeated the vows. As he did so, he looked at each one of the lords and ladies in the entire hall. He even gave passing glances to the senators and politicians who also sat at attention. "I, Edwyrd Eska, hereby declare that I will serve Gladonus to my fullest potential. That I will remain impartial to the needs of any one particular nation. And that the Power bestowed on me on the day of Passing, by the Twelve who have First Blood, will remain mine and mine alone through the abstinence of love and marriage and heirs. To all of this, I swear in the presence of the Ancients, the Twelve, and the families in power."

"What words do you have to defend your actions?"

"Every one of my Powers that I have received from the Twelve remains mine. I have no offspring with Conseleigh Iycel. We never married."

"But did you love her?"

Eska snapped his head in Luvan's direction across from him in front of the other podium. His conseleigh's eyes bore into him. Clearly, Luvan was using any necessary wording to convict Eska. Where had he gone so wrong? Why did propriety matter so much to Luvan? Was it because he lived here in the upper echelon of society? He had been born in Epoch, so what fueled the man's animosity?

"I already said that we have been intimate."

"Yes, but do you *love* her?"

It panged Eska to see that his conseleigh felt so betrayed, as if Eska should have loved all of them equally. Loyalty was beautiful in Eska's eyes and what he loved most about Tundra—her unwavering, undying loyalty. He didn't have any love for outdated decrees, even if that did mean casting aside his own propriety.

"Yes." Eska looked around the room. "What is love? Love is understanding. Love is sacrifice. Love is loyalty. It doesn't end. It never vacillates. It never dies. Love does not seek its own; love seeks only to give. It does not delight in the devils of this world. Instead, it seeks truth. And love protects that truth. It protects hope. And it always perseveres.

"Who are the Twelve to say I cannot love? Who are the Ancients to say that I cannot love? Being gifted with the longevity of the Twelve through the Power of the Guardian, I have seen my family pass away. I have seen nations rise. I have seen nations fall. I have seen more things than anyone else in this room, but I had never seen love until my time with Conseleigh Iycel. And why should I not be able to experience that intimacy so close to the conclusion of my Guardianship?

"Conseleigh Iycel and I connected over the loss of our loved ones, her husband and the sister I lost before my Trials even began. We found comfort in one another's melancholy, we understood each other perfectly, but never in my time with Tundra did I forsake my vows of being impartial to Gladonus. Never have I not given my all to Gladonus.

"When Deimos ravaged the land during my first Pirini Lilapa, I helped keep the nation of Mistral afloat. I chained the beast along with the Twelve on the Plains of Valor. I helped usher in an age of technology that could peacefully coexist with Power. And whilst it fills me with dread to hear of wars, I know it is not my right to interfere in their politics. My sole mission as Guardian of the Core is to serve the nations of this system, to protect them no matter the cost, and to not abuse the Power given to me by the Twelve."

"The very Power you have abused, Guardian Eska. Time and time again. And a Power you have consolidated all for you own."

Luvan still stood next to his podium, hunched over, hands gripping the sides, leaning on it even though he didn't need to. His gaze never wavered from Eska.

"Some of you may think that my actions on Mount Volan were an attempt to consolidate my Power. To get rid of the Twelve and commit the most utter act of apostasy, but none of you were in the situation I was in. None of you had the ability to do what needed to be done.

"When I arrived on Mount Volan that evening, Luenar was using his might to bring the moon of Onkh closer to the planet's atmosphere—something, I admit, that even I cannot do. The force being used upon that mountain was like an earthquake with every clash. It was tearing the mountain apart. Can anyone tell me what is significant about Mount Volan? Olivia, perhaps you know seeing as you are the lady of Gar." Eska turned his attention to Gar's section.

"It is said that Mount Volan holds a pathway to Axiumé," Lady Aprah said. "Same as Mount Klaff in Chaon."

"That is just a myth, though, my Guardian." Lord Zalos Kapache stood up. "To purport such a thing is—"

"It is not a myth, Zalos." Guardian Eska interjected. "I have seen the path for myself on Mount Klaff. A path that takes you inside the mountain and upwards."

"Did you enter?"

"I took the first few steps. I noted how steep the steps were. How narrow. How dark it was save for the sparse light moss that covered the walls, and I decided not to continue. If you do not believe me, that is your own prerogative, but if you climb Mount Klaff someday, you will see what I saw." Guardian Eska turned back to Lady Aprah. "Yes, Olivia, to Axiumé. If the fighting didn't stop, Mount Volan would been disemboweled. A gateway to Axiumé syphoned off, and those who believe in the Ancients would have lost a symbol of their presence.

"If the moon came closer and perhaps even crashed upon Mount Volan, how many lives on Onkh would be taken? An incalculable number. The Twelve, spurred on by centuries of loathing and bitterness for their hatred of the other tribe, tensions still high from the Great War, had no plans to stop, so I had to intervene. I had to make that decision. I made it, and I do not regret sealing the Twelve. I assure you that the life essence of the Twelve is still around; they are still alive, and I can call them back at any time I choose. They are safe, locked within jewels." Guardian Eska eased the tension in his shoulders, letting his words dispel into the crowd. He would have hoped for more silence and time for rumination, but Luvan Katore spoke once again.

"What Guardian Eska is not telling you is that he dismembered a few of the Twelve before placing them in those jewels. He engaged in aggressive combat with his dragon in order to stop them. He did not merely just restrain them as he suggests."

Guardian Eska scoffed and shook his head. "When you are not only fighting for your life but for the life of all of those on Onkh, Luvan, things are bound to get bloody. Orekus came at me, knives large enough to sever my torso. I fought back. Not only was he a threat to me, he would have been a threat to the other Twelve as well."

Lady Liliana Voux stood up from the Mistralian section. "Guardian Eska, I, for one, know how hard it must have been to make that decision and to experience another Pirini Lilapa. All of us are still thankful for your efforts against Deimos, but from talking with some of the other lords and ladies here, I want to voice a concern for everyone. How safe is safe when you mention the jewels? Please explain more about the binding process. Is it similar to what holds Deimos captive? We wish to understand more about the efficacy of your tactics."

"Lady Voux, you bring up a good point. I have scattered the twelve jewels throughout all of Gladonus. To where, I will not say, but it should come as no surprise that I do keep one on the Core by my person. I have no intention of bringing harm to these jewels in my own self-interest, as the Power of the Twelve is also my own Power. If one were to be syphoned, then my own energy would be syphoned, so I can assure you that all of these jewels are in locations perilous, treacherous, and impossible for normal individuals to reach. And because they are scattered all over the system, the chances of them coming together are nearly impossible. Even if they were collected, though, we must remember that the Twelve are of First Blood. A normal weapon cannot kill them. Therefore, even if a jewel happens to be smashed by accident, let's say, whichever god or goddess of the Twelve that is sealed within that jewel wouldn't die; their life force would be merely split into separate entities, all of which can be easily undone."

"And at the time of your Passing?" Lady Voux asked.

"At the time of my Passing, my apprentice will bear that responsibility. Apprentice Mourse will have the Power necessary to release the Twelve should we agree that they be released again, but I do not see that being necessary for at least another one-hundred-and-fifty years."

"And why is that?" Lady Liliana followed up.

"Because that is when the next Pirini Lilapa is set to occur, if, in fact, it does occur. Perhaps their strength will be useful then, but outside of that event, their life-force is just as advantageous as their physical forms. How many of you actually communicate with the Twelve on a regular basis?"

No one raised their hands. Eska had suspected as much.

"When was the last time any of you saw the Twelve?"

Eska expected no one to stand, so he was a little surprised with Aiton Paen stood.

"My father took my brother to see Pearl before the Trials began, Guardian Eska."

"And Pearl is no longer with us thanks to your brother."

"It wasn't his fault!" The outburst brought all eyes in the chamber to Aiton. The little lord cowered under the gaze of so many. "Excuse my outburst, my Guardian."

"I am sorry for bringing up past wrongdoings, my lord. Now what other—"

"What would happen should all the jewels be destroyed?"

Eska paused for a moment. He tilted his head towards Aiton. "Why do you ask?"

"You mentioned that the Twelve could be reincarnated if brought together. But what if they were destroyed? What would happen?"

Eska had expected this question, but not from Aiton. In truth, he was glad no one had asked him thus far, but now that it was out in the air, Eska could either lie or tell the truth. The harsh truth. He tapped the sides of the podium. All eyes looked at him now. He could feel it, even though he kept his gaze on the podium in front of him.

"Deimos would eventually be released."

Gasps surged through the Hall.

"What do you mean by eventually?" Lord Kapache and Advisor Vesk both stood up at the same time.

"It was the Twelve and I who bound Deimos in the Plains of Valor. Without the Twelve's life-force, only mine would remain to keep the bindings intact."

"And is that enough?" Errion Vesk raised a hand.

"Until the Passing were to occur, yes. Once I pass, though, and give my Powers to Eirek, my life force will also fade away and so will the last remaining bond on Deimos. But Apprentice Mourse will be capable of finishing Deimos in a way of which I was not capable."

"And what makes you think we should have any hope in your apprentice, my Guardian? He only barely managed to get enough votes for his Coronation."

Guardian Eska flicked his eyes to the new voice in the room, Lady Farah Scule from Lurid. Short silver hair hung just below her ears. Pale skin, as if she hadn't seen a dash of daylight, gave away her heritage.

"Apprentice Mourse is..." Guardian Eska toyed with the idea of telling them all of his bloodline, but decided it best not to. Instead, he picked the next word that came to his mind. "*Special.*"

"Special?" Lord Kapache scoffed. "In what way? He has yet to even thank Chaon for the gift we offered him after Coronation. It seems he is already lacking in propriety and manners."

"Apprentice Mourse is much more competent than at the time of Coronation. Furthermore, Zalos, I want to mention that my Trials aimed to test things that cannot be taught, they aimed to test here." Eska pointed to his chest. "While the previous Guardians did test for Power, combat skills, and intelligence, these are all things that can be trained. Partnership, however, cannot be trained. It is a moral that one is brought up with. As is fortitude. The idea of equality."

Luvan scoffed at Eska. "Equality? You dare to preach to us here on the idea of equality?"

Eska's patience was wearing thin for his ex-conseleigh, but he kept his face still, channeling his frustration into fingers that tapped the side of the podium.

"Is that so difficult to believe? You know as well as I that it is something I tested in the Trials. It is how Apprentice Mourse came to be picked over Prince Hydro Paen."

"True. It is very much the test you used to choose your apprentice, but it was only a riddle. Hardly anything extraordinary about it. But the reason I bring this up, Edwyrd, is because equality is another vow disregarded. Aren't you supposed to remain impartial?"

Eska nodded. He was unsure where Luvan was going with this.

"Then why did you deny Lady Scule's endorsement for the Trials? When it was time to scout contestants for the Trials and each of us brought our selections, I remember you denying Celeste Silver of Lurid from competing in the Trials. You claimed earlier this was for the sake of Gladonus, yet I still do not see why. She was a highly competent individual."

Lady Farah Scule of Lurid stood. "Celeste is a member of my Zircha Guard now, Guardian Eska. There is no doubt in my mind she will become their leader. Why was she denied?" Lady Scule shook her fist in the air like she held a gavel.

"Lady Scule," Luvan went on, eagerly seizing on her anger, "it gets even more interesting than that. Celeste would have definitely outperformed the contestants I put forth. In fact, according to the Guardian of the Core, one 'didn't even show,' if I remember your words correctly. And the other two were 'a prince that didn't even win a single Trial, and an apprentice who needed much refining.' All three of them incompetent in the eyes of our Guardian. So why, Edwyrd, was Celeste Silver denied?"

Eska bit back his tongue. *Never cross words with politicians, much less Mistralian ones.* Features as placid as he could make them and his voice in as sincere as he could muster, he said, "Because of the prophecy."

"The what?" Lady Scule and Luvan asked simultaneously.

"The prophecy," Eska repeated. It was likely only his mentor was aware of it. Guardian Eska flicked his gaze towards Lord Omyon and saw, to his surprise, a slight nod in return. The brief acknowledgement was all Eska needed.

"When the position of Guardian was created, a prophecy flew on the winds. It goes like this:

> Chosen will be blood from all five domains.
> Hope they will bring through chaos, anger, and pain.
> Twelve will lose favor, four will regain form.
> Bringing with them more death than the Great War.

"The domains in the prophecy represent each planet in this system."

"And you know this for certain?" asked Lady Scule.

"No. Prophecies are often up for interpretation; however, at the time, I was fairly certain about that line, and I made a conscious effort to avoid such a catastrophe. I do not want to be responsible for another Great War."

"You said, *at the time*. Does that mean you no longer think this way?" Luvan was quick to ask.

"Recent information and enlightenment have allowed me to see the prophecy in a new way. While I still believe that the domains represent the planets in the system, I no longer believe this prophecy was concerned with contestants in the Trials."

"So your cause for Celeste's denial was unfounded?"

"You may see it as that, Luvan." Eska stared at his conseleigh for an intense moment, until Luvan broke eye contact. Then Eska surveyed the whole auditorium. "But I want to remind you all that I am human. I make mistakes. Sometimes I say things that I learn to regret later." He hoped Luvan would catch that line. "While my intentions at that time were good, I understand that I did, in fact, let my bias show."

"Like the bias you showed against my nation recently?" Lady Aprah stood, arms crossed over her breasts.

"Bias, Lady Aprah? I am not sure I understand."

"You required twenty-five of my elites, half of my force, to help Conseleigh Iycel on a mission in Sereya. She returned with only two of my men. What in the Ancients' good name could have been so important and so deadly?"

Eska breathed in and exhaled. Finally, it had come to this. If he successfully navigated this, he wasn't sure how much more they could bring against him. With a courteous nod in Lady Aprah's direction, he acknowledged her sentiment. "Yes, Olivia. Conseleigh Iycel's actions were my actions. She did not request any of Acquava's soldiers because of the recent turmoil that Hydro has caused throughout the nation and the family. While I may not make the best decisions at times, I am not heartless. I didn't want Acquava to go through any more trouble than it already had. I told her to depose Lord Grime should evidence be sufficient of his—"

Whittiker Grime stood up and cursed out Tundra. "When is deposition the same as beheading?"

Eska's eyes flared, but he reined in his anger. He couldn't afford another outburst, but to put up with such a derogatory term infuriated him. He shot his eyes to Whittiker. "I cannot say what caused Tundra to go to such extremes; however, she told me that your father directly threatened her life and my own. *That* is something that is not acceptable. She is not heartless; she is loyal. And loyalty beats all."

"Loyal or not, the actions she took against the Grime family in Sereya were brash and severe. Why was she also not dismissed? Do her actions not warrant the same repercussions as mine? Does your intimacy with her make you biased and blinded to her actions?" Luvan asked.

Eska formulated his rebuttal in his mind. Severe actions were not the same as disobeying a direct order. If anything, Tundra was following it to the letter, for Eska had asked her to take care of him. Perhaps he should have been clearer on that. As he was about to respond, though, Whittiker asked a different question. "Are you afraid of my father, my Guardian? He can hardly hold a cane. How do you think he would manage to defeat you? Words are water, are they not?"

For once, he was glad Whittiker had interjected. While he had a defense ready, he would have not liked to answer Luvan's question. Instead, he ignored it and focused solely on the last words spoken. "Yes, words are water, Whittiker, but you also forget that actions are ice. Conseleigh Iycel found that your father had been working with a man named Doctor Genus Cere, who I know to be directly responsible for influencing the Trials and causing Zain to refuse the position. *That* is a serious offense, one that affects every single person here, for without the tampering, the true Trial candidate most likely would have been chosen. Astor then—"

"I heard your hedge phrase. You said *most likely.* We have no way of knowing if Zain Berrese would have accepted or not."

Eska turned his attention away from Whittiker. Senator Numos stood alongside Luvan, sharing the podium with him. "No, we do not. There is not an alternate reality we can perceive as to whether or not Zain would have said *yes* to my offer should Cere not have interfered. However, by having ties with Cere, Astor was then held as an accomplice and deserved the punishment. Also, from what Tundra had told me, in dealing with Cere, he also neglected his duties as a militia advisor to Tundra while she was the lady of Sereya. Astor Grime had two wrongs against him."

"And that still does not make it right," Senator Numos boomed.

*This is going nowhere.* Eska allayed his mind and reached out to Eirek. *Eirek, are you outside?*

*Yes, my Guardian.*

*And are you ready?*

*I will try.*

That is all Eska needed. "Aye, I cannot say what is right and what is wrong. That is what all of you are here to decide. I have spoken my piece concerning all the allegations brought before me. I am only human. I, too, fall susceptible to biases at times, improper recourse to others, have done things that I wish I hadn't, but if you are going to judge me, then judge me now and be done with it. And if you find it fitting to strip me here of my title today, then I believe my apprentice is ready to take over my role, regardless of whether he was the true winner of the Trials and regardless of what Luvan Katore quoted earlier. In the months since Pirini Lilapa, Eirek Mourse has made great strides, and I do believe he may be an even better Guardian of the Core than I could ever be."

Senator Numos guffawed. "I've already demonstrated how incompetent Apprentice Mourse is. I saw it for myself during the Trials, Guardian Eska. You may say that he is ready to take your role, but how will we ever truly know?"

"You won't ever truly know unless I am impeached today, but you can see it for yourselves and judge accordingly."

Numos frowned, clearly suspicious.

*Eirek, it is time to enter.*

"I wish to bring forth my apprentice Eirek Mourse."

The double doors of the Hall of Voices opened wide.

CHAPTER 11

# SELF-WORTH

Having never visited Mistral, Eirek didn't have any expectations when he entered the Hall of Voices—but anything he could have imagined would have been shattered. Hundreds of people cut from the finest cloth filled the circular auditorium, groomed to be alphas from a young age, Eirek was sure. This was the upper echelon of society, only allowed to those with names and status bred over centuries. He had never seen so many important people all at once. Well, he supposed that wasn't entirely true. The Hall of Voices would have been even more spectacular had he not already gone through Coronation on the Core and seen the Palace of Power on Mount Volan. Those events would serve him well here, he hoped, as he faced the highest stakes of his life. If they impeached Eska, the weight of Gladonus would fall on Eirek. Was he ready for that? Could he handle becoming Guardian of the Core so early?

Eirek ignored the bright beams of light that shone down from the auditorium's ceiling, casting a spotlight around the stage and the doorway from which he entered. Whispers overtook the room, clawing over one another in an attempt to see how this turn of events would play out. For many, Eirek supposed, it was a chance to finally put a face to Eska's apprentice, to finally gauge his worth. And for the lords and ladies here, it was a chance to evaluate his growth during the time on the Core. Would he live up to their standards?

Eirek continued forward. Senator Numos and Luvan were frantically talking away from the microphone on the second podium, casting Eirek furtive glances as he made his way towards Guardian Eska, who never stopped looking at him. Eska turned back to the microphone when Eirek had approached the center stage. "I give to you, my apprentice, Eirek Mourse. Judge his competency to take over for me should you dismiss me here today." Eska gestured for Eirek to stand alongside him.

When he did so, everyone rose to their feet. The sign of respect flushed Eirek's face. He noticed Linn had joined this meeting, and her presence gave him more confidence. She smiled at him, and he gave an appreciative nod to her. Then he looked out around the room, making sure to exchange nods and glances with all the lords and ladies present and those he didn't know but assumed were filling in for the lords or ladies who were absent.

"My Guardian, this is outlandish. Apprentice Mourse is not on Trial. You are the one who is to be impeached."

Eska whipped his head to Senator Numos. "This is a hearing, Senator. I am allowed to have witnesses. You have brought forth allegations that my Trials were too difficult and that it broke the psyche of my contestants. Here is one of my contestants. Evaluate his psyche, ask him of the Trials, and let it be known..." Eska stared around the room before continuing. "Let it be known that while I may have signed off on the individual Trials, they were not designed by me. And, in truth, winning the Trials didn't matter at all."

"Excuse me..." Lord Kapache stood up, scratching his chameleon's chin. "Did I hear that correctly? The Trials did not matter at all? Then why have them?"

Eska dipped low to speak into the microphone, but Eirek pushed forward and spoke first. "Guardian Eska's Trials were a test of who we were. He wanted to find out about us here." Eirek pointed to his heart. "The man who actually won the Trials, Zain Berrese, secured no points during the event. To the Guardian, though, he had showed something more than what merely winning a point may do."

"And what was that?" Lady Liliana Mistral asked.

Eska answered, drawing the microphone closer to him and leaning forward. "Zain Berrese showed grit. He showed the ability to analyze situations. He showed compassion for the lives of others, and that is the main reason I chose him."

"And what is it, then, that this apprentice showed?"

The voice came from Empora's section, but it wasn't Victor Zigarda. Eirek knew Eska had dismissed him the day before, but he could not recall the name of the substitute, though he had seen the man in the Web.

"A humble heart." Eska turned to Eirek and smiled.

"One riddle showed you that?"

Eska swung his head towards Senator Numos, who quickly followed up his outburst. "For those of you who are unfamiliar with the situation, Guardian Eska chose Apprentice Mourse to be his apprentice based on one riddle. That is it."

Eska drummed his thumbs on the side of the podium as gasps rippled through the Hall. "Senator Numos, do you still recall the riddle I asked?"

"I do, my Guardian."

"Please do me the favor, then, and repeat the riddle for everyone here. Let's see if anyone can guess it."

"What is it the Ancients never saw, the Twelve seldom see, but what we see every day?"

"Very good. Yes, after Zain Berrese denied my offer, I made my selection between Prince Hydro Paen of Acquava and Eirek Mourse of Cresica upon this riddle. Can anyone tell me the answer? My apprentice will let you know if you are right."

Eska backed away from the microphone and glanced around the room. A few shouted answers to which Eirek leaned in the microphone and said, "Incorrect." Eska tapped him on the back, and Eirek looked up. Eska gave him a nod, so Eirek leaned forward once more. "The answer is actually—"

"An equal."

"Yes, actually. Lady Aprah, that is correct."

Eska took the microphone from Eirek's grasp. "Do you see how many people got it wrong? Only one here got it right. And do you know why that is, Senator? Do you know why that is, Edwyn?"

The man who filled in for Zigarda stayed quiet. Senator Numos, on the other hand, gesticulated toward the seated auditorium. "Enlighten us, my Guardian."

"No. Eirek will do that. He knows the answer." Eska stepped away from the microphone and gave Eirek a pat on the back.

The token of confidence didn't make Eirek any less nervous. Eirek felt the enormous amount of stares on him. It grew so intolerable and the silence so awkward that Senator Numos guffawed.

"It seems he isn't as capable as you—"

"Give him some more time, Senator. He will surprise you. He has certainly surprised me time and time again."

Eska's overarching confidence in Eirek had never been so rewarding, but right now it seemed hardly applicable. Eirek could not understand why Lady Aprah had known the answer. She had been born into her title. She hadn't ever worked for it. But then Eirek remembered Cadmar talking about the Passage and how it symbolized the journey that Lady Aprah's parents went through to make Gar the nation it was today, and there, that was the answer.

Eirek took the microphone and cleared his throat. "The people of Gar know what it's like to not be rulers. To not be equals with the other nations here."

Eirek bought himself some time and looked from Senator Numos out over the auditorium to the other lords and ladies. His eyes fell last upon Lady Aprah, who stared intently at him. The same intent stare she had given him while examining his next move in their chess duel before he was taken to the Sacred Passage. Eirek recalled what she said that day. And now that he thought more about that match and the advice she gave him afterwards, he understood fully why she, out of all the people in the auditorium, would solve the riddle. With a beaming smile, he turned to Senator Numos.

"Before I attended the Meeting of the Twelve, I played a chess match against Lady Aprah. During that duel, she told me that the colors on the board were how she chose her sigil colors, and that the silver on her sigil symbolized the need to constantly achieve something greater. To know that you are never truly first, only second. It is a humbling color. And she humbled me that day as well by beating me in the chess match. I thought her use of her lady early was brash and foolish, but she beat me nonetheless. She told me to never ask someone to do something you would not do yourself. You have to earn the respect below you, rather than always pleasing the people above you. Every piece across her board she saw as equals. And as Guardian of the Core, one must be humble, one among equals, to serve and protect all the nations." Eirek looked out across the room. The silence from Senator Numos made him smile.

"Well spoken, Apprentice Mourse. You know our colors well and have re-membered the little lessons I gave you." Lady Aprah gave him an appreciative nod and a slight clap.

Eirek's smile widened upon the approval. "It is my duty to know, Lady Aprah. Thank you."

Linn Clayse stood up. "No one knows Apprentice Mourse like I do. Before the Trials, he was bumbling, awkward, shy. The Trials didn't break his psyche, as Senator Numos must have pointed out in the previous meeting. Instead, I can honestly stand here today and say that I do not even recognize the man I see upon the center stage."

Eirek blushed at her words.

"It is Apprentice Mourse who gave me the advice that I needed to do what was expected of me after the incident on Syf."

"Apprentice Mourse told you to declare war on Epoch?" Lord Evber's advi-sor roared from the Epoch station.

Linn shook her head. "No. But he gave me the courage to be equals with those who would be fighting. To fight alongside them and add my valor to their strength should our war culminate in violence. And while others may have criticized the apprentice for being discourteous, I have found him nothing but the opposite." Linn turned to the rest of the audience in the chamber. "After Pirini Lilapa, Eirek visited my family to offer his condolences. As I mentioned previously, he has grown much from when I first saw him before the Trials began. Even at Coronation, he struggled with his words, but I see today the confidence needed to take Guardian Eska's spot should the vote fall towards the Guardian's impeachment.

"I say this not because I believe Guardian Eska should be impeached. I say this because it is clear that Guardian Eska and his conseleigh have raised Eirek to lead well. So while there may have been past grievances, there has also been much progress made under the training. It makes me believe that Guardian Eska is fulfilling his role, despite any vows that may have been broken."

"What you say, Lady Clayse, comes from a place of privilege," Lady Aprah said. "While I can appreciate how the apprentice has blossomed, it does nothing to alter the fact that Eska's conseleigh took half of my best men north and only come back with two of them. Lives were lost, and that is something you cannot understand."

"My mother's life was lost during Pirini Lilapa. Apprentice Mourse lost his uncle. Do not speak to me, to either of us, about lives lost, Lady Aprah."

"I agree with Lady Aprah, Lady Clayse. Your closeness to the apprentice, while touching, blinds you to the fact that Guardian Eska did not act in the name of equality. Cresica had a chosen applicant; Lurid did not and for foolish reasons, nonetheless," Lady Scule added.

Eirek couldn't watch Linn get lambasted by the other ladies in the room, so he spoke up. "Ladies and lords," he started, drawing attention away from Linn and back onto him on the center stage. "Since the Trials, I have grown a great deal. Many of you saw me at Coronation. I was as Lady Clayse has portrayed me, but I hope you can see that has changed. I have stood face-to-face with the Twelve; I have trained under Guardian Eska and his conseleigh for months; and I have learned much through all of my experiences with him. What vows he has broken in remaining impartial were broken because he wanted to avert disaster. The Twelve he sealed on Mount Volan to avoid a greater catastrophe. Whether you would like to see it or not, Guardian Eska has acted with pre-science to save lives.

"I gave Lady Clayse advice on how to lead, advice I learned while spending time with Lady Aprah. But when I heard that she had declared war on Epoch, I felt partially culpable. I doubled my training efforts on the Core and have advanced greatly in combat and in Power, and I did this because I wanted the chance to enter the next phase in my training, which is living in each nation for a year so that I can begin building rapport with the regular citizens and families of Power. But do you know what?" Eirek paused now and looked around the room. The three ladies still stood, caught up in his words. "He denied me that chance. I wanted to go to Epoch or Cresica so that I could talk them out of this war. War that Lady Clayse entered, I believe, due to the social pressure put on her from other families of Power. A war born from revenge, and revenge is never a good motive for anything.

"He denied me that chance because I don't yet know enough about your cultures. And, to be honest, I am still not as strong as my Guardian, either. I am better, yes, even I can hardly recognize myself, but I am not yet ready to be Guardian of the Core, whether Guardian Eska thinks that or not. Because being Guardian of the Core means knowing each nation's situation, knowing its people, and knowing how to best defend them from any catastrophe. So, no, Lady Scule, Lurid may not have had a contestant in the Trials, I may have very well taken that person's spot for all I know, but he did it for the greater good. And Lady Aprah, while I don't know the details concerning your elites and Guardian Eska, I do feel as though he did it for the greater good as well. After all, he sealed the Twelve on Mount Volan for your safety. Do not forget that."

"Touching, Apprentice Mourse," Senator Numos spoke. "You certainly have changed much since I've interviewed you on the Core, but I believe I heard you say you are not ready to become Guardian of the Core. If Guardian Eska is impeached here today, I take it that you rescind your rights to being Guardian of the Core."

"I..." Eirek's throat tightened. Caught up in the moment, he hadn't thought about the implication of those words. Senator Numos continued, offering him no time to correct his statement.

"Let us be clear, then, that the vote here today would officially remove Guardian Eska *and* his apprentice, the Guardian of the Core based upon the charges against him and the apprentice on his own lack of willingness to enter the position."

Guardian Eska snatched the microphone from Eirek. "Do not attempt to twist my apprentice's words, Senator Numos." He turned his attention to the rest of the auditorium. "I want to make it clear that by removing me from my position *does not* remove my apprentice. My apprentice said he doesn't feel ready to take my position, not that he is *unwilling* to take my position. The hearing only concerns my actions. I merely brought my apprentice here to show you why I conducted the Trials as I did and how training has improved the boy's performance dramatically. Should you wish to continue holding my actions against me, then so be it. I have nothing more to say." Guardian Eska spared no glance for Senator Numos as he turned around to face the back of the stage. "Speaker of the Hall, let us begin the vote."

Neil Raiden got up and exchanged places with Eska. Numos remained stationary, obviously unsure as to whether Eska had outmaneuvered him. After a long look from Neil Raiden, Senator Numos removed himself and returned to sit alongside Luvan.

"There is much information to take in," Raiden said, "and the consequences of this vote are immense. I am using my authority as Speaker of the Senate to issue another recess. Lords and ladies, you will have the night to gather your thoughts. Tomorrow, the Guardian of the Core's fate will be decided. You are all dismissed."

After the dismissal, Eirek and Guardian Eska went back to their hotel room in the heart of Briseas. Because Mistral floated in the sky, nighttime came later here than it would to the nations on the ground, so by the time the hearing adjourned for the day, darkness still had yet to set in. Guardian Eska had congratulated him on his performance during the ride back, and after a dinner of potatoes, vegetables, and meat, he and Eirek devised a set of contingency plans should the vote go against Eska.

"If that were to happen, I'm going to ask for a year extension in my Power. I want to be able to properly transfer the knowledge you need to fulfill my duties, Eirek."

"Do you think they would grant you that?"

"If they are smart, they will. There are many things I have yet to show you."

"Like what?"

"We'll discuss that when the time comes." Guardian Eska smiled, but the sigh that followed told Eirek it was forced. Then Guardian Eska undid his reimaje and let its pure blackness unravel before him. "This will show you anything that you need to know from the previous Guardians of the Core, but if you do not know what to search for, it is useless. Some of the things I have yet to tell you about are better shown. I hope you understand."

Eirek's eyes never left the reimaje. He had only seen Eska take it off one other time, to teleport himself to Mount Volan during Pirini Lilapa. Eirek nodded. He paused a little and then asked, "Did I mess up today?"

Eska put the reimaje back on his head. "No. Senator Numos is doing what politicians do, twisting words and finding loopholes. It is in a Mistralian's blood like fire is in my own and water in an Acquavan's." Eska clasped his hands behind his cape. "I've decided I'm going to remove him from his position tomorrow as well. After the vote."

"Isn't that—"

"Yes. It is. But at this point, what does it matter? He took advantage of my generosity during the Trials to take the blood of my contestants, isn't that correct?"

Eirek nodded. "He took mine at least."

"I have no way of knowing where that blood is. He may have given it to Victor Zigarda, he may not have, who knows. The lord somehow managed to get Gabrielle's blood already, so I assume Numos had some role to play in it. Regardless, it is a grievance I cannot allow."

"Why not just arrest him?"

"Because everything is circumstantial. There are too many open ends to say for sure whether the senator was in collusion with Victor Zigarda. And there is always perhaps the idea that he did, in fact, use it for verification purposes as he purported. It is too hard to say what has become of that, but I cannot allow it to go unpunished. He should have notified me before he conducted those interviews. But enough of that for now. I am going to step outside for a bit."

"Why?"

"It's dark out finally and I want to see if I can find something." Eska said.

"Like what?"

Eska chuckled a little. "Maybe someday I will tell you. Get some sleep, Eirek."

"Can I join you?"

"Not this time." Eska shook his head and walked out the door.

Eirek didn't go to bed right away. Instead, he had turned off the lights and then crept over to the window and peeled back the curtain slightly. Eirek's heart sank. It didn't matter. They were too far up in this hotel to properly see down below, but that also meant Eska couldn't view him either, so he drew back the curtains and looked at the sky. The city lights were slowly dying, but without moons, the nighttime sky was brighter than ever, perfect for star-gazing. Ever since his uncle told him one star held his name, Eirek had always been curious how he might determine which one was his, but he supposed that was just another tale his uncle used to tell. How would he know which one it was? How would one call out to it? The whole process caused his brain to hurt even more than it already did after the day's events. He pushed himself up from the side of Eska's bed and went back over to his own, tucking himself underneath the covers, ready to sleep. Or, at least, try. An hour or two later, when he was on the verge of doing so, Eska came back into the room, but Eirek didn't get up. He heard Eska pull the curtains inward and slide into his own bed. Within moments, Eska snored. Did he have no qualms about the vote? Or perhaps he was resigned to the idea that he could do nothing to change the outcome and was resolved not to worry about that which he could not control. Eirek wished he could have the same paradigm as Eska, one of cavalier confidence, but too much was resting on the twelve lords and ladies and the vote. Tomorrow he would either remain apprentice or become the next Guardian of the Core.

CHAPTER 12

# THE INNER SANCTUM

Hydro stood in a cavern that shouldn't have existed. Not by any laws of nature, anyway. As soon as he had submerged, the force of the whirlpool pulled him forward. Knowing he could breathe underwater thanks to the mermaid's kiss, being pulled apart by the strength of the whirlpool or devoured by Gaia were his primary concerns. He considered himself lucky not to be plucked out of the ocean like a fish. And the vortex was unlike the devilssand he experienced in Chaon. When he entered the vicinity of the whirlpool, he didn't have time to feel anything. Instead, it yanked him under and pulled him to the cavern he now stood inside. Where Gaia had risen up from.

*Will she return?* Hydro tapped his foot impatiently, looking up at the blue ceiling that spread out over the circumference of the cavern, like a watery mouth opened wide, sticking out its blue tongue. The water spilled out from no other place, pooling there as if held by some invisible force. If Hydro hadn't been from Acquava nor had he ever seen the Watery Path or where Pearl lived, he would think the cavern odd, but he was sure that the same Power that prevented the Watery Path from spilling over to the Hall of Lords was the same Power at work here.

*No time to think about that.* Desmós moved him to the lower levels of the cavern, to where the split splat of the water no longer misted him. *The jewels are what matters.*

*That was a Creature of Legend. That was Gaia.* Hydro forced his body to keep stationary.

*And Gaia is nothing.* Desmós pushed against Hydro's will, maneuvering him off the cliffs where he had entered.

*Would you stop doing that?* Hydro braced himself, keeping Desmós back.

*There are more important things than Gaia, Hydro Paen. We should go.* Desmós overpowered Hydro and forced him to move farther into the cavern.

Hydro gasped as his body moved against him. The sound echoed about the cavern. He couldn't keep fighting Desmós. Not like that. *I will search for it, just let me do it. Okay?*

*Very well, Hydro Paen.*

Hydro raised his arm and shook his leg, testing his body. Hydro huffed but continued walking forward. If he was to search for a jewel, it would be on his own terms. And while he was conscious. He didn't want to black out again like he had after Crestal's Palace.

*Are there other creatures as powerful as Gaia?*

*Gaia's might is nothing compared to mine.*

*How?*

*I know all of my father's creations. None of them can stand to me.*

*You are related?*

*I already told you; she is my sister.*

*Is that why she attacked us?*

*Yes. Now, the jewel.*

Using his right hand, he pinched his eyes and nose and then brushed over his face and ran his fingers through his hair, removing any water and allowing him to scan the area properly. A natural glow emitting from the red moss clinging to the walls radiated across the expanse. It allowed him to see the constant drip of water from the stalactites around the cavern, although the gushing of the water from the upper reaches of the chasm overpowered any splat he may have heard. Without the machine, there was no way of knowing if the jewel he was searching for was actually in this cavern, but he assumed that it was. After all, where else would the vortex suck the jewel?

Luckily, the water only spat out at one spot throughout the spacious subterranean cavern, directly to a stone pillar composed of other smaller pillars that made the center of the hollowing a large pedestal. Hydro was on a lower level but not yet on the cavern's floor. Before descending farther, he walked around the perimeter of the stone pedestal on the third level and stopped when he had noticed a glow filtering out from a cavern hallway, similar in size to two other spots he had observed earlier. There, basking in the glow from a patch of red moss, was the jewel he had given to the little girl.

Hydro pounced onto the lower level. His footsteps reverberated throughout the cavern. Shadows danced in the glowing hallway the jewel lay before.

Spying a large rock, Hydro dove and hid behind it. Back pressed against the stone, breathing heavily, he listened to the footsteps. There was a certain click to the cadence and a gentle thumping as well. Intrigued, Hydro steadied his breath, turned around and lifted himself so his eyes were just barely over the ridge of the stone.

A creature walked towards the jewel. Large thighs made for jumping long distances supported a muscular frame with long, sinewy arms. The creature had no palms, merely large talons. A huge sickle-shaped claw on each of its hindfeet clinked whenever it tapped the floor. Behind the beast dragged a heavy tail. It bent over, lowering its long, low head with an upturned snout towards the jewel. It sniffed it for a moment and then grabbed it with its talons and darted back from where it came.

Hydro turned back around, contemplating his next course of action. It was clear he would need to follow the beast into the cavern in order to retrieve his jewel; what wasn't clear was how dangerous the trek would prove. He didn't have time to think about either of these things. His chest surged with heat, and Desmós forced him onward.

*They will not hurt you, Hydro Paen.*

*I told you not to control my body.*

*You are wasting time.*

*I will go.* The fire in his chest faded. The sudden decrease in heat sent shivers rippling through him.

In his current predicament, Hydro felt less confident than usual. A necklace could overtake his body. A large earthen bird had just tried to pluck him from the sky. And now a creature he had never encountered before with razors for claws and feet held his jewel. He pushed away these thoughts, though, because to think allowed Desmós to know his plans. He needed to shore up the boundary between them.

In the hallway, Hydro moved cautiously, always keeping one hand on his hilt and taking his paces slow and steady, being careful to not make any noise that would give away his position. As the hallway descended, the heat rose, and the colors of the wall changed from brown to maroon. He pinched his nose against the burning sulfur invading his nostrils. Deeper and deeper he went, no longer able to hear any of the creature's movements.

Hours passed. Perhaps days. The only way Hydro calculated the length of time was how hungry he felt, but even hunger was replaced by an overwhelming anxiety crawling within him with each step of his descent. When he noticed the descent leveling off, he paused and strained to hear. Sure enough, there seemed to be movement up ahead, flapping, something roaring continually.

Hydro crouched down and put his hand on the wall to steady himself.

The wall moaned.

Hydro yanked back his hand, jerking his body along with it, and crashed into the wall behind him.

The other wall moaned.

Faces pushed through the wall. Hands pushed against it. The walls were alive, as if people, souls, were trapped inside, waiting for someone to free them. The sound deafened him, paralyzed him in a state of inaction and awe. A scurry of footsteps advanced on him from around the bend in the hallway. Hydro scrambled to his feet, but before he could withdraw Purge, the clawed creature stood before him. Above, a large, brown spider descended on a web and twirled before Hydro, yellow eyes boring into him.

Involuntarily, Hydro began conversing in a language he didn't know he knew. The dialogue exchange lasted for minutes, and it ended when the spider, using one of its eight legs, cut itself free from its dragline and crawled between the larger creature's legs, disappearing down the tunnel. The other creature gave a deep barking cry before turning around and following.

*Follow, Hydro Paen.*

*What did I say to it?*

*I told them you are here for the jewels.*

*And they will give them to us?*

*If you pass their test.*

*Test?*

Hydro didn't have time to react to the necklace's words, for he was forced forward once more. He entered another large chasm, this one large enough that a wide river flowed through it off to another part of the cave that extended deeper still. Stalagmites and stalactites gave the chasm eerie, inhuman features. Red moss that sat at the base of either formation illuminated the large chasm and the serrated edges of each one made it looks like fangs, ready to clamp down and eat whole anyone not worthy enough to be allowed into this spacious sepulchral sanctum. Farther back, a large group of stalactites had come together in such a way to make a makeshift throne bathed in a fiery glow from an oven of flames behind it.

The creature with the tail jumped over the river that cut through the center of the chasm to land effortlessly on the other side. It barked something.

Hydro stopped at the river's edge and looked down. The flow was sluggish, the waters as black as tar. It reflected none of Hydro's likeness; on the contrary, it showed a skeleton. Flesh peeled away, his heart glowed a bright red which slowly turned to black as if the river itself seeped onto it, covering it in slime. Enthralled, Hydro lowered himself to the tar-like liquid.

Skeletal hands shot out of the river, attempting to drag him in. He flipped himself on his back and pushed with his heels to scoot himself away.

"What was—"

A barking howl cut through his words. Hydro jerked his head upright to see the creature had returned with something. Or someone. Hydro didn't know what it was or how to describe it besides a living skeleton. It climbed onto the makeshift throne, a sick silhouette from the glowing fire behind. In its hand was a long onyx staff inlaid with silver vines that ran up its shaft. A jewel rested on top of it.

Hydro blinked. *What is that?*

*It's a lich. Do as it says, Hydro Paen.*

As Hydro put one forced stepped in front of the other, he chewed on his lower lip. Had he perceived a trace of fear from Desmós? Feigned obedience or not, Hydro now carefully surveyed the obsidian eyes that bore into him. They flared with red embers, dancing like hellpits. They gleamed and ran over him like a predator would prey. Hydro stopped many bodies' length away, at the edge of another river of black tar that crawled through the sanctum.

The lich rustled and shifted itself atop its stalagmite throne. "Welcome to the Inner Sanctum." He spread his skeletal hands wide, still gripping the staff in one hand. "I heard you want the jewels that were given to us from above." A sick smile spread across the lich's decayed face. "To get them, you will have to come closer, my child. Much closer." The lich raised his free hand and curled his bony fingers inward, urging Hydro forward.

CHAPTER 13

# THE VOTE

E irek sat in the back of the auditorium, tapping his foot and wiping the sweat from his palms onto his legs. Eska exuded composure, posture perfect as he waited for the voting to begin. He seemed thoroughly confident, or perhaps he had learned better to not dwell on things he couldn't control. After all, that was one of the lessons he had taught Eirek. The theory behind the lesson was sound. Life-changing, really, but the practicality of it and how someone actually might learn to let themselves remain unaffected by the actions and comments of others was a different story. Eirek thought it may have been a ruse, a strengthening of his visage to impress others, but after Guardian Eska initiated a conversation with Senator Numos as quorum came to a close, he realized Eska's confidence was genuine.

"Senator Numos," Guardian Eska said while still looking ahead.

"Yes, my Guardian?"

"You are officially removed from your position in the senate after this vote occurs."

"You have no justification."

Eska turned his head to Numos. "You forget. I don't need any justification. I am Guardian of the Core. But, to amuse you with politics, it has come to my attention that you have syphoned some of Eirek's blood for *identification* purposes. I do not know whether that is truly what it was used for, but you didn't mention you would be conducting an interview in such a format before you arrived on the Core."

"And must I inform you of everything?"

"Yes, actually, you must. You were present thanks to my generosity. So consider yourself dismissed when this vote sees me acquitted."

"The vote hasn't even happened yet."

"I am not worried. You need a two-thirds majority. Do you really believe eight of these nations will find me guilty?"

Silence.

Neither spoke again as Neil Raiden brought the calling of quorum to a close. "Now that quorum is established, I will go in alphabetical order. When your nation is called, please stand and announce your vote either in favor of or against the impeachment of the Guardian of the Core, Edwyrd Eska. First nation, Acquava."

Eska turned his attention to Aiton Paen, who stood upon a chair and leaned into his microphone. "I... I find Guardian Eska negligent in his duties as Guardian of the Core. I vote to impeach." He sat down quickly.

Eska furrowed his brows and punched his cheek with his tongue. Had he really thought Aiton would vote for him after his actions against Hydro? Now that Eska had made such a substantial claim to Senator Numos, he hoped Acquava wasn't one of the nations Eska had been relying on to win.

"Guardian Eska is negligent in his duties as Guardian of the Core. I vote to impeach as well." Lord Zalos Kapache sat down.

"Next, Cresica."

"I find Guardian Eska a worthy Guardian of the Core. He has demonstrated great respect in sending Apprentice Mourse to us to offer his condolences. I absolve him of wrongdoing."

Eirek beamed at Cresica's vote, though it did not come as a surprise. A vote to impeach would have made things very awkward between the two of them.

"The vote stands at two to one in favor of impeachment. Next, Empora."

Zigarda's advisor stood. "Empora stands to impeach Guardian Eska. This monster must be stopped from abusing his Power further."

Eirek had expected as much. The advisor would have courted scandal and ruin if he had gone against Zigarda.

"Next nation, Epoch. How do you stand?"

"I, Nathan Alois, voice for my lord, Daven Evber, find Guardian Eska guilty. He should be impeached immediately."

*That is certainly interesting. Did what I say to Cain influence the decision at all?* If Linn hadn't been here, would her advisor have voted differently? Would he have turned against Eska as well, seeing only the devastation Eska created after the Trials? Eirek shifted in his seat, not wanting to think about the answers to those questions, now even happier with Linn's support.

Guardian Eska still remained stoic even as the fourth vote against him was cast. Only four more and Eirek would become the Guardian of the Core. His stomach knotted further, if that was even possible.

"Those in favor of impeachment are four. Those against, one. Let us continue. Lady Aprah of Gar, please rise and cast your vote."

"Guardian Eska, this was a difficult decision for me. I stayed up all night contemplating it. After all, you saved our nation from disaster when the Twelve fought upon Mount Volan. And while I like your apprentice and find him capable and respectable enough, and while I also abhor the deception Victor Zigarda employed to call this hearing, your actions have thrust Gar into a war with Sereya. Your decision also resulted in the negligent waste of good and loyal men. That mission was undertaken for your own agenda, to the benefit of no one else. It has taken Gar out of one coal mine and put them to work in another. Therefore, I am sorry, my Guardian, but I vote for your impeachment."

Eirek's mouth hung slack. Guardian Eska shifted in his seat. *That is certainly surprising.* Eirek drummed his fingers on his thighs. He sensed Guardian Eska attention on the remaining lords and ladies sharpen.

"Edwyrd, I believe you overestimated your clout," Luvan muttered under his breath.

Eska didn't respond to the bait.

"Let us move on to Ka'Che. Please stand and vote."

"By the authority granted to me by Lord Vangle, Ka'che absolves Guardian Eska of any wrongdoings."

"Very well. Those in favor of impeachment, five. Those against, two. We continue with Lady Farah Scule of Lurid. Please stand up and cast your vote."

"Guardian Eska, you claim to uphold your vows. However, one of those vows is showing no particular favor to any one nation. Supposed prophecy or not, you overlooked one of our finest in Lurid from competing in the Trials. In fact, you ignored all of Pyre if what was told here is correct; therefore, I cannot absolve you from wrongdoing. I find you guilty of disavowing the pledge you took upon your Coronation."

"Those in favor of impeachment, six. Those against, two. Lady Liliana Voux of Mistral, please rise and cast your vote."

"Mistral would not be a nation today if Guardian Eska had not saved us from Deimos long ago. I do not want to see that beast return. And if it ever should, I know that you will be able to keep us from harm's way once more. Guardian Eska, I vote against impeachment."

"Those in favor of impeachment, six. Those against, three. Next, Lord Garett Omyon of Nova."

Guardian Eska tilted his chin to the left. From the back of the auditorium, Eska's mentor stood. Stoic, he gave nothing away. Eirek noticed Eska's breathing had stalled, as if everything came down to this vote. As if nothing else mattered in this hearing.

"Edwyrd, I am not one to be drawn into foolish lies. I am not one who believes in the necessity of war, for I have seen the greatest war ever to occur. What I care about is propriety. You know that more than anyone. I do not find you guilty of stepping over those boundaries. You do not have any heirs, you have not passed along your Powers, you did what you needed to do to protect the citizens of Gar, and although Lady Scule does not believe in such prophecy, I know of its existence, and I understand why you chose the contestants as you did. I believe that the Trials did their job in selecting the right one. He has grown much since I saw him at Coronation, and I believe under your charge, he will only continue to evolve into the next Guardian of the Core this system needs. Apprentice Mourse..." Eska's mentor turned to look at Eirek. "You will always be welcomed in Nova, just as your mentor. Edwyrd, I absolve you."

Eirek felt warmth rush over his body. He hadn't expected to receive such a compliment, but he was glad another had noticed his change and the achievement of his mentor's consistent training. Eirek knew that anything he could do now was because of Eska's patience with him and his constant guidance. As he shifted slightly to look at Eska, the Guardian's lips curved upward and his posture wasn't as rigid anymore. Had that one vote shifted the tides in Eska's favor?

"Very well. Those in favor of impeachment, six. Those against, four. Will Lord Astor... excuse me, the sons of Astor Grime, how do you vote?"

Not a second went by. "Impeach." They both pumped their fists in the air.

Eirek gulped. *Seven.* He had been too caught up to keep count, though Sereya's vote had been no mystery. Eska stood on the precipice of impeachment. Eirek looked to his mentor, who tapped his fingers on his knees and bit his lower lip. *Who else has to...* Luvan's words cut off Eirek's thought.

"This is it, my Guardian," Luvan said.

"That is the last time you may have to call him that," Senator Numos added.

"Will Lord Rhagoh Requart of Therus please cast the last vote."

Eska shifted in his seat. Lord Requart stood. It felt strange to Eirek seeing him without his massive enkine by his side. Eirek had no idea how Lord Requart would vote. Lady Scule had voted against Eska, and Lord Omyon had voted for; both were from Pyre as well.

Eirek's breathing steadied. Time stood still, slowed to a halt, so visceral that he could feel his heart pump. This was it. He didn't allow himself to blink. Everyone in the auditorium shifted their attention to the lord of Therus, watching in eagerness as the last vote was set to be cast.

## CHAPTER 14

# THE LAST VOTE

"It is interesting to be in this predicament," Lord Requart began. "Never did I imagine that I would have such sway in Gladonus. The other nations on Pyre are divided, and this division reflects my own. While I do wonder why no one from Pyre was chosen to compete, who am I to cast doubt on a prophecy? Even if his choices can be criticized, though, I know that Guardian Eska made up for that in other ways. He held the fourth trial in Therus and tested something that I do believe a Guardian should have—fortitude. Without fortitude, one may cower in the sight of peril, war, or the next Pirini Lilapa. As I know, none of the contestants he chose cowered in that trial. According to my advisor, all of them rode out to their defeat or victory that day, and that means one thing to me: success. It means that Guardian Eska created a position, created the *want* for the position, I should say, that individuals were willing to die to obtain it. I commend Guardian Eska in his creation of the trial and am glad to have had the chance to host the final event. Guardian Eska, I absolve you from wrongdoing." Lord Requart sat down.

Eirek let his breath go and slumped slightly in his chair. *Thanks be to the Ancients.* Eska grinned. Luvan and Numos sat as still as statues, expressions rigid.

"Very well. Those in favor of Eska's impeachment, seven. Those against, five. A two-third's majority is not met. Therefore, Guardian Edwyrd Eska retains his title as Guardian of the Core."

Voices broke out in the hall. Overwhelming susurrus filled the room.

"This is outrageous. More people voted against you than for you, and you're still Guardian." Numos spat and jabbed the fist that clutched his cane towards Eska.

Eska stood up and pulled on his glove. "I would suggest an amendment to the law, Nyom, but you can't do that anymore. Have a good day. Luvan, may the wind blow in whatever direction you go. I do hope it is not further along that path. Bad company ruins good morals." Eska nodded. "Eirek." Eirek stood up and left the bickering duo of Mistralians to approach Senator Raiden with Eska. "Neil, thank you for being such an unbiased individual at today's meeting. I would like to inform you that I have taken the liberty of removing Nyom Numos from the senate. He is no longer allowed within this Hall of Voices, is that clear?"

"Yes, my Guardian. Of course." Neil Raiden flicked a furtive gaze to Nyom Numos and then back to Eska. "I am sorry things were so close against you."

"Close never matters. I am still Guardian. Have a good day." Eska waved his hand at everyone. Eirek waved as well, his eyes falling upon Linn, whose gaze lingered, as if she needed to speak with him. Or Eska. He didn't really know. "Come on, Eirek, let's go."

Eirek waved to her and mouthed the word *bye.* Then he followed Eska outside the Hall of Voices in a hurry, the voices of Numos and Luvan fading as they went. But they hadn't gone far before another voice called for Eirek to stop. Eirek turned to see Linn running after them, the first one out of the chamber.

"Apprentice Mourse, Guardian Eska, wait. Please. Wait." She reached for him as she came close.

Eirek raised his brow. "Linn, what's wrong?"

"Lady Clayse, thank you for your support today."

"Of course, my Guardian. I know Eirek has been trained well under your charge. I have seen it so much. It is a shame the others do not."

"In the end, it didn't matter. What may we help you with?"

Only a body's length away, she looked back. People were only now starting to filter out of the assembly. She blushed and lowered her head. Twiddling her fingers, she looked from Eirek to Eska. "If truth be told, nothing makes sense anymore after Pirini Lilapa."

"It rarely ever does. I know that more than most."

"Yes. And that is why I want to talk to you, my Guardian. That is why I am here instead of in Edgefield."

Eirek cocked his head a little. She had abandoned her army in the midst of a war in order to seek out Guardian Eska. What could be so important to do something so brash?

Clearly confused, Guardian Eska cocked his head as well. "What do you mean?"

"I want to know more about Pirini Lilapa."

"What about Pirini Lilapa, Lady Clayse?"

"How does it work?"

"Every one-hundred-and-fifty years the suns converge."

"But what does that mean?"

"It marks the anniversary of the culmination of the Great War."

"When the Ancients left us?"

"Yes."

Linn crossed her arms and tapped her foot. She bit her lower lip.

"Is there something else, my lady? My apprentice and I have errands that need attending to while here on Agrost."

Linn straightened. She looked up at Guardian Eska and held his gaze. "How many Ancients are there?"

Eirek blanched. *What in...*

"Why, two, of course. Ancient Lyoen and Ancient—"

"You lie."

Guardian Eska stopped, his features growing taut. "What do you mean?"

"There are three, aren't there?"

Guardian Eska pushed his tongue against his cheek. He looked over at Eirek. His eyebrow arched. Eirek shrugged his shoulders and shook his head. He was just as confused as Eska about how Linn had come to this realization.

"Let us talk about this matter in a more secure location. Follow us to the transport."

Inside the transport, Linn explained the story once again of what she saw during Pirini Lilapa. For Eirek, it was nothing new, but Eska furrowed his brows and constantly bobbed his head, thoroughly engaged in her retelling.

"And you are certain this entity was gold?"

"I will never forget that image in my life, my Guardian."

"You saw him."

"That was the third Ancient?"

Guardian Eska nodded. "It was."

Linn slouched, putting one elbow on her crossed legs. She bit her nails.

"What is it, Lady Clayse?"

"I declared a war on Epoch due to the urging of my advisors and those around me. But now I understand that war isn't necessary. How do I avoid it? I don't want my men to die."

Eirek's heart swelled with elation. "Then don't do it." He jumped into the conversation, unsure whether he should have. With the words already spoken, it was too late to take them back, so he bore the stares of them both. "War with Epoch isn't necessary," Eirek reiterated.

Eska remained silent, watching the conversation play out between the two.

"But I've already declared war. What can I do? My leaders will think that I am weak if I stop now. Everyone is asking for atonement for what happened that day."

"What you did in the past doesn't have to define your future. You can change it." Eirek chuckled. "Look at me after all."

Linn smiled and tucked a strand of hair behind her ear. "Easier said than done, Eirek."

"And sometimes words are the best tool that we have. The pen is mightier than the sword, as the Mistralians said. That is why they wanted to convict Eska, because to do so by force isn't possible." Eirek looked at his mentor, who gave an appreciative nod, noting how Eirek had taken his last piece of advice to heart.

"So I should write a letter to him?"

Eirek shook his head. "I don't think it needs to be taken so literally, but I do think you should talk to him and admit wrongs. Talk. And stop the war before it escalates to bloodshed."

"How?"

"Go to him directly."

"I don't even know where he—"

"His force is in Lorian."

"How do you—"

"I spoke with Cain a little before the hearing. He told me he and his father were in Lorian. I assume they are still there. Asking those to give their life is the ultimate sacrifice. I can understand. You must talk to Lord Daven Evber and set things straight with him."

Linn breathed in deeply and sighed. "Thank you, Eirek. Truly, Guardian Eska has done wonders for you. I am glad you can continue learning under him."

Eska smiled. "Your vote helped me keep my status, Lady Clayse. I thank you for that. It is nice to see my apprentice coming into his own as well. There are many things I have yet to teach him, but he has grown wonders in analyzing situations and providing feedback. As I said in my hearing, we all make mistakes. But we can always atone for those mistakes."

"It is unfair for them to treat you as they did. They almost—"

"Life isn't always fair, but we must learn to deal with injustices the best way we can."

Linn nodded. "You're right. I will make plans to talk with Lord Evber. Thank you." She turned to Eirek. "Eirek, it... it was nice to see you again. I wish you the best of luck with your training." She leaned forward on her toes and waited patiently for a moment.

"Thank you, Linn." Eirek nodded.

Linn blushed. She shook her head and tucked strands of hair behind her ear. "I... I should be going now. My officers are probably wondering where I am. Take care." Red in the face, she left the ship.

When the ship door closed again, Eska chuckled.

Eirek spun around to face his mentor. "What is so funny?"

"You may be good at giving advice, but I dare say we need to work on your social cues with the opposite sex."

"What do you—" Eirek blushed now.

"She wanted a hug from you before she left. And for you to say how good it was to see her."

"I..." Eirek's neck tightened. "But... the vows."

Eska laughed. "You forget that I just set a precedent for acknowledging those vows are outdated." Eska beamed. "Don't think so much about her. You will see her again. Let's go. There is something I want to show you and someone I want you to meet. It's time you start learning the secrets of the Guardian." Eska left Eirek and went to the pilot's seat of the ship, and a moment later, they were off, the Hall of Voices silently drifting away in the distance behind them.

Through a whirlwind of clouds emerged a floating isle, like a green pupil encircled by a cloudy iris. It hovered there perfectly, always being exactly the same distance away from any side of the cluster of clouds encompassing it.

"What is this? Who lives here?"

Eska did not respond. He continued steering the spaceship until it hovered slightly away from the floating island. As soon as Eirek stepped onto the aventurine floors of the cavern isle, he felt the buffets of breezes that seemed determined to push him off kilter and away from this place. Not yet inside, the wind smacked him and cooled him. Through all of this, Eska didn't say anything; he merely walked inside the cavern. Eirek followed.

Inside, Eirek saw a polished floor and pillars that held the cavern's ceiling up. Blue moss clung here and there, washing it in light.

Eska surveyed the area and then turned to Eirek. "How do you feel?"

"Fine." Eirek shrugged. "Better than outside. What is this place?"

"Fine? Are you sure?" Eska raised an eyebrow.

Eirek gulped and nodded his head, unsure what Eska was getting at. "Uhm m... yeah?"

"You don't feel out of breath?"

"No. Not really. Should I?"

Eska frowned. "Follow me. Stay behind. Hand on hilt." Eska turned on his heel and stalked down the cavern's hallway.

Eirek had rarely seen Eska so serious, so alarmed, and he did as he was told. Were they in danger? Eska crept forward with his sword withdrawn. Eirek crept behind Eska like a shadow, eventually making their way to a large cavernous mouth that held five swirling portals.

Still hunched, ready to lunge and strike, Eska surveyed the area, one hand holding his sword and the other arm back behind him, keeping distance between himself and Eirek. When it was clear that no one was in the cavern, he let his posture relax. "Zeph?"

Silence.

"Zeph?" Eska called again.

Nothing.

"Is something the—"

Eirek stopped his sentence short when Eska darted around the cavern, searching for someone, or something, that clearly wasn't here. Near the wall where five portals swirled, he stopped and swooped down, examining something on the floor. Eirek crept closer, unsure what was going on.

"My Guardian, is everything okay?"

Guardian Eska pinched his fingers together and sighed. He stood up and shook his head at Eirek. "It would do me no good to lie to you, Eirek. My actions already have shown this is not what I expected."

"What did you expect?"

"I wanted you to meet someone here. Her name is Zeph."

"Who is she?"

"She is the mother of Naydeia. She is the wife to Ancient Bane."

Eirek's eyes bulged. He stammered, trying to think of something to say. Stumbling over his thoughts, he managed to push out. "You mean she is my...?"

"Yes. I believe she may be your great grandmother. Maybe even older than that."

"But why does she live here?"

"Perhaps you can ask her that yourself some day, but as Deimos rampaged the land during my first Pirini Lilapa, she called me here. I didn't know who she was either. I never knew this place existed."

"So the other Guardians?"

Eska shook his head. "Not that I am aware. To be honest, I don't know why she chose to make this her dwelling, although I do have my speculations. But this island, Eirek, is a secret that only we know about."

"What is it? What are those things on the wall?"

Guardian Eska nodded. He glanced at the floor, shifting his posture slightly, and then gestured for Eirek to come over. As furtively as possible, Eirek glanced downwards, hoping to see what had stolen Guardian Eska's attention. *Is that...* Eirek eyed the red that Eska had tried to conceal. *Blood?*

"These are portals that will take you to other planets instantaneously."

"Like wormholes?"

Guardian Eska shook his head. "No. Much more efficient than wormholes, Eirek. These will transfer you directly to the planet, not the atmosphere. Each planet has a set drop point, and each planet has a series of portals like this. They are hidden from the naked eye or blend in such a way with the environment that it would be impossible to actually determine them. I didn't know they existed until I met Zeph."

"Where are the others?"

Eska shook his head again. "That, I do not know. I only know of this location because Zeph has only ever revealed this location to me."

"Which one leads where?"

Eska pointed to each portal, naming the planet each led to. "Imagine this portal similar in function to the reimaje, but less effective." Confusion clearly apparent on Eirek's face, Guardian Eska continued. "The reimaje allows me to visit any place on any planet that I have been. This portal allows the same transportation but at set locations, which cannot change. I want you to use this one to return to the Core." Eska pointed to the middle portal.

Eirek stared. "Me." He pointed to himself. "Now?"

Eska nodded. "Yes. It will give you a first-hand experience as to what traveling will be like through the reimaje."

Nervously, Eirek stepped forward. "But... what about Zeph? Where did she go?"

"That doesn't matter right now. What matters is you taking another step forward in your training."

Eirek gulped, and he stood in front of the portal. The walls spun before him like a continual whirlpool. He looked back. "Where will this drop me on the Core?"

Eska smirked. "There is only one way to find out." And he pushed Eirek forward through the portal.

CHAPTER 15

# PLAN B

Hostility fought tension for control of the room. Cronos seemed unaffected. Cavalier in his expression, his hand gripping his Ether Staff, the other Sages behind him, silent and stoic as usual. Lord Zalos Kapache, as well, seemed to be oblivious as he sat stroking the chameleon perched on his shoulder. However, two others in the room exuded enough silent hostility and anxiety to make up for their lack. Numos stood in contemplation by a bookshelf, looking out through a window, lost in aspirations and dreams, Zakk supposed. Zigarda paced around the room, hands locked behind his back, chin tilted downward, hood covering his face, impossible to decipher if not for his pacing, which told Zakk he, too, was contemplating options. Edwyn stood next to Zakk, thrumming his thumbs on the top of the couch, no doubt wondering what would happen in the wake of the vote's failure.

Finally, Zigarda stopped in front of Cronos. "You told me the vote would work. It didn't. Eska is still Guardian of the Core. I don't even have a title anymore thanks to this plan."

Numos turned around and took the knuckle of his index finger from his lips. "Neither do I."

"Titles are pointless. To complain about losing them makes you a hypocrite."

"And how do you suppose that?" Numos leaned on his cane.

"This plan was meant to elevate your position. Victor, you wanted to become Guardian of the Core, yes? And you, Senator, wanted to become Lord of Mistral, yes?" Both men nodded. "Then you would have lost your positions, anyway. To lose them now means nothing."

"But now I am no longer a senator, nor will I be Lord of Mistral. Lady Liliana isn't dead."

"I told you she will die, senator. Have patience." Lord Kapache looked up from his chameleon to the senator. "It is happening as we speak."

Numos strolled over to join Zigarda in the middle of the room but then turned to Lord Kapache. "When I see it, I'll believe it," he spat.

"Have faith, Senator," Cronos said. "You will still be Lord of Mistral, I see it."

Numos torqued his body around to face the Sage. "Hmmm," Numos purred. "Somehow I don't trust your staff's vision. It was wrong about the vote, after all."

Numos and Zigarda looked down at Cronos, and he stared back at them, one of his bicolor eyes focused on each. "The vote would have gone as planned had Linn Clayse not been present. That was unexpected. This deviation is a whim of fate."

"Another deviation?"

"Yes."

"These deviations have cost me a lot. When will your staff ever be right?"

"Foresight shows me many things, Victor. Things I search for. Cresica's vote would have been different if she wasn't there."

Zigarda paced a few steps before stopping once more. "So what happens now?"

"Plan B. Kill Eska."

Zakk's eyes widened. He knew that this had been the contingency plan all along, but to actually implement it was something entirely different. The logistics of impeaching him from his position required nothing physical, just intellectual prowess and manipulation, and Zakk knew how close the vote had been. To depose him by force, though, even Zakk was interested in how that was truly possible.

"If you are referencing the jewels, that plan has gone awry. I can no longer contact the Paen boy to see if he is still alive. He stopped communicating with me before the initial meeting ever began."

"You, too, must have faith, Victor. Like the senator. It will be done. You do not need to see everything to know it is happening."

An intricate pattern of knocks sounded on the door.

Lord Kapache's head piqued at the jingle. "It is done. Senator, go get our guests."

Zakk furrowed his brows, same as Senator Numos. The obese man waddled over to the door, looking through the peephole unnecessarily before opening it. "Longwei..." The senator bowed.

The man with the crippled hand entered, and behind him were four other individuals. One had the furunculous face and droopy skin of a shapeshifter. The other three, though, were clothed in brown and green rags, as if they were trying to blend in with a forest. Two of them carried swords at their hips, the third one a bow. Each were lean and built, but the one with the bow was less muscular than the others. The slighter stature told Zakk this assassin was a woman. All carried packs on their backs.

Senator Numos closed the door and scooted around the newcomers. "So?"

"The entire family is dead." Longwei forced a smile and strolled over to stand behind Lord Kapache.

"How?"

"I told you not to worry, senator," Lord Kapache said. "The assassins of the Bonded Guild in Chaon are the best in the system."

"My lord, there is more that you should know."

Lord Kapache titled his head from his chameleon to Longwei. "And that is?"

"Gaia."

Zakk didn't understand the name, but it caused everyone else's head to turn to the man.

"Gaia, you say? What about her?"

"We saw her. On our return here."

"You're certain?"

The assassin with a bow stepped forward. "I am, my lord." She had already let down her sack from her back. Out from the bag crawled an animal that made its way up the woman's leg as if it were a tree, to perch upon her shoulder.

Zakk furrowed his brows. *A chameleon.* It licked the woman's face, showing its warmth. Zakk felt a slight stab of jealousy at such an open display of affection. He wondered how any person actually managed to find their bonded animal.

"I am originally from Cresica. In the north. I grew up with stories about Gaia all my life. To see her, though, well, no one has seen her for centuries."

"How—"

"Lilyth also claims to have seen a child on her back."

"Gaia has bonded?"

"We only saw the animal for a brief second, my lord, as it came up from below and flew off above the clouds. It nearly hit our ship, but I thought I saw something."

"Something we should keep our eye on, but nothing that concerns us here."

"I believe it was a child. Perhaps I could recruit her to the Guild?"

"You think you could do such a thing?" Lord Kapache stood up, he strolled over to stand in front of Lilyth.

"I do, my lord."

"What do you need?"

"Your leave. To track her down and find her."

"Hmmm... Take Ryo with you."

"I can do this myself."

"There is safety in numbers, Lilyth. Take Ryo. Or don't go at all."

"Yes, my lord."

Lilyth turned around and stalked past the others. One of the other assassins followed her out of the dwelling.

"Gaia, well, wouldn't that be something to have on our side?"

"What do you need?" Zakk asked without meaning to.

Lord Kapache was about to speak, but Cronos spoke before him. "Gaia is one of the four Creatures of Legend. They are only bonded to those who are worthy."

"And how does that happen?"

"It is a matter of blood and a feather."

"Feather?" Zigarda turned around. "Feather? Didn't you steal some sort of feather?"

"It cannot be just any feather, Victor," Cronos said.

"And this one isn't. It twists and turns on its own."

Cronos shifted his position. "May I see it?"

"Zakk..." Zigarda waved his arm.

Zakk came closer to Cronos. He kneeled down before the old man and lifted the necklace over his head, revealing the feather he had taken from Zain when he came to the Web. Gingerly, he handed it over to Cronos, who grabbed it by the strands and dangled it before his eyes. Longwei and Lord Kapache both peeked around Senator Numos to get a glimpse of what was happening.

"Well?" Zigarda asked after long enough silent admiration from Cronos.

Ignoring Zakk, Cronos flicked his eyes to Zigarda. "This is exactly what is needed now."

"What do you mean?"

Keeping his eyes locked on Zigarda, Cronos handed the feather back to Zakk. "With that feather you will be able to bond with Rhayna if she finds you worthy enough."

"And do you believe me to be so?"

"It matters not what I believe, Victor. What matters is your blood and your Power. And you have both. Remember, I endorsed you for your own Trials two-hundred years ago. Bonding with Rhayna will be the only way to level the playing field with..." Cronos heaved forward. He clutched his staff. A part of him grimaced. His eyes flared.

Zakk reeled back to stand alongside Zigarda and his advisor. No one spoke. No one made any moves. A moment later, Cronos stood up. He turned around to the other Sages and said something to them that Zakk couldn't comprehend.

Turning back to face everyone in the room, Cronos said. "We have to leave now. Other matters call to us." Cronos maneuvered his way past the furniture but then turned around. He pointed his Ether Staff towards Zakk. "Take that one along with you, Victor. Getting to Rhayna will be difficult. Two heads are always better than one, for bonds always come in two."

The Sages left.

Zakk stuffed the feather back into his black snakeskin suit, aware that the curious gazes from Longwei and Lord Zapache lingered. Zigarda pivoted to stand in front of Zakk, hood down, lidless charcoal eyes boring into him.

"Let's go, boy. We have a bird to catch and a Guardian to kill."

Zigarda turned and exited, and Zakk followed like a subservient shadow.

## CHAPTER 16

# AN ANCIENT'S POWER

With Eirek gone, Eska removed his foot from the bloodstain on the floor. He followed its trail to the portal that led to the Myoli domain. It was the easiest domain to pick out because, out of the five portals, it spun the opposite way, congruent with how the planet rotated. That also meant that she was dropped off at Valor in Chaon.

Eska tapped his foot and looked at the blood on his fingers. First Blood. He bit his lips at the predicament. He wanted to keep this from Eirek, at least for now, but he suspected Eirek had managed to catch that something was amiss. If not by Eska's actions at Zeph's absence, then surely due to his natural astuteness.

The blood meant that a fight had occurred in the cave, which in turn meant someone had known about this cave's location—and, more concerning, that someone was actively tracking the jewels. If they could find such a reclusive island, surrounded by a storm of clouds, could they find the others? Second, how had said battle concluded? Did Zeph retain possession of her jewel? This mattered less; Eska had given her an empty shell that contained no god or goddess. Regardless, he assumed the answer was *no;* otherwise, she would have stayed in her home and he would have found the perpetrator's body. The absence of such a body led Eska to the most troublesome bit of insight—the hunter carried an Ether Weapon and was considerably adept in its use. Zeph relied on her overwhelming Power to control everything—Eska suspected she had no physical weapon—which likely meant the blood was hers.

The culmination of all these insights meant only one thing: Hydro Paen was collecting the jewels. Eska already knew the man had the Power of the Zas Necklace, which meant he had the Power of Desmós. Eska also knew Hydro had stolen his father's Ether Weapon on the night he killed his family. What Eska didn't know, and could only speculate on, was how Hydro was managing to track the jewels. It now also occurred to Eska why Hydro had been last spotted by the Hown outside of the Sacred Passage. He didn't need Tundra's report to know the jewel would be gone from that location as well. This ability to track the jewels meant one thing—Hydro colluded with Victor Zigarda. *But when would...* Eska pulled his gaze away from his fingertips, stopping in mid-thought. Tundra had spotted Hydro in Mendeck, but he had eluded her.

Eska let his hands drift behind his head, and he took one more lap around the cavern, searching for any other clues. Anything. But he found nothing. He stalked back out to where his ship waited for him. There was one more piece of business to attend to while on this planet. One he would deal with alone.

"Destination reached."

Eska drew his fingers into a fist and breathed outward. Before him lay the Sages' Palace, an estate of obvious but understated wealth.

Guardian Eska surveyed the estate from his cockpit for a moment, taking in its exuberant modesty. While it was painted in gold, he had seen larger. Certainly, it was only one-third of his own palace on the Core, but size didn't matter. Nothing truly mattered here besides answers, repercussions, and justice, and Eska would deal with each of those in its own turn. First, though, he was unsure whether to be wary. If Cronos truly could see the future, then would he anticipate Eska's arrival? If so, would he hide?

He sighed. "This is it."

He unbuckled his seat and exited the ship. He approached the estate with caution, keeping alert. His right hand kept his cape close to his side, hiding his sword. Although he wasn't afraid of Cronos, he was worried about the other three that always remained mute. Was Cronos merely the acting fraction of their Power? If they chose, could all four band together and overwhelm Eska? Cronos had an Ether Weapon, so armor didn't matter.

Tempted to merely knock on the front door in an act of feigned ignorance, Eska decided against it. Instead, he circled the estate, looking for anything suspicious, trying to gauge if anyone was home. To Eska's dismay, most of the curtains were swept shut, blocking what little light filtered past the canopy of the forest and the clouds overhead.

After two trips around the estate and nothing to show for it, Eska decided to knock.

Nothing.

Keeping alert, he knocked again.

Nothing.

*I will just cut my way in.* He pulled out his Ether Weapon.

His eyes shifted.

Gold.

Eska side-stepped. A golden sword coated with flames jabbed through the air where he had been standing. It pierced the door with ease, leaving burn marks around the skewered wood. Behind him, a being with wings of flames and gold plates appeared. *The Third One.*

It removed the sword from the door and swiped at him. Eska ducked. He jumped sideways off of the porch, and the Ancient flew towards him. *"Maa."* A pillar of dirt gave him a moment of separation. He landed on the ground.

Fire overtook the wall of earth, eating it as greedily as dry leaves before engulfing Eska. The Ancient sped towards Eska, sword raised. Drenched in flames, the two battled each other, Eska always on the defensive.

"How can you withstand the flames?"

Eska didn't reply to the croaky voice. It seemed partly dead, as if it were missing a piece to make it complete, to make it as angelic and pristine as the master who owned it. Even though the Ancient's Power didn't overwhelm Eska entirely, to reply meant death. Eska had only needed such concentration one other time in his life—against Deimos. He prioritized concentration on combating the Ancient through physical strength, though he was clearly outmatched, and through his battle with Power, which was quickly waning as well.

Eska continued ducking and parrying the blows. An unexpected sidestep combined with leveraging Power to his advantage caused the Ancient to stumble. Eska came down on the flesh of the wing with Adonis. But it just clanged on the wing as normal steel would clang on stone. The reverberated shock made him recoil, loosening his grip. A golden fist impacted his sternum, and Eska flew back, hitting hard against the trunk of a tree, his sword skittering across the ground halfway between him and the Ancient.

The Third One flew towards him. Eska flung up a barrier of earth using Power. *I just need a second.* He tore off the glove over his left hand. The barrier broke. The Third One closed in on him. Sword first, it jabbed towards Eska. Eska twisted his body out of the way. He brought a left fist straight into the stomach of the Third One.

Eska drew upon his remaining stamina. *"Voima."*

The Third One flew backwards towards the mansion, stopping itself before it collided with the estate by opening its wings. Eska used the precious moment to scramble and pick up Adonis. Then he ran towards his ship, determined to get away. But a spire of earth impaled it, ripping it in two.

Eyes wide, breaths heavy, Eska halted. He felt a trickle down his left side. He turned around.

"So the absence of the Twelve hasn't diminished your Power, has it, Guardian of the Core?"

Eska's skin prickled. The Ancient made no move to rush him. Instead, it set itself down on the grass, one foot and then the other. Eska stood just on the outside of its shadow. Orange eyes engulfed with fire watched him in surety of Eska's demise. After all, the Ancient had Eska trapped and without a ship. There was only one chance left for Eska, and he hoped beyond hope that it would work. But against an Ancient, who knew what was possible?

"Do you really think you can win this fight of ours?" The Third One flared its wingspan, as large as Vesel's. With the sudden movement, embers were flung up into the air, falling down like red snow, dying on the ground, leaving nothing but pockets of burnt grass. "Even with that Ether Weapon of yours, you have no chance."

Eska looked from the Third One to his weapon. He sheathed Adonis. "I know I cannot beat you." He put his glove back on. Buying time. Setting up his next move.

"Then this is the part where you die."

Eska shook his head. "No. This is the part where I kill your son."

Purple flames erupted around the Third One's visage in a display of ire Eska never had experienced before. The Ancient yelled, causing Eska to step back a few paces, but also providing him the cover to say his spell.

"*Tuuli.*"

The Third One flew towards him but was caught in mid-air, halted, as if an invisible leash prevented the Ancient from going any farther. Quickly, Eska undid his reimaje and threw it out in front of him, thinking of the Core. He felt the earth underneath him start to shake. He jumped forward towards the reimaje's wormhole, avoiding a spire of earth that would have made his body an echo of the ship's. Launching feet and body first into the portal, he brushed the top of it with his hand, taking the reimaje with him, leaving the Ancient in its wake.

Evening had already descended upon the Core. He had been thankful more than ever for the necklace around his neck. If he couldn't have casted wind, he would have died. Perhaps it truly was a word of Power so coveted that Bane had only ever spoken it to his wife. Perhaps it didn't truly exist, save in the necklace around his neck. If that was the case, it was one of the most powerful words in existence.

Keeping one hand on the wound at his side, he made his way towards the estate, limping. Before too long, Vesel flopped down in front of him, roaring a silver flame into the air.

"I am alright, Vesel. I am alive."

The dragon snorted.

"You saved me today. Again."

It flapped its wings, gusts of air pluming against Eska.

Eska smiled at the warmth. He had never been more thankful for the ability to withstand flames thanks to his bond with Vesel.

Vesel rubbed his nose into Eska's chest.

"I know. I know. I should be more careful. But I faced an Ancient today. I am lucky to be alive."

Vesel jumped up into the air and flew around, breathing silver fire into the purple nighttime sky. Soon enough, he came back to Eska and beckoned for him to get on.

"The Ancient won't come here. I told him I was going to kill his son; he will be more worried about that."

The lie had been a necessary diversion to keep the Ancient from following him. He was not certain of its ability to travel through the portal, as the Ancient was clearly not at its full strength. Had it been, Eska wouldn't have lived to see the night, but he didn't want to take any chances. It was clear now that Hydro would have to die, slaying Desmós along with the ill-fated prince. Doing that would ensure the Ancient could not exceed its current strength until Pirini Lilapa and, while still far above others in skill, couldn't open personal wormholes and threaten the entire system. At least, Eska didn't believe so. *Perhaps he gave that ability to Deimos when the beast was created?* Eska bit his lip; he would examine that idea later, but the gash in his side concerned him more.

Eska bade Vesel farewell and bypassed him to get back to the estate. With one hand on his side, he limped up the stairs.

A voice called after him. "Guardian Eska, is everything okay? I heard roars outside."

Eska stopped on the fourth step. He didn't turn around. "Everything is okay, Eirek. It was only Vesel, happy to see me return. Go back to bed." Eska climbed a few more steps.

"Where are you going?"

"Work," Eska lied. "Go back to bed." When he didn't hear Eirek retreat, he turned around. "What is it?"

"I... it's nothing." Eirek shook his head and slunk off.

Before Eirek retreated, Eska called him back. "Eirek." He waited for his apprentice to return. "Where did the portal spit you out?"

"Gamrol Cliffs."

"And how was it?"

"I felt my body stretch and tighten all at the same time. My heart beat faster."

"Was there pain?"

Eirek thought about that for a moment. "Not pain. Maybe discomfort."

"That's good. We will talk more about it tomorrow. Go back to bed now. I am sorry for waking you."

Eska watched Eirek until he retreated back to his room. Then, Eska turned around and continued limping up the steps, letting his posture slip a little now he was alone. On the last step, Eska closed his eyes, paused, and breathed in heavily. *That battle took more from me than I imagined.* His endorphins and the adrenaline began to fade away.

"Edwyrd?" Tundra stood on the second floor wrapped in a light blue nightgown that matched her hair. "You've returned." She took another few steps towards him.

"I have."

"And you're hurt."

"I will live."

"What happened?"

"Another day." Eska hoisted himself to the last step. "Can you help me to the apothecary?" Tundra nodded.

While walking, she asked. "Was it Hydro?"

Eska didn't respond. When outside the apothecary, he pushed a button that would summon the head adored. Tundra helped him sit in a chair.

"What happened to your reimaje?"

Eska blinked. He looked down at his hand. He had forgotten to put it back on his head, so he quickly did that before Adored Amiti arrived. "I needed it to escape."

"Escape? Escape from where? From who?"

"The Third One."

"Edwyrd! He did this to you?"

"Yes. Keep your voice low, Tundra."

"I'm sorry." She bowed her head.

"It is all right."

"What does that mean?"

"Guardian Eska, such a late call. What may I," Adored Amiti yawned and stretched as he walked forward down the hallway, "do for you?"

"I need you to look at a scratch. Perhaps stitching and blood clotters."

Adored Amiti spun his arms in circles, waking up his body. The adored scanned his hand on a pedestal and opened the chamber. He proceeded inside. "It'll be just a few moments to get prepared."

The doors closed. Eska turned his attention back to Tundra. In a whisper, he said, "I am unsure. But I will get the answers tomorrow."

Tundra folded her arms over her chest. "How? From whom?"

"The Crypt. I believe it is time to show Apprentice Mourse to the past Guardians. It's time we reopen Gladima."

CHAPTER 17

# REDEMPTION

*C*  *hild? I am no...*

Hydro didn't finish his thoughts. He was forced to move closer. His lips sputtered, *"Maa."* A bridge formed that bypassed the large river.

*Walk.*

Again, staggered step after staggered step, he came closer, as if tied to invisible strings.

*I will do it myself.* Desmós's influence diminished, and Hydro approached the horde of creatures that had gathered around the lich. Bats flapped overhead, and spiders hung off the stalactites, dangling on their draglines.

"So you can use Power, can you? And I hear you can speak our tongue?" The lich stood up and circled Hydro once, enveloping Hydro in the scent of death, so much so that he wanted to retch, but he held his breath and fought back the urge. While circling Hydro, the lich spoke something in a language Hydro couldn't comprehend but replied to all the same.

*What did he say?*

*He wants to know how you know this tongue. I told him the Twelve taught you.*

The lich sat down again. "My master, Orekus, has not shown here for a while."

"That is because Orekus is locked within one of the jewels I seek. Along with the other Twelve."

"Why do you need these jewels?"

*Tell it you want to free them.*

"I want to free the Twelve."

*And you want to open the jewels and break the bonds tying them.*

"I will break the bonds sealing the jewels by opening them."

"How do I know you are telling the truth?"

"What need do I have for jewels?"

"Everyone needs something. Jewels. Power. Wealth. Isn't that so?"

Hydro shook his head. "Not everyone."

"No?" The lich tilted his chin back and tried chortling, but the laughter came out rough and maniacal. He jerked his head forward again, dead obsidian eyes fixed on Hydro. "Enough talk. You are here because you want something, but I must ensure you are worthy to have it. So we are going to play a little game."

"Sounds fun." Hydro forced a tight smile.

"If you answer my riddles correctly, I will give you the chance to obtain your jewels and you get to keep your soul. But if you lose, well, I will consume you and your Power and shepherd you myself to the Soul Sanctum." The lich pointed his staff down into the chasm to where the black rivers of tar flowed.

His lips twitched.

"Not fond of the conditions I take it?"

Hydro tsked his tongue against his teeth. "On the contrary, I love them. I expected something more *challenging*," Hydro feigned.

"Excellent." Red embers flared in the lich's eyes. "Answer me this riddle: I am greater than the Twelve and more evil than the Ancients. The poor have me, yet the rich do not. If you eat me, you will die. What am I?"

*Hydro Paen, this riddle makes no sense. The Twelve are the evil ones, not my master.*

"I will answer this. Not you."

The lich cleared his throat, but it only sounded like a rattle of bones. "Well, I certainly won't be giving you the answer, unless you fail. In that case, your soul is mine."

Hydro glared at the lich.

"Although," the lich continued, "perhaps you have already lost your soul." It leaned in closer to examine Hydro. "Why are your eyes black?"

"Unless you have just changed your riddle, you do not get to know that," Hydro retorted.

The lich's sick smile flattened. "Very well. I suppose it matters not. Now your answer?"

Hydro focused on the lich's riddle. He would prove to it, to Desmós, to everyone that he could solve riddles by himself. That he didn't need help in solving these riddles as he did on the Sacred Passage. He would prove to himself that he could do such a mundane thing, something he had failed at against the Commoner.

*The Commoner. What did he have?* Hydro bit his lip and tapped his foot and thought about the man who beat him for apprenticeship. He had no combat skills, he had cast no Power, and he had no name. No title. Nothing.

Hydro furrowed his brows. *Nothing?* While the Ancients were certainly greater than the Twelve, someone who had been blessed by Orekus wouldn't see it that way. He would see the opposite. The poor would have nothing, and the rich have the opposite. If one ate nothing, one would die.

Hydro touted his chest. He laughed. "That is simple. Nothing."

Unmoved, the lich tapped his staff on the ground, sending a small tremor throughout the cavern. The other creatures around the lich departed. Its eyes flared red. From the furnace behind the chair, something dropped.

"Very good. I'll make this one more challenging. Here it is: Give me food and I will live. Give me water and I will die. What am I?"

*Water to make someone die? How can water kill? It is the source of life. Only...* His mind drifted back to his sister, Anya, who had died when she fell into the water. The water killed his ability to cast Power to save her. It killed his fire.

Hydro's eyes widened. *That's it.* Smirk on his face, he snapped his finger. "Even easier. It's fire."

Again, the lich tapped his staff to the ground, causing another ripple to flow through the chasm. "Indeed, it is. Let us see how much food you are willing to give to obtain your goals." The lich stood and motioned for Hydro to join him directly before the furnace, where a great fire raged. Inside the furnace were two jewels.

"If you want them, you must climb in and retrieve them yourself."

"Why are they in there? They should be mine."

"And they are yours, assuming you can get them."

"That isn't fair."

"Why, it most certainly is. I said you had the chance to obtain the jewels, assuming you answered my riddles correctly. I am a man of my word."

Hydro shuddered at how this thing still thought himself a man. He tapped his foot and spat on the floor, feeling stupid for not catching the caveat earlier. "So I just need to retrieve them?"

"Yes. Something quite simple for someone such as yourself, I am sure, but I should tell you first that the fires here and below burn anyone without First Blood. My master had charge of the fires until today. Now it is my duty. If you truly are worthy of handling something so precious, retrieving them should be easy for you."

Hydro pushed his tongue into his cheek. *Too many tests.* He stared at the crawl space large enough for him to enter on his stomach. He wouldn't have to completely enter to retrieve the jewels, but they were far enough back that it would require his arms to be fully encased in the blue flames.

"Not as eager as you once were?"

Hydro harrumphed and began to climb into the furnace. A prickle in his chest stopped him. The lich blocked his way forward using the scepter.

"Oh, and one more thing that I should mention before you climb in there. If the flames touch you, and surely they will, then make sure on your voyage from this place that you never look behind you, no matter what. What was brought out of the fires should never return to the fire. To look back is to be consumed and engulfed by the flames when you perish from your world."

"Charming." Hydro hustled forward, crawling on his stomach towards the flames. As he came closer, he saw miniature flames inside the larger flames dancing around the jewels, yet they had no effect on the gems. *Eska must have coated them with magic before dispersing them.* As he looked from jewel to jewel, he wondered if his Ether Weapon could actually cut through them or if a ward had been placed upon them. Did such a ward even exist?

The flames licked toward his face. All he needed to do was stretch out his arms and grab the jewels. He wiggled his fingers, testing them, warming them up for the quick dash. Hydro plunged his hands into the flames. He clutched the jewels.

Screams manifested from the flames. Awful screams, as if someone were burning alive. Scenes of his mother and the Night flashed before his eyes. Scenes of Hydro pouncing on her, smothering her in her own vindictiveness, her own loathing for her child. Hydro lay there, hands in the fire, burning, but he couldn't pull away. He was fixated on the scene playing out before him as his mother lay burning and burning in her own bed as the fire raged on the third floor.

*Hydro Paen!*

His arms were yanked out of the fire. The topaz he had lost was now safely back in his possession, along with another opaque jewel. A thick line of red, the color of rust, ran down the center of the maroon gemstone. He looked back to the fires, no longer special, just ordinary orange and yellow flames with hints of blue and white. He dropped the jewels, their heat singeing his palms. The pain drew him back to reality. Pulling the bottom of his sleeves over his palms as best he could, he grabbed the jewels again and began to slide back from the furnace.

It wasn't until after he was outside of the crawl space that he examined his hands, only to find that they had not been affected at all. The lich grabbed his hands and flipped them over, revealing the two jewels.

"So you managed to retrieve them?" He flipped the hands over. "And without burns, I see. Who are you?"

Hydro ignored the question. "What is that place? What did I see in there?"

The lich leaned on his staff and smirked. "You saw the regrets of your heart."

"My *heart*?"

"Yes. This place, the Inner Sanctum, reveals that. Beyond this is the Soul Sanctum, which reveals truths about yourself you may not even know." The lich extended his hand to the pathway that followed the river downwards. "Do you care to venture?"

"No." Hydro shook his head. "I should be going now."

"Do I get the privilege of your name, human? I have never seen such a thing as you before, retrieving something from the fires without burning. That means you have First Blood. Is that why your eyes are black?"

*First Blood is nothing compared to my blood.*

"No," Hydro said.

"Then how did you manage to escape unharmed?"

"It doesn't matter." Hydro turned to leave. He walked a few feet before a great stone barrier was erected in front of him.

"Orekus implores me to learn the names of all who come here."

*His master is nothing. Tell him. He doesn't deserve my name.*

Hydro talked to the wall of stone before him. "Your master is nothing. Even if he could receive it, he doesn't deserve my name. Now remove this wall."

"You are not in a good place to be making demands, regardless of if you can speak our tongue or not."

Around the cavern, the creatures from earlier regathered around his position. The wall vanished as easily as it had come, and Hydro stared at a pack of creatures that barked and howled at him.

*Tell him if he solves a riddle, he gets my name. And if he doesn't, he dies and we leave this place.*

Still facing the exit, Hydro relayed the message to the lich.

The lich laughed. "Now it is my turn? Go ahead. Amuse me with your words."

As the riddle was told to Hydro, Hydro passed it to the lich. "Who makes it but has no need of it? Who buys it but has no use for it? Who uses it but can neither see nor feel it? What is it?"

"Too simple. Death. The Ancients made it, but they can never die. People buy it and kill others. And those dead cannot see it nor feel it. I thought it would be more—"

"You're wrong." Hydro's mouth pushed out the words faster than he could. It was clear Desmós had taken over control. Despite his objection, Hydro's body spun around. "It's a coffin. Now you die."

The lich laughed. "Humans have no Power over me."

Hydro's hand jerked on his Ether Weapon and pulled it from its scabbard. At the same time as the steel shone, the lich's eyes widened. "I am more than human."

"Who are—"

Severed in two, the lich's body fell to the ground, staff clanking on the stone next to him.

"I am the one who is going to kill your master for his heresy. You lose."

In the last fits of life, the lich laughed and coughed up black blood. Choking on its thick, tar-like consistency. "I've already won." The lich muttered even as the last of his undead life fled.

Hydro's body spun back around. Brandishing the sword in the air, he used it like one would use a torch at night to keep away the darkness. It kept the shocked creatures at bay.

*Use my Power to help you escape.*

"*Maa.*" Hydro formed another bridge and went to the other side.

Only looking forward, he began his ascent, casting a spell of Power over the exit behind him, keeping his efforts focused on that. However, that soon became hard to do as the surrounding walls moaned and groaned in euphoria. *Take me with you. Save me. Grab my hand.* These phrases inundated Hydro in a sea of requests, none of which he could oblige. At one point, Hydro tripped over a stone and went crashing to his knees. Hands pulled his tunic to the wall, but he pushed away from them as fast as he could. The sudden distraction lifted his spell of Power, and he heard rumblings from down below, little tremors ascending to meet him.

*It is time to run, Hydro Paen.*

*I thought you could control them.*

*Not yet.*

Hydro darted up the incline. He ran and ran and ran. Never stopping. Adrenaline fueled him, and the vibrations, the clacking and cawing and howling that seemed to crawl up the cavern with him, never let up. To rest here was to die.

Eventually, he returned to the origin. "*Maa.*" Nearly succumbing to exhaustion, he cast Power and lifted himself directly to the third floor. From the other side of the cavern, the larger side, he saw creatures advancing on his position, including a beast with three heads. Hydro didn't want to think about what kind of animal that was, so he called to the water. "*Vesi.*"

The vortex formed a mouth and sucked him up into its essence. There, Hydro focused on keeping his control of the Power to fight the current that threatened to pull him back in. He didn't need to worry about breathing, so he swam until he finally reached the surface. Above the water, he gasped for fresh air and brushed the water out of his eyes. He focused on the surrounding area, quickly locating the earthen pier he had dived from.

Hoisting himself back onto dry land, he heaved up his stomach contents. He walked and half limped towards the ship. *The ship.* Hydro was surprised to see it unharmed. Unlike the Hown, perhaps the machine wasn't understood as a threat by these people. But what about Gaia? Had it ever tried to battle it? What had happened after he dove into the water? One thing was for certain, the bodies were gone. Bloom was nowhere in sight, nor was anyone else on the island. Before entering the ship, Hydro rummaged through the makeshift houses of felled tree timbers, looking for any sort of sustenance he could find. Settling for dried and preserved meat along with some bread, Hydro ate enough to fill his stomach. No one came, and while that was certainly odd given the state of disarray, he was thankful for it. It allowed him to concentrate and to calculate. To meditate on what had just happened.

*I just killed a lich. I killed an undead.*

*Now he is truly dead.*

*But what about me? You turned me around. I wasn't supposed to be—*

*Do not believe in such lies, Hydro Paen. Myths and fairy tales, that is all that place was. I am real.*

Hydro didn't respond. He sat silently on a wooden stool inside of an empty house, looking at the ship parked outside. He chewed on bread, ruminating. Ever since the ice palace, Desmós had been able to fully take control of his body whenever he felt like it, and while its actions had saved him, Hydro wasn't sure what the latest involuntary movement may have cost him. Would the lich really have just made something like that up? The fires and what he saw in them, they were real, so why wouldn't his words of warning be, too?

Hydro swallowed the bread and tore off another bite. Before plopping it into his mouth, he looked at it, then placed it in. He did it again. Desmós never interfered. It was in that state of organic, natural flow that Hydro was safe, where he neither thought nor planned what he did; he simply acted. And he would have to be in that same mindset if he wanted a chance to loosen the noose around his neck.

## CHAPTER 18

# TRIALS BY FIRE

After failing to best his father in the initial duel, Cain wasn't allowed to retest immediately. Instead, Brenton had told Cain to rise like the phoenix from the ashes and be born anew, and only after that was done would they face each other in combat once more.

It was a moment of humility for Cain. Humbling, but humiliating all the same. He, who had been born within the castle walls of Thoth to the greatest dynasty of Epoch, a Trials participant in his own right, had failed to best a man twice his age who lived in the middle of nowhere.

The day after the combat, Cain reflected on everything that went wrong. His wariness of the Ether Weapon in Brenton's hand, the fire that had consumed him just moments before, and the crowd of onlookers. Although the Ether Weapon compared to his own staff was certainly cause for concern, it wasn't so much any of that. It was that he had to fight Brenton in a pit of warm charcoal with no shoes on. Brenton had glided on the pit as if it was nothing but rocky sand; to Cain, each movement was if he stepped on shards of hot glass. The fight was over in less than a minute.

He had grown to accept his father's words. Even the name Brenton the Protector sounded like something from a novel, like one of the many heroes Cain modeled his destiny after. Maybe he had gotten his fancy for heroes from him? He wasn't blind to the physical traits they both shared. Anyone could see that. So while Cain wanted to continue living his lie, he knew that he needed to let it go. He needed to be reborn. Like the phoenix. While he may have been the son of fire, he wasn't fire. Not even close.

To correct this, Cain had acclimated his feet to walking on the bare ground over the next few days. Only minutes at a time for the first day, then an hour, and then eventually multiple hours on end. Now he walked barefoot. The felsic floor underneath him didn't bite at all. It would prove invaluable in the upcoming trial. Even though Cain's feet had gotten used to the heat, he didn't challenge Brenton. His father had told him he would only have two chances. There was never a third. The first was meant to humble him, and the second one tested if he learned from his mistakes. Cain would show his father he had.

And that is why he spent the rest of his days watching his father interact with the people around the village. He took it upon himself to integrate in this society, to lodge himself in their culture and customs. And through it all, Cain felt as though he was becoming more of who he was meant to be, a True King. A King who would look after his people; a King that would put their needs in front of his own; a King that didn't answer to his past.

The day when he emerged a True King came faster than anticipated, as four days after his disappearance, two riders from his other father's party found him.

He had been returning from a hunt with Brenton as they scoured the lands for firefoxes and flaming boars. He had killed a boar with his own halberd, and as they had been returning, their party had come across a couple of firefoxes lapping at a nearby flame hole at the bottom of a slight depression. Brenton had seen the foxes from the ridge and slowed the party.

"Watch closely." An instant later, he kicked his horse's side and ran down the slight hill, down upon the pair of foxes. The pair darted away at the sudden start of an intruder, making their way across the low-field. While on top of his horse, Brenton threw his Ether Spear and impaled a fox seven meters away. The other one escaped up and over the small hill. Cain's eyes had bulged at the accuracy.

Cain kicked his horse's sides, rushing towards his father, who now remained at the flame hole in the depression. "How did you do that?"

"You must never see where something is, Cain. Always see where it will be. Guilty men live in their past. Fools live in the present. And leaders live in the future. Remember that."

Cain nodded. He would. And he would use that advice sooner than Brenton would realize. The three others from the party joined Cain and Brenton.

"Nice shot, my king," one of them said.

"Let's retrieve our prize, shall we?" Brenton took his reins and was about to kick his horse's sides when Cain interjected.

"I'll go grab it for you."

Brenton nodded and gestured for him to go.

Cain rode out to the firefox, glad Brenton allowed him this opportunity. It would be invaluable to feel the Ether Weapon in his hands. It would allow him to know the weight of such an object and that would give him insight into his next fight with Brenton. Cain needed to do anything to gain the edge, especially when fighting against such a weapon.

What Cain didn't expect, however, were the two Epochian soldiers that happened to come up over the hill just as Cain took the spear from the fox's carcass. They rode down to him. Cain looked back. Brenton's party now rode towards him as well. His past and his future were colliding, and here he was, in the present moment, stuck in the crossroads.

"My prince, is that you?" The rider drew nearer. "Prince Evber, it is you. It is."

Cain's eyes flicked towards Matthew. Then to Ian, the scout alongside him. They were two of his father's personal scouts.

Ian flung himself off the saddle and strolled over to Cain. "Thank the Twelve you are alive. Matthew, savages are coming. Send for backup. My prince, we have to leave now. They won't take you again." Ian wrapped one arm around Cain's shoulder and turned him back to his horse.

Cain resisted. "They didn't take me. I chose to be here."

Matthew came to a halt at Cain's words. "My prince, look at how disheveled you are. You don't even have shoes anymore. It's clear they've made you their slave."

"They've done no such thing."

"Ignore him, Matthew. The prince is delusional. It's the heat. Prince Evber, let's go. Come with me." The man pushed Cain forwards, putting more of his weight into the movement. It was no longer a suggestion. It was a demand.

"I'm not going." Cain outmaneuvered Ian's grip. He stuck the Ether Weapon in the ground and gripped it with both of his hands. "Don't do this."

"Son, who are these—"

"Son? He is Prince Cain Evber. Son of Lord Daven Evber, not kin to some filthy savages like—"

The man never finished his sentence. Cain impaled him with the Ether Weapon. Blood shot over his face. Cain's eyes flicked towards Matthew as Ian's body crumpled.

"My... My..." Matthew kicked his horse and turned around. He galloped off.

"He's getting away," said one of his Brenton's party.

Hooves clacked on the felsic floor. Brenton's men would eventually subdue the man, but Cain didn't have time for eventually. He didn't know how close he had been to sharing locations with reinforcements or contacting someone. He didn't even know where other troops were. Instead, he removed the spear from Ian's body, wiped the blood from his eyes, and calculated where the man would be, not where he was. He aimed. And threw.

The Ether Spear struck the man straight through the neck and spine, popping his head right off. The body stayed on the horse for a few more trots before it fell. As the hoofbeats faded, he heard Ian cough. The scout was fidgeting with his telecommunicator. Cain withdrew his halberd and sliced off the man's wrist before he could connect the call.

The man wailed. "You... What is wrong with you?"

Cain stared down at the man. Blood oozed from his decapitated hand and from the hole in his gut. He would die in minutes, but Cain would be more merciful than that.

"Dead men tell no tales."

The man coughed blood. "Have you gone mad, my prince? What fire has—"

"I am no longer a prince."

The man stammered for words. Through fits of bloody coughs and gags he managed, "What?"

"I'm a King."

Cain came straight down on the neck with the halberd.

Brenton came up alongside Cain. "Are you all right?"

Cain shuddered momentarily at what he had done, but he accepted it. He had to do it. There had been no other option. "I'll be fine." He looked at Brenton.

"Leaders have to make tough decisions sometimes."

"I already knew that."

"You threw my spear well."

"Thank you." Cain bowed his head.

"They were your own. Why did you do it?"

From the way Brenton examined Cain, he knew that this was an evaluation. "Dead men tell no tales."

"Oh?"

"Leaders look to their future. Only fools stay in the present." Cain repeated the words he knew would catch Brenton's attention. "If either of them would have escaped, the entirety of my father's force would be on this place."

Brenton gave an appreciative nod. "You took my lesson to heart rather fast."

"I'm a quick learner."

"Is that so?"

Cain nodded. "It is. And I want to challenge you again tonight."

Brenton smirked. "I accept. Tonight will be your trial by fire."

Nighttime came quicker than expected.

As before, an arena of charcoal was made before them. Embers underneath danced, showing they were still warm and ready to burn anyone not worthy. That wouldn't be Cain. Not again.

On the opposite side of the arena stood Brenton. Scars on his chest and one cut on his abdominal that Cain had given him were his armor. They told the story of a fearsome man, a man who didn't cower at his enemies, a man who stood over those who opposed him, a king. In an effort to mimic Brenton, Cain took off his shirt, revealing similar proportions but less rugged. There were scars on his arms from the Trials, but he didn't have the forest of hair on his chest like Brenton had. His skin was still soft, whereas Brenton's was hardened and toned, bred for exactly this purpose: trial by fire.

There was no pretty introduction. No initiation. Just simple acknowledgement of what brought these individuals to the center of the ring. When the charcoal court was assembled, Stannon came over to Cain with a flagon of firewine. This was the only requirement before stepping into the arena. Cain took the flagon by the handle and gulped down as much firewine as he could stomach before he felt the heat rising in his chest. Stannon took the flagon and walked around the court, offering it to Brenton as well. The man took it. All. Cain knew this because Brenton deliberately turned the flagon upside-down so that Cain could see no liquid spilled. It was all bravado. Cain knew that. Brenton was trying to intimidate him before he entered the arena, but palace life had accustomed Cain to such sweeping and ostentatious gestures.

Brenton stepped forward.

Cain followed suit. Unlike the last time, he didn't squawk at the heated coals beneath his feet. Now that he had been walking around on the felsic for days, the charcoal actually soothed him. It was now nothing more than black grass beneath his feet.

All around him, villagers watched. But none of that mattered now. The only thing, the only person who mattered was the man in front of him. And this time, Cain would force him to submit.

They stood five body lengths away from one another. Cain held his halberd, Brenton, his Ether Spear. In this trial, no Power could be used. Brenton claimed True Kings didn't need Power, the bond with their creature and their weapons was the only thing they needed. That was their identity. And Cain had thought about that a lot over the past few days; it had also given him an insight on how he might win the battle.

Last time, the charcoals under his feet had been a problem, and his constant acclimation to the conditions negated that now. But Cain had also been overly cautious of the Ether Weapon, knowing that it could split him in two with a simple stroke. The battle hadn't even progressed to that level before Cain succumbed to the coals underneath his feet, but as he thought about his strategy now, he reexamined that statement about weapon and wielder being bonded. Brenton thought of himself as his weapon. He had first introduced himself as Brenton the Protector, and if he was as true to his words as Cain thought, that meant that he wouldn't be aggressive in combat. On the contrary, Cain needed to make the assaults and breach his defenses, and the more Cain thought about this, the more he realized how accurate that logic was. After all, it was only if Cain attacked the Ether Weapon and Brenton defended that his weapon wouldn't break. Not the other way around.

Firewine worked its way through his blood. He didn't know what exactly the substance did to his body, but it warmed him. Made him more focused and alert. Confidence crept into him as well. It was almost as if the elixir allowed him to perform at his optimal potential.

He charged at Brenton, running on the charcoal with ease. Brenton readied himself. Cain launched an assault with a rapid succession of strikes. Slash. Swing. Sweep. Jab. The dull end of Cain's halberd caught Brenton in the chest. He stumbled back. Anticipating a recoil swing from Brenton, Cain ducked and swept Benton's legs from underneath him.

Susurrus and movement in the crowd stole Cain's attention. Was it done? Had he dethroned Brenton? He noticed a party of ten Kane men, hunters and scouters, wander off. Cain's heartbeat. Had he been too late in stopping the men from earlier? Were there more here now? How many?

A flash came to Cain's right. Instinct raised his weapon. It protected him, but at a price. His halberd was sliced in half. Now he held a baton in one hand and an axe in the other.

"Focus!"

Cain furrowed his brows. *Stupid!* He spent the next several minutes regaining his ground and maneuvering his way out of Brenton's blows. They weren't as refined as his, but with an Ether Weapon in his hand, it didn't matter. Any blow could be a lethal blow. He knew what he needed to do.

Shuffling back a few paces, Cain gave himself a moment of rest from Brenton's onslaught. Stuck in a stalemate, both eyed the other, waiting for the next move in the game. Cain took the time to formulate his next series of moves and countermoves. There was one way he could win and only one way. His luck and his evasive maneuvers would eventually fail him, and he would succumb to the same fate as so many others.

Swinging with both halves of his halberd, Cain attacked Brenton as if he was steering oars on a boat. One after the other in successive motion, waiting for Brenton to stop his advance. He did. As Cain's axe descended upon Brenton, he held up his Ether Spear to block the assault. Noticing the block before it came, Cain adjusted the trajectory of his axe slightly so that the throat of the axe would land on the Ether Spear, not the head of the axe. Instead, the head of the axe landed just above, and with a little coordination and spinning on Cain's part, he scooped the Spear, and in the process of doing so, contorted Brenton's body, hunching him, arm turned backwards still clutching his weapon. Cain took the full force of his baton and slammed it down on the exposed forearm. The impact caused Brenton to drop the Ether Weapon. Cain kicked it away, and as Brenton went to scramble after it, Cain met his throat with his halberd.

"Do you submit?"

Brenton's eyes twinkled. "I do."

Claps and cheers erupted from the villagers around. Cain hadn't expected that. He would have figured they wanted to see Brenton win, but perhaps they cheered for the opportunity to see such a duel occur or the fact that Cain proved worthy in this trial by fire. The waves of the cheers fell to whispers when the soldiers Cain noticed earlier came back.

"Sir!"

The appreciation for Cain's success fell from Brenton's face. Staid, he faced the returning party.

"We caught this group sneaking about the lands here."

"More from before?"

A voice tried to rise amongst the men from within, but it was quickly quieted.

"I don't know, sir. They seem different."

"Different?" Brenton crossed his arms over his chest. He glanced over at Cain. "Cain, Protector is yours now. Pick it up."

Cain gulped, but he didn't question it. It is what he had wanted after all. Who didn't dream of owning a fabled Ether Weapon? Throwing down his halberd to the charcoal court, he picked up the Ether Spear and felt the familiar weight in his hand. He got lost in its cloudy amethyst beauty. A woman's groan dragged him from it.

He couldn't see who it was—Brenton stood in his way—but Cain stepped around the man to survey the newcomers. The captured.

"What should we do with them, sir?"

Brenton turned to Cain. A smirk on his lips. "Well, my king, I believe this is your decision to make."

Cain gulped. His eyes widened. It couldn't be possible, could it? In front of him, on her knees, was Linn Clayse, Lady of Cresica, the one who had started the war with his father.

CHAPTER 19

# THE GUARDIANS

Eirek had been sitting in the hovercraft for a little more than an hour now, drumming his thumbs on his thighs all the while. Guardian Eska was taking him somewhere, but he had not revealed the destination. What Eirek did know, though, is that whatever was about to happen was serious. Seemingly overnight, Eska had changed from a stoic mentor to one who now held a look of determination on his face that could only herald the coming of something awful.

When the hovercraft stopped, Eirek found himself before a large, tri-colored pyramid of gold, silver, and copper. For the most part, the surrounding mountains isolated it from view, the gold at the top of the pyramid blending in with the peaks. While most of the pyramid was entrenched between the surrounding mountains, Eirek saw the middle level of the pyramid was silver and the base was copper.

"Follow me."

Eska left the hovercraft. Eirek hurried out and walked alongside Eska down a narrow pathway that served as a divider between two mountains. The sheer magnitude of the mountains and the impending entity of the pyramid made Eirek feel small.

A carved-out tunnel led them into the base of the pyramid, whose shadows soon dwarfed Eirek and the Guardian. "What is this place?"

"This is the Guardian's Crypt, Eirek." Eska undid his gloved left hand. It glowed brightly until Eska clenched his fist, suppressing the light.

"What is it?"

"This is the location of the Passing Ceremony, something that will take place when I hand over my full Power to you, fifteen years from now."

"Why are we here now, then?"

"We come for understanding. Hopefully, we will find it." At the end of the hallway, two statues holding unusual weapons animated themselves. Eska opened his gloved hand and immediately the two figures eased their stances and lowered the weapons barring entry from the door.

With the weapons removed, a mark on a copper slab was now visible. It looked like a pyramid with a G in the middle of it, splitting the triangle into three equilateral triangles. Eska put his gloved hand on this icon and the slab of copper shook and slowly pushed itself upward, granting access to Eirek and Eska.

As Eska led Eirek down a copper path lit with electric moss, Eirek looked back to see the slab closing shut and the statues step once more in front of it. "What were those things?"

"Guards, Eirek. If someone other than me tries to approach, they will protect the Crypt."

Eirek turned his attention back to the Guardian. He had stopped before a vast open space. In the center of the hollowed Crypt was a shrine and, on either side of the shrine, a slight depression that held a large pool. On the left side of the shrine, rising from the center of the pool, was a silver pedestal holding a silver bowl above it. On the right side, a copper version mirrored the silver. Outlining the shrine, ivory columns rose up from golden plinths to support a massive roof. There were three levels of stairs before the shrine, with stone statues that surveyed Eirek but spared no glance at Guardian Eska.

"What do they do?"

"They are part of the shrine's protection. They do not recognize you. If I was not here, they would kill you, or try to at least."

"What is here that needs such protection?" Eirek walked past the bull statues on the second level and then eyed the lions on the third.

"The crypt and throne."

Climbing the steps, Eirek pointed to the different colored pedestals sitting in the middle of the shallow pool. "What are those?"

"That is how one would reopen Gladima."

Eirek's eyes widened. "How?"

"As it was the Ancients who sealed Gladima from view, only one of their blood can reveal it again." Eska climbed the steps.

Eirek stopped. He looked at his hands. "Like mine?"

Eska halted and turned back, looking down on Eirek from above. "That, I do not know, but I intend to find out. That is later. Come, now." Eska waved Eirek to join him.

At the top, two golden statues sat on thrones of fire behind two crystalline tombs. When they came within two hundred meters of the thrones, the statues sprang to life.

"Guardian Eska, who is this that you have brought with you. You know it is—"

"Forbidden," Eska cut in. "However, I believe you will see it as an appropriate exception, Guardian Raule."

"What is your name?" The same statue leaned forward in his chair.

"Eirek Mourse, Apprentice to Guardian Eska."

"You bring us your apprentice, Eska?"

The other statue on the right spoke. Since Eska had identified the first statue as Guardian Jorey Raule, Eirek assumed that this second one was Eska's mentor, Guardian Matthau Crevon.

"Who else would he bring here?" the other statue bickered.

"But it is not time for the Passing yet."

"No, it is not. However, my apprentice and I are here for your council."

Guardian Raule nodded. "Proceed."

Guardian Eska told them everything from the past Pirini Lilapa—which received a harsh diatribe for his actions—to Galan's death and then about the prophecy and how perhaps it had been misinterpreted all along. After, he paused, as if he was deciding how to continue. Finally, he pulled Adonis from its sheath and showed it to the previous Guardians.

"Do the Ether Weapons have special abilities?"

Both Guardians leaned forward in their thrones. "They can cut through anything. Isn't that an ability?"

Eska shook his head. "Beyond that. Beyond just their Ether nature. Do either of you know if they have alternative functions?"

The two Guardians sat back in their thrones and looked at one another. Guardian Crevon spoke, "What makes you think such a thing?"

Eska then proceeded to talk about how the Sages were conspiring against him to return home. He offered the evidence of how the Emporian ship happened to be outside of Hown at the precise time to require an immediate landing. He talked about how Hown was no more. How the jewels were being sought.

"This betrayal is certainly something to take into consideration. Have you reprimanded the Sages yet?"

Eska opened his mouth to speak but then shut it. He hesitated and then said, "I haven't been able to locate them. This further makes me believe that they can anticipate actions to a certain extent with their Ether Staff, Foresight."

Guardian Crevon put his forehead into his fingertips.

Guardian Raule sighed, releasing a little puff of fire. "It seems as though things have certainly spiraled out of control since this last Pirini Lilapa."

Eska bowed his head and sighed. "For that, I am sorry." After a moment, he continued, "The last time I spoke with you, I mentioned how I suspected the Third One has plotted all the past Pirini Lilapas. It seems with Galan now dead, and the Twelve locked away, this one is no different."

"Except with how you handled it. You disavowed those who charged us with this duty!" Guardian Raule slammed his golden fist onto the throne of fire, pushing out a blast of hot air.

"Guardian Raule, it was not Guardian Eska's fault. I suggested they be used. Guardian Eska did what he needed to do in order to save more of Onkh."

"Be that as it may—"

"A thought just occurred to me, Edwyrd."

Eirek and Eska and even the statue of Guardian Raule looked at Matthau Crevon.

"A rather sickening thought, I want to add, but a thought all the same."

Eirek leaned in, shuffling his feet.

"What if, and I daresay, this is a ridiculous thought, but what if perhaps the Third One is Cronos?"

Eska tucked his right arm around his torso and propped his left arm up as a pillar for his chin to rest upon.

"How would that be possible?" Guardian Raule turned to his counterpart.

"From what the Twelve told you about the last moments of the Great War."

"Many of them vanished before its finale."

"Yes, but *who* didn't?"

"The Sages..." Guardian Raule's jaw dropped now as well. He closed it, expression turning thoughtful.

"What do you mean?"

Guardian Crevon acknowledged Eirek, but ignored his question. He stood up from his throne of fire and walked around it, hands behind his back. "The Great War ended with Lyoen and Bane fighting one another. A massive fight that brought stars closer together, tore planets apart, and threatened to wipe out the rest of the universe. Upon seeing the Third One seal Lyoen and Bane away, the Twelve left, in hopes of escaping before the Core fully formed. The Sages came after them. By some miracle, they had defeated the Ancient and showed the Twelve its armor and lifeless body as proof of its defeat."

"But how?" Eska asked.

One hand on the back of his chair, the other pointed upwards as though in epiphany, Guardian Crevon spoke fast, hands animated throughout the explanation. "Chronology is important here, and our only source comes from the Twelve and their telling of the War during the explanation of our position. But they mentioned that Bane had cast a spell before he was locked. It was a wicked spell that made saying the Third One's name impossible. Sealing Bane before he could cast more Power may have syphoned the Third One's energy enough that the Sages could have overtaken it. After all, the Third One's strength was already diminished without Desmós. This act of sealing the other Ancients may have syphoned it of all its strength."

"Then how do you explain the Sages being the Third One?"

"Because the Third One, Apprentice Mourse, is also known as the Bonder. He created the process of bonding and was the first being to ever do it."

"Matthau, are you suggesting that perhaps during the altercation between the Sages and the Third One that the Bonder transferred his energy into them at the moment of defeat? Is that even possible?"

"I do not begin to question if anything is possible when the Ancients are involved, Jorey. Those three did miraculous things. Terrible at times, but miraculous all the same." Crevon's voice tapered off, and he turned his attention from his counterpart to Eska. "Edwyrd, you have been silent for some time. What is on your mind?"

A light lifted in Eska's eyes like he had finally cleared away a fog. "What Guardian Crevon believes is true."

Guardian Raule shifted on his throne. "You know this? For certain?"

Guardian Eska looked at both of them, then to Eirek. He nodded. "I do. Recently, I conducted some investigations on Agrost. I went straight to the palace of the Sages in Epoch to confirm my suspicions about their betrayal. They weren't there. The Other was."

Eirek choked. The other Guardians did as well, releasing little puffs of flames in their astonishment. Eirek's face twisted in confusion. He gave a furtive glance to his right, but couldn't notice anything off with Eska. If he had been in a confrontation with the Third One, he hid his wounds well. *Is that why he came back so late?* Eirek bit his lower lip.

"Did you say the Other, Edwyrd?"

"Yes, Guardian Crevon. It fought me."

"And you are still alive? How?"

Eska nodded. "Luck."

"The Other is a part of them? How does that even work?" Guardian Raule asked.

"Again, I agree with Guardian Crevon. It is not for us to understand the Power of the Ancients, but I am certain of what I saw and what I faced. My Ether Blade didn't harm it at all. There is only one reason for that."

"I believe Guardian Eska."

All the Guardians looked at Eirek.

"When I was on the Sacred Passage, Pirini Lilapa occurred. And when it occurred, Cronos was off by himself, speaking nonsense, muttering something. Almost as if he was in a different place."

"How do you know this?"

"I was with him. I disrupted him. His eyes were afire that day. That whole week he had more energy than usual."

Eska's neck tensed. He looked at the other Guardians. "It cannot be happenstance. Cronos, the other Sages, the Third One. They are all connected." Eska raised his hand to the air. "And that is why..." Eska murmured. "Victor..." He chuckled to himself briefly.

"Edwyrd, what is it?"

Eska shook his head. "How could we all be so blind?"

"What are you talking about?"

"Victor Zigarda. It all makes sense now. His distaste for me."

"That stems from your own Trials, Edwyrd. You and I both know how that ended."

"Partly, yes, my Guardian. But I believe the Sages have been using Victor, kindling his hatred towards me, guiding him to what could have been my ruin."

"Ruin? What do you mean?"

Eska told them about the hearing and vote that had occurred on Mistral. "If I had been absolved of my Power, Victor may have set his sights on Eirek and taking the Guardianship for himself."

"After all this time you think he still wants to be Guardian?"

Eska didn't respond. Eirek surveyed each of the three Guardians as they sat or stood in a silence so complete, Eirek could hear his own breath.

"Maybe. I do not know," Eska said. "But if the Sages... if Cronos is the Other, then with Victor as Guardian they would have access to the Core. As Guardian, Victor would know of this place and would know its purpose. And if he had Eirek's blood, which it seems that he does, he could reopen Gladima. And then..." Eska's eyes widened.

Guardian Raule gave Eirek a dubious look. "Edwyrd, you are sputtering nonsense now. To reopen Gladima we would need—"

"The Ancient's blood of Lyoen and Bane. I know. And we have it. Here. In my apprentice." Eska stood alongside Eirek, arm wrapped over his shoulder.

Eirek tensed as the other Guardians observed him.

"What do I need to do?" Eska asked.

They looked at him, dumbfounded.

"Well?"

"You are telling us your apprentice is the offspring of Naydeia and Galan?"

"I have very good reason to believe so. Now, what do I need to do?"

It was clear that both Guardians had more questions to ask, but the immediacy in Eska's voice overpowered their desires to get more answers.

"Blood needs to be given."

"How much?"

"A few droplets."

Before Eirek could pull away, Guardian Eska seized his forearm and rolled back his sleeve. Eska had pulled a knife from somewhere and held it to his skin. "Eirek, I will—"

"But that isn't all Edwyrd." Guardian Raule cut in. "There are spells of Power that need to be said. Power from the Ancient Language."

Keeping a steady grasp on Eirek's forearm, Eska looked back at the Guardian. "Surely, the reimaje could tell me everything I need to speak."

All the while Eirek waited with bated breaths, tense as a tightrope about to cut loose.

"Yes, it certainly may. But reopening Gladima is only one issue, resurrecting Ancient Lyoen or Bane is a completely different issue, and for that we have no precedent; it was before our task started. Reopening Gladima may do more harm than good if it brings the Third One another step closer to his goal."

Eska relaxed his hold and put the knife away. His shoulders slumped. "And what of the Ether Weapons, then? Did the Twelve mention any special function they may have?"

"The evidence you provide is interesting but not convincing," the statue of Guardian Raule said. "You have access to every memory that ever entered that reimaje, Edwyrd. And in all that time, I guarantee there is no such thing mentioned."

Eska furrowed his brows. "I understand, my Guardians. Eirek, let us leave." Wasting no time, Eska spun around and descended the steps.

The Guardians returned to their inanimate features. Eirek hurried down the steps after the Guardian. He didn't fully catch up to his mentor until halfway out from under the pyramid's shadow. Eirek tugged at his arm so that Eska would stop.

"Why did you rush out of there so quickly?"

Still in the shade of the pyramid, Eska glanced from Eirek to the pyramid. "You see the pyramid, Eirek?"

Eirek turned around and nodded.

"What are the colors?"

"Copper, silver, and gold."

"Yes. Denotations of all three Ancient Powers, and that is why this pyramid is the pathway to Gladima. We are in a game of Ancient Power, Eirek, and the field for the game is changing. I will be the one who makes the first and final move." Eska walked towards the hovercraft and jumped in. "Hurry up. Let's go. Time has never been more of the essence."

Eirek hesitated, looking up to the tri-color pyramid. He glanced down at the sword at his hip and played with the orb of energy that sat above the hilt with his thumb. He flicked it to and fro, but it never deviated too far from its center, as if it was invisibly tethered to the hilt. *What is your name? What is your ability?*

"Eirek, let's be off. There is nothing else here."

Eirek exhaled. With slumped shoulders and a frown, he turned around and made his way back to the hovercraft, plopping down in the seat beside Eska.

"What is on your mind?"

"I..." Eirek pushed his lips to one side. "I can't figure it out. Everything makes sense in there. Well, almost everything."

"Like?"

"Well, I believe everything you mention about the Ether Weapons. I think they do have abilities."

"What makes you think that?"

"Just my own sword here." He showed Eska the hilt of his sword. "You see how that orb isn't attached at all. I always wondered what kind of trick did that. Now I'm thinking perhaps it has something to do with its special ability."

Eska leaned in closer, seemingly just noticing the orb for the first time. "That is certainly odd. Adonis doesn't have anything like that."

"Did you name your sword?"

"No. It already had a name when I inherited it from Guardian Crevon. And even before him with Guardian Raule. The Twelve told Guardian Raule its name when he first took up the mantle as Guardian."

"I wonder what mine is called."

"I could use my reimaje and see if there is anything to help you, but I am sure you will know in time."

Eirek sighed and put his sword away. "All right."

"Is that all? There seems to be something else."

Eirek turned to his mentor and said, "Surely Cronos knows who I am. If the Twelve figured it out. If you figured it out. Surely, he did too. Yet, he trained me. He had me close enough to him that he could have killed me at any time. But he never did. Why?"

"Perhaps he was worried that he needed your blood to reopen Gladima. Perhaps he was worried about the repercussions for killing you."

Hand under his chin, Eirek thought for a second. His eyes lit. "You?"

"Yes. And while I may have not been able to harm the Ancient, my Ether Weapon could definitely kill Cronos, and if the Third One is using him as a momentary life support system, it makes sense that he wouldn't try something so brash."

Eirek gulped. "I... I just realized something."

"What's that?"

"The Twelve grew upset when they saw me. Perhaps he needed me to be at Pirini Lilapa to sow dissent amongst them. To make you fight them and syphon your own strength." Eirek leaned forward, putting his elbows on his knees and his head on top of his palms. "With you out of the way..." Eirek twisted in his seat. "What would happen?"

"Chaos." Eska pushed the button of anitron, hoisting the hovercraft into the air. Saying no more, he turned the hovercraft around and headed back to the estate.

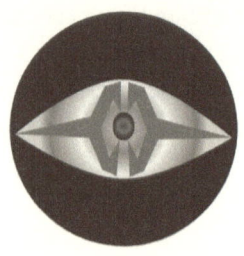

# INTERLUDE 1 - WRONGLY ACCUSED

A bittersweet feeling Cadmar couldn't quite describe hung in the air. And, in truth, this feeling had been with him the whole time since he began the Passage. Perhaps it had been due to the good and the bad happening to him while he undertook the quest. The good had come in the form of friendship with a man named Fayser. Out of the five that had begun the Passage, he was the one Cadmar most closely connected with, despite his southern heritage. Cadmar was of the north, but his mother lived in the south. And there was the rather morbid fact that he connected with Fayser most because he was the only one left to connect with. Ninety-four days later, a day's ride from Visis, the Goddess Flower in his good hand, the horse's reins in his other, he finally would return. *Father will be proud of me. I know it.*

Cadmar had given his all on the Passage. He had lived up to his grandfather's name and his father's name, and even more. His father had returned in one hundred and eighteen days, just shy of four months. Cadmar had set out to break that record and show his father that what had happened in the past wouldn't happen again. And he did it. Yes, he had done it.

"Let's stop here for the night," Cadmar said.

"You don't want to get there tonight?"

"What be one day, Fayser? We have already missed our chance to beat Horm's record."

"I don't believe anyone be beating that record."

"Neither do I. That man must be faster than a horse." Cadmar chuckled. He got off his own steed and stretched. "Let's tie the horses here." Cadmar pointed to a group of trees, all without leaves as the beginning of winter blanketed the land. "You pitch the tents, I'll go look for some stones."

Cadmar walked through the snow, kicking it up with his boots. It was easier to do so here than in Sereya. And after what he experienced in the true north, this cold didn't bother him at all. Even the polar bear fur wrapped about his body and the sling on his arm felt warm now that they had returned to Garian territory, and the bright lights of Visis off in the distance gave him the reassurance that everything would be all right. Tomorrow would be a new day, a day he would finally look into his father's eyes. The Passage had taught him what his father and his grandfather had experienced, how it made a person cold, how it strengthened the strong and killed the weak. And he understood now that his father had never given his respect because Cadmar had never earned it. Tomorrow, that would change.

Within the time it took Cadmar to gather stones for containing the fire, Fayser had set up the campsite. The leafless tree branches next to the horses would feed the fiery beast. Inhaling, Cadmar breathed in the smoky air; he listened to the crackle of the twigs sacrificing their energy to provide them comfort. His eyes drifted from the city lights shouting for attention to the luminescent moon, bright and nearly full but seemingly closer than it ever had been now with the silhouette of Mount Volan as the companion to its scenery. His mind stayed in this sweet state for a moment. While in that moment he saw the reward of his efforts so close to him, like the moon, that he could reach out and grab it at any time he desired. But when that moment began to slip, like it always did since the incident on Peril's Pass, the crackling of the twigs turned to swishing water, the snowflakes' caress became heavy burdens that made his body shiver. And that moon. That moon. That damned moon too close to the planet would remind him of how it affected the water and how it made Perils' Pass that much more perilous and how, because of him and his vanity and his need to beat his father, Garth had been swept away by the tide.

"Don't think about him."

Through the fire, Cadmar looked to Fayser. "I be trying not to, but I can't." Cadmar's head fell. Keeping his head down, he pointed at the moon. "Whenever I look at that thing... The memories be returning."

"But that don't mean they should be staying. Garth chose to go with us..."

"But I convinced him."

"He wanted to be better than others, too. And the only way one be earning a record time on the Passage be going through Peril's Pass."

"I..." Cadmar sighed. "I suppose you be right."

Cadmar maneuvered off of the pile of stones he sat on to the blanket Fayser had laid out for him. He sprawled out, the light snow underneath giving him a little extra cushion. He twirled the Goddess Flower in front of him once, seeing the fire shimmer off of its petals before putting it aside away from the fire—he still needed to present it to Lady Aprah on the morrow in pristine condition. Eyes closed, he hoped tonight would be one of the nights where he wouldn't get dragged back to the sea yet again.

"Get up!"

Cadmar felt a slight poke to his chest. He opened his eyes. A man stood above him, sword drawn, pointing towards him. The fire had died. Still groggy, Cadmar couldn't see much of anything else.

"I said get up."

Cadmar yawned and blinked, his vision slowly adjusting to the grave of night. The man in front of him was a soldier of Lady Aprah, but not an elite. He could tell by the clothes.

Pushing his good elbow into the ground, he leveraged himself upright. "What be this about?"

"What be your name?"

"What it be to you?"

"Your name! Now!" The man jabbed Cadmar's chest with the sword, enough to irritate, but not enough to puncture skin.

"Cadmar Briggs. And my friend Fayser."

"You be hearing tha, Ross? We finally found Cadmar Briggs. I thought it be him. Do it."

The man named Ross pushed Fayser over to Cadmar and then stepped away from the trio, doing something with his wrist. As the man began speaking, he trailed off, inaudible to the others.

"What he doing? What this be about?"

The man laughed. "Like you don't know."

"I don't."

"Yeah, sure you don't. And I be from Acquava." The man laughed some more.

Cadmar exchanged a glance with Fayser. His brows and shoulders went up together. Distracted by the call his partner made, the man's hold on his sword was sure to be weak. A fatal flaw. With as little movement as possible, Cadmar gestured towards the grip, hoping to catch Fayser's approval. Fayser nodded.

Stepping carefully, Cadmar used force and momentum to break the man's grip, grabbing the man's sword from him and then pushing him back and down.

The scuffle did not go unnoticed by the other man, who immediately rushed to the scene, sword drawn, but Fayser greeted him with axe in hand.

With one knee pressed into the man's stomach, Cadmar pushed the sword to the man's throat. "Now, what this be about?"

"Act dumb, it won't be mattering once the Elites arrive. You be paying for what you did to Lady Aprah."

Cadmar furrowed his brow. Fayser looked at him with the same perplexity. Cadmar turned to the man and sighed. "I be sorry for this."

"Sorry for—"

Cadmar let the sword drop to the ground and then punched the man hard in the side of the head, knocking him unconscious. By the time Cadmar got up, the other man had crumpled under the strength of Fayser's chokehold.

Cadmar moved his bad shoulder, a little agitated after the confrontation. He stood up. "What that be about?"

"I be wondering the same thing."

*What happened to Lady Aprah?* Cadmar flicked his gaze towards Visis. The lights called to him like a fly to a light post. If he went too close, would he get zapped?

"We have to move."

"I agree," said Cadmar.

"If they be looking for us out here, they been scouring Visis, too. What happened?"

"I... I don't know..."

"What about your aul man?"

"He would know... but..."

"But, what?"

Cadmar felt a stone in his stomach. The relationship he had with his father hadn't ever mended fully. After the first incident with the Passage, his mother left, and his father disowned him. In hopes of mending it, Cadmar sought to become Guardian of the Core. But that failed as well. Guardian Eska gave him another chance for the Passage and another chance at making things right with his father. And he had been on the threshold of that respect until this. Whatever this was.

"Cadmar, we need to be leaving."

"You don't need to come with; they never said anything about you. You can still make it to Visis like you be never with me."

"Cadmar, I not be leaving you now. Not after what we went through."

Cadmar smiled. The friendship reminded him of Eirek and all they went through during the fourth trial.

"Okay. Then let's get our horses. We ride for Visis. Have your weapon ready."

The modern-day mountains of Visis were close now, large skyscrapers that had sprung up from the affluence of Lady Aprah's reign, the rebellion of her parents, and their sacrifice, their martyrdom. Secured tight to his chest thanks to the polar bear sling he had made while on the Passage, his arm didn't bother him the slightest as he bounced up and down in cadence to his horse's trot. Alongside him trotted Fayser's large draft horse.

Although he didn't know what was going on, he was certain that he could explain everything if he could only get the chance. That chance, Cadmar realized, was coming sooner than expected.

Three hovercrafts sped straight towards him and Fayser.

"Up ahead," he shouted to Fayser.

"I see them. Why they be out here?"

A question Cadmar wanted answered as well. Surely the men that had woken them up a few hours earlier had contacted reinforcements and had given away their position. After they rendered both men unconscious, Cadmar and Fayser decided it would be best to approach Visis by going through one of the less traveled routes, not the main road. They had split off on the road that led directly to Visis, going farther south first, towards Banad, and from that minor city they would approach Visis. However, the hovercrafts that sped towards them completely disregarded the airroads and specified pathways, cutting through earthly expanse like a fissure.

"Let's stop. We can't be outrunning them anyway." Cadmar pulled back on his reins, bringing his horse to a stop.

Fayser stopped alongside him. "Who do you think it be? How could they find us here?"

Cadmar didn't answer. He already knew who he thought it might be, and he needed to concentrate on the following encounter.

Within minutes, the three hovercrafts surrounded them, each carrying two men. All six disembarked and approached Cadmar and Fayser, hands on the hilts of their weapons. Chest out, the E on their chest clearly labeled them as Elites. Four of the Elites stayed back, leaving the elder two to stalk towards them. Cadmar knew them both. Breaths heavy on the air. Boots crunching on the snow. Horm, Lady Aprah's top guard, looked from Cadmar to Fayser. Alongside him stood Lady Aprah's second-in-command, Cadmar's father.

"It be time to come in, Cadmar."

Cadmar's neck tensed. His brows furrowed. His father hadn't even acknowledged their familial relationship.

"What this be about, Pa?" Cadmar pivoted his eyes from his father to Horm.

"You be wanted for questioning by Lady Aprah..."

"But why?"

"How did you get that sprain?" Horm cocked his head, pointing his chin to Cadmar's wrapped arm.

"A polar bear that be on the Passage."

"Or perhaps a rough landing from an escape off a balcony?"

"I don't know what you be talking about."

"Cadmar, you be wanted for the attempted assassination of Lady Olivia Aprah. It is our duty to bring you in. If you resist, we will have to resort to force." His father opened his stance, positioning his legs farther apart. He moved his hand to the throat of his axe. "What will it be?"

Nothing made sense to Cadmar at that moment. He hung his head down, trying to contemplate what reality he had awoken into. When he glanced up again, he noticed all eyes continued to stare at him, even Fayser. In turn, he looked at all of them, turning to his father last.

"Lead the way."

# INTERLUDE 2 - THE PEOPLE OF KANE

On her knees, Linn looked up at none other than Prince Cain Evber. Her breathing hitched. Her eyes widened. *Is the heat playing tricks on me?* She blinked and shook her head. Cain stared back at her with the same face of disbelief. *What is he doing here with all these people? Is that an Ether Weapon?* Linn tried processing all the information, but it muddled around in her mind.

She struggled against her captors. "Cain! We need to talk."

"You know these people, son?"

*Son? What in Abaddon's name...* She glanced from Cain to the man who had spoken. Her mouth hung slack as she saw the similarities.

"Prince Evber, please tell these men to release us." Her father next to her struggled against his bonds as well.

All eyes were now on Cain. He stared at them, seemingly dumbfounded by the attention. It was a long moment before he spoke. "I know them. Get them up."

Linn was brought to stand, though the large man behind her did not let go of her wrists. Trying to escape would be futile, so she hoped instead that Cain would listen to her reasoning. Would hear her out.

"Why are you here?" he asked.

"We were on route to your..." Linn paused. She looked towards the other man. "Father?"

"Daven is still my father. What business do you have with him?"

"The war. I owe him an apology. This war doesn't need to happen."

"You came to surrender?" Cain arched an eyebrow.

"No. Surrender would imply this war has even started in the first place. I'm here to call off the war before it starts."

"What has made you change your mind?" Cain eyed her and her men.

"Epoch didn't attack me."

Cain chuckled. "Now you finally see it. When did you come to your senses? How?"

"Guardian Eska."

"You lie. He is currently in Mistral."

"I just came from Mistral not two days ago. The hearing is concluded."

"You went?" Cain's breath staggered. "And?"

"And we should talk."

Cain nodded. "Brenton, may we use your hut for our discussion?"

"It is your hut now, son."

Cain looked at Linn awkwardly, a little flushed in his cheeks. "Kai, you may let her go. Lady Clayse, follow us."

The man released her, and the other captors followed suit. Linn looked back at her party. "Stay here while I talk with Prince Evber."

"My lady, you don't want us—"

"No," she cut off Roland. "Not this time."

Her personal guard took a step back and bowed his head.

"Linn be careful."

"If they wanted us dead, it would have already happened, Father." She smiled and acknowledged the others in her party before going to Cain's side.

"The others are not coming?"

"Not this time. There are many things I think that you and I need to discuss." She glanced from him to the other man who strolled in front of them.

Cain opened his mouth, prepared to speak, but then closed it. "Very well, Lady Clayse. It is time we talk."

Inside a clay hut, Linn recapped the events of Mistral. She had been timid at first to do so, seeing as the other man, who had yet to introduce himself, was still present. He said he wouldn't leave, and Cain made it clear she should continue. Cain was curious as to why Epoch voted against the Guardian, but he showed relief to know that the Guardian still remained in Power. It wasn't until Linn told him of the Third Ancient that his eyes widened.

He coughed into a fist. "Three?"

"Here is some fire tea for you." The man set two clay cups on the table in front of them and poured an orangish tea into the cups that he had been busying himself with earlier. After, he returned to the stove and busied himself with cooking something while humming.

Linn glanced awkwardly at the man and then at Cain. Cain just shrugged his shoulders. Sighing, Linn leaned in closer, hushing her voice. "Yes, Three. And it was the Third Ancient who attacked my city."

"What did it look like? What exactly happened?"

Linn recapped the event, finishing with a description of a great firestorm that came to Syf that culminated in the appearance of a fiery golden entity with angelic wings.

"Where is it now?"

Linn jumped back in her chair a little. As she spoke, the man must have abandoned his cooking. He now stared down at her with eyes of fire, similar to what she saw that dreadful day.

Stammering, Linn said, "I don't know. It flew off afterwards with Angal's body."

The man clicked his tongue and returned to the stove.

"You can't just leave the conversation! What do you know? How do you know about the Third One?"

The man ignored Linn. Linn turned to Cain, her eyes pleading.

"Father?"

"I have ears. I am finishing your food. You will need it. Especially you, son. You need to keep yourself strong for Chantico."

Linn cocked her head at Cain. "Chantico?"

It was Cain's turn to divulge the information he had just learned. By the time he finished his story, the man had returned carrying two clay plates with an assortment of red rice, cooked meat, and a two halves of a red pepper, grilled and lathered with paste the color of clay.

"Eat."

Linn followed Cain's lead in trying the meat first for it was the safest thing on the plate. It was overcooked and tough to chew. "Now what do you know about the Third One?"

The man returned with his own plate of food. He didn't answer right away, preferring to eat a few bites first. When satisfied, he set his fork and knife down and cupped his hands together. He looked from Cain to Linn. "Did you know that back before the Great War that a True King was chosen to rule each planet?"

Linn looked at Cain, who didn't seem phased by this information. "I... I... No, I did not, but I do not see the relevance."

"You will. Let me explain."

The man told a story of how each True King was chosen. They were as strong as the Twelve, but because of their heritage and lack of First Blood, they were unfit to join them in Gladima. Rather, they remained on their own domain. This had made them reject the Ancients and loathe the Twelve until one day they received a visit from an entity plated in gold. The story went that he gave each one a feather of Power and created an animal especially for them to bond to, so that they could show the Ancients how strong they could really be.

"Are you referring to the Four Creatures of Legend?"

"I am." The man nodded.

"Father!"

The man held up a hand to silence Cain. "I am not finished yet." He turned his attention back to Linn. "These creatures were powerful beyond comprehension, much more powerful than the Kings they were bonded to. The strength they received went to their head, and they thought they could do anything—even exterminate a plague of wild animals..." He muttered the last part to himself, but Linn still heard it. Before she could ask, he continued. "That is what happened to the ruler of Pyre, Andrej. He wanted to save his village from being ravaged by hordes after hordes of local animals, and so he called upon the beast, Chantico, to help him and he waged war against creatures you have never heard of or have ever seen in your life. Creatures with boulders for bodies and nails like scythes and large, shale-shaped monstrosities... Well, not even he had enough strength to defeat them all, so they killed him, and when they did, the volcano erupted due to Chantico's rage, and it threatened to wipe out the entire village. One man, however, saved that village by leading them through a special portal. This man had been a bard, and he told us he had come from Gladima."

"A bard? What was his name?"

"*That*, I do not know. The man insisted on my forefather's tribe not knowing his name."

"Why?"

"He came to us in the midst of the Great War. Maybe before, I am unsure. He mentioned to my forefather that he was not safe there, so he needed to get away." The man looked at Linn. "Now, whether that danger was because of the Great War or something else altogether, I do not know, but this bard you mention in your story, a bard with the strength to halt the Other, my guess is that it is the same individual."

Linn coughed. *Angal? Angal? A bard from before the Great War. Is... is that why he always joked about how old he was?* Linn started connecting bits and pieces of his narrative. If it was true, then what did that make Eirek?

"How could you possibly know all of this?"

"My name is Brenton. I am the True King of Pyre. Well, now Cain is." Brenton looked at Cain and smiled. He turned back to Linn. "The Third Ancient is responsible for giving my lineage its Power. He is responsible for the Power of all of the True Kings, and he created the Creatures of Legend. They were some of his first."

Linn eyed him skeptically. She had finished her food, not enjoying the dryness of it all. The tea was bearable, although much too hot for her throat, so she could only take it in little sips.

"You still do not believe me?" Brenton asked after scooping rice into his mouth.

"Guardian Eska has told me only a handful of people know about the Third One. One should you be one of them?"

"Because the people of Kane stayed true to their history. To their roots. Stories get passed down from one generation to the next here, not distorted in books or fairy tales or in the gossip of other civilizations and peoples. We have remained pure to our past in order to achieve the glory we once held at the proper time. And that time is now. With Cain. You are ready to bond with Chantico, son."

Cain nodded. His birthright gave him confidence. "I will."

"And I will give you the means to do so."

"Wait. What about your father? I mean Lord Evber? I need to call off this war."

Cain opened his mouth to say something, but Brenton spoke for him. "Cain cannot return to his father. Lord Evber would try to confuse him and prevent him from reaching his destiny."

Linn looked at Cain. "So the war must continue?"

Cain bit his lip. Glazed over eyes told her he concentrated on something deeply. Why else would he be so silent, so reserved at a time like this?

"No, Lady Clayse," Brenton said

Linn looked to him. "Then you and I will go to Lord Evber while Cain escapes off planet. I need to speak to the lord as well."

"No!"

Linn and Brenton turned to Cain now. His placid demeanor had been replaced with one of intent.

"Cain, you must go and claim your destiny."

"And I will, Father. But I will not allow you to speak to my father the words that I need to speak to him. Doing that would be running away from my problems. And that isn't what a hero would do. That isn't what a King would do. I will go to my father, and I will tell him the truth."

Brenton crossed his arms over his chest and nodded towards Cain. "That is the son I expected you to be."

Linn locked eyes with Cain. No longer seeing a man abashed at what he had learned, but a man who had accepted the task that lay before him. A man who had come out from the shadows of others to live in the light of his own story. She saw a King.

# PART II - PLAN B

CHAPTER 20

# MANTRAS TO LIVE BY

The red cloud of Mendeck came into view as Zigarda's ship went farther into the atmosphere of Myoli. Zakk sat in the middle compartment by himself, biding his time by watching the screen on the wall show him what the cameras on the ship saw. As they approached Mendeck, Zakk heard the voices of Zigarda and his advisor, Edwyn Lyze, intensify from the cockpit.

"What will happen to Empora now?"

"Nothing will change. It still needs a strong ruler."

"You heard Guardian Eska himself. Everyone heard it. He stripped you of your title."

"What of it?"

"That means Empora needs a ruler, my lord. I can help do that."

"They won't need your help, Edwyn. They have me."

"Denying Guardian Eska again? That may result in your death."

"Death." Zigarda scoffed. "What do you know about death?"

There was an eerie silence. Zakk shifted on the bench, trying to hear if the conversation had become only whispers. It hadn't. It had stopped completely. When Edwyn continued, he eased back into his position, arms over his chest.

"I know nothing," Edwyn continued. "I admit that. But I am your advisor. With your power stripped, I can rule as a surrogate in your place while you remain behind the scenes. Perhaps it's best to let me off here? Who better to continue your legacy than—"

Coughs. Zakk scooted a little closer to the door that separated the two compartments.

"Why did you..."

More coughs.

The compartment door slid open.

"Zakk, come in here."

Zakk arched his eyebrows and stood. Lord Zigarda's advisor lay on the ground, a stab wound in his stomach, mouth and lips and face red with blood. He coughed again, spitting up more of the red substance. Zigarda moved into the pilot's seat and pushed a button.

"Throw this one out of the cargo hold."

The back of the ship yawned. Air berated him. Zakk braced himself, resisting the vacuum that threatened to suck him out. Zigarda's advisor lay on the ground, still alive, but bleeding and panting heavily.

"Do I have to ask you again? Throw him out."

Zakk took the feet of the advisor and dragged him to the back of the ship. The sound of the wind overpowered his senses. It was too hard to maintain a standing position at the mouth of the ship, so Zakk went to knees to push the man out. As he did so, Edwyn grabbed Zakk's forearm. He pulled himself up.

"You dog. You're nothing more than his pet." The man spit on Zakk's face.

Face twisted in disgust, Zakk pushed the man off of the ship, succumbing to his furor and impatience at the man's name calling. Zakk didn't bother trying to look to see where the man fell. He knew that journey all too well, but chances were this man wouldn't fall into a lake as Zakk had. Had fate saved him from a certain death? Did he survive to bring some sort of purpose to the world? He'd yet to find an answer to those questions, and the tumultuous torrents of wind offered nothing.

Getting up from his knees, he staggered back to the front of the ship and went inside the cockpit.

"It's done." Zakk took his seat.

"Good." Zigarda pushed a button. The door closed behind him.

In front of Zakk, a castle in the north came into view.

"Take out that feather of yours."

Zakk reached inside his shirt and pulled the feather out. It pointed to the west and slightly north. After noticing the feather's position, Zigarda turned the ship in the same direction. While continually looking at the feather, he turned the ship to the northwest until the feather straightened out, then he put it on autopilot.

"Where are we going?"

"Wherever the feather tells us to go. You can let it go now."

Zakk let the feather drop to his chest. Before him, the ship traversed plains that slowly went from green to white and became hilly.

Zakk shifted in his chair and gave a furtive glance to Zigarda. "Why did you do that?"

"What?" Zigarda kept focused ahead.

"With Edwyn."

"You heard him, didn't you? He wanted to be dropped off in Mendeck."

Zakk focused ahead and bit his lip. He resisted the urge to cross his arms, not wanting his body posture to betray him. Coolly, he said. "Not that. Kill him."

Zigarda turned his head towards Zakk. Lidless charcoal eyes boring into him. "Do you have anything to say about the matter?"

Zakk turned to meet Zigarda's gaze. "No."

Zigarda's lips stretched in a crooked grin. "You lie. But that is okay. Sometimes it's necessary to lie." He turned back to the front and then spared a glance at Zakk's chest and then once more back ahead. "It seems that Rhayna may be on the Frozen Pass."

His feather curled upwards, pointing to the mountain that loomed before them. Zigarda angled the ship towards a castle that came into view near the foot of the mountain range.

"Why do you think I lie?"

"Because otherwise you wouldn't have asked the question." Zigarda let his words settle for a bit before speaking again. "Do you know what is wrong with most people nowadays?"

Zakk kept silent and let Zigarda answer his own question.

"They say things they think others want to hear instead of truly speaking their minds. It's almost as if they are fighting for the other person's good will before championing their own needs. My brother was like that. I despised him for it." Zigarda clicked his tongue.

"Fight for others, then fight for yourself," Zakk repeated the Gazo's mantra.

"Is that some kind of mantra you live by?" Zigarda scoffed. "The most important person is yourself. Your goals. Your ambitions. Your dreams. Speak what you mean and mean what you speak. That is what it takes to be a successful and powerful ruler. When people stand in the way of that goal, you let them go. We will land in Lokigh." Zigarda tilted the steering wheel down towards the castle and make our journey through the passage from there.

"Why not take the ship?"

"I don't want Rhayna to know we are coming. The best element isn't water or fire or electricity or earth, it is surprise." Zigarda turned to Zakk. "I've told you this before, yes?"

Zakk nodded.

"And that vote would have worked if not for the Lady of Cresica. I'll pay her back eventually for that, but now it is time we surprise Rhayna and gain her strength and her favor. Then I will go to the Core, and this time it will be my turn to surprise Edwyrd." Zigarda laughed to himself.

Zakk could not remember ever seeing the man so lost in his maniacal mind. Was he going mad? Zakk bit his lower lip. He hated surprises.

For the most part, the castle was empty, for Marquis Desmier's men had left on orders to take over Pelopon. While some soldiers who remained to look over the keep attended to Zigarda's requests to prepare supplies for the journey north towards the Frozen Pass, he used that time to make a few calls from Marquis Desmier's telecommunication chamber.

His first call was to Marquis Desmier himself. The marquis answered on his telecommunicator.

"My lord. How do things fare? You are in Lokigh right now?"

"Yes. Business draws me north to the Frozen Pass, so I am taking some of your supplies and horses to maneuver up the mountain. Has Castle Semson been overtaken?"

"Yes, my lord."

"Everyone is dead?"

"No. Some managed to escape the castle walls and the city before we overtook it, but we have laid siege to the castle successfully."

"That is good to hear. It is your castle now. You are the Lord of Ka'Che."

"I am honored by the title, my lord."

"You earn what you deserve."

"It would not have been possible without your plan or the..."

"Yes. The shapeshifters. Were any lost in battle?"

"Only a few. There are still a handful left."

"Good. Make sure you keep tabs on where they are. *Who* they are."

"Most will maintain the same identities they've always had."

"Good."

"What draws you north, my lord?"

"I am going to bring you reinforcements should an attempt be made to take back the castle."

"Reinforcements from the north?"

"Rhayna."

Marquis Desmier coughed. "Rhayna, my lord? The Creature of Legend?"

"You heard correctly, Rowan. I've learned how to bond with her recently, and I intend to do so to finish the last part of the plan."

"That will be a glorious sight to see, then. I look forward to your arrival."

"It will not be long now."

The connection cut. Zigarda typed in another seven digits of a telecommunicator number. A hologram of a woman with brown hair and shelves of books behind her appeared on the telescreen.

"Hello? My lord? Give me a second."

The connection cut. A few minutes passed, and the connection resumed. Behind her now were tall green hedges which swallowed her small face. It darkened her features as well.

"My lord? What is it?"

"Has the boy returned from the meeting yet?"

The woman nodded.

"Start making plans with Rhemu. The plan is going ahead as scheduled."

"That man failed?"

"I suspect so."

"I will reach out to Marchioness Puwl then," the woman said.

"Keep your eyes on the little one."

"He has already gone away."

"Gone. Where to?" Zigarda asked.

"I do not know. They left by ship a day ago."

"Then it may be the perfect time to plan something. Keep an eye on him when he returns."

The woman frowned slightly. "It will be much harder as he is bonded now."

"Bonded?"

"To a horse."

Zigarda did seemed unperturbed. "Use this time to your advantage, then. Do not fail."

"I will begin planning things."

"Good."

The connection cut.

Zigarda turned on his heels. "Let's go. We have a bird to catch." He pushed open the door and exited the telecommunicator chamber.

Zakk rushed out after him. "My lord," Zakk called out, stopping Zigarda as the man moved down the second story hallway.

Zigarda pivoted. "What is it?"

"Do you intend to head off for the Frozen Passage now?"

"Yes. There is no time to waste."

"I suggest we stay here for the night. Dusk is approaching."

Zigarda hustled back towards him. Charcoal eyes alight with the fire sconces on the wall, he asked, "Are you afraid of the dark?"

Zakk shook his head. "Always see every brush stroke of battle, for it determines the war's portrait."

"Is that another mantra of yours?"

Zakk nodded. "Gazo's taught me. If we leave now, we may not make as much progress tomorrow due to fatigue. You have been busy these past couple of days, wouldn't you agree?"

Zigarda sighed and clicked his tongue. "I suppose you have a point. What is one day?"

"Nothing."

"Exactly. We head north for the Frozen Pass tomorrow. Make sure you're ready."

"As always."

"Then find a place for yourself. I will go find my own. I will meet you at the courtyard tomorrow at dawn." Zigarda stalked away down the hallway, footsteps reverberating the cadence of his determination.

Zakk didn't move until Zigarda left his sight. Then he strolled down to the open-air courtyard, the stones awash with a light coating of snow. The white crunched underneath the heel of his boot. A cool wind lifted up the feather necklace, and he caught it as it floated in front of his face. Holding it by its quill, he studied it, and it twisted slightly left and upwards. Zakk followed the pointing feather toward the mountain that loomed as the backdrop of the castle. There he stayed, holding the feather and looking towards the summit, wondering what other surprises waited for him at the top.

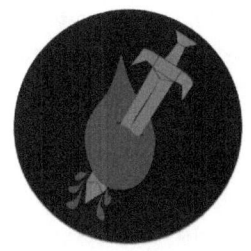

CHAPTER 21

# RETURNING TO THE LABYRINTH

A s Hydro looked upon the next location for the jewel, he tapped his foot
incessantly on the ground. *I don't have time for this.*

He looked back at the ship behind him. "You are sure it is in there?"

"My scanners indicate so."

Hydro turned around and crossed his arms. Shoulders sinking, he exhaled
deeply. This was the last place he had wanted to see in his adventures. He had
returned to the labyrinth.

Its ominous walls of sandstone stared back at him. Unlike the first time
visiting this place, there was no one else around him, and an eeriness set in,
even though it was only noon. The smell of rain mixed with dirt and worms
was absent from the air. By all means, these things should have been a boon to
Hydro, and the knowledge that he had killed all the creatures in the labyrinth
himself should have provided some sort of comfort, but it didn't. Nothing could.
Not when this was the place where everything had begun for him.

*Why are you waiting?*

*I am not particularly fond of this place.*

*You found me here. You won a Trial here. All of these things should make you
proud.*

Hydro bit his lip, forcing his mind away from the thoughts that formed next.
He didn't want the necklace to know. Now that Desmós could control him, the
protection of his thoughts was the only thing he had left. But even those were
not impervious and free from prying. If he truly wanted to be free, he needed
to be spontaneous.

*This time will be easier.*

Hydro spat on the ground. *I do not believe you.*

Securing the first jewel on this planet had nearly taken his life, but it had provided extremely valuable information as to the extent of Desmós's Power. Hydro firmly believed that without the necklace's help and command, he would have died, and for that, he was thankful. If he had died, then he would have died with the fate of his brother's life still looming over him. Furthermore, the battle had invigorated a part of him. Now that he had a taste, he wanted more. He wanted a worthy opponent like Zeph. Perhaps it was the necklace slowly seeping in and mixing with his pride, but he wanted more. He would not find it here, though. He had killed what remained of those living in the labyrinth almost a year ago.

Hydro still had no idea how long he had spent traversing the Abyss. Days? Weeks? He had been oblivious to any fragment of time while down in the Abyss, but that in and of itself had been an adventure that started with a Creature of Legend. The match of wits with the lich proved an interesting challenge in itself, seemingly innocuous now, but another part of Hydro still wondered what ramifications would come of that encounter. Perhaps the lich had just been bluffing. Hopefully, that was the case. But Hydro did best not to dwell on that; it didn't matter now. He couldn't change the past. All he could do was not let his brother down, so he would complete this inane task of gathering the jewels for Aiton's sake and his sake alone. *Damn the Ancients and the Twelve to Abaddon itself.*

Wind brushed against Hydro, paralyzing him, choking him. Struggling to breathe, Hydro surveyed the terrain. Was it her? It wasn't. He let a deep exhale go. She was one woman Hydro did not want to see again, and it made him really wonder about the strength the people of First Blood possessed. He thought back to his battle with Pearl. Hydro had won because the necklace had helped control the mermaids, otherwise he would have succumbed to her might as well. *Is everyone who was born on Gladima as strong as the Twelve or Zeph? Or am I just not as strong as I think I am?* Hydro bit his lip.

*Do not doubt yourself, Hydro Paen. My Power is only as strong as my host's capabilities.*

For whatever reason, that didn't reassure him. In truth, the word *host* sent another prickle up Hydro's arm. He spat on the ground again.

*Let's get this done.*

Hydro walked forward towards the labyrinth. Unlike the first time he entered, he knew the labyrinth's secret—Power did not function there. Well, normal Power. But he had Power beyond normal. So, while flicking his hand, he said, "*Maa.*" As if he were a baker splitting hot bread, the labyrinth walls tore apart in front of him, allowing him to walk directly to its center. He didn't know if the jewel would be at its center, but he assumed that it would be, as Guardian Eska would not have expected anyone to have the ability he possessed.

As he walked through the labyrinth, he spoke to Desmós, curious about the logistics of the location.

*How did you manage to get sealed here, anyway?*

*That is a long story, Hydro Paen.*

*Then make it shorter. I am curious.* As he walked through the opened labyrinth, he looked down the endless aisles. *This necklace would have made the first Trial much easier.*

*Yes, it would have.*

*Shit.* Hydro stopped and regrouped. Thinking about nothing, he continued. When he saw a black tar pit, he stood over it, remembering the feral creatures that had attacked him and the Garian while they were partners. When nostalgia sickened him, he sidestepped the pool of tar and continued. *So, will you tell me?*

*I believe you already know the answer.*

Hydro looked ahead. The circular, central chamber slowly came into view with each step. And, as it came into view, Hydro became more and more cognizant of the tomb in the center. He stopped. *I believe I do not.*

*What happened when you tried to use Power the first time you were here?*

*Nothing. I could not use Power until I held the necklace.*

*And that is why I was put here. Lyoen made this area a deadzone for Power, thus hoping to bind me to this place through Beno.*

*The monster I killed?*

*Yes. The man who was the first to taste my Power... And abuse it... With him on guard and being the sole individual to use my strength, he was an adept sentinel to making sure I was never taken. What better place to secure me: a creature who can use all Power, locked in a place where no Power can be used, yes?*

*Not all Power...* Hydro furrowed his brows. He noticed another pool of tar close to his feet. Preferring that to the center of the labyrinth, he walked over to it and looked down. *That man, that Beno, warned me of the girl with black hair. Is that because she is you? Is her name Desmós?*

*No one has that privilege. I am the only one.*

Hydro's chest surged with pain, crippling him to his knees. He held himself up with one hand while the other clenched his chest. He winced and closed his eyes. *Forgive me, Desmós.* The sensation stopped. With a heavy inhalation, he took in the smell of dirt and decay, still present in the derelict deadzone. Pain gnawed at his hand. He opened his eyes. The tips of his fingers on his right hand had settled in the pool of tar.

"Aahh!" Hydro yanked them out and wiped them on the sandstone wall, removing the black substance.

Sitting down, he examined his hands. Parts of his index and middle finger had eroded and decomposed. His chest surged once more and the force inside him flung him onto his back. He writhed in pain for a brief moment. When it stopped, he looked up at the large islands floating in the sky. He brought his hand over his face and saw two black marks in place of where the flesh had been eaten away.

*What is this?*

*I cauterized your wound. I healed you. Let's continue.*

*You... what?*

*Healed you. That's all you need to know.*

If only that was all Hydro needed to know. Hydro resisted the urge to retreat back into his mind. Instead, he observed with presence and picked himself up off the ground. He moved his tongue around his mouth, punching both cheeks as he left the pool of acid behind and continued towards the labyrinth's center.

*Of course, no one is you. But who is she? Why could I see her sometimes?*

*She is the daughter of the man who slayed me.*

*If you are dead, then how can you communicate with me?*

*Because of the girl, Anne.*

*But how—* His chest surged, and he dropped to his knees again, this time in front of the tomb. "Aahh!" Only the sky and the tomb heard his scream. He punched the floor with his fist. The scales of the necklace dug into him even more, extracting blood. He tore open the top of his tunic, looking at his fresh wound. The blood crawled up his skin, past his neck to his cheek. There it stayed. He couldn't see it, only feel it. His lips quivered. *What is...*

His cheek flared in pain, as if he was being branded. He collapsed to the ground. His lips touched dirt, and a tear slipped down one cheek. Hydro inhaled the noisome labyrinth floor. He coughed, blowing up dust into his eyes. He rolled onto his back. *What... what happened... what did you do...* Taking his fingers, he rubbed the right and left sides of his cheeks, still numb.

*You ask too many questions, Hydro Paen. Do not forget the jewel.*

For the second time in his life, Hydro felt as if he needed to cry. He lay there immobilized. As he patiently waited to regain his breath, his chest surged again.

*Get to your feet.*

Unwillingly, Hydro stood. As he marched toward the tomb, he balked at the new pain spreading up his arm. *What are you doing to me?*

*Using my control to make sure that you obey. Do not forget why we are here.*

*I will. I will. Let me go.*

Hydro felt himself regain control as the burning sensation died away. He breathed. Now, he stood over the tomb, the very same tomb that he had picked up the necklace. It had called to him. She had called to him, webbing him with her voice. His fingers grazed over the names etched onto the top of the tomb. Perhaps they had been there before, but for some reason, Hydro had not noticed. He read the list: Beno Begare, Anne Banegul, Kent Pavos, Troy Pavos, Hydro Paen.

His eyes widened. He stumbled back. Falling to the labyrinth floor once more, he kept his elbows tucked to avoid clanging his head against the floor. To the right, Beno's skeleton and what remained of any piece of him lay in the pit of crushed labyrinth sandstone. The pungency of death now enveloped the circular chamber like a layer of atmosphere.

Hydro stood again, trying to ignore the smell and the body as best he could. *Why is my name on this tomb?*

*It shows all the people who have ever possessed the necklace and all of those affected by it.*

Fingers scrolling the tomb once more, Hydro read the names carefully to himself. *But all of these people are dead. Except me.*

*Everyone must die eventually Hydro Paen—only the Ancients are immortal. Bane and Lyoen are gone. Even they aren't.*

*My master still lives, though. And with your help, we will be reunited again.*

Hydro stared at the wall in front of him. *Are you telling me that there is a third Ancient?*

*I have been telling you that all along, Hydro Paen. Do you think any mere being could have the Power that I have?*

Hydro thought back to the things he had heard while on his trip. Or even the things that Anne had said to him. Or was it Desmós through Anne? He was beginning to be unsure if that little girl had truly said anything herself or if it had been the dragon the whole time. But he did begin to understand much of what was said and the hints she had given. *Master... On Mount Volan, the stained glass not shattered... that... that was the Third Ancient? Wasn't it?*

*It was indeed, Hydro Paen. It was indeed. And when we are reunited, Gladonus will tremble at the fury we will show it. We will bring a new age of reckoning.*

Although the tomb's cover had already been moved a little backward, Hydro shifted his weight onto his right leg and pushed the tombstone back. He waddled each side back until he could see the golden topaz inside. He glanced down at it and reached towards it, unable to keep his gaze from the pedestal where he first discovered the necklace. If only he could return the necklace to the tomb.

His body still halfway into the tomb, he grabbed the jewel. He brought the jewel up with him and twisted it in the scant sunlight that crept through the nation above. The golden topaz reflected the marks now on both of his cheeks. Black marks, like tattoos. Both looked like a circle with an equilateral triangle inside of it. He took the jewel away from his face and brought it down to his side; the decayed corpse of Beno Begare was once again in his line of sight.

Preferring not to look at the cadaver, Hydro untied the satchel on his hip, where it rested next to his sword. Seven jewels stared back at him. One of the Twelve lived inside each one. In a matter of days, he would find the last three, and split them all in two with his sword, Purge. Only that could kill the Twelve for good. Only then could he leverage the playing field with Guardian Eska to his advantage and be ready to take the final jewel and win his freedom.

Slowly, he put the jewel away.

As fast as he could, Hydro took his sword from his scabbard and brought it towards his neck. Within inches of it touching the necklace, his arm froze. His neck tensed. He tightened his abs, squeezed his muscles, and did everything he could to bring Purge to touch the necklace. But he couldn't move.

He screamed out and tried harder. The blade moved just a quarter of an inch.

*Hydro Paen! What are you doing? Stop!*

His chest burned. Hydro yelled, ignoring the voice. He had no energy to waste answering. Every fiber of his being focused on bringing the sword to his neck and removing the necklace stuck to him. The burn in his chest intensified. Still, he held onto his sword and edged it closer. He was almost there. Another yell surged through him as he fought against Desmós's strength. Blood rushed to his head. His skull throbbed, beating like the palpitation of his heart.

The scales bit into his chest, drawing blood and further intensifying the pain. Blood traveled up and down his body, but all Hydro could do was watch, locked in a stalemate he needed to win. He saw it on his forearm, sitting there in a congealed pool. Where else did it go? The liquid bubbled and sank into his skin. Pain devoured him. He was being burned and branded alive. He dropped his sword and crumpled to his knees. His back surged in spasms, paralyzing him. His fingers locked into clawed shapes, unable to close.

Alone in the labyrinth, he echoed the same scream his mother yelled on the night he killed her. He writhed and rolled on the ground, trying to douse the imaginary fire and the very real pain which now overwhelmed his body. Minutes passed like hours as Desmós harrowed his mind.

*You try to betray me?* Hydro spasmed. *You try to kill me?* A terrifying throe took his body, twisting it in ways thought unimaginable. *After all I have done for you and given you. After I vowed to give you the strength to protect your broth-*

*er? After I told you of the adventure you would have?* With each statement, Hydro convulsed in a new direction, obtaining aberrant postures to make even a contortionist cringe. Pain passed its threshold. Hydro's world went black as his eyes closed. And like that, they remained.

Eyes fluttered open. It was nighttime, and his eyes adjusted rather quickly. He bent down and grabbed the sword from the ground, sheathing it immediately. Feeling the satchel on his side, he counted to make sure all the jewels were still there. They were. He turned around. Arm outstretched, he said, *"Maa."*

Sandstone split for him at his whim, like the deity he was. He walked back to the ship, his confidence and determination swelling beyond anything he had known before. Four more jewels awaited him. He didn't need to know where they were. He would secure them regardless. Whatever contraption had brought him here would do its duty and find them like it had in the past. Nothing would keep him and his master apart. Not time nor space. Not a miscreant prince. Not any whims of fate. And certainly not the Guardian of the Core.

CHAPTER 22

# RUINS

"**N**ever let the air we breathe grow stale, drench us in the flames we use, make solid the water which helps us stand, and liquefy the earth to produce our grains. Ancients, to this we pray."

"Very good, Zain. You remember more every day."

"I do as much as I can, Mrs. Sonetta."

"Do you know why we say it?"

Zain looked out to where the murky waters of the Krine Sea met the shores of Empora. They had been at sea for two-and-a-half weeks. Zain assumed they were making great time, as no winds had sent them back; in fact, the winds had, on most days, pushed them forward as if fate itself wanted Zain to succeed in his quest to make his family whole.

"It's tradition."

"Ah, but it's more than just that, Zain Berrese. It's history. That prayer started with the Ancients, and Grace reformed it to be her own, one that she taught her daughter Gracie and the same one that has lived with this academy since its inception before the Great War."

"Why is it called Gracie's then if everything started with her mother?"

"Her mother never lived long enough to see it completed. At least, that's what has been said."

"How did she die?" Zain turned back to the headmistresses.

"Land ho. Land ho."

Zain spun to face the bow of the ship. Sure enough, the Anga Mountains loomed in the distance. The same mountains that had haunted him for years after Eva's death.

Issac appeared from the staircase to the left. "Zain, I need to speak with you about which port we are going to use."

A hand came to Zain's shoulder. "We will continue our discussion another day, Mr. Berrese. You have the words, now you have to find the strength to believe them. Gabrielle will be proud to know your progress."

He nodded. "Thank you for helping me."

Carla Sonetta returned the gesture. With her hands locked in front of her, she returned below deck, leaving the two men.

"Another lesson? How did it go?"

"I know the words now."

"Why is that all she is teaching you?"

"It's what I lack and what she claims is the strength of Gracie's Power."

"Prayer? A source of Power?" Issac chuckled. "Do you think it's true?"

Zain exhaled and thought about the question. "I'm not sure, but it's worth a shot."

Issac studied him. "I'm hoping it hasn't caused you to lose your edge."

"What makes you think I have?"

"I haven't seen you practice with your sword since you got ill on deck. Did you ever find out what caused it?"

Zain shook his head. "No. I just. I dunno, Issac. I haven't been in the mood recently."

"Because you've been spending too much time with them."

Zain's breath hitched. It was true. He hadn't been practicing. When asked, he had blamed it on the stomach flu. Or he blamed it on the fact that he didn't have his *Gift*. Not since Zakk had melted it down to the bag of gems on the floor of the dungeon in Zigarda's Web. Both reasons were merely excuses. In truth, he could have borrowed a sword or used the one he had taken from Empora. But it didn't feel right. A lot of things didn't feel right anymore. Maybe it was the freedom the sea provided, maybe it was the teachings of Carla Sonetta or his conversations with Gabrielle, but something was changing inside him. He could feel it. And he hoped it would help.

"I've had a lot on my mind." Zain feigned a smile and hunched his shoulders.

"Well, with that kind of attitude, you'll lose an arm, or worse, your life if you're not careful."

"There are things worse than death." The words came to his lips before he could stop them. They were one of the phrases Carla Sonetta and Gabrielle repeated time and time again.

"What was that?"

Zain tightened his neck. "Nothing. Now, what did you want again?"

"The captain told me to ask you which port you wanted to dock at. We have three options: Berson, Mox, or Anganin."

"Anganin. It's the closest. We can dock there in a matter of hours."

"Mox may be a better choice, Zain. It's a larger city. It will have more supplies for us on the road ahead."

Zain shook his head. "That is where the other ships will be docked. These vessels aren't equipped to handle an entire fleet there. It is better we dock at Anganin and make our way to Mox to help out by foot or hovercraft. We can surprise Empora that way. Also, we haven't gathered our full army yet."

"What do you mean?"

"We're going to Stel. Gazo's is there. They will help us."

"What makes you so certain?"

"Faith." Zain locked eyes with Issac until he looked away.

"Anganin it is then. I will tell the captain."

Zain didn't immediately go below deck. He fidgeted with the cremain jewel on his finger. *I'm almost home, Dad. I'm almost home. I'll protect Mom. Don't worry.* Zain clenched the side of the ship and pushed off from the railing, heading below deck to pack.

The port of Anganin was a few hours from the mountain range by caravan. In the past, when his father had taken him here to see some of the jewel excavation sites in the northern part of the city, he and Zain would always stay by the port. Zain had enjoyed those nights together, dining with his father in lavish restaurants and seeing unique performances from the flora of culture that made this port unique. The city streets had been pleasant to walk, despite the smell of fresh fish, squid, kraken, and other wildlife in the area. Traders and visitors from all over Ka'Che—sailors, foreign businessmen, miners, fisherman—all made Anganin one of the most unique ports in Ka'Che save Mox.

Here. Now. There was only ash. Smoke. Fires had long since devoured the wooden houses. The town had been razed to ruins. Even though only half a pier remained, Zain still made port there despite the advice of Issac and the ship's captain. If Anganin had been taken so violently, then he could only imagine what lay in store for them in Mox. His skin prickled thinking about it, and so he tried busying himself with unloading, ferreting for any remnants of supplies, and coordinating efforts to find any survivors.

But he found none. There were no survivors. Only meager supplies remained.

"What are we going to do?" Issac asked after Garie finished relaying information to Zain.

"Mr. Berrese, what is going on?"

Zain glanced past Issac and Garie. Carla Sonetta approached them, Gabrielle linked on her arm. Cleaver came with them, the large man on the other side of her.

"What's our strategy here, tactician?" Cleaver crossed his arms and grunted.

"Same. We journey west."

"How are we going to get there?" Cleaver raised an eyebrow.

"Garie, what all was found again?"

Garie relayed the information for all of them to hear. Less than a handful of hovercrafts remained, but only three were operational. No horses remained. They had found supplies, but little that would be of much use.

As the party waited on his decision, Zain put his hands to the back of his head and turned away from Carla and Gabrielle. *Why?* Zain cast a glance upward and then closed his eyes and inhaled deeply. On the exhale, he once again asked himself, *Why?*

"Zain?"

"I just need some time to think." He waved off Gabrielle, even though he knew she couldn't see his gesticulation.

Hands behind his head, Zain paced in front of them. He tapped his head while continuing to breathe and think. When that posture didn't work, he put one hand underneath his elbow and put his right hand under his jaw. Closing his eyes, he pushed out the thoughts around him and only focused on now. And himself. He was present. His father's cremain ring dug into his jaw. He stopped and stretched out his hand in front of him. His gaze drifted up towards the mountains.

*Would they still be...?* Zain bit his lip. *It's worth a shot.*

Zain spun back around. "Cleaver, you will take Garie and Issac up towards the mountains. My father's factory lies in the north of this city, near the start of the mountain range. It was where one of my father's excavation sites was located. Chances are the army didn't go farther north. There should be some more supplies, weapons, and hovercrafts we can salvage from there." Zain turned towards the women. "Mrs. Sonetta and Gabrielle, I need you to come with me."

"Zain, you're not coming with us?" Issac asked.

"I told you why we came this way. I need to gather the rest of our army."

"Army?"

Zain turned to Cleaver. "In Stel. There are men who can join us. I will get them and bring them back here to help shepherd our troops to Mox."

"That'll take more time."

"No other choice right now with the city as it is."

Cleaver grunted. "How do we get to this excavation site, then?"

"Follow what remains of this road up to the north and veer right when the path splits. Another twenty minutes or so, you'll see the factory."

Cleaver left, not saying another word. Issac and Garie followed the large man.

"Stay safe, Zain."

Zain nodded.

"How are we able to help with Gazo's, Mr. Berrese?"

"If I can show Gracie's forces support me, Gazo's will too."

"Are you so certain of that?" Carla Sonetta arched an eyebrow.

"No. But I have faith. And that's a start, isn't it?"

Gabrielle beamed at his answer.

Carla Sonetta's lips curved into a smile. "It certainly is, Mr. Berrese. It certainly is."

CHAPTER 23

# PRIDE AND EGO

To Zain's surprise, Stel was entirely untouched by war, but he supposed Zigarda's strategy was to keep his forces together and focus on Mox, the second largest city in Ka'Che, before splitting up to clean up the smaller cities on their way north to Pelopon. Zain wondered if Stel even knew an army had invaded. Had they already sent their men? Would they find only the neophytes at the Academy?

Zain paced back and forth in front of the metal gate that looked like multiple swords driven into the ground. Beyond, he could see the large-oval shaped structure where classes took place and the outdoor training grounds behind it. To the right of those were the Habitat Arenas, a collection of indoor training areas where trainers could vary their reality, making sessions easier or more difficult. These arenas were surrounded by four dormitories for the men who lived on campus.

"Nervous, Mr. Berrese?" Carla Sonetta arched an eyebrow. She waited patiently beside Gabrielle, looking bored, one arm draped across her body and the other holding her chin.

Zain paced another lap before answering. "Not nervous. Anxious," he corrected. "It has been centuries since one of Gracie's has been to this town."

"Too long, in my opinion," Gabrielle said.

Carla Sonetta pursed her lips. "And I'll hold mine until after we speak with Headmaster Barrata."

"Have you spoken with Headmaster Barrata before?"

"Klum and I have talked once or twice. Only during tournaments, mind you. He would boast of his titles, and I would feign admiration." She scoffed.

Zain tensed. That kind of talk would only hinder any peaceful negotiations. "Let's try to keep titles and prestige out of it for today."

"Why, of course, Mr. Berrese. I assume you didn't bring us here for that, anyway."

*Does she know my agenda?* Continuing to pace, he flicked a furtive glance at them and bit his lower lip. He had brought them here under the pretense to show the support he had already gathered, but his reasoning actually went much deeper than that. Gazo's and Gracie's held bad blood with one another for wrongdoings of the past, but he hoped that the presence of the Gracie headmistress and their star student—maimed and vulnerable after what one of Gazo's own had done to her—would induce an empathy to join the cause.

He changed topics, feeling uncomfortable. He stopped his pacing and looked at Carla Sonetta. "You never finished your story from the ship. How did Grace die?"

Gabrielle turned her head in the direction of her headmistress. "You told him?"

"Not all of it yet. We were interrupted."

The gates opened.

"And it seems we have been interrupted again, Mr. Berrese." She pointed towards the academy. "Are you ready?"

Zain nodded. "Let's go."

Carla Sonetta gestured him forward with one arm, the other still linked with Gabrielle. "We follow your lead, Mr. Berrese. You are the man, after all, and we are visitors in your home. Please accept us into your academy."

Zain shook his head. "Right. Follow me."

Zain walked up the five steps that led to the revolving doors to the lobby. Inside, he saw the same circular silver walls. A chandelier hung from a cupola above the lobby and the students passing beneath. A tiled mural in the middle of the room depicted the Gazo's logo—a circle with a sword piercing diagonally from the right to the left. The main office lay to the left of the mural, next to a section of the wall that had a mailbox for each student registered in the academy.

"Follow me." Zain walked towards the office when someone called out to him. Squinting, he searched for the voice. "Kendel? Is that you?" His former trainee pushed through the crowd, which had grown still once they realized two women were in their presence.

"Yeah."

Zain's eyes widened. The scrawny man he used to train, who could hardly hold a shield, now had a larger, more muscular frame. He had grown another few inches in height, almost meeting Zain at eye level. The only things that hadn't changed were the shaggy red hair on his head and the lack of facial hair.

"You've—"

"Grown." Kendel laughed.

"I noticed." Zain surveyed his trainee once more. "How—"

"Mr. Berrese." Carla rested a hand on his shoulder.

Zain shook his head. "Right. We will catch up later, okay? We have to see Headmaster Barrata. Do you know where he is?"

Kendel shook his head. "Ask Lauryen."

Zain nodded. "Thank you, Kendel."

Kendel smiled. "Bye." He looked towards the headmistress. "Bye..." He extended his hand.

"Headmistress Sonetta."

"From Gracie's?"

"The very one."

"I—I—" His eyes shot to the woman who clung to her arm. "Who is—"

"It's very nice to meet you, Kendel." Carla looked towards Zain. "Mr. Berrese?"

Zain entered the office. Behind the desk sat Lauryen Smotter—an old lady with a hearing problem. More importantly, though, she was the only woman who ever consistently stepped foot in Gazo's Academy.

When a bell rang, signaling their entrance, Lauryen looked up from her papers, pushed her glasses up her nose and said, "Mr. Berrese, finally."

Zain raised an eyebrow.

"Your mail here has been—"

"It doesn't matter, Lauryen," Zain swiped his hand. "Where is Headmaster Barrata?"

She swiveled back around on her chair, grabbed a clipboard to her left, and flipped through the pages. "The Habitat Arena. There is open enrollment still for the next hour."

"Thank you."

Zain pushed off the counter.

"Your companions."

"They're with me, Lauryen. It's fine."

"They will need to wait here, Mr. Berrese. You know our policy. Women are not allowed past the lobby."

"Excuse me?" The headmistress put a hand to her chest. "I'm Headmistress Carla Sonetta."

Lauryen stared at her blankly, not saying anything for a few minutes. "Is that name supposed to mean something to me?"

Zain thought he saw a faint glimpse of ire and surprise on Carla's face, but if any had existed, it disappeared in an instant.

Carla Sonetta sighed. "Forgive my intrusion. It wasn't very decent of me. Is it all right if we wait here?"

"Please. Take a seat." Lauryen stood up and offered her hand, motioning to a red leather couch. Both women sat.

"I will be back as soon as possible," Zain said.

"I know. Go."

Zain darted through the halls leading towards the classrooms. The Habitat Arenas weren't located in this building, but there was an exit at the end of the corridor. Only a few unfamiliar students roamed the halls.

It had been months, almost a year, since he had entered this place. At twenty-four, he had almost graduated from the Academy and would've been on the market to serve as a member of a Royal Guard, war council, or the such. The Trials, and everything after, had disrupted that, and in truth, he wasn't sure if he would ever complete his time at the Academy, but it didn't matter. Not anymore.

A few minutes later, he hurried through the courtyard toward the Habitat Arena. Once inside, he saw the four various arenas that comprised the building. Each could be changed to hold a variety of habitats and also featured an area for people to watch the fights if they didn't want to stand outside the large glass window that extended the length of the arena. Zain peered inside each one until he found Klum Barrata.

A boy no older than seven was testing. He wielded a lance and fought a hologram. From Zain's recall, he was two-thirds of the way into the testing process. The first was simply a display of skills using a weapon. The second, a mock fight to show those skills in action, and third was a series of exercises to test your senses, culminating in a blindfolded test where one must be able to strike plates tossed in the air. That one Zain remembered vividly for it had halted his acceptance into the program until Zakk told him the pattern. It was something Zakk had never allowed him to forget.

The hologram knocked the boy to the ground. Buzzing. The lights dimmed. The boy had failed.

The group of evaluators waited for the next participant to prepare himself as Zain entered, stealing the attention of everyone in the bleachers. Two senior instructors sat with the Headmaster—a man who had come to the Academy from Chaon fifty-six years prior to teach the capstone course for tacticians and another whose fiery hair marked him as a native of Pyre, a retired fireson who taught the capstone for combatants.

Klum Barrata narrowed his gaze on Zain and stood up. Shorter than most, the Headmaster's stature was lean and strong, corded with muscle. For his density and his age, being sixty-four years old, his agility had impressed Zain when he had the rare opportunity to see Headmaster Barrata spar one evening at Gazo's.

"Mr. Berrese, you have returned. To what do we owe the pleasure?"

A side door opened, and a boy of eight years old entered, sword in hand. His brows shot up as he saw Zain.

"We are in the middle of enrollment, Mr. Berrese. Whatever you have to say will have to wait," said the fiery-haired man to the right of the headmaster.

"It can't."

"We are sure it can," said the man to Klum's left. Ignoring Zain's presence, the man continued, "Okay, so Devon—"

"I've brought Carla Sonetta and Gabrielle Ravwey with me. We need to speak."

The words spread, quelling all movement in the arena. All three men looked at him for a long moment, and then they whispered amongst one another. The boy just stood in the middle of the arena, rocking back and forth on his heels, looking between Zain and the others, oblivious.

When the whispering died, Klum Barrata stood. "Devon, these two men will instruct you on the proceedings."

Under the glares of the other two men, Zain left the arena and waited for Klum Barrata to meet him outside. When Klum did join him, they walked together.

"Do you have any idea what you have done bringing Mrs. Sonetta here?"

"I do."

"Never has a woman from Gracie's stepped foot in our academy. Certainly not two. And now you bring their headmistress and their famed student into our halls?"

"And if it was under any other circumstances, I wouldn't need to."

"What do you mean?" Klum Barrata stopped walking.

"The Trials and everything that has happened since. There are reasons I haven't returned to Gazo's."

Klum Barrata raised an eyebrow. "I have always wondered what had happened to you and Zakk Shiren."

Zain nodded. "You're about to find out."

In his office, Klum Barrata sat on a leather chair. Behind him, a sword hung on the wall. Above the sword was a saying painted in black on the burgundy walls: "Nothing is impossible, when I'm possible." Carla Sonetta and Gabrielle took a seat together on the leather couch in front of the desk while Zain paced back and forth.

"Headmistress Sonetta, how... *nice*... of you to join us."

Carla Sonetta scoffed. "Thank you for the... *warm greeting.*" She smiled. "Are you always so *decent*?"

Zain bit his lip at the innate tension.

"Only when I treat with ladies from your school."

"So, you are never decent, then?" The headmistress chortled.

"Enough, both of you," Zain broke in. "Put your rivalries aside for one moment and listen."

Both settled back into their chairs, easing their posture.

"Zain, go ahead," the headmaster instructed.

Zain recapped what had happened to him after he received his invitation letter. The fallout with Zakk. The Trials. Zakk's resurgence. His father's death and the war that was already in Ka'Che.

Leaning back in his chair, Klum Barrata raised his elbows and put his hands behind his head. "We already know about the war, Mr. Berrese."

Zain spun. "You do? But everything seems so normal here."

"That's because everything *is* normal here. There is no reason for Gazo's to participate. This isn't their war. This is a war between Chaon and Ka'Che."

"So you'd let Ka'Che fall just because this isn't your war?"

"Zain, I understand your predicament. This nation is your uncle's nation. Now, try to understand our position here at Gazo's. We may be stationed in Stel, and in this nation of Ka'Che, but we are a *sovereign* facility. The members of this Academy represent all nations. We shouldn't go to war just because war comes to us. See each brush stroke of battle—"

"For it determines the war's portrait," Zain finished. He clenched his fist but held his tongue. Silence dominated the air, mixed with hostility and tension. A small but confident voice in the back of the room shattered it.

"What if you can no longer see? How zen would you be able to determine the war's portrait?"

Klum Barrata turned his attention to Gabrielle. "What do you mean, Ms. Ravwey?"

"I mean zis." Gabrielle removed her glasses, showing her blindness to Klum Barrata. "You know from Zain's story zat Zakk did zis to me. Wasn't he one of your students?"

"Yes. And capable. You both went into the duel knowing the stakes, if I understood Zain's story correctly."

"We did. I understood, and I still remain undefeated zanks to ze Ancients."

Klum Barrata scoffed at that. "You remain undefeated thanks to skill. I have seen you fight before in tournaments."

"Zat isn't za point. Za point is zat you are blind right now. You don't see za war's portrait as you claim."

"Is that so?" Klum Barrata leaned back. "And you are capable of seeing more than me? Please enlighten me."

"Yes. Zere is also an attack on Pelopon from Empora in za norz. Chaon is attacking from za souz. Togetzer zeir jaws will clamp down upon you, and za sovereignty you zink you have will vanish. Zigarda ordered soldiers to attack Gracie's. What makes you zink zat za same fate won't befall Gazo's?"

Klum Barrata narrowed his focus and shifted in his seat.

"You remain za best weapons academy *because* of your sovereignty. But if Empora comes to ransack Stel—no, when, not if—it comes to take zis city, what are you to an army?"

The Headmaster leaned forward and steepled his hands.

"Zey would make you either join zeir army or kill you for resisting. Zen zis Academy would have a new Headmaster, and za school's prestige would fall to za ranks of Tempest in Mistral or even Finesse in Acquava."

"Preposterous. We would never let such low-caliber people into this facility."

"If you're dead, you wouldn't have a choice. Join us in stopping zis war while we can."

"Klum, listen to what Gabrielle is saying," Carla Sonetta said. "Truly listen. Empora has forced our hand and drawn Gracie's into this war, and the women that are with us do so by free will. One academy of just women may not have the adequate strength to shift the tides, but if we had Gazo's as well, if we had your *manpower*, then I believe we all could truly fight for others, as you claim so in doing."

Klum Barrata had stood while the headmistress spoke. Hands cupped behind his back, he faced the wall where the sword hung just above him. "Fight for others, then fight for yourselves," he muttered. He reached up and grabbed the sword. Back to them, he stood there, stroking the flat part of the blade as if lost in a trance. Klum Barrata put the sword back on the wooden pegs and turned around. "I will make an announcement for volunteers. We wouldn't want the ladies of Gracie's going unprotected; that wouldn't be very *decent* of us."

Zain's heart leapt. Gabrielle and her headmistress stood up with smiles on their faces.

"No, it wouldn't be." Carla Sonetta smirked.

"It's time to show the world Justice once again."

"And we will surely send our Prayer into the hearts of many," Carla Sonetta retorted. "Good day, Klum. Thank you for receiving us. Let's go." The head-mistress pulled Gabrielle alongside her as she went to exit. Zain turned to leave, too, but Klum Barrata called him back.

"Zain, sit down." Zain obliged. Klum Barrata sighed. "I feel awful for what has happened with Zakk. I feel responsible."

Zain shifted in his seat. "What do you mean, *responsible*? Why should you feel responsible?"

Silence seeped into the room before Klum Barrata spoke. "Did you know I sponsored Zakk for the Trials?"

"You what?"

"I sponsored his original application."

Zain had always wondered how Zakk had been accepted for the Trials. Zain's uncle had sponsored him, and his authority as Lord of Ka'Che was sufficient to get Zain recognized.

"You are wondering why not you."

Zain shook his head. "No. No. I knew Zakk was always better than I was. He would never let me forget it when we lived together." Zain laughed.

"I was impressed to hear that Gabrielle beat him. I had always wondered who would've won, if in the same divisions." Klum Barrata strolled around the desk to the front and leaned back on it.

From his spot on the couch, Zain said, "I... I want to tell you something."

"What is it?"

"Although I lost the weapons tournament in the Trials. I still won the ap-prenticeship."

Klum Barrata pushed himself off the table and studied Zain.

"I didn't accept. Once I knew I hadn't killed Zakk, I needed to find him again, to try and make things right."

"Spoken truly. I am impressed. You gave up so much."

*You have no idea.*

The Headmaster continued, "It makes me wonder why he even joined Zi-garda in the first place. What was he looking for?"

"I know that answer now, too."

"You do?"

Zain nodded. "Yes. It's the same reason I denied the apprenticeship... Fam-ily."

"Family?"

"It makes sense why he came to you for sponsorship. You had always been a father figure to him. My dad was always gone on business, and he couldn't truly call Lord Vangle his family, when he hardly knew him. And when I let him go that night..." Zain flexed his fingers. "When I let him go that night, I betrayed his trust in the only thing he had. The only brother he had. His faith in family was taken away that night."

"Faith." Klum Barrata scoffed. "You have been hanging around with Gracie's too much, Zain. Be careful. Keep your edge. Keep your steel. That is what is going to protect you out there in the coming days. You know that, right? Where is yours anyway?"

"Melted. Back in Empora."

"What do you use now?"

"Just something I picked up. It's sufficed so far."

"Would you like Justice?" Klum Barrata turned around and strolled back to the sword on the wall.

"No. No. No. I couldn't. That was Gazo's original sword. It's yours. You're the head instructor here."

"I insist." He held it out.

"I cannot." Zain pushed back.

"Very well. I will have the forgers make something for you. I will also relay your message to the students here in the Academy and see how much money we can raise to fund buying additional hovercrafts for the war."

Zain's eyes widened. "Really?"

Klum Barrata nodded. "Yes."

"I'll go tell the others."

"Very well. I will see you tomorrow then, Zain."

"Goodbye, Headmaster."

Zain rushed out the door. He found Gabrielle and Carla Sonetta waiting for him outside the sword gate.

"What was zat about?"

"We talked about Zakk. Headmaster Barrata is impressed you beat him."

Gabrielle chucked. "Zat was all?"

Zain shook his head. "No. He said he's going to try and raise money for more hovercrafts to help with the war."

Gabrielle looked at Carla Sonetta, then both of them looked back at Zain. "Perfect," Carla Sonetta said. "Our plan went even better than expected."

Gabrielle giggled.

"Plan?" Zain asked, dumbfounded. "What do you mean?"

"You men have so much to learn."

"Za way you were talking to him wasn't convincing. You gave him facts, expecting to feel somezing. Za only zing men feel are shots to zeir pride and ego."

"What do you—"

"Zere is a reason why I mentioned Tempest and Finesse, Zain."

"And there is a reason I mentioned needing help *being protected*."

"Pride."

"Ego."

"Pride and ego," Zain muttered under his breath.

"Mr. Berrese, you must learn that a battle can be fought with more than just steel. True strength comes from utilizing all of your weapons. That is the third pillar of Gracie's Academy." She walked away towards the hovercraft parked outside of the Academy.

Zain reached out for them. "Wait, how many pillars are there?"

Carla Sonetta didn't bother turning around. One arm locked around Gabrielle's, she used her other hand to hold up four fingers. "Four, Mr. Berrese. And if you want to stay alive, you'll learn to use all four of them."

Flustered and dumbfounded, Zain ran to catch up, wondering what else he might learn.

## CHAPTER 24

# THE TRUTH

C ain stood in front of his father. The redness in his eyes had dissipated, as did the tears. Joy slowly ebbed as well. His father was coming to the conclusion that something was amiss, though surely he had deduced it to some degree from the cavalry Cain rode into Lorian with. Linn's party waited in a tent opposite this one, attended to and watched over by some of his father's Owl Guards. Only Linn and Brenton had accompanied Cain into the tent with his father. His father's lead guard, Castor, also remained at his father's side, hand on the hilt of his sword, studying Brenton. Also in the room was the baron of Lorian, Roger Yung, and marquis of Vale, Soren Mesh.

His father released Cain from his embrace, and Cain saw the man in front of him turning from father to lord with every passing second. First, he observed the Ether Weapon that Cain held in his left hand, running his fingers over it to make sure it was real. Then he looked into Cain's eyes, maybe first noticing the cut on Cain's cheek from one of his duels with Brenton. Surely he also saw more fire in Cain's eyes now, too. Had he realized the solipsism that now strengthened Cain?

He would wait for his father to catch up, to start putting things together and asking questions, for he had already completed his transformation and had learned to accept who he was. The real question was, would his father be as willing?

"Cain, what's this about? Why are you here with... with..."

"One of them." Castor finished his father's sentence, nodding to Brenton with his chin.

"And her." His father's eyes shot over to Linn.

"We've come to have a talk with you, Father. And one that I think best for only our ears." Cain flicked his eyes to Castor.

His father didn't turn around. "Everyone, leave."

"My lord, I will not abandon your safety."

"There isn't any danger here. My son is not in handcuffs, and I am sure you've seen his Ether Weapon. You may go. Wait outside the tent flap. Make sure no one else lingers."

"Lord Evber, what is—"

Lord Evber turned his head to the marquis with a sigil of a nightingale bird with wings outstretched on a lavender background. "Soren, it is nothing. I will be fine. I need to speak with these individuals privately."

All three around Cain's father shifted their weight, casting uneasy glances at the foreigners in the room, but after his father gestured for them to leave once more, they complied. With everyone out of the room, Cain's father surveyed each of them in turn. "Now what is it, Cain?"

"Father, I believe it's best if Lady Clayse speaks first."

"Very well. Speak, Lady Clayse."

"Lord Evber, I have recently discovered that there is no reason to go to war with you. Epoch did not attack Cresica. Nor did it launch any attack that resulted in my mother's death."

"So you've finally realized the truth? What spurred this revelation?"

"A talk with Guardian Eska while he was in Mistral."

Lord Evber raised an eyebrow. "You attended the meeting?"

"I had to get answers. And that is what I did. Guardian Eska made it clear to me that the thing that attacked Syf was no entity of Cresica, and so I came here to tell you and to call off this war personally, in front of you, because that is the respect you deserve."

Lord Evber bobbed his head. "I appreciate the virtuous sentiment, Lady Clayse. I, too, am happy we can avoid bloodying the pages of our stories. Tell me, how did you come to this conclusion?"

"As I traveled through Kane to speak with you, I met Brenton and your son." Cain saw his father's eyes shift and scan Brenton now that he had a name for the face. "Brenton confirmed to me what Guardian Eska told me in Mistral."

"And that is?"

"The third Ancient did this."

It took a second, but Cain's father shook his head after a delayed reaction. "A third Ancient? Did I hear you correctly?"

"You did."

"The Ancients Lyoen and Bane have been gone since the Great War. And now you purport there is a *third* one as well? One that no one knows about? Do you hear this, Cain? Am I crazy?"

"I hear, Father. And no, you are not. I know, too. And I know it to be true."

His father had wanted to laugh off the idea, but his jaw hung slack now, his face lost again in tides of truth. But this was only the shallow water. Would he drown once he learned the whole truth? Cain wiped the sweat from his palm onto his leg and steadied his breathing. His turn to speak would come soon enough.

"It is one of the secrets kept by the Guardian of the Core."

"Then how does this man know?" Lord Evber pointed to Brenton.

"Because that is how my family has received the majority of their Power."

"What Power can a chieftain from such a small territory like Kane hope to have?"

"Power beyond your wildest dreams."

Brenton told the story of the Native Kings of the planets and of the feud between the Ancients that he heard from the bard. Linn chimed in, retelling the story of the catastrophe that was her birthday. As they spoke, Lord Evber's posture slumped, his confidence with it. His vision darted over the floor, lost. His thumb moved to his mouth, and he nibbled it incessantly. Tiny drips of perspiration began lining his father's brow. He was beginning to drown in uncertainty.

When finally finished, Lord Evber didn't speak right away. Instead, he gathered his thoughts and then turned his eyes towards Brenton. "Brenton, is it?"

"Yes."

"The feather that you mention in your story, the key to your Power. Do you have it?"

"I no longer have it."

"Then how am I supposed to know that this story is true?"

"Because I have it, Father. And you've seen it with your own eyes." Cain plucked the feather out from behind his shirt.

His father's face tightened. Lips slightly agape, he looked up at his son. "Cain? You... you believe all of this."

And now it would come. The inevitable deluge. Would it be best to inundate his father and then hope he would somehow claw his way to the top? Or would it be better to slowly push his head down below water and see how long he could hold his breath?

Looking at his father, Cain exhaled, ready with the choice he made. "Yes, Father, I do."

"What do you—" His father's mouth hung aghast at Cain's admittance.

"Do you deny yourself the truth because you think living a lie is that much easier?" Brenton cut in.

"I don't know what you mean," Cain's father spat. He crossed his arms over his chest.

"Certainly, you do. You just did it again." Brenton walked closer to Lord Evber, who leaned back, trying to avoid the towering figure. "Why don't you ask yourself where your son got the necklace?"

Lord Evber remained speechless. He flicked his eyes to Cain, as if calling out for him to help. Cain frowned. He shook his head, saying nothing more.

"Probably because you cannot face the fact that it was your wife who gave it. Probably because you cannot face to hear the truth of why your wife named your only child after a despicable *savage* country that your forefathers cast away. And it's probably why you are afraid to wonder who it is that gave Dawn the necklace? Or how it came to be in her possession? Is that so?"

With great fluidity, Lord Evber drew his axe, swung it, and stopped it to rest upon Brenton's throat. Lord Evber breathed deeply. "How do you know my wife's name? What lies have you filled my son's mind with? No more games!"

A rustling from behind made Cain glance over his shoulder. Castor had poked his head into the tent and entered. "Lord Evber?" his hand reached for his weapon.

"Leave. I'll call you if I need you."

"My lord?"

Lord Evber looked back to Castor. "I said leave!"

Castor backed away and sealed the tent once more. Cain turned back to his fathers. Both of them. He saw the trembling of his father's arm, and he saw the strength Brenton showed in the face of a man who could so easily end his life. His father seethed, and now it was Cain's turn to heal him. To tell him the truth.

Cain stepped forward and put a hand on his father's raised arm. "Lower your weapon."

"Cain, this man. Don't believe this man. You are my son."

"I am your son. But I am also his son. Please. Stop this."

His father's eyes welled with tears once more. He sniffled. "Cain? Son? What do you—"

"You raised me, but I am not your son. Brenton is my true father. And mother received the necklace from him and gave it to me so that I would remember. So that this day would eventually come. So that I would seize the destiny that is meant for me."

His father stumbled back. Strength left his arm. The axe clattered to the ground. He clutched at his chest as if he was having a heart attack, the same way Cain clutched his own chest after drinking the flame wine for the first time. Would he be invigorated or enfeebled? His father braced his back and arms on the table, doing all he could do to stay upright. His posture slipped, but before he hit the ground, Cain had ducked under his father's slack arm and hoisted him up.

"I have you."

"How?"

The question was barely audible, despite his father's breath pelting Cain's face.

Cain walked his father around the wooden table, where a map of the surrounding territories had been sprawled out. He set him down on a chair, and then Cain perched upon the table. There, Cain told him how he had wandered to the stump after the meeting when they had first arrived in Lorian. He told him of the information that Eirek had mentioned to him, information that was similar to what Brenton told him. He finished with the story of his and Brenton's first meeting, and at the end of it all, Cain stood up and moved to stand beside his real father and took off his glasses.

"How can you deny what is so clear to see? Brenton is my father. My other father."

"But? Our family. Our reputation. Our name..." His father's lower lip quivered. "I'm a fraud." His father took off his glasses and rubbed them incessantly on his shirt. He put them back on his nose and ran a hand through his hair.

Cain went over to crouch alongside his father again, bringing himself to eye level. He reached out for his father's hand and took it in his own. "You are anything but a fraud. You are the man who raised me. Who educated me."

"But I lost you. You're with him now."

Cain could tell by his father's trembling voice that he was doing all he could to hold himself together. Cain continued to hold his father's hand and rub his knuckles with his thumb. "You haven't lost me. I didn't lose you. I only gained another father. One who finally explained to me why I've felt so lost lately. One who could explain to me what is going on."

His father flicked his gaze to Brenton with wounded eyes. Gathering what must have been the rest of his strength, his father stood and pointed at Brenton. "You think you are superior to me because of your blood? You think Cain is your son? My family has been—"

"I know." Brenton raised a hand. He waited for Cain's father to relax back into his chair before continuing. "That is the reason why I chose to do what I did. Any child that would be born in Kane would have access to limited resources and knowledge, but your wife gave my people a way out. From one king to another, are we not ruled by the needs of our people? Are we not driven to keep them safe?" Brenton stepped around the table and kneeled as well. "That is how you and your forefathers have been able to keep your name for so long, is it not?"

"But now that title will be..." Cain's father couldn't finish his words, preferring to massage his forehead instead.

"Changed. For better or for worse. I may have given him my blood, but you gave him so much more. You gave Cain the access to knowledge, life lessons, combative training, and Power training. Most of all, you gave Cain the morals that he now has in life; *that* I can never take away from you." His father stopped massaging his forehead to look Brenton in the eye. "And that is why I came before you today, to see the type of man that you are, so I can know the type of King my son will grow to be."

Cain's father looked from Brenton to Cain. He didn't speak for a long while. Cain waited, content to let him speak first, to find his voice, to rise up through the deluge that had nearly drowned him. When he finally spoke, he asked, "So, what happens now?"

"I must return to Castle Thoth, Father. From there, I will leave for Pyre. And I will bond with Chantico."

"But here... the war."

"I thought there was no war." Linn came back into the conversation. "I told you that I wanted to call it off."

"I've already sent Joshua and the troops up towards Ambit to lure your army that is surely moving across the outskirts of Kane."

"When did you send them? How long have they been gone?"

Cain's father shook his head. "I... A week or so now at least."

Linn bit her lower lip and rolled her eyes upward. "They're close. You have to call them off now. Where is your communication chamber?"

Cain's father nodded. "I'll take you there." He turned back to Cain. "Son, I... I can still call you that, can't I?"

Cain smiled. "Of course, Father."

He sniffled. "That is good to know. Thank you for telling me." He turned his attention to Brenton. "You as well, Brenton." Then, turning back to Cain, he continued. "I... I hope you find Chantico... I hope you become the hero you've always wanted to be."

"I'll become more than that, Father." His father's mouth hung agape for a moment. His eyes searched Cain's for an explanation. "I'll become a King."

CHAPTER 25

# RETREAT

I f red clouds didn't hang to the west, Zain would have thought this morning would have been a good morning. Everything was going right. A thousand men from Gazo's volunteered to join Zain's cause. Now this makeshift army consisting of those from the Scorpions Rebellion in Empora, women from Gracie's Academy, and men from Gazo's began their approach to the south, keeping the Shrouded Gulf within sight to their east. Klum Barrata had gifted Zain a zircha blade. All of these things made it seem that this day was bound to be auspicious as the graceful winds blew them from Empora to Ka'Che, but that soon turned out to be far from the truth by midday, a few leagues away from Mox.

There were seven others in Zain's hovercraft, but he only knew five of them: Klum Barrata, Issac, Nyrin, and Garie, and his former trainee, Kendel.

As Zain passed his time by changing the sword between uploaded calibrations of various axes and lances and even knives, Kendel looked on in amazement at the show. All but Klum Barrata watched. The headmaster sat to the left of Zain with his eyes closed and arms folded across his chest.

"Have you ever wielded a zircha blade before?" Kendel asked.

"Only in training at Gazo's." Zain rubbed his jaw, reminiscing about the blow Hydro gave him during the Trials. *Shield.* The halberd in his hand turned into a round shield. "I've fought against them, though." Zain raised his arm.

"Woah. It can change into a shield, too?"

Keeping his eyes closed, Headmaster Barrata spoke. "That zircha weapon has been calibrated with every weapon, Kendel."

"What about a bow?"

Headmaster Barrata opened his eyes and furrowed his brows, giving Kendel a dubious look. "No. Not a bow. No zircha weapon can replicate that. At least, not yet." He closed his eyes again.

"Can I try?"

"Sure." Zain handed Kendel his blade. "Hold it here." Zain pointed to the metal sensor on the hilt. "Think about the weapon you want it to change to and hold it still."

The weapon changed into a sword. Then into a lance. Then into a mace.

"Cool. Why can't I have one?"

"Kendel, what must we do before focusing on the fight?"

"Know ourselves left to right and right to left, Headmaster."

Klum opened his eyes, looked at Kendel, and smiled. "And can you fight with both hands yet?"

"No, Headmaster."

"So it seems you have your answer." He leaned back again, returning to his position of rest.

Kendel gave Zain back his weapon. "That was a stupid question. I should've known."

Zain smiled to himself. It was one of the first lessons that Gazo's taught, but many people grew out of ambidexterity and focused on just the left or right and usually a specific weapon of choice. Zircha training was for more advanced students who were being vetted to become trainers or graduate from the Academy.

Zain changed the mace into a sword and sheathed it on his right hip. "You still have time to learn. I... What are you doing here? You're only fourteen. You should be at home with your family."

Kendel leaned back and crossed his arms over his chest. "I'm fifteen now."

"Still—"

"Gazo's is my family, Zain. It's a brotherhood. After my failure when you were my trainer, I committed myself to practicing more and eating better."

"I can tell. You are strong now."

"You inspired me. When I heard you and Zakk had gone off to the Trials, I realized I'd had a special instructor, and it made me feel like a failure that I still hadn't passed, even though it had been my fifth time."

"Kendel..."

He chuckled to himself. "I'm possible, right? That's why I'm here."

"You could get yourself killed."

"So could you!"

"But this is my battle."

"And we fight for others before we fight for ourselves."

Zain opened his mouth in retort but then closed it. He couldn't. Kendel's confidence and demeanor had increased greatly since he had last seen him. Zain wouldn't cast a shadow over that.

In the silence, Klum Barrata spoke. "Lots have changed since you've left, hmm Zain?" a twinkle shone in the headmaster's eyes.

"Yes, it has, Headmaster." He looked back towards Kendel. "Thank you." Then Zain turned his gaze to the rest of the people in the hovercraft. "All of you, thank you." There was a loud harrumph from the men and they all pumped their fist in the air, even the drivers.

The bravado of the men died just as quickly as it had come, though, as Issac stood up and pointed to the east. "Zain, look."

He turned around. Everyone did. The port of the Shrouded Gulf overflowed with the fleet of Emporian ships. A quantity so vast it made Zain's stomach crawl. This is why Aeston hadn't given Zain's company any problems. This is why Anganin had been razed to ashes. And he wondered if he was too late. Smoke billowing up in tongues of gray told him more than he cared to know. The wind cut his skin more than it should have. Prickles lifted the hair at the back of his neck. Was he too late?

Movement off to the west attracted him. "There!" He shouted.

Klum Barrata turned towards where Zain pointed. "Daniel, take us west."

"Yes, Headmaster."

Soon, the mass of movement Zain had noticed earlier became clearer. "It's the army."

Issac stood beside him, forearm over his brows. "Looks that way to me."

"What are they doing?"

"I'm not sure."

"We should check." Zain turned. "Can you have him fly lower?"

Klum Barrata nodded and tapped Daniel on the shoulder. The hovercraft turned off the airroad and started a slow descent to the ground fifty meters below. As they were the lead hovercraft, the others followed suit and when the soldiers below saw a long train of hovercrafts from their flank, their hands went to the ready position, and they halted.

The hovercraft stopped at the head of the group. The other hovercrafts formed two columns that stretched backwards to half of their army. At the head of the faction, every man stood, hands on their hilts and visors up to clearly see Zain's party.

A voice called up. "State your name and your purpose here."

Zain's ears twitched. "Uncle?" Zain jumped over the railing of the hovercraft onto the ground.

"Zain?" The broad-shouldered man immediately waved his hand. The men behind him released the grip on their weapons. "Zain, what are you doing here?"

Zain embraced his uncle Lukas. "Why would I be back there?"

Lukas pulled back, squeezing Zain's shoulders. A red line scarred his cheek now that Zain hadn't seen before. "Before I left for Callumbra, there was news of your return from Mendeck."

Zain stiffened. "What do you mean?"

Lukas's upper lip twitched. He pulled away completely now from Zain. "A story for another day. We need to leave. Mox has fallen just like Callumbra."

"Fallen?" He didn't need to look to the south to know the words his uncle spoke were true. He had already seen it on the gray pillows of smoke stacked above the city like tombstones. "It can't fall. We are here. We came to—"

"Callumbra's fallen?" Nyrin pushed his way to stand beside Zain.

Lukas shifted his focus. "Nyrin. Yes. I'm afraid so. Listen, we don't have much—"

An explosion thundered in the background. The gray tombstones of smoke were obliterated by a large mushroom cloud that quickly gathered in size.

"We need to leave. That is our exit plan."

Zain choked on his words.

Lukas had already turned around and began barking orders to continue marching north. "How many of us can you shepherd to the capital?"

Zain continued watching the expansive mushroom, engorging itself on the sky, as gray as the Krine Sea.

"Zain? How many are you?" His uncle shook him.

Issac took over. "Three-hundred hovercrafts. Nearly seven people a piece."

"Your crafts are going to get a lot cozier." He turned around. "Men find a hovercraft and get in. Spread the word. We go north."

"Wait! What? But the battle is there." Zain pointed to the south. The air felt warmer now. Dry, too. Heat clawed at him. Or was it just his imagination?

"The battle there is done for the moment, Zain. We head north. We must return to the capital as quickly as possible."

Zain stammered. "Wha... what do you mean?"

"You. Here. It doesn't make sense. I'll tell you more on the way. For now, we retreat."

His uncle didn't say another word. He hoisted himself over the side of the hovercraft and took a spot next to Garie. He didn't sit right away, though. Instead, he stood up on the bench and observed his men getting into the hovercrafts over the next half hour.

By the time he sat down, Zain had returned to the hovercraft, sitting opposite of him. Klum Barrata looked between Zain and Lukas.

"Your orders, Zain?"

"We head north," Lukas shouted.

The headmaster ignored the man. "Your orders, Zain?" he repeated.

Zain looked from Klum Barrata to his uncle. "We go north," Zain muttered, at a loss for words for anything else.

His stomach felt queasy again, like it had that day on the sea. It wasn't as severe, but something definitely gutted him. Was it the mass destruction he had just witnessed in the distance?

Zain curled up and put a hand on his forehead, trying to keep himself from vomiting. In his awkward, bent over position, Zain noticed Lukas clutching his stomach as well and biting his lower lip. Had his uncle sustained an injury? It didn't matter now. There would be time to heal and time to talk on the Long Pass to the north. But Zain didn't like that. Zain didn't like any of this. How had a day so perfect gone so completely wrong? If Pelopon was truly taken, what of his mother? And Abraham? Would he arrive too late to do any good? Would he always be one step behind?

## CHAPTER 26

# THE CROSSING

By nightfall, Zain's group had made it just over The Crossing, a narrow bridge that had been designed before the Great War to connect the northern half of Ka'Che to the south. Before the technology of hovercrafts and spaceships, this bridge made seizing the north nearly impossible as it, being only two lanes in width, bottlenecked any advancement from southern armies. Now, though, it merely marked the last outpost before traveling the Long Pass north to the capital.

Normally the Long Pass would take a few days to travel, even by hovercraft, but Zain suspected with an army of this size, it would take them nearly a week now that the hovercraft were weighed down with double the amount of men.

Zain's uncle had effectively taken control of Zain's forces, and as the suns descended in the east, Lukas gave orders for the hovercrafts to land side by side in a half circle just north of The Crossing. This would halve any traffic coming from the south, as well as any traffic coming from the north, unless that traffic happened to be spaceships.

Zain objected, "Stopping here will do nothing. The Crossing isn't a bottleneck anymore. They can still fly over us with spaceships."

"They can't." His uncle put one hand on the railing and leapt over the hovercraft, beginning to bark orders at his men as soon as the other hovercrafts touched down.

Zain jumped off the hovercraft after him. "What do you mean? Mox and Callumbra both have spaceports."

Lukas didn't spare a glance at Zain. "*Had* spaceports. Dras, Oscar, Collins, spread the word to form a perimeter around the Crossing."

"Sir!" Each one saluted and went out.

Zain put himself into his uncle's line of vision, not quite ready to accept the horrible truth Lukas had uttered. "Had?"

His uncle stared at Zain, expression unwavering. He stayed silent.

"That was..." Zain put his arm to his stomach. "The explosion earlier?"

His uncle didn't respond. He grew disinterested with Zain and barked another order.

"Sir Vangle, why have we stopped? What is going on?"

Marquis Daran Moxxie strutted forward, gesturing toward Zain's uncle. As did Marquis Brynn Ropis of Callumbra. Each marquis was attended by their receivers and advisors as their escorts.

"Zain, why have we stopped? What is going on?"

Zain twisted his head to see Gabrielle led by Carla Sonetta.

"We are making a barricade before we head north," his uncle answered for him.

Klum Barrata stepped into the scene as well. "Do you intend to fight here, Sir?"

Before Zain knew it, their small circle had quadrupled in size, each leading authority wanting to understand what was happening amongst the calamity of formation protocols now being carried out.

"No. We don't have the forces or the battlements for it. Not with the numbers I've seen. This is our best line of defense in case they happen to catch up to us."

"Well, at least you have sense enough to see that."

"And who are you?" Zain's uncle whipped his head around.

"Klum Barrata. And you?"

Lukas turned to Zain. "The Gazo's Headmaster? Zain, this is your doing?"

Zain nodded. "I recruited Gazo's and Gracie's to help once I heard Empora was attacking Ka'Che."

"That would explain her," his uncle muttered, gaze drifting to Carla Sonetta. "How about the big man there?" His uncle tilted his chin to Cleaver.

"Cleaver." He snorted and spat on the ground.

"Pleasure to meet you all." He turned to Zain and smiled. Another man rushed to Lukas's side. "Sir, our battalion is in place."

"Good. The others?"

"Close, sir."

"When it's finished, Collins, bring Dras here."

"Yes, sir."

Carla Sonetta stepped closer. "Now are you going to tell us what is going on here, sir? Or do you have a name? Why are you—"

"Carla Sonetta. Everyone. This is my uncle, Lukas Vangle. Brother and head guard to Lord Vangle."

The Cleaver, Carla Sonetta, and Klum Barrata surveyed his uncle. Gabrielle had even turned her head as though she studied him. The two marquises tapped their feet impatiently, arms crossed over their chests.

"Lukas, are you going to tell us what in Abaddon's name we are doing here?"

"Resting, Daran. It is nearly nightfall."

"Do you think it wise with so many soldiers chasing us?"

"I think it is wiser than being exhausted the next day."

Klum Barrata butted in. "Always see each brush stroke of every battle, for it determines the war's portrait."

"Headmaster Barrata, enough with your philosophical maxims. You denied our request for help, yet, here you are... helping. What has swayed your mind? We could have used you earlier."

"And you could use a lesson in manners. Perhaps the women at Gracie's can teach you patience. Everything in its due time."

"My apologies, good sir. I didn't realize you were so close to Zain."

Zain kept his mouth shut as Headmaster Barrata apologized. He and his uncle actually weren't so close. They shared blood, but Zain had spent a majority of his life away from castle walls, and whenever he did see his uncle, he was never an uncle. He was always only the head guard for the lord.

"That doesn't matter now. The Gazo's instructor is right, Daran, we must look at the bigger picture. War isn't just a single battle. It's multiple, and we won it in Mox."

"You sent men to their deaths!"

"And we sent many more Emporians and Chaons to theirs. Do you not see that?" Zain's uncle fumed.

"I see my city in ruins and a spaceport blown up."

"Two spaceports blown up," Marquis Ropis corrected. "And our army scuttling back with its tail behind its legs. Why don't we fight for a change?"

"Did you two buffoons not listen?" "This open field would be a disaster for our men!" He didn't like raising his voice, but he didn't like much about the situation as it stood anyway. The two marquises glared but stayed silent. Zain noticed Gabrielle stepping back a pace. Had he frightened her?

"Zain. It's fine," his uncle said. "I am Lord Vangle's voice right now. We do what I say. If we had stayed in either of your cities, we would have been swallowed whole. We go to the capital to save it and to have a chance at warding off this enemy." Lukas glared at the two marquises. Each of them fumed, Zain could tell, but they also knew who held more rank and kept their mouths shut.

"Zain, I didn't realize you'd be here. Why are you here? You are supposed to be in Pelopon with your mother."

"What do you mean?"

"Aeneas and the Sea's Commander set off from Empora months ago. You should have been back a month or more now. Did you come from the north?"

His stomach churned at the news. Zain shook his head and, with a heavy sigh, said to his uncle, "I think it's time I catch you up to speed."

Zain took what must have been an hour updating his uncle and everyone else about everything that had happened since leaving Pelopon with Gerald Starshine. He explained about the shapeshifters, his imprisonment in Mendeck and what they had to go through in Empora to get here, including their underground route from Terran to Soeco, where they met the Cleaver, to their journey from Aeston and reports of how Anganin had been razed to the ground.

"You wanted to see me, sir?" A man came up beside Lukas, who had listened to Zain's story intently while keeping his arms crossed over his chest.

"Dras. You and Oscar take a handful of men each and head north. Don't take the Long Stretch, take supplies that you'll need and cut through, making your way to Hollan. From there you will go west to Cotterall and Oscar will continue north to Arwood and Snowmelt. All forces will assemble at Pelopon."

"Yes, sir."

"Leave within the hour."

"Yes, sir."

"Dismissed."

Dras disappeared back into the sea of men. Lukas turned to Zain. "Continue."

Zain shook his head. "That is it. After Anganin, I went to Stel to recruit Gazo's and then came to Mox, hoping it wasn't too late. But... but what happened?"

Lukas pushed his lips to one side and sighed. "We underestimated the enemy, Zain. That's all there is to it."

"What do you mean?"

"A month ago, Ryder Scarus contacted us." Lukas gestured towards the receiver, standing to the left of Marquis Ropis. "Callumbra had fallen under attack. Chaons came up from the south. Fifty thousand of them. Sieged the city. By the time we assembled forces to go there from Pelopon, the damage had been done. We managed to fly there on ships, but the Chaons took out our spaceships while we were busy fighting them in the city.

"They had flanked us from the north, expecting aid to come to the rescue, and then, once we did come, clamped their jaws down on us. Some of our men managed to cut our way through and make it to Mox, relying on the hovercrafts we had taken. When we got to Mox, we regrouped with the army there and told them of the Chaon force coming from the south. What we didn't expect was the barrage coming from the east."

"Empora...," Zain muttered.

"Empora." Lukas nodded. "We fought them in Mox as best as we could, but time was against us. It would only be a few days until the Chaons would be upon us again and join forces with Empora, so we decided to halt their progression."

"The bombs?"

"Aye. We set the spaceship port to self-destruct so that they couldn't use the vehicles there to go directly to the capital. If they storm Pelopon, they'll either come by ship or come by the Long Pass. Either way will take them significantly longer, wear out their supplies and their troops. It would have given us a chance to regroup with the northern forces and band together in the castle and capital. But now... now I'm not so sure."

"Because I'm here?"

Lukas bit his lower lip. "Yes. Because you're here. And now that you've mentioned shapeshifters... and Hector... I... I have a bad feeling about Pelopon."

Zain gulped. "Do you think—"

Lukas shook his head. "I don't know what to think right now, Zain. All I know is that we need to get north as fast as possible. Pelopon could be under attack or already fallen." Lukas turned to the others. "If things went according to plan, the bombs we detonated in Mox should have crippled most of the Emporians. Chaon will still be coming for us, and whatever remains of Empora may join them by foot or will travel by boat. Regardless, they will need to regroup. I've sent men ahead to gather recruits up north to join us in Pelopon. If the castle has already fallen, then we will need more men to take it back, and we will need to take it back before the southern army advances on us. We can't hold them here, despite the bottleneck strategy, but in Pelopon, we have a chance."

"How large is the Chaon forces?" Zain asked.

"Maybe thirty thousand now. Joined with what remains of Empora, it could be forty. I'm not sure."

"Tactician, how many do we have?" Cleaver asked.

"Just over four...," Zain muttered.

"What was that?"

Zain cleared his throat. "Just over four thousand now with my uncle's troops."

"And we're going to be fighting against forty? We need to find Zigarda, boy. Cut the head, and the body will fall. Why are we wasting our time doing anything—"

"He will be at Pelopon."

Everyone looked at him. Zain didn't cower under the weight of their gazes. A good lie showed confidence, so he made sure he straightened his spine by puffing out his chest.

"You know this for certain, Zain?" Lukas asked.

"Yes," he lied again. "That is the head of Ka'Che. It makes sense he will go there if it has already been taken over. Most likely, he'll have my other uncle captive."

"In the best case."

Zain tried his best to ignore Lukas's words, but they still gutted him, regardless. He put one hand on his stomach and another on his forehead.

"I sent men ahead. If we can recruit the force of Cotterall, we have a chance. Total forces from the north will recruit us another twenty-five."

Cleaver pushed up his upper lip, crinkling his nose. "Not the best numbers, but I've seen worse."

"Don't forget you have us," Carla Sonetta reminded.

"And us," Klum Barrata added. "We aren't regular recruits."

"Nor are we," said Carla.

Zain groaned at their sibling rivalry. He had enough of politics. He had enough of all this vanity. None of that mattered right now. Couldn't they see that? Zain turned around and walked away from the party, preferring to be alone. He walked south until the lights of the hovercrafts were no longer present, and darkness swallowed him.

He stood on a shallow hill that overlooked the large Krine Lake directly ahead of him. The placid waters were the only good thing about the lake, but eventually nostalgia beckoned him back to peer out over at Trent's Forest across the lake. Luckily, he could barely make it out with the fading light. That would save him from more guilt than he cared to admit, but he still felt the pain in his side and the wound on his hand. And now, with everything else happening...

Zain retched onto the grass. There was nothing much to his vomit, for he had eaten little. But whatever his stomach had contained was emptied onto the grassy knoll.

"Zain, are you okay?"

Zain wiped his mouth with his forearm and looked back to see Gabrielle, Carla Sonetta at her side as usual.

"It'll be fine, Gabe."

"Why did you leave?"

"It's just..." Zain looked from Gabrielle to Carla Sonetta, who gave him a quizzical stare. "It's nothing."

"Tell me." She reached out to him blindly.

Zain took Gabrielle's hand. He looked past her to the headmistress. "Can you work together with Gazo's?"

"If they can work together with us, Mr. Berrese."

"They can. Just try to put rivalry aside. For once? We need to be together now. More than ever."

Carla Sonetta sighed. "Will do, Mr. Berrese. Ladies should be decent, after all. I will... I'll leave you two alone." Carla Sonetta turned and walked away.

Gabrielle cuddled up close to Zain's arm, squeezing his hand. "What are you doing out here?"

"I... My stomach doesn't feel right."

"Like on za boat?"

"Not as bad as then. I just... I can't help but think we're too late."

"Have faiz, Zain. Zings will work out as zey should." Gabrielle caressed his cheek.

Zain shook her hand away. "Sorry. I just... Things don't seem to be going the way they should."

"And not everyzing in life does. Za Ancients test us."

"I wish they wouldn't." Gabrielle didn't respond. Zain stood there, hand clutched with hers, heads supporting one another. He exhaled deeply. "Tell me the rest of the story."

"Story?"

"Carla Sonetta never finished telling me how Grace died."

"Gazo killed her."

"But I thought Gazo died chasing—"

"Not her husband, Zain. Her son."

"Her son killed her? Why? How?"

Gabrielle was quiet for a moment. She nuzzled his head with hers and squeezed his hand tight. "He didn't have faiz, Zain. He didn't believe."

## CHAPTER 27

# THE POWER OF BLOOD

T though the moments in the Guardian's crypt had been intense and challenging, Eirek was thankful for them as the monotony of training resumed in the days that followed. There was no life outside of it. For two more weeks, he woke up to morning runs, then trained on the stone court, then in the Habitat Arena under the supervision of Guardian Eska, and then both Eska and Tundra would train him in the evening, focusing on exercises in Power. Words couldn't describe how his body and mind felt, but he understood why they pushed him so far. A war was coming. That much he had gleaned from what started with a simple prophecy. It was a war they wanted to make sure he was ready for.

Eirek ducked underneath Guardian Eska's swipe. "*Maa.*" Eirek made a small platform of earth under Guardian Eska's feet rise.

Eska jumped from the platform to the stone court, sword overhead. Eirek rolled out of the way and swiped at Eska's legs. Eska raised the closest leg to avoid the blow, then followed through with another strike overhead. Still kneeling, Eirek put his sword above his head and braced. The shockwave from Eska's might would have crippled him if he had not held his sword with two hands. Now they were locked in a stalemate.

"*Maa.*" Eirek tried the same tactic.

"*Maa,*" Eska echoed.

Around the two, the stone court shook and trembled, not knowing whose command to obey. Eirek struggled in overcoming Eska's grab for Power. *Move.* He commanded it. A slab of earth erupted out of the ground, but just as quickly, it retreated. *Break. Split.* A fissure worked its way between their bodies. A deafening split cracked the air. Then it stopped and budged no farther.

Sweat snuck its way into his eyes. His heart pounded. *Split!* He reached deeper inside. The ground shook and pulled away. One inch. Two. It caved inward once again.

Eirek collapsed on the floor. He coughed for air. Legs tired from holding such a position, mind tired from battling for the command of Power, and arms and shoulder tired from his stalemate with Eska. "How... how much of your strength were you using?"

Since beginning to train Ether Weapons and Power with Eska, he had been curious to know just how close he ever came to seeing Eska's full strength.

"Fifty percent," Eska replied.

"Still?" Eirek sighed.

"Once you start training with Vesel and me, you will see my other fifty." Guardian Eska laughed.

Eirek chuckled, now understanding why Eska had always said only fifty. "How often have you and Vesel fought together?"

"You saw us at the Meeting of the Twelve. That has been the only time."

"Really? But the other Pirini Lilapa? Your fight with Deimos?"

"The Twelve helped me there. There has been no occasion before or since where I have required him. But that doesn't mean I haven't used his help in other ways."

"What do you—" Eirek's wrist beeped and vibrated. He furrowed his brows. "It's Cain." Eirek pushed *accept.* "Cain?"

"Eirek." Cain paused. "I mean, Apprentice Mouse, I am sorry for disturbing you. Is this a bad time?"

Eirek looked towards Guardian Eska, who nodded his approval. "We can talk briefly. What is it?"

"I want you to know that I know who I am now. You were right after all. I have blood from the True King of Pyre. The necklace around my neck is my birthright. It means that I can bond with Chantico."

Eirek shook his head. "Slow down. Slow down. Did you say True King?" Eska's stance shifted.

Cain nodded. "It is a long story. But they and their descendants are the only ones who can bond with the Creatures of Legend."

Eirek looked towards Eska. "Are you hearing this?"

Eska nodded.

"What should I say?"

"He said Pyre?"

Eirek turned back to Cain's hologram. "You said Pyre?"

Cain nodded. "I know it to be true. That is why I didn't sweat during the fourth trial."

"We knew that he may have been from Pyre, but this is far more than I imagined." Guardian Eska folded his arms across his chest. "What does he want?"

Eirek repeated the question.

"I am going to Pyre to bond with Chantico, yet I do not know where she is or the process involved. Does Guardian Eska have any advice?"

Eirek waited for Guardian Eska's answer. Eyes glowing, Guardian Eska paced the stone court, hands now behind his back, preventing his cape from drifting too far. *Who is he communicating with?* After two full laps, he stopped before Eirek.

"You will go meet Cain on Pyre. I have just informed Conseleigh Inferno to be expecting both of you. Before his time as a conseleigh, he was the previous lord of Therus and is bonded to an animal himself. He will be Cain's best contact there to not only guide him through the process, but to locate Chantico as well."

"Am I ready to go?"

"*That* I am unsure of, but you must go nonetheless. You are not so helpless anymore."

Eirek pursed his lips, then nodded and looked back at Cain. "Guardian Eska is allowing me to leave the Core and meet you on Pyre. Conseleigh Inferno will meet us as well, and he will be your guide."

Cain nodded. "Where do we meet?"

Eirek raised his eyebrows to Guardian Eska.

"You should meet at Fernis. It will give you easy access to all of Therus, and it's an access point to Lurid, should you need to visit there."

"Fernis, the capital of Therus," Eirek said.

"I will see you there. When should I expect you?"

"Tomorrow."

"Then I shall see you soon, Apprentice Mourse."

Eirek smiled. "You will, Prince Evber."

The connection cut.

"Make sure your things are ready and visit the apothecary before you leave to get a bag of ard leaves. Assuming the encounter is successful, they will be useful after the bonding is complete."

Eirek sat with his elbows hung over his knees. *Cain is the True King of Pyre.* A part of him couldn't believe it. But the other part knew it was naïve to deny it. The evidence was clearly there, and now that Eirek knew, it made his conviction regarding the chosen individuals for the prophecy that much more solid. Still, a thought nagged at him.

Eirek got to his feet. "Why am I going? My training?"

"You are capable enough. Your goal was to help Cain find himself. Now it is time for you to see it through to its completion."

"But am I ready?"

"No." Eska furrowed his brows and looked intensely at Eirek. "The truth is that you may never be ready. No one really ever knows until they are thrown into the situation whether or not they can survive, which reminds me, do you have the mithril armor still as well as that quartz ring from Lady Aprah?"

With one eyebrow arched, Eirek nodded. "What will I need those things for?"

"I want you to be fully equipped. For anything and everything that might happen."

"And what might happen? It's only Pyre."

The muscles in Eska's neck grew taut. "There is a possibility that you may run into Hydro Paen while on Pyre."

Eirek gawked. "Hydro? Why would he be on—"

"I do not know what is propelling him to track down the jewels we sealed the Twelve in, but what is more problematic is that he is succeeding. Conseleigh Inferno has a jewel on his person."

"So you are using him as bait?"

"I didn't intend to, but now, yes. He knows the role he plays in drawing Hydro out. Hopefully, he will do this to our advantage."

"Advantage?"

"In the best-case scenario, Eirek, it will be you, Cain, Chantico, and Conseleigh Inferno against Hydro. The odds will be in your favor, and you will finish this once and for all, for you and you alone have the blood to destroy that necklace Hydro wears forever. To sever his connection with Desmós."

"My blood?"

Eska nodded. He walked to Eirek and put a hand on his shoulder. "Whatever faint trace of Ancient blood that remains in your veins, Eirek, has the Power to end this. Only Ancient Power can fight Ancient Power. I understand that more than ever now. Ever since my run in with the Other on Epoch. I believe Desmós is using Hydro the same way the Sages are manipulating Victor. Have manipulated him ever since our Trials together."

Eirek looked at his mentor, eyes wide with curiosity. Eska rarely talked about his Trials. "What do you mean?" Eirek asked, hoping to spur his mentor into finally divulging his past.

"It starts with our why. Do you know your why, Eirek?"

"Why?" Eirek stammered. "I am unsure what you mean."

"Why did you participate in the Trials to begin with?"

"My uncle said I should."

Eska shook his head. "No. There was a deeper reason. I am sure. Why did you obey him? Why did you even choose to want this position?"

The question brought back nostalgia of nearly a year past. He had been in his uncle's presence, and Linn's mother had asked him the same question. "To support those who haven't been supported. That was my why."

"And have you done that yet?"

"I am not Guardian yet."

"Your why doesn't just start when you become Guardian, Eirek. It propels you. It is what propelled me."

"What was your why?"

"To not let my sister's sacrifice be in vain." Guardian Eska looked at Eirek for a long while, and with a heavy sigh, he finally let loose his past. "She died right before I attended the Trials. Vesel killed her. But that instance brought us together, and it is only because of Vesel that I am here before you today."

Eirek's mouth hung slack; he felt tears form in the corners of his eyes.

"The last trial was a duel between Victor Zigarda and me. I should have lost that duel, Eirek. Victor overpowered me. But my bond with Vesel made me immune to his Power. Well, his blue flames, anyway. After I was swallowed in his blue flames, I reached out to Vesel, and he gave me his strength. I swallowed Victor in flames of my own."

Eirek put a finger to his lip. His eyes went wide. "That's what you meant when—"

Eska nodded. "It is indeed. I have called upon Vesel's strength like that only a few times. It terrified me in the beginning, but as I trained with Guardian Crevon, I learned to harness that Power, until now Vesel and I fight with equal ferocity. We understand one another now. Like Victor understood me the day of our trial. At least, to the best of his ability, he understood me."

"But why does that matter?"

Guardian Eska stared deep into Eirek's eyes. "Because when you understand someone, Eirek, when you truly know them, their thoughts and goals, their weaknesses and their strengths, when you understand that person so well that they are almost like kin to you, that is when you are powerful, for you have the knowledge to love them," Eska paused, "...or annihilate them. And now that we know all the pieces on the table, it is time to do just that."

CHAPTER 28

# THE FROZEN PASS

In the week since Lokigh, the air had gotten colder the farther north they went. Beyond conversing over directions, talk didn't exist. Zigarda had insisted on keeping the feather in his possession during the ascent up the mountain, and he led his horse to follow its twisting indications. While hovercrafts would have taken them to the base of the mountains faster, they would have been practically useless during the assent, so horses were taken from Marquis Desmier's stables. Even with the horses carrying a majority of their supplies, Zakk still wore a trekking backpack to carry the rest: fur cloaks, animal hides, sufficient food, snow boots, and all other essentials for their voyage.

The suns darted behind the banded horizon, blanketing the white land with darkness. Moons hung lower tonight than Zakk had ever cared to notice. Maybe it was the location, within a valley and large snow-covered mountains all around, ice and rock under their snow boots, but something made the moons look majestic, as if being here brought him closer to the heavens of Axiumé. And maybe that was why the feather called them this way, why Rhayna had chosen to make her home somewhere in these mountains.

Wind howled and slapped him in the face. He rubbed the ruby ring on his finger, one of the trinkets Zigarda gave him before going north. It allowed them to keep warm, which then allowed them to make better time. But it also produced a careless negligence in Zigarda, believing warmth would offset their inability to see, and so even in the waning twilight, Zigarda continued on ahead. Zakk couldn't continue like this.

"The suns are behind the mountains now. We should make base while we still have what little light is left."

His comment went ignored.

Zakk kicked the sides of his horse and caught up to Zigarda. "We should camp while we have light."

"We will camp when I say."

"The light."

"I will make us light. We press on for another hour."

Zakk twitched his lips in disapproval but said nothing. With limited light, the footing for the horses could get worse, and pitching the tent would be more difficult as well. Impossible, if Zakk even used that word, but it wasn't allowed in the Gazo's vocabulary because nothing was impossible when living by the mantra *I'm Possible*.

After climbing another slight incline, Zigarda pulled on his reins, stopping his horse. Before them, a pass extended up between two mountains. Blue rock and snow covered the cliffs, but Zakk understood why Zigarda had chosen to go another hour now. The wind here had died to almost nothing. Perhaps the man knew more about terrain advantages than Zakk had given him credit for.

Zakk took the cue to set up camp. After tying the horses to the closest trees, he laid out a few furs for blankets. Then he pitched the tents and by the time he had finished, Zigarda had started a fire. With a real fire in their midst, Zakk deactivated his ruby ring and sat down on one of the furs. He rubbed his hands together, stretching them out in front of the tongues of fire; Zigarda, on the other hand, kept his hands close to him, twirling the feather before his eyes, enthralled with its Power. No matter how he twisted it, the feather pointed towards the pass behind them.

"How did you start the fire?"

Zigarda let the feather fall to his chest. "Power."

"Most fires are orange."

"Yes, that is because they are weaker. Blue is the hottest and reserved for the strongest of Power casters."

"But how?"

"You're either born with it, or you're not. If you've never cast by now, you most likely don't have it."

Zakk knew that. He had been tested while in Gazo's, and when he and Zain couldn't cast, they passed them into the tactician's branch of the Academy. There, they learned to cultivate strategies to use terrain, materials, formations, and even the natural elements to the advantage of the men they led.

Zigarda rubbed his hands in front of the fire for a moment before obsessing over the feather once more, leaving Zakk in silence. While he sat there, he sought out the constellations, trying to find the star that might be his, as the old folk-legend went. This far beyond city lights, the stars were brilliant. Zigarda's voice called him back to attention.

"What do you know of Rhayna?"

Zakk blinked for a moment, dumbfounded that Zigarda would venture further conversation with him. "I... I haven't seen her before. Zain claimed he saw her once, though. Legends say she is the most beautiful animal in existence. That she is known to bring good luck." Zakk chuckled.

"What is so funny?"

"Luck. There is no such thing. At least, good luck."

"Luck." Zigarda snickered. "That may be the first thing we agree about. Power. Skill. Intelligence. Those are the things that make a man. Not luck."

Arms wrapped around his bent knees, Zakk asked. "What do they say in Empora about Rhayna?"

"They see her as hope. That she was sent down from Axiumé to lighten the world."

Zakk raised his brows. "Who's they?"

"Everyone who isn't me."

"And what do you say?"

"She's just another animal. Beautiful or not, she will..." Zigarda coughed and continued coughing for another few minutes. He hobbled to his horse, took a flask from his saddlebag, and drank a little, killing his cough. Zigarda sat back down. "Beautiful or not, she will serve her purpose."

"What is that?"

"Power. That's why animals were created. Power."

"Who told you that?"

"Cronos."

Zakk nodded. The man had an Ether Weapon and bi-color eyes, and the way that even Zigarda respected the old man, made Zakk realize looks could often be deceiving.

"Why do you need more?"

"Because of this..." Zigarda pulled down his hood, exposing his marred face. No hair covered his head, and wrinkles coursed across his skin. Lidless charcoal eyes bore into Zakk. "I will repay him for it," he finished in a cold, hard voice.

"How did Eska overpower you—"

"He didn't overpower me!"

The blue flame that had been keeping them warm shot outward. Zakk kicked back, plopping off of his fur mat into the wet snow in order to avoid the gush of blue flames coming from the fire. Eyes wide, Zakk looked to Zigarda. The man breathed in deeply, and with his exhalation, the flame receded.

"He didn't overpower me," Zigarda repeated, calmer this time. "It should have been me."

Zakk had no idea what the man was rambling about. Cautiously, he stomped out the small fire that had eaten half of his blanket and returned to sit on what remained. Silently, he waited for Zigarda to continue, or not, but he didn't want to be the one to cause another outburst. Zakk knew enough about past hurts to not pour salt into wounds.

After looking into the fire silently for some time, Zigarda turned his attention to Zakk. "What makes a man? Were you listening?"

"Power. Skill. And Intelligence."

"Correct. Edwyrd had all three, although not nearly the same caliber as my Power or my skill."

Keeping his voice noticeably docile, Zakk asked. "So how did he—"

"Because animals are made for Power. Before he came to the Trials, he had found his animal to bond with—a dragon. I didn't know it then, not until after we fought each other in the last trial. His dragon hadn't been with him at all; he had kept it back home." Zigarda tucked the feather away underneath his robe. He tilted his right hand, palm up, and soon a blue fire came to it. With his other hand, he created water. "Even though we both fought with fire, he drenched my flames as if he was using water." The water leaped from his left hand and put out the fire on his right. "A dragon came out of the flames that day. I'm not sure how he accessed the Power of his bonded animal so quickly or from so far away, but he did and that is why he won. And because of that dragon's special ability." Zigarda muttered the last part.

"Ability?"

"When you bond with an animal, they grant you an ability. Because of Edwyrd's dragon, my flames didn't affect him. No flames affect him now. Fighting him with fire is useless."

"He knew of his dragon's ability?"

"I am unsure."

"Then how does that make him more intelligent?"

"Because he never showed signs of having a bonded animal."

"Would the outcome have been different if the dragon had been with him? Wouldn't he have been stronger?"

"Stronger. Definitely. And that is why I need Rhayna to combat him now. But he also would be weaker. For when you bond, a part of that animal is with you, forever, until it dies. I would have gone for his animal first, and then I would have finished him while he was at his weakest. That is what I will do after I bond with Rhayna."

"And then?"

Zigarda let go of the feather again. "And then?" His face stretched taut, as if he were trying to raise non-existent eyebrows.

"What will you do after you become Guardian?"

"Do something no other Guardian has done before."

"What is that?"

With sick fixation, Zigarda stared at Zakk. "Cheat death."

Zakk shivered. "Only death defeats you, nothing else," he muttered.

"What was that?"

Zakk shook his head. "Only death defeats you, nothing else. It's a Gazo's mantra."

"Get those family values out of your head. They won't help you survive."

"Have you ever had a family?"

Zigarda laughed at that. "No one needs a family. I've been alone all of my life."

"You never had any siblings?"

"A brother. Younger. Weaker."

"What happened to him?"

"I killed him. After my Trials and my disfigurement, my father skipped over me for the family's inheritance and would have passed it on to him. I couldn't allow that to happen. He would've destroyed Empora."

Zakk shook his head, doing a double-take. "You did what?"

"Killed him. I put a knife in his spine and let the poison do the rest."

Zakk coughed. He immediately reined back in whatever disbelief he had shown, not wanting to give too much away. But it was already too late. Zigarda had seen him and answered the question his body language asked silently.

"Why? Because sacrifices needed to be made. You'll understand one day. That's enough idle chit chat for tonight. We start early tomorrow. Go to sleep." Zigarda covered his head again and laid down on his furs.

Zakk followed suit. Although he wanted to ask more questions, he was content with not knowing more than he needed. Perhaps the best way to live was to forget everything he had ever known.

CHAPTER 29

# A CHANGE IN STRATEGY

B ound and gagged on top of the battlements, Zain's mother and uncle stood next to Marquis Pillian Desmier of Empora. Hector and Sheamus stood behind them, weapons raised to their throats. Alexyer was also along the top of the battlements with the hordes of arches, bow at his ready but not drawn back.

Zain didn't know which emotion to honor. Rage in the betrayal that had happened. Horror in potentially witnessing his mother's death. Calmness in knowing she and his uncle were at least still alive for the moment. The kaleidoscope of emotions quickened his heart and pushed sweat out from his body, despite it being nearly evening. They had just arrived in Pelopon after a four-day journey on the Long Pass. Normally, it would have taken half the time, but with a party their size, coordinating routes and facilitating order to avoid collisions meant slower progress than usual.

It hadn't been even an hour since they set up camp outside the city, outside of the range of any archers. Using a voice projection, the marquis had called Zain to come forward to negotiate surrender terms. Zain obeyed but took Lukas to accompany him, as well as Cleaver. The three of them would be the most intimidating in the negotiations, and it was better if Empora didn't know yet that Gracie's and Gazo's Academy had joined the fight.

"Mr. Berrese, how nice of you to make it this far. And who is that I see amongst you? Your uncle, is that it? And... who is that portly fellow?"

"Where's Zigarda?" Cleaver bellowed, ignoring the man's question.

"He isn't here. Business calls him north, but that doesn't matter. You won't be seeing him, anyway."

"Is that so?" Cleaver clicked his tongue, and Zain tensed under the enormous man's gaze.

"They're lying," Zain whispered. "I sense Zakk. It's a ploy."

Cleaver raised an eyebrow to Zain yet remained silent with his arms folded over his chest.

"Let my mother and uncle go!"

"Such a tall demand for someone so small and whose army has no way of matching our own."

Lukas stepped forward. "What are your terms?"

"Lukas!" Zain whispered. Lukas hushed Zain.

"Quite simple. End this little charade of yours. Lord Vangle here is quite stubborn, you see. He believes somehow that you are actually going to be able to rescue him." Marquis Desmier laughed. "Outrageous thought, and while I could have killed him earlier, I didn't want you to miss anything. Surrender yourselves to Empora. Declare Ka'Chean land now an entity of Empora. Lord Vangle will die a quick death, as will his family members, but that doesn't mean it's the end for you. You and your," the marquis searched for a word, finally coming upon, "followers... don't have to suffer the same fate."

"And what makes you think we would trust your word? Zigarda already betrayed us in Mendeck."

"Betrayed implies that Zigarda and you had an agreement to begin with. You didn't. These are our terms and conditions now. Take it. Leave it. Or watch your mother and uncle die now, here, in front of you." Marquis Desmier nodded towards Hector and Sheamus, and they shuffled the prisoners forward.

His uncle and his mother both squirmed under the grasps of the two betrayers behind them, but their attempt to break free was futile.

"You have until the count of three. One."

Zain's eyes widened. His mother and uncle were pushed closer to the precipice.

"Two."

Hector and Sheamus dangled his mother and uncle off the parapets, holding them by the back of their clothes, their feet scrabbling for purchase as they futilely tried to right themselves. A noose around each neck was tied to the battlements. *They're going to hang them.*

"Thr—."

Zain rushed forward. "Stop!"

"Zain, don't! You can still do this. I know you can. My life is gone either way but—"

Marquis Desmier nodded. Sheamus let go of Zain's uncle but caught the rope with two hands. The move was just enough to cause his uncle to stop talking.

"Surrender, or we hang them, Mr. Berrese. It is as easy as that."

"I..." Zain's heart pounded. He collapsed onto his knees. "Just let them go."

"As you wish, Mr. Berrese. Release them both."

Zain's mouth widened in horror and shock as his uncle and his mother tumbled from the battlements. They fell. Rope around their necks. Through the air.

"No!" Zain rushed forward. "Mah—" Zain stretched out his hand. Arrows shot out at him. Earth shielded him and obscured his view. *What the...* Zain lowered his hand and as he did so, the arrows fell to the ground that had been blocked by the shield. *What just happened? Mom?* Zain looked up and saw two earthen pillars erected underneath the feet of both his mother and his uncle, saving them from a hanging.

Hand held upright in a fist, Marquis Desmier shrank back a little. Shaking his head, he regained his position. "Tomorrow morning you will have an answer for me, Mr. Berrese. I will not ask again, nor will I spare their lives again. Tomorrow morning, you surrender, or they hang. This time there will be no earth under their feet to save them. Bring them up."

Before Zain knew what was going on, arms swooped underneath him and dragged him back. His uncle and his mother were being raised up the wall on the earthen pillar that the marquis must have made. Once his mother and uncle were safely on top of the battlement, Sheamus and Hector lifted the nooses from around their necks.

"Zain! Do you have any idea what you just did?"

Zain blinked. He looked at his hand. *Did I... Or was it?* The battlements were empty. The party had already disappeared behind the walls. He rotated his hand left and right.

"Zain, do you hear me?"

Shaken, he blinked and looked at his uncle. "Sorry. What was that?"

"Do you realize what could have just happened?"

Using one arm, Zain pushed himself to his feet. "Yeah. They could have killed mom and Abraham, but they didn't."

"And you! Those arrows..."

Zain looked at the arrows once more on the ground.

"When were you able to cast Power?"

"Power? Did I?" Zain looked over his hands while walking back to where they had set up camp a little while ago. He expected to find something more than scars of past regrets, but he didn't. "No. Impossible. I'm..." He shook his head, not wanting to say the word. He continued surveying his hands. *Did I? No... It was the marquis... He must have split his spell.* Wishing for the scars on his palms to disappear, he clenched his fists. "No. I'm Denied, Lukas. I can't cast."

"Denied?"

Zain tensed. Cleaver came around him, blocking him off from the camp.

"So this whole time you've been lying about being able to sense Zakk Shiren?"

"Oh..." Zain flew back and stumbled to the ground as Cleaver's fist hit him square in the face. Tinnitus disrupted Zain. The sound of withdrawn steel brought him back to focus.

Lukas had stepped in front of Zain, weapon withdrawn. Cleaver, too, had his weapon out. "You punched my nephew."

"Your nephew lied to me."

Zain rubbed his jaw and felt his nose. Red coated his hand. One elbow propped on the dirt, he noticed the two men in a fierce stalemate. Their bodies leaned forward, as if they were ready to pounce. Zain's eyes widened. The standoff had gained the attention of the camp.

Zain pushed himself to his feet. "Uncle, it's fine." Zain squeezed Lukas's shoulder.

Lukas ignored it. "Zain, he hit you."

"He had a right to."

Confused, Lukas looked at Zain, a frown on his face. His tense shoulders slouched sightly.

"Cleaver," Zain said. "I—"

"Zain, what's going on?"

Zain lost his words. Klum Barrata had pushed his way to the front of the crowd. Carla Sonetta appeared soon after him, holding the hand of Gabrielle.

"You're bleeding, Zain. What happened?"

Zain shook his head. Too much attention was never good. "Cleaver, please, let's talk about all of this in private. I have some explaining to do."

Cleaver looked at Zain and then at his uncle. He grunted and sheathed his sword. "Lead the way."

The five of them filed into the command tent. Zain didn't waste time. Before sunrise tomorrow, they had to come up with a strategy or his mother and uncle would be hung in front of them. Then everything that Zain had worked for would be for nothing.

"Cleaver, you have the right to be angry. I—" He never got to finish his apology, let alone start it, for Cleaver had already interjected.

"Angry? Angry ain't the word. The world lives by codes. Men live by codes. My rebellion, Guy's rebellion, lived by a code. That is how we were able to stay alive for so long. That is what drove us. Fueled us. We respected them. I joined this fight thinking that Gazo's men had a sense of code as well. It's clear that you don't have any such codes. So, angry? No. I'm disappointed." Cleaver snorted and spat on the ground. "You can fight this army yourself. The Scorpions are finished here." Cleaver walked towards the tent's exit.

"Cleaver, wait! You haven't even let me explain!"

"I don't care for your—"

"Zain never lied to you."

Zain twisted his head towards Gabrielle, who was closest to the exit. "Gabrie—"

Cleaver turned on his heel and approached Gabrielle. "The blind lady wishes to say something now?"

Gabrielle didn't cower. She stood straight, less than half the size of the man in front of her. Next to her, Carla Sonetta had her arms crossed over her body, her left hand coming to rest on the hilt of something hidden beneath the table she stood around. Zain gulped.

"Zis blind lady wishes to refresh your memory. I told you zat Zain and Zakk were brozers. I told you zat Zakk would be at Zigarda's side wherever he was. Zat Zakk was his lapdog."

"Yeah. And Zigarda ain't here."

"I never said he would be. I said we'd find him after we take back Pelopon."

"And you said it would be through him." Cleaver raised his arm in the air and pointed to Zain. "That man is Denied. He couldn't even find Zakk if he wanted to."

Cleaver threw him a glance of vehemence. Being Denied had never bothered him before, but when Cleaver uttered the word, it made Zain's skin prickle. He shuddered underneath the label.

"But zat isn't your issue. Your issue is zat Zain lied to you. He did no such zing."

"Then it's you who have no code."

Gabrielle laughed. "You know nozing about our code at Gracie's."

"Then enlighten me, Blind One."

"You have to be decent, but deceitful, before you can show form, yet also be formidable," she recited. "I never once lied to you. I said zat zey were brozers, which is half true. Zey are adopted. And I said zey have a bond togezer, which zey do. I never said it was a blood bond. You merely zought zat yourself."

"You little..."

Carla Sonetta shifted. Gabrielle put her hand up. "I don't need your help. I could take care of zis man myself. Even blind."

"Oh, yeah?" Cleaver growled.

"Yeah."

Cleaver looked down. He stepped back.

"Zis Blind One could have just sliced your femoral artery or cut off your manhood."

Cleaver sneered.

"Now, if I'm not mistaken, you pledged your troops to our cause in order to find Zigarda afterwards. And we will find Zigarda afterwards, zat I promise, but first zings first. It is zis battle. So if you intend on leaving now, Cleaver, it is you who does not have honor."

The tent went silent. Everyone's gaze fell upon Cleaver, wondering what the large man would do. If Zain hadn't seen it with his own eyes, he wouldn't have believed it, but the large man cowered under the weight of the stares. He grunted but returned to his position around the waist-high table.

He cleared his throat. "So what are we looking at in terms of troops inside the castle?"

The change in tone and comment indicated Gabrielle had won. Zain's heart pounded, and tingles crept over his body. If only she could have seen the smile on his face. He wanted nothing more than to kiss her and hug her then, but he knew it would be foolish to do so with so many eyes watching.

Headmistress Sonetta raised her hand. "Mendeck has a population of five million. Only a small percentage of that, though, is military. You may have up to forty thousand."

Zain's eyes bulged. "Forty thousand. That isn't—"

Carla Sonetta put up her finger. "Zain, your escape wasn't planned. Most likely, Zigarda left abruptly and didn't have a chance to call for all the soldiers to accompany him, maybe only those in the Web's grounds or near its perimeter."

Lukas put a hand under his chin. "So, where does that leave us?"

"Anywhere from three to ten thousand."

"That is a pretty large range."

"And it is more likely to be higher in the range, Klum."

"And why is that?"

The headmistress turned to Lukas. "When our party was escaping from Empora, Zigarda called forces to hunt us down. We barely managed to make it out of Rydel in time. And by the time we reached Terran, he sent hunters for us specifically."

"And I know there are at least four shapeshifters within the castle. That'll make things even more dangerous," said Zain.

"Shifters, Zain? Again with this?" Lukas craned his neck to Zain.

Zain nodded. "Uncle, I am positive one of those shifters was me. Was my father. That is how they overtook the castle in the first place. Hector, Alexyer, and Sheamus, they betrayed us while in Mendeck. I'm sure they helped this castle be overrun."

Lukas crossed his arms over his chest. "Then those three will receive a traitor's hanging when we are successful." He glanced around the room, his attention falling on Zain for the longest.

Zain raised an eyebrow. His uncle looked away and continued. "So, there are at least four shapeshifters and ten thousand soldiers. Dras contacted me just before we settled down. He reached Cotterall. Marquis Sesso is sending troops to us; we should have them by our second sunrise."

"That isn't fast enough!" Zain pounded the table. "You heard what they will do."

"They are bluffing, Zain. Hang your mother or the lord and they no longer have any bargaining chips should we overwhelm them."

"Did you not see what they did today?"

"They toyed with you. Psychological warfare is just as deadly as actual violence. They want you to make a brash decision. But I'm telling you now that if we storm that gate tomorrow, we won't break through. Not with the forces we have now. And not unless we want to lose a considerable amount of men in the process."

Carla Sonetta cleared her throat.

"Excuse me. Men and women," Lukas corrected. "The castle sits on a hill, forcing us to approach over difficult terrain, and the parapets above would make us easy targets for archers. I suggest we maneuver towards the bluff located past the city, where we keep our fleets. There are stairs there leading up to the castle. It's sure to be heavily guarded, but it will be much less suicidal than trying to barge through the front door."

"You have Gazo's with you." Klum Barrata raised a fist. "Levels of our men are trained in close-quarter combat. We can send them—"

Carla Sonetta scoffed. "You men and your blades. Your plan is illogical, if I may be so blunt."

Lukas crossed his arms over his chest. "I know this city and this castle better than any of you. I've been born and raised here. This is the only viable option."

"That's because you don't see all the other viable options," Carla Sonetta corrected.

Lukas chuckled to himself and shook his head. "Amuse me, then. What do any women from Gracie's know about the fortifications of the castle?"

"As much as the men from Gazo's know about decency, but I do know there is more than one weapon we can utilize."

"Such as?" Lukas raised an eyebrow.

"The cliff approach has merit, but you have to realize that the city is most likely overrun. Did you not observe all the traffic flowing away from the city as we approached?"

Lukas grunted and inclined his head. "Go on."

"I don't know anything about this city, but you made it clear that these ports are located behind it, meaning we need to make our way through it before we even reach the heavier defenses at the castle. Surely, many of our numbers will be lost there."

"So, what do you suggest?" Lukas asked.

"Our ladies can enter tonight and scout the city. They should not consider us a threat."

"Why is that?" The Cleaver asked.

"Because men never do." Carla Sonetta smirked. She turned her head towards Zain. "The fourth and final pillar, Mr. Berrese, is *life is a play, act accordingly.* This goes hand-in-hand with our third pillar." She focused around the room. "The men who have overrun the city and the castle are from Empora. When we scout the city, I will make sure only some of our Emporian ladies go. Their accents shouldn't give them away, and the fact that they are ladies will make them less inclined to consider them a threat."

"Your women are willing to do such a reconnaissance for us?" Lukas asked.

"Gabrielle and I will talk to the women and see what small force we can muster."

Gabrielle turned her head to the headmistress's voice. "Lady Sonetta?"

"You do not have to go with them, Gabrielle. These women respect your voice, though. You and I can talk with them."

"All right." Gabrielle nodded.

"And after?"

"We will let you know if your plan is viable or not."

"I believe, for once, Carla is right. Winning a battle is having more men. Winning a war is having a better strategy and using what you have at your disposal. Until the Ka'Chean reinforcements come from Cotterall, we do not have the numbers to win a battle, but we are smarter and have a myriad of different talents. We can win the war, but we need to work together," Klum Barrata said.

Lukas glanced around the room, one hand cupped under his chin in thought. "Very well. It's settled. Headmistress Sonetta, I appreciate your efforts. Ka'Che owes you."

"And I will take your lord up on that offer after we rescue him. For now, let us focus on getting the castle back before the south closes in on us."

"Agreed. Everyone is dismissed. Zain, I would like to speak to you alone."

Everyone else in the tent gave Zain a momentary glance, but they all vacated soon afterwards. As everyone left, Zain looked at his uncle. Nothing showed on Lukas's face. His stoic nature caused Zain's stomach to clench.

"Zain."

"Yes?"

"What happened earlier today?"

"What do you mean?"

"The Power you cast. Was that you? I thought you were Denied."

"I told you I didn't cast. I couldn't have."

"Those arrows should have hit, but they didn't. Do you want me to believe that the marquis split his spell in two in order to save you? He wants you dead."

"I..." Zain fidgeted. He tried to remember what had happened earlier. His eyes widened. "It must have been Abraham. He can cast."

Lukas sighed. "Maybe." He bit his lip. "Yeah, maybe." He paced a few steps, hands clenched behind his back. "Just be more careful next time. You could have died today."

"But—"

"I know what you saw today was hard. It was for me, too, but I understand how this game is played. They want to torment us into making rash decisions. We can't afford to do that."

"And we can't afford to lose my mom and Abraham."

"No. We can't."

"Then let's think of a strategy."

"I've already told you storming the front door would be next to impossible given our amount of troops."

"But so will overtaking the city."

"We don't know that yet."

Zain tapped his fist on the table, trying his best to not let his emotions overwhelm him. "No. I guess you're right." He exhaled through his nostrils. "But are you really going to take a chance? We are sitting ducks out here. Do you think Empora is just going to wait for our reinforcements?"

Lukas didn't answer for a long while. When he finally spoke, he said, "That is what my gut tells me as well. They could easily raid us. But what do you suppose we do?"

"We use today as our example."

"The shields?"

Zain nodded. "How many of your remaining men can cast?"

"All of the men wearing maroon helmets. Maybe twenty or so."

"We spread out the Power casters and form groups. When arrows fly, they summon the earth to form a shield over us. That'll get us to the walls."

"Domes of Power are a great defense, but we won't be able to see inside them. Spellcasters might loosen the spell in order to advance, only to be shot dead with arrows."

Zain snapped his fingers. "Then why not split our factions?"

"What do you mean?"

"Each group is paired with a Power caster and someone who has a telecommunicator. We'll leave someone here at the command tent with a telecommunicator, as well as a few Power casters on the edges of the battle, telling them when it is safe to storm ahead again. They can be our eyes. When they say to move, we do it."

Lukas pushed his tongue into his lower lip. "That might actually work."

"Then I'll tell the others of the plan."

Lukas raised his arm. "Zain, wait. Let the women do their reconnaissance tonight. If that option isn't available, we can try this one."

"But we're putting them in unnecessary danger."

"*They* offered to do this," Lukas corrected. "And we would be putting everyone in even more danger by not at least exhausting all of our other options first."

"Fine." Zain stalked away, prepared to leave the tent, when his uncle's voice called him back.

"Zain, I want you to know that your uncle would be proud. I'm proud of how far you've come as a tactician and the zeal you show for the cause. Tomorrow, keep your wits about you. You said it yourself that there will be shifters in there. Don't trust anyone."

Zain nodded to acknowledge Lukas's comment but proceeded out of the tent into the nighttime air without saying anything more. The time for talking was over. Now it was the time for action.

# INTERLUDE 3 - AN UNEXPECTED CATCH

T undra hated this place. If not for her love of Edwyrd, she would have never agreed to return to this cursed palace. As it was, though, Tundra stood outside double doors of brumal hues that waited for her to open them. And when she did that, she would once again step into a room of crystalline mirrors, reflecting herself in a million different ways. But there was only one mirror in that room she hoped to avoid. If she could resist the temptation.

Tundra sighed.

Gripping both handles, she pulled open the doors to Crestal's Palace and stepped inside. At first, nothing seemed out of the ordinary. The place was crystal and ice. It wasn't cold to her; she had been born in this climate and had lived all of her life in Sereya until abdicating her position of Power to take up her role as conseleigh by Edwyrd's side. It had been what she saw in the mirror that day that made her realize how broken she was inside after her husband's death. It had been the reason why she joined Guardian Eska's conseleigh when the opportunity presented itself, and after she had learned about Edwyrd's own tragic misfortune with the loss of his sister shortly before his own Trials, they had bonded. And that bond had grown into a relationship hardly acceptable for someone of his position and for someone of her lowly stature.

She had opened up with him once about the mirror and how she saw the worst parts of her life reflecting back to her. How she saw a decrepit woman with gaunt skin and tassels of hair falling out. For that mirror had revealed to her what she felt on the inside after her husband's death. After her ascension to Power, Crestal had called her to this place to meet with her in person, a privilege that had been reserved for her husband. It was during that first meeting that Crestal led her over to the mirror and told her to look inside. And it was after that first meeting, not barely a week into her rule as Lady of Sereya, that she knew she wanted to quit that life.

She hummed to herself in the mirror, reliving her past yet trying not to relive this tower at the very same moment. What would the mirror show her now?

Now in the vestibule of the chamber, she realized she would never have a chance to know the answer to that question. The mirror had been shattered. Shards of it lay scattered, mixed with the chandelier that had crashed to the floor as well. Her eyes widened, and her hand went to the hilt of her icy scimitar. The sword had been a gift to her from Crestal over the years of service as Lady of Sereya. Like the tower itself, it had been formed of pure ice. Crestal had blessed it with her own words of Power, and that is why it was nearly the same caliber as an Ether Weapon. While it couldn't break due to the mixture of pure ice and her blessing, it did not have the cutting power of Ether Weapons, and that was the differentiating factor. Still, any weapon to hold its own against an Ether Weapon was one she cherished.

A quick scope of the interior, though, showed no signs of movement. There was no place anyone could hide in this chamber. One of the crystalline walls would have reflected the intruder's presence. As it turned out, the only intruder in this place was her.

She reached out with her mind. *Edwyrd, I'm here.*

*And?*

The response was instantaneous. Had he been waiting for her? Had he been thinking of her like she thought of him? The moments not by his side were some of the hardest in her life, but so far, everything had worked out well for them. Edwyrd hadn't been absolved of his duties as Guardian, Victor Zigarda had finally been dispossessed of his Power, and Dr. Cere had been dealt with. Who else was there that they needed to fear? Cere's final words came into her mind. Cronos. The Sages. Yes, they were the manipulators of Zigarda, but that plan had failed. Surely, Edwyrd would be in the clear now, and once he managed to track the Sages down, they would be dealt with personally for their transgression.

*Tundra? What's wrong?*

*Nothing, Edwyrd. I am fine. Merely lost in thoughts. Someone has been here.*

*The jewel?*

*I will look for it.*

Tundra spent the next hour making lap upon lap of the small vestibule, looking for a jewel. But she had found nothing. She had stayed away from the shards on the floor of the mirror, for fear of the temptation to pick them up, but every other piece of debris had been nothing.

*There is no jewel here, Edwyrd.* The Guardian didn't respond to her for quite some time. Enough time that she had to ask again. *Edwyrd?*

*Are the other matters taken care of?*

*Not yet.*

*See to them and then report back here immediately. Tundra, thank you for doing this.*

*My honor and duty, Edwyrd.*

The connection cut. Tundra expected to leave right away, return to her lover's beckoning, but she stood there. For what purpose, she didn't know. Perhaps curiosity had finally gotten the best of her, and she went over to the mirror and looked at herself in the parts of it that remained.

Her seventy-three-year-old body looked back at her. White and blue hair. The same lines on her face she already knew well. Icy blue eyes that had lost their sheen over the years examined her, but it was her. Had she overcome the demons inside of her, or did the mirror no longer reflect her innermost self due to the damage done to it? She walked back to her ship knowing she would never know the answer. Some things were better left unexplained.

Inside her ship once more, she set a route for Mount Volan. There, she would bury the bodies of the Hown soldiers who failed to capture Hydro. Or had succeeded but had somehow failed. It all seemed too confusing for Tundra. How had Hydro overpowered them? All of them? There were at least twenty of the best-trained men in the system hunting down Hydro Paen. The man possessed an Ether Weapon, but a single man with a single blade could not outperform twenty of the system's highest pedigree soldiers. How did he escape? A survey of the site would do her good, and it would also give time for Lady Aprah to settle in from her return from the hearing.

A day later, Tundra looked upon the mass of carcasses in black neurofiber armor, the golden H of their station pinned to each chest. She had found the bodies of General Satorus and Chase Arwayn near a flipped over hovercraft. The general had been pinned down on top of it, Chase thrown from it. A black net lay nearby, large enough for a body. She picked it up and rubbed the material between her fingers.

While holding it, she said, "*Maa.*" Power didn't obey her. Then she tried, "*Vesi.*" Nothing.

She ran her tongue over her upper teeth. *Interesting. Edwyrd never mentioned anything like this before to me.* Did it matter that he had withheld secrets from her? Not particularly, but a net that didn't allow one to use Power. Well, that was certainly unique. What other pieces of technology did Edwyrd not share with her? What other secrets had he kept for himself?

She took the net and put it in her ship. Then she went back and examined the rest of the bodies. None of them had died from a sword wound, an unexpected development. Instead, mouths full of red blood mixed with bile that overran their lips was the culprit of their death. Like Oliver Thane, they died with their eyes open in shock and terror. Some had scratch marks on their neck, showing how they had tried to claw their suits off of them. But not of that mattered. She knew they had  succumbed to the same blasted virus that had killed the other Hown with her while on her mission in Sereya. Whatever that virus was, though she had no idea.

Despite so many years on this planet, she was beginning to realize just how little she knew about the powers at play. What struck her as odder still, though, was that two of the soldiers died with large holes through their chest, as if a laser beam or something fired straight through them. But did that kind of technology even exist? She knew lasers existed. They were crucial in most engineering feats, but to weaponize it? She would take one of those bodies back to Edwyrd to get his thoughts. And then there was one final body that had been pulverized to a pancake. The flattened body rested within a slight recess, like a footprint but much, much larger. Thrice the length of Tundra's entire body.

*What in Abaddon's name?*

She surveyed the area and quickly saw another slight depression. Something had been moving. A giant? What else could it have been? Had they left their post in the Sacred Passage? Why? What could have called them out?

These were questions that she couldn't answer on her own. There were certainly still larger forces at play here, and if Hydro was in league with giants, well, what did that mean for Edwyrd? He was strong, but he was only one man, and even he had failed to take on Deimos by himself. Even if giants were half the strength of that beast, could Edwyrd handle them?

Worry prickled her skin. Her heart pumped in ways she didn't like to admit. She needed to finish her business on this planet and return so that she could get him this crucial information. Using Power, she rolled and walked the bodies one by one into the Sacred Passage to the first alcove and buried them. Each of them deserved more than just a mere mound of dirt, so she put them in a place where they would be remembered for their service yet rest undisturbed all the same. Even by speeding up the process this way, it was still nightfall by the time she had finished her task. She would go to the nearest town and rest there for the night and make her trip to Visis in the morning.

Two hands before noon, Tundra met with Lady Aprah. This was to be a tense meeting, she was sure, but perhaps it would be the only good thing to come out of this blasted trip. If she could at least reconcile with Lady Aprah, apologize, and win her back to Edwyrd's cause, that might make all the difference in the war to come, whatever war that was.

She did this out of propriety. And because she felt she owed it to Edwyrd, given her brash actions in the north and the possible fallout. While it may not have been the most careful expedition, she did get the result she wanted—Dr. Cere's death. Although she wished she had been able to glean a little more information from the man before he passed. What mattered now was doing this and perhaps being able to bring Edwyrd some piece of good news, considering that everything she had done so far had been far from pleasant.

With how the beginning of the visit started, she thought that this was bound to be more of the same. Bad things came in threes, as the old proverb went. When she arrived, she had been ushered into the estate by Lady Aprah's receiver and placed in the lady's chambers. Alone. And she stayed there, alone, for at least an hour. No guards. No servants. No one came to check on her.

At first, she merely thought this was a formality. No doubt Lady Aprah was busy tending to another matter. But as the minutes passed by, her suspicions grew. A glass of water in her hand, she had been musing over everything that had thus far occurred on this trip when she noticed a few chips off the cabinet. She ran her fingers over the chips of wood and then continued examining the room. Even though the floor was carpeted in thick burgundy, she spotted red splotches of different coloring. Had it always been there, or had there been some kind of struggle in this room? What exactly was going on? Why hadn't Lady Aprah come back yet?

She was in the midst of kneeling on the carpet, petting the hardened bloodstains, when the door opened. Immediately, she stood, hand on the hilt of her scimitar as Lady Aprah entered, accompanied by three large men. Lady Aprah expression was unamused, and her eyes drifted down to Tundra's hand. Tundra didn't let go, though she kept the sword sheathed. One by one she glanced at the men and then let her posture slip when she recognized the one farthest to the right.

"Cadmar?"

The man didn't say anything. Instead, Lady Aprah's hardened face broke into joy and tears. She rushed Conseleigh Iycel and, before Tundra knew it, embraced her in a hug. "Conseleigh Iycel, it is so good you are here. So..." She pulled back, keeping her hands latched onto Tundra's upper arms. "So, fortunate, actually."

"Excuse me?"

"I'm sorry to keep you waiting, but matters dragged me away. You will hear about them later. Horm, pour Conseleigh Iycel and myself a glass of whiskey."

Without questioning the demand, the largest man stepped out of formation and went over to the dresser where a vase of water lay amongst other decanters more full than empty. He brought over two cups of whiskey.

Lady Aprah took it and smiled at Conseleigh Iycel. "To health and to life." She shot it back.

Tundra looked at the glass. *What is going on?* When Lady Aprah gently nudged her drink, Tundra took it as the cue to drain it. She did so and coughed afterwards. She hadn't had a hard liquor like that for a year, perhaps even longer. Through her coughs, she repeated Lady Aprah's toast and then asked, "What is going on? Why?"

"Sit first. We have many things to talk about, Conseleigh Iycel, and I am happy that fate finds me standing face-to-face with you now. Why are you here? Wine or water? Or more whiskey, perhaps?"

Tundra settled into her seat across from Lady Aprah, still confused. The brief buoyancy Lady Aprah had demonstrated quickly faded, replaced by her usual decorum. She sat with her back straight, legs crossed, and one hand on her lap, loosely clasped around her other arm that supported her head.

"Water is fine for me."

"Water and another whiskey then, Horm." Lady Aprah snapped her fingers.

The large man poured the drinks and brought them over.

Bumbling for words, Tundra eventually managed, "I am here on behalf of the Guardian of the Core. I want to..." Tundra exhaled deeply. "I want to sincerely apologize face-to-face for the repercussions of my actions in the north. I, well, I know that it is one of the reasons you voted against Edwyrd. I mean, the Guardian, at the hearing."

Lady Aprah looked at her, calculating. "You can call him, Edwyrd. I know about your intimacy. It was quite touching the way he stood up for you in the hearing." She looked down to her whiskey and swooshed it around. "As for the incident in the north, well, it was most unfortunate. I lost many good men there."

"Boras is he..."

"He's busy on another assignment."

"Already?"

"While only third in rank, he is our best tracker. That is why I sent him with you to the north. He did his job there, and hopefully, he'll do his job here."

Tundra eyed Lady Aprah curiously. She fingered the lip of her glass.

"You'll hear more about that later. Anyway, what else do you have for me?"

"Besides my apology for being reckless with your men, I want to ask you not to take my actions and hold them against the Guardian. Edwyrd needs all the support he can get currently, and nations like yours, strong nations with the determination of youth, are what is needed now more than ever."

Lady Aprah pushed her lips to one side. "Is that so? Why?"

"Edwyrd believes there is a war coming. Not just to Gar. Or to Acquava or Sereya, or any other nation on the other planets. But he believes the war will be on all planets. A system-wide war."

Lady Aprah shifted in her seat. She sipped wine. "Isn't that already what is happening?"

"I beg your pardon?"

"Tensions between Sereya and Gar are high after your show in the north. We will go to war, that much I am certain of. It is just a matter of when and if there is a further catalyst, beyond the removal of Astor Grime's head. Ka'Che, from what I hear, is defending itself against Chaon and Empora. Cresica and Epoch are going to war. It seems the only planet so far unscathed is Pyre, but why have war when those inhabitants constantly battle their environment every day? However, I want you to know, Conseleigh Iycel, that I forgive you for your actions."

Tundra cocked her head. "You what?"

"Forgive you. If you couldn't tell by my lavish embrace, I do not hate you. Not anymore. While you put Gar into quite the predicament, you have also saved my life. And maybe even the life of Mr. Briggs behind me. Time will tell."

Tundra fumbled for her words. Before she could formulate any, Lady Aprah continued.

"The day I came back from the hearing in Mistral, Cadmar Briggs came back from his Passage."

"That is good to hear."

"Perhaps." She clicked her lips. "At first, I thought it happened to be just mere happenstance we returned together, but when I consulted with Horm and found out that his time was ninety-four days, well, I grew suspicious. That is nearly as good as Horm. And that is better than his father."

"I don't see—"

"Let me finish, please. At the meeting, it was clearly demonstrated how Victor Zigarda had employed shapeshifters to falsify records for some of the Trials participants. It made me think back on your words to me before you went north, describing how Cadmar Briggs's blood may also have been compromised. So, while Mr. Briggs most certainly could have returned to Visis the same day as I did, it seemed almost too coincidental for my liking.

"As propriety demanded of me, though, I met with him, tired and sleep-deprived as I was. I was mulling over a glass of wine when he came to my chambers. When he entered, I looked at him up and down and saw him in an outfit that he most likely would have worn for the Passage."

Tundra flicked her gaze to Cadmar, who still stood silently alongside his father. He had since lost the furs he had draped over his shoulders when happenstance allowed them to meet on the Dunes of White in the days of Pirini Lilapa.

"Cadmar, come over here. Let Conseleigh Iycel examine you."

Cadmar came to stand by his lady's side. His eyes looked at Tundra pleadingly, as if everything she said determined his fate. What had happened?

"Conseleigh Iycel, is this the man you saw on the Passage?"

"He didn't have a sling when I saw him."

"I got it after—"

"Quiet." Lady Aprah held up a fist. "Now, Conseleigh Iycel, do you happen to know whether or not Mr. Briggs had secured his Goddess Flower for me?"

"He did." Tundra nodded.

"Interesting..." Lady Aprah purred. She glanced casually at Cadmar. "He seems to have lost it somewhere in his Passage."

"Your men be finding me outside Visis and me and Fayser—"

"Yes. Yes. Yes. They were destroyed. I know."

Cadmar slumped his shoulders.

"The problem is, Conseleigh Iycel, is that this is also the man I saw after I returned from the hearing. He didn't have a broken arm at that point, though, and there was a change of clothes, but that could be altered easily. He didn't have a Goddess Flower. And that is what struck me as odd. Besides completing the Passage that is the *only* thing they should really care about returning to me. Yet, he nor his partner had one."

"The arm?" Tundra asked, nodding to it with her chin.

"Yes. Well, when I noticed that that Cadmar or this Cadmar," she tilted her head to her right, "came to me without a Goddess Flower, I grew suspicious. I talked with him, but could realize nothing off with his speech, so I offered him a seat to rest after such a long Passage. He denied it. This made me more suspicious. Remembering your words, I tried to find something else wrong with this Cadmar, so that I could prove he was fake, but I couldn't. Instead, I embraced Cadmar and slipped a small quartz ring I carried into his pocket. It's new technology we are developing here, but being quartz, it is wired to electromagnetic currents and, thus, is trackable. We like to know where all of our technology is here in Gar.

"After the short embrace, I told him 'Surely, you must be thirsty. At least let me get you something to drink.' I turned my back to get him a glass of wine for his accomplishment, but I never got to serve that wine. When I turned my back, Cadmar stabbed me with a knife. Here." Lady Aprah twisted her shoulder and pulled down the strap of her dress, revealing a large gash near her left shoulder blade. She turned back around and pointed to the side of her ribcage. "Then he stabbed me here. By this time, two guards entered. I had my wine glass in my hand and smashed the side of his head with it. He stumbled back. A guard of mine through a knife into his chest, wounding him, but the man still managed to escape out through my balcony window."

Tundra looked to the sliding glass doors, not having seen anything out of the ordinary.

"I already had it repaired. Seeing as it was Cadmar who just tried to take my life, I told Corrigan to track his son through Blood Bonding, just in case that ring had fallen out. Corrigan returned to me with this one."

"I be the real one," Cadmar said, his voice hoarse with emotion.

"Son...," Corrigan cautioned.

"Why would I be returning to Visis if I just be trying to murder Lady Aprah? It be making no sense. And what be about Fayser?"

"Fayser could have been waiting outside city limits. You both could have been changed during your passage. The Passage's cruelty brews resentment in some."

Tundra spared a glance at everyone in the room. "So what happens now, Olivia?"

"Now, we wait. For Boras. The best-case scenario is that my tracker brings back the *real* culprit and clears Cadmar's name. And in the worst case, Cadmar is hanged for treason."

"How much longer are you—"

The doors burst open. Corrigan and Horm spun at attention, weapons already in the air. Muffled shouts reached Tundra's ears. She raised an eyebrow and cautiously stood up.

Lady Aprah bolted up. "You're back? And?" She darted around the couch to greet Boras. "Well, well, well..." Lady Aprah turned to Cadmar. "I am sorry to have doubted you, Cadmar."

Tundra maneuvered around the couches to stand beside Lady Aprah. There, on the floor in front of her, writhed a man within a net sack. A gag prevented him from uttering anything other than grunts. "Boras..."

"It be nice to see you, Conseleigh Iycel. I didn't know you be here."

"Is that..." Tundra's words faded into nothing. Her mouth hung open as she stared at the man on the floor. He wasn't Cadmar. Far from it. He seemed ordinary. "Are you sure that it is him?"

"There is only one way to tell. Boras, Corrigan, Horm restrain him."

As a collective unit, the three large men brought the man up to his knees. Through the netting, Horm held him around his throat and waist with thick forearms. The other two held his arms. The man glanced feverishly as Lady Aprah approached him. He squirmed, but he was no match for the men who held him. Coolly, Lady Aprah pushed her hand through the netting into the man's pocket. She pulled out a ring and held it in front of her face. Terror now filled the man's eyes. He struggled against his yokes but to no avail.

Tundra stepped alongside Lady Aprah and watched as she put the ring back on her finger. "So, this is truly the shapeshifter, then?"

"Yes, Conseleigh Iycel. I believe that it is."

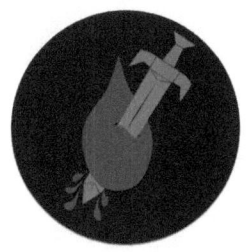

# INTERLUDE 4 - SEAGUARD

After such an emotional hearing, Aiton had thought that he could have had a few moments of reprieve to collect himself, but fate wasn't so kind to him. A few days after Aiton had returned, Sachiel Rio, the elected senator of Acquava who resided in Mistral, had called Aiton with news to make his dreams dashed once again.

"When does this stipulation come into effect?"

"It already has been passed, Receiver Dornell."

"Why such urgency?" Elias asked, hunching forward in his chair.

"Lady Liliana Voux's family has been abruptly killed."

Aiton's eyes bulged.

"Killed?" Darien asked.

"Killed," Sachiel repeated. "We are unsure yet as to what spurred it. Rumors say an assassination. Others say simply a tragic ship malfunction."

"Well, that is certainly unfortunate. Suspects?" Darien raised an eyebrow.

"None yet. But there has been talk now of implementing new stipulations to lay claim to the family in power here. If anything, it might help our lord's claim."

"By what do you mean?" Darien asked.

"There is a movement to make the voting process democratic, not just limiting it to those families of Power."

"Is that so? Who is leading such a thing?"

"A new politician from Mistral, Audra Toso."

Darien hummed to himself. "I have never heard of her before. What does she want?"

"I do not know either, but I think it may help the lord's claim regardless."

"Yes, I am thinking that as well," Darien said. He strummed his chin a little. "Very well. Good day. Thank you for keeping us afloat in this sea of information."

The connection cut.

"A whole family dead? War between Gar and Sereya again?" Professor Haruko sighed. The whole system is collapsing, I feel." He rubbed his forehead with one hand. The other supported his bent over body. Aiton's tutor looked over at Aiton. "I am sorry that you have to reign in times such as these, young lord."

"As am I," Elias said. "Your father ruled during prosperity."

"This incident only makes our need to find the lord an adequate advisor that much more pressing," Darien took control of the room again. "We must think of options."

And so, for another few days after the pressing news, in addition to listening to all the complaints and pleas from denizens who came to the castle, Aiton sat in tedious, long meetings with his council with the aim of making this appointment. Elias, Haruko, Darien, and Korth each nominated a viable option to replace the late advisor, Len Posair, and they went back and forth contemplating the advantages and disadvantages of each. This was exceedingly dull, with many points rehashed as endlessly as a sea would continue to swell onto the shore. In the end, Aiton just decided that the best man to be his advisor was the one Korth had suggested, Drake Pilar. While he had many great attributes, none surpassed the fact that Korth nominated him, meaning he was native to the Hart Isles. If this person was to be giving him advice all the time, at least it would be pleasant to his ear. While not the most scientific method for choosing, Aiton figured it would work, and so afterwards, they prepared their things and took to the sea to visit the man and make the selection official. If the man accepted, an inauguration ceremony would follow.

Four days into their departure from the capital, while sailing through the Hartless Strait, Korth pointed out a city on the southern tip. "You see that there?"

"Uh huh? Where is that?"

"That is called Seaguard, Aiton. That is where I am from."

Aiton chuckled.

"What's so funny?"

"And now you're an acqua guard. You haven't changed much, have you?"

Korth guffawed at Aiton's pun. He rubbed the boy's hair. "I guess it was my birthright."

Hands gripping the side of the ship, Aiton continued looking at the port-side town. "Do you have any family still there?"

"A father, I think. My mother has already passed."

Aiton turned to his guard. "You think? What do you mean? Don't you know?"

"It's been a while since I've seen him last. He's old and doesn't use technology."

"Can't you track him through blood?"

"I can. And I do, from time to time. Let me try now." Korth closed his eyes. A little while later, he opened them, flashed a quick glance at Aiton, and then closed his eyes again.

"Is everything okay?"

Korth opened his eyes a moment later. "I... my lord, would it be possible to make a stop in Seaguard for a moment?"

"Your father?"

"His pulse is weaker than normal. I want to know what's wrong."

"We stop."

Aiton left Korth and found Elias and Darien with the captain of the ship, Caspian Arno. "Caspian, dock at Seaguard."

"My lord?"

"Aiton, we have plans for Deider."

"We will get there in time, Darien. I've never been to the Hart Isles. I want to see Seaguard."

Darien looked at Elias and then back to Caspian.

"Well?" Aiton tapped his foot.

"Very well, my lord." Caspian spun the wheel to the port side.

Aiton ignored the comments of Darien and Elias as he walked away. However, they followed after him, hounding him for answers.

In Korth's presence, Aiton turned around. "Korth's father may be sick. It is our duty to look after one another, is it not?" He looked at each of them, waiting to see if either would try to refute his authority.

"It'll only be for a moment, Darien. I just need to see how he's doing. His pulse feels weak."

"Korth, I'm sorry. Of course. Take the time you need."

Within the hour, the ship docked at Seaguard, and Aiton followed Korth into town. Elias came as well, carrying his medicines in case there was something that needed to be done. Darien stayed back on the ship and made sure the ship's hands didn't travel too far while on a momentary reprieve from duty.

Seaguard was a quaint minor bay side town situated within the fjords of the straight. The houses along the bay were constructed of white walls and pink slate roofs. Above the city, on the terraced landscape of the high rocky hills that encompassed it and hid it from all points of view, were ancient walls that stretched the length of the city, helping to fortify it and protect it from land invasions.

The spellbinding landscape, though, wasn't as impressive as the number of cats in the city. And the variety. As Aiton walked through the old part of town full of simple folk, he noticed that cats outnumbered the people. At least, that is what it seemed from how many strays were wandering around the city's brick roads.

"This city is beautiful," Aiton said.

Korth nodded. "It is."

"Why are there so many cats, though?"

"They protect the city from the mice and rats and snakes of the mountains and the sea. They are our Seaguards." Korth chuckled. He bent down and pet a stray cat that rubbed against his boot.

"Interesting."

"It certainly is." Korth stood again and went down another alleyway that was narrower than the main road. "We are close now."

Within a few minutes, Aiton found himself inside a humble dwelling without any electricity. Instead, it relied on the natural sunlight that came through the open windows, wooden shades having already been rolled up. A fat cat lay on a wooden table, too lazy to scurry away even as Aiton wandered through the small abode with Korth and Elias.

No one was present in the living room. A rocking chair lay vacant in the corner, next to it a large tome, a blue feather inside to mark the current page.

"Pa?"

A cough. Korth jerked his head. He moved towards the adjoined kitchen and ducked through a low doorway. Past the kitchen, he went down a few steps to a room in the back of the house. Aiton and Elias followed closely behind, stopping as Korth hesitated behind a door that was slightly ajar. Korth rapped twice.

"Who's there?"

The door creaked opened with Korth's push. "Pa?"

"Delilah?"

Korth rushed inside and sat on a nightstand by a bed. An old man, even older than Elias, sat upright in the bed, wearing nothing but wrinkles that told his age. The woolen bedsheet covered his legs, leaving his upper body naked, exposing liverspots and a sunken ribcage. Frail arms lay at his side, one of them clutching a white cloth stained red. Korth's father looked and squinted at the movement in the room.

"Delilah, is that you?"

Korth took his father's right hand. "Delilah is dead, Pa."

"Korth?" The man leaned to the side and coughed into the handkerchief once more. More blood. "Korth, is that you?"

"Yes, Pa."

The man heaved into his handkerchief once more. After, he turned to look at his son with glassy eyes. He put a hand to Korth's jaw. "It is you."

"Of course." Korth pressed his own hand against his father's.

"Good. Now I can..." Korth's father coughed. "Rest." He smiled and closed his eyes.

"Pa?" Korth nudged his father gently, to no avail. "Pa?" Then again, with the same result.

"Aiton, let's go," Elias whispered in Aiton's ear, then tugged the collar of his shirt.

Aiton left Korth with his father. It was only proper to give him time alone. Aiton knew what it was to be at a dying father's side.

Aiton went with Elias to the living room, and while Elias went over to sit on a couch, Aiton moved towards the rocking chair. Next to it lay an untitled, leather-bound book. Casually, Aiton opened the book to the page the feather was marking. The feather began to float, and he slapped his hand down to keep it in place, then eyed it. He looked around and noticed the window shutters weren't shut. *It must have been the wind.*

Keeping his hand on the feather, Aiton moved it aside and began reading, or trying to read. The pages were filled with scribbled notes, each dated. *A journal.* Aiton's eyes grew wide, and he flipped through the pages, seeing a copious amount of entries, some long, some short, and others that were hardly legible as ink smears overran the pages in question.

When Aiton heard the shuffling of footsteps, he put the book back into place beside the rocking chair.

"My lord?"

Aiton straightened his posture as best as he could on the rocking chair.

"Perhaps it's best if you and Elias go along ahead with Darien and Haruko. I need to take care of some things here."

"Do you need any help?"

"It's no such thing for a lord to do. I will be fine. I need to visit some others who knew him, too."

Aiton glanced at Elias, who gave a subtle nod.

"We can pick you back up on our return from Deider. Will that be enough time?"

"It will suffice, my lord."

Aiton pushed himself off the rocking chair. "Is there anything I can do?"

Korth kneeled down on the ground to Aiton's level. He forced a smile. "Do you remember what I taught you?"

"You've taught me a lot of things."

Korth chuckled. He wiped away a tear from his eye with a thumb. "Warriors still standing do not stand still. I will keep moving, and so should you. We are true Acquavans, are we not? Are we not water? Do we not flow?"

Aiton smiled. "We do."

"Then there is nothing else that needs to be done. A broken heart is just the start, but I will get through this, and I know you will, too. Go to Deider and convince Drake to be your advisor. He is a solid businessman and, like all of us on the Hart Isles, he's resilient."

Aiton nodded. He flung himself around Korth and hugged him. "I will keep moving."

"You best, Little Lord. For the sake of Acquava, you best." Korth stood up. "Elias, did you bring anything to prepare my father's body for burial?"

"Yes. I can do that now if you'd like."

Korth nodded. "Please. I trust you more than other adored in the city."

"I shouldn't be too long." Elias disappeared into the bedroom.

Aiton went back to the rocking chair. "Is this your father's journal?" Aiton tapped the leather-bound book.

Korth strolled over to the book and weighed it in his hands. He examined the cover and then flipped through the pages. "My family's journal, actually. My father and his father and his father always kept an account of important things that happened in their lives."

"Why don't you?"

Korth smiled. "Well, I guess it's my turn now after all these years." He leafed through the page, stopping at the blue feather. "Do you want to see something fascinating, Aiton?"

Aiton's eyes lit up. "Yes."

"Take this feather and watch it closely."

Aiton took the feather by the quill and held it in front of him. At first, nothing. Soon, though, he noticed the feather bend slightly. He furrowed his brows and then looked outside. It wasn't windy at all. He continued looking at the feather as it gradually swayed on its own.

"It moves."

"It does. My grandfather told me the story that his grandfather told him and that his grandfather told him. Or something like that. I don't remember exactly how many generations we've kept this feather, but it is the reason why my family started the journal."

"It is?"

"Malik Irvine found this one day while he was at sea. Well, actually, it was in the stomach of an enormous fish that he had netted. A fish as big as this house, the story goes. Maybe even bigger. It was so big that it took up the entire net, and it had a sword on its head.

"Cutting that fish open, he found the feather. Undigested. Everything else in its stomach was clean or partly dissolved, but not this. Then it started moving by itself as if it had a mind of its own. Malik wrote down his thoughts about that day, and ever since then we've kept writing entries in that book when something significant happens. Or lucky.

"He claimed it was a magic, lucky feather. He gave it to his son, who eventually gave it to his daughter, Cordelia, once upon a time when she was accepted for the very same Trials that Guardian Eska won."

"Cordelia?"

"Well, let me continue my story, Little Lord. Cordelia did not succeed at the Trials, but she passed it on to her own daughter, Sabrina, who married my great grandfather, Douglas Centill. And then it was passed down to my grandfather, Calder, then to my father, and now I guess it is mine."

"So a member of your family almost became Guardian?"

"I'm unsure how close Cordelia came to succeeding in those Trials. But that is how this feather came into our possession and all of that is written in that journal. And more."

Aiton's eyes bulged at the journal. He couldn't wait to read it. If Korth would let him, that is. Aiton drew his attention back into the feather. "So this is like a Power feather?" He spun its quill between his index and thumb.

"Sure. You can call it that if you want. Aiton, I want you to have it."

Aiton fumbled with the feather. He caught it again. Mouth open, he looked at Korth. Stammering for words, he finally pointed to himself and said, "Me? But it's your family's heirloom."

"Aye, but I have this." Korth held up the book. "And that's all I need. You should have the feather. It's lucky. And as a lord, you need all the luck you can get. Am I right? Especially now, in the aftermath of the Curse and the meeting with Drake in a few days."

He wouldn't get to read the book, then. The fleeting sadness lasted only a handful of seconds. Aiton knew he shouldn't be greedy. He already had more support than he could have asked for with Korth, Darien, and Elias. He didn't need the feather and the book as well. Watching it bend and curve as it spun it between his fingertips, Aiton glanced at Korth. "Are you sure? What if I lose it?"

"Don't lose it. Give it here. I'll make a necklace for you."

Aiton handed the feather over to Korth. Korth disappeared into the kitchen and returned in hardly no time at all. In front of Aiton, he pulled tight on some fishing line to form a chain that he laced through the quill of the feather.

"This should hold. It'll be your lucky feather now." Korth dropped the necklace over Aiton's head. "You do have luck by your side, after all. You found Zarya. Aiton Paen, the luckiest lord in Acquava." Korth nudged Aiton's arm.

Aiton smiled, and he held the feather up in front of him, twisting it by the quill before stuffing it under his shirt. "I will keep it safe." Aiton hugged Korth.

"Good. And it will keep you safe, too."

Elias returned, passing through the kitchen to join them. "Korth."

Korth let go of the embrace and stood up. "Is it done?"

"It is. The minerals I put on his body will delay decomposition for a few days, but that should be more than enough time."

"Thank you, Elias."

"My pleasure. Aiton, are you ready to go now?"

"Yeah. We must keep moving."

"Spoken like a true warrior." Korth laughed. "I will see you in a couple of days, then."

Aiton nodded. He and Elias left Korth and wandered back through the city streets, littered with cats. Aiton walked fast, wanting to continue moving forward and never becoming still, just as Korth suggested he should do. He would become a lord as great as his father one day. He knew it. And now, he had luck on his side to help.

# PART III - PLANS AWRY

## CHAPTER 30

# A DARK, HOT PLACE

D arkness enveloped Desmós. The sounds of animals prowling, thirsty and hungry, stalked him. He maneuvered through stalactites and stalagmites to the constant dripping of boiling water that came from the land above. Desmós had driven the ship as far into the darkness as he could take it, causing him to abandon it for the time being outside a division of the cavern too narrow and shallow for its body. The monitor had showed a blip and dot twenty kilometers to the northeast. He walked in that direction now.

He hadn't known this place existed. It hadn't existed the first time he'd come. He'd known only the land above, full of heat and sulfur. The combination would bite most noses, but not his. And while sulfur still lingered here, it wasn't as prominent. Darkness was prominent. The lights had faded twenty kilometers from the city, and since then, darkness had been his only companion—darkness, but not silence. Magma streams rumbled above, boiling water dripped, hissing, from the cavernous ceiling, and he could hear the shuffling steps of creatures, creatures that would fill most men with fear. However, he wasn't most men. And unlike most men, the darkness didn't bother him either, for he could see perfectly fine.

This darkness, and the things it hid, were, he assumed, why Guardian Eska had chosen to scatter a jewel here. If one could not see it, one could not obtain it and use its power. Or abuse its power.

Up above, in the land he knew, he had found the previous jewel within great, volcanic towers in the north. Magma had oozed from them like drool. Occasionally, the mouths would spit gobs of fire, and those would fall near him, even splashing his skin at times, but he didn't feel any pain that would have normally followed. Ash fell down around him like snow.

The deep red jewel cut like a diamond had been located on one of the volcano's cliffs, in a nest that belonged to a wyvern. Splotches of black, almost like trapped soot, could be seen within. For most men, it would have proven a precarious jewel to obtain. However, he wasn't most men. Using Power, he had cracked the felsic floor underneath him and ridden it like a platform. It gained girth and elevation when it needed to, eventually coming to rest eye-to-eye with the nest of stones where wyvern laid their eggs on a bed of ash and soot.

Hatchlings had cried and hissed and fluttered around him. Hardly baring teeth, they posed no considerable threat. The threat came in the form of the mother swooping down from another of the towers. He remembered the green, toxic fire it spewed in the air as it approached and its roar as it called a warning to him. Any good mother would have done the same for her children, and he was pleased by this resolve of the creature. Within one hundred meters, though, the threat ceased. The wyvern recognized who it was with her hatchlings and stopped its calling, staying silent while circling above him. Her hatchlings joined, and soon it seemed that he had a halo of creatures over him, protecting him and watching him. Like many of the animals that encountered him, they watched history. They viewed their origin, and soon, when all the jewels were collected, they would see history come back to life, and with it, proper reign and rule.

In truth, there were only three types of creatures that he needed to worry about. The first were any other humans who had bright ideas of interrupting his reunion. The prince whose body he occupied had come too close to severing his bond, and he couldn't allow that to happen again. The next were animals bonded to humans who no longer served their True Master and Creator, but the false one they adopted as their own. And the third were his direct sisters: Rhayna, Chantico, Thalassa, and Gaia. They had been gifts to the Kings of old to dismantle any sort of attempted hierarchy the other Ancients tried to thrust upon the domains they created. They listened to no one but those who were chosen to be their rulers, the True Kings.

He doubted he would find any of those entities here in this dark, hot place. He paused and scanned the surroundings. He twitched his lips to one side. The boiling of water echoed off the cavern walls, now noticeable because his footsteps no longer drowned them out. *East.* He looked down and noticed a tiny rivulet running near his feet. *That will lead me to the water. Perhaps it is there.* Using the knowledge that he had seen while the prince had acquired the other jewels, the Guardian was sure to have had it placed somewhere near impossible for an ordinary man to get to. If darkness wasn't enough, within boiling water that a normal man couldn't see would surely do the trick. However, he wasn't most men.

He followed the rivulet east and noticed it grow in girth and strength. While he walked, he moved his hand down to the side of his leg to pat the satchel tied to the belt on his hip. Now and then, he took a moment to reaffirm its secureness and the number there: nine. Soon to be ten.

He then took a moment to wrap his fingers around the leather hilt of the Ether Weapon. It was a decent blade, Purge, but it paled in comparison to some of its brothers and sisters and was nothing compared to his master's blade. He knew he was lucky that the man had never unlocked its true potential, as that would have ended his quest. But he didn't have to worry about him anymore.

Bats and other mammals with wings hung from the ceiling. In the shadows where his vision didn't quite reach, he noticed golem-like figures slink away into more darkness. Every so often, he would pass a gargoyle that clung to a stalactite with their stone claws, red eyes fixed on him. Besides the slight movement of their neck and head as he passed, they continued holding onto the stalactites, wings outstretched. In truth, all animals noticed him, as they should. Most, however, were too timid to bother him, or they approached close enough to smell his scent, then retreated in fear of his authority.

After half an hour of walking by the stream, it led him to a giant bubbling and hissing pool. Steam escaped to the ceiling and then crawled outward as it tried to find more space to continue its upward travel.

He bent down and bounced on the balls of his feet. The continual bubbling of water burst in front of his face. The steam that rose from the pool didn't burn his face or make him close his eyes like it would most men. In fact, his vision allowed him to see directly into the pool of water where an orange jewel shone fiercely in its depths. *Perfect.*

"*Vesi.*"

The water spilled over the floor and slowly dissipated from the pool, leaving just a dried-out well and an orange jewel that glowed as if fire burned inside. While keeping control of the spell, he jumped into the well and bent down to pick up the remnant and put it in his satchel. *Two more to...*

Thud. Thud. Panting, like the lapping of a tongue.

*Hmmm...* He stood up and looked around. Three sets of yellow eyes peered at him from the distance. They moved forward collectively, a little vibration accompanying them each time. Soon enough, the whites of their teeth showed. Eventually, he came to realize that it was not three separate dogs but one dog with three heads and fur as dark as the blackness that enveloped him.

With the use of Power, he elevated his position so that he could be face-to-face with the beast. It stopped in front of him, teeth barred. A low growl. The show didn't alarm him enough to put a hand to his hilt. He stood there, letting the cerberus evaluate him. When all three heads had the chance to look into his eyes, pitch as the surrounding area, it knelt in fealty to its superior. *Good. This will make things easier. In time all these animals will serve me and my father.*

He mounted the great beast and whispered in its ear. It roared and moved back towards the ship in great, giant leaps that showed the muscle and might of the animal. As it bounded back to the ship, the other creatures scattered to and fro, paws pumping on the ground or wings whipping the air, trying to escape its ferocity.

Within an hour, he found himself back at the ship. Its lights were off, but he didn't need light to see its silhouette. As he approached, the ship turned on automatically, realizing the shell had returned.

He hit the ground, shoulder first, head second. For a moment, his vision blurred. His head spun. The clattered steel from his scabbard reverberated throughout the caverns. Still on the ground, he noticed the great beast twist and turn in violent throes in the glare of the headlights. It roared then fled, seeking the darkness it much preferred.

He looked at the ship with disdain. He spat on the ground and stood. After a quick padding of his shell to check if the jewels and sword were still intact, he went to the belly of the ship and entered.

He sat down in the cockpit and let his muscle memory take over as he looked at the foreign control panel. A blip occurred to the south. It was close. But it was moving. He stared at it for a while longer, trying to figure out its direction. *Had an animal swallowed this next gem or is the ship malfunctioning?* It moved northeast, towards the access point above. He curved his lips and furrowed his brows, then pushed a few more buttons. *It can move all it likes. I will cut it out from the belly of whichever beast swallowed it. Then I will go to the Core. Once I collect that, my brother will be free, and everyone will see greater things once again. They will see things like I have seen and will revel in the beauty and divinity that is restored. They will say my master's words: ajid volintasey fuan and truly find themselves, for the first time.*

CHAPTER 31

# CHANTICO

I n Lurid, the morning came without the dawn. As the nation was underground, Cain slept in darkness and woke in darkness. Anxiety and anticipation were his bedfellows as he sat on the edge of his bed, shoulders slumped,
head down, and forearms resting on his knees. *Today is the day.* In time, his
fingers made their way up to the necklace and tugged the feather free from
beneath his shirt. He twirled it. *Today I meet Chantico.*

He had left everything and everyone he had known to get to this point.
His father he had left in shock and confusion. His mother he had left in tears
of joy and adulation. In hope. For he had come back to the castle, finally
understanding who he was. All his life, she had been telling him of his birthright,
making sure he always took care of the necklace she had given him when he
was only five. She had given him book upon book of heroes to read, cultivating
in him a drive to become his own hero. For all those years, he had been too
blind to see what it truly meant. And Brenton he had left with pride filling his
chest. He had only known the man for a fortnight, yet Cain felt as though their
relationship spanned a lifetime already.

A knock came at his door.

"Cain, are you ready? It is breakfast."

"I will be out shortly, Eirek." He remained sitting on the bed.

As if he were back on Epoch, he looked out the window and saw only
blackness. Why they had a window in this inn was beyond him to begin with,
but he assumed it was for travelers who needed some semblance of their home
life, and from it one could see the faint glows that the city cast. In a different

room, he would have been able to see much more, but this faced only the Silver Road.

Conseleigh Inferno had explained that because of how new the nation of Lurid actually was, the people that lived here only lived in major cities or the capital. The major cities lay a day's ride or more by hovercraft from the capital, which was located in the center of the nation. To make traveling safer down in this abyss, each major city controlled a very powerful silver beacon that washed over not only the streets and homes, but flooded for miles and miles and miles each direction. These lights that shot into the darkness were called the Silver Roads. It was the Luridians attempt to create an artificial feeling of sunlight for those who moved here from up above, and to some degree it worked, but Cain would have much preferred to have woken to the smell of his family's garden and actual light from Freyr and Lugh.

Cain tucked the necklace back into his shirt and stood up. He walked to the desk in his room, grabbed Protector, and slung it over his back. Then he went downstairs to join the others for breakfast.

"Did you sleep well?" Eirek asked.

"Not really," Cain admitted.

"Nerves are to be expected, Prince Evber." Conseleigh Inferno scooped what appeared to be a porridge with white worms into his mouth. After swallowing with a slurp, he said, "But you should dispel them as quickly as possible. Bonding is much like controlling Power."

Cain twisted his face at the sight of such a treat. It gave too much away.

The conseleigh leaned forward and spoke in a whisper. "Also, as King of Pyre, you will most likely need to acquire the taste for the cuisine here. I suggest you start with these." He pushed forward a different plate that contained some biscuits, a pool of red paste, sliced purple fruit dotted with many tiny seeds, and a steel bowl that held the same porridge.

"Right." Going with what appeared to be a safer option first, Cain took the biscuit, sliced it in two, and slathered the red paste over the flaky surface. When he bit down, the distinct taste of cinnamon hit his palate, followed by the familiarity of the semi-stale bread. "Sorry for my behavior earlier." Cain took another bite. "The food here is not that bad."

"I agree. Growing up on Pyre my whole life, I understand that the food here is a little dryer than one would typically expect. The heat robs the bread of its moisture, but the dragon fruit on your plate and the soup are good as well."

"Thanks." Cain gave an awkward laugh. "What were you mentioning about bonding?" He buttered the other side of his biscuit.

"Bonding is like controlling Power." The conseleigh looked at Cain first and then Eirek, arms extended outward like he was telling a story. "There needs to be confidence. Power does not lend itself to just anyone, only those who know they can use it."

"Chantico will try to judge my worth, then?"

Conseleigh Inferno shook his head. "Not try. Will. And we should refer to her by *She* now. You never know what ears are listening." He motioned his head backwards to a few other people of light red skin and some completely pale, who also sat in the dining room.

"What will it feel like?"

The conseleigh didn't answer right away. Instead, he looked out one of the windows in the dining room. Cain noticed a quick flash. Through open doors came a phoenix that perched itself on the conseleigh's shoulder. He stroked its head and answered in a voice lost in reminiscence. "Every animal is different, of course. But for me, it was a moment of intense satisfaction when I bonded with Nil. Like I finally found a new part of myself that had been hidden and I could do anything."

The words brought a smile to Cain's face. A second later, it flat-lined as the conseleigh continued.

"But you can't. Remember that." He took the finger that he used to pet Nil and pointed it at Cain, then at Eirek. "Both of you."

"What do you mean?" Eirek asked.

"You will have increased strength and stamina. Nil here gave me all of that, and I can only imagine what *She* will bring you. You must be wary, though, Prince Evber. That is how the last King fell because he thought he could do anything."

Cain gulped. "Could you tell me about him? What do you know?"

"He lived in what used to be Vatu Village. After countless raids, the village was destroyed. The King couldn't do anything about it. You see, when the Third One bestowed *Her* upon him, he did so with the condition that he could create more creatures to fill the planet with, one for every person. Some animals like the phoenixes were peaceful, but other animals like the zubin were malicious animals. Constantly, they besieged the city and eventually they stole away the King's son. When he found him next, the boy was already dead. Soon to be a brother, too, for his mother carried a baby within her. Determined not to let this happen again, he declared a genocide on the zubins and they were almost completely wiped out with the help of *Her.* But other creatures helped their fellow brethren and soon the King became overwhelmed and died. That is when *She* disappeared, and that is when Vatu Volcano erupted last." He lathered a slice of bread with red paste. "Until recently, of course."

"You mentioned yesterday that if the bonder dies, then the animal does as well. Why didn't *She?*"

"I have two possible explanations. Well, three. First, and most unlikely, is that *She* is dead, and what you saw, Prince Evber up on top of the volcano during the Trial is your imagination. Second, *She* is powerful enough to live by herself. But, I think the third option is that a new heir had already been conceived by the time of the King's death. In the story, the wife is pregnant at the time of her husband's death and gives birth shortly thereafter. Because of this, I think the third option is the most reliable." Conseleigh Inferno finished his bread and then tidied his lips. "Are you finished?"

Cain nodded. Eirek did as well.

The conseleigh stood. "Then let's go. Lady Scule has supplied us with a special hovercraft to making driving in Lurid easier, harnessing the light of the Silver Roads. Now that they shine, we should go."

Cain noticed that light had blanketed the city during their lengthy discussion. He and Eirek followed the conseleigh to where a different hovercraft was stationed alongside the conseleigh's. Similar in size, the only real difference could be seen in the reflective panels attached to the roof and sides, making the hovercraft look like a suit of armor. As they drove, the light ricocheted off the hovercraft's panels, giving them all a full view of the area while driving.

"How long until we reach the Forge?" asked Eirek.

"A few hours. Normally it would be longer."

"Why isn't it?"

"After supper last night, I arranged a meeting with Marchioness Corvina Delaynie of Colby, who met with me to give me this hovercraft from Lady Scule. She also mentioned that Lady Scule informed her of our request to access the Forge so she made sure no workers will be there today."

Cain glanced at the conseleigh. "Didn't she ask why we are traveling there in the first place?"

"Of course. I told her regulations on the Forge and labor rights have come into question with Guardian Eska. I needed to say something to make it justifiable why the area should be evacuated." Keeping his hands on the steering wheel, he turned to Cain. "More importantly, Prince Evber, I needed a way to arrange a private meeting for you with Chantico, and that is what I did."

"No one will suspect anything?"

"Well, I don't know about that, but why should they? I am Guardian Eska's conseleigh, and a previous Lord of Therus. They have no reason to suspect anything. More importantly, I wanted to protect you, both of you, and the people."

"The people?"

"In case there are any *surprises*."

Cain arched an eyebrow. "Surprises? Like my inability to bond?"

"Something like that."

"Do you think that will be the case?" Cain asked.

"Confidence breeds compliance. If you question your ability to control her, things may go awry. But from my observations of you, and the fact that you do indeed have a feather much like the one in the stories, I believe you will succeed. When that happens, we will need to discuss with Guardian Eska how to release such information."

"Why is that?"

"Privacy at the Forge today is a two-edged sword. It will protect many but may delegitimize your claim, as the only witnesses privy to the event will be Apprentice Mourse and I. Although our credibility is not questionable, some may not agree entirely with Guardian Eska and may see the move as usurping the current lords and ladies of the planet. There are more families in power that are at odds with Guardian Eska currently than those that are for him."

Cain knew what the conseleigh was referring to. He had no idea why Nathan Alaois had chosen to vote against Guardian Eska, but Cain couldn't help but think it had been something he said. Regardless, when Linn told him that Guardian Eska managed to retain his authority, even if by the slightest of margins, Cain had been relieved.

"In a single breath, Prince Evber, you will become more powerful and have more authority than anyone else on the planet, even more than I have. A change like that in such a short span of time may cause an imbalance. I hope you are ready for that. I hope the system is ready for such a flux in Power. Who knows what other Kings or Queens are out there."

"You believe there are more True Kings? Ahh Queens?" Eirek asked.

"I believe there is the possibility. After all, there have been numerous sightings of Rhayna on Myoli over the years. If rumors are true, Gaia has just shown herself again on Agrost. Chantico here. The only one who has yet to make an appearance is Thalassa."

No one responded. The depth of the information consumed them. At least, it consumed Cain. If he was a King, and there were others out there like him, then what did that mean for the system? Would they live in war or in peace with one another?

Up ahead, miles off in the distance, a faint glow split the darkness. Soon the light radiating from the hovercraft congealed with the natural light from up ahead.

Cain leaned forward and pointed. "Is that the Forge?"

"It is." The conseleigh nodded. His brows furrowed and lips became a straight line. "Your importance, both of you, goes without saying: an apprentice and a potential True King. Moments like these are one of the reasons I wanted to become part of Eska's conseleigh."

"And the others?" Eirek asked.

"Because of Guardian Eska. Growing up, knowing that the Guardian of the Core was from our planet, it created a sense of entitlement for many citizens here. I realized, earlier on, however, that the Guardian's role was rather exclusive to the Core and that he didn't interfere or visit planets or nations as much as I once thought. I had never been the Therus-born fighter like you see in Lord Requart now, or the firesons trained to protect him. I enjoyed the more elegant things in life, not the brutality of it. I suppose I was a disappointment to my father. Who knows?" He sighed. "Anyway, after conseleigh Ariel Scule of Lurid died, I took the opportunity to try for a position that better suited my skillset and my interests and allowed me to realize my dreams of meeting Guardian Eska."

"You had not seen him before?"

"Twice. Once at my father's funeral. The other time at my wedding."

"Do you regret it?" Eirek asked.

"Never. It has kept me busy, but not so busy to prohibit me from seeing my wife and children. We are almost there."

"Is that why you're here?"

"Guardian Eska gave me a special task after Pirini Lilapa, Prince Evber." Conseleigh Inferno repositioned his grip on the steering wheel. "And now he's tasked me to help you bond with Chantico."

*Hmmm... Is he hiding something?* Cain didn't want to overthink anything. Overthinking, he feared, would cause him to doubt his legitimacy. Instead, he counted the stalactites and stalagmites that passed them by, emptying his mind of everything, so that he could be prepared for anything.

Cain shifted in his seat. "You mentioned that the area we are going to today was evacuated due to your demands, correct?"

"Certainly. Why do you ask?"

"Well, if Chantico really lives here, why hasn't she shown herself to others before? Why has she allowed them to use her home?"

"You pose a good question. Let me explain. The Forge doesn't actually use any of the magma, like the surface uses. Zircha forging is much too delicate of a procedure to produce mass quantities. The pieces of metal are dipped into the Forge, held under for a minute or two, and then brought to the surface for fitting. A single zircha weapon undergoes this process several times, for after each fitting, the characteristics are saved in the storage unit, then fitted again with the characteristics of a different weapon. Many times, these weapons are made-to-order, meaning the buyers have a specific set of weapon types they want the model to carry, and if they would like more, they have to send the item back so that it can be put in the Forge once again."

The hovercraft slowed down. Cain could see five anvils, tall enough to be work stations if sitting down, and many tools. Flames darted up a wall at the back of the area, higher and higher, showing the curve and depth of the wall and lighting the area below it as if it were the backdrop to a play. Two cranes, attached with steel chains and, from those chains, steel boxes, sat near a cliff that cut off the expanse of the area. Bursts of fire licked the air in front of them, casting their brief shadows onto the backdrop.

The hovercraft stopped. Conseleigh Inferno exited; Cain followed. "How many actually work here, then?"

"Perhaps twenty. It isn't much. Any casualty, though, is bad. Remember that Prince Evber, because soon you are about to become this planet's protector. Are you ready?"

Cain furrowed his brows. He tightened his core. *I am fire.* He reached behind his back and withdrew Protector from his sheath.

"An Ether Weapon, Prince Evber? Why haven't I noticed that before?" Conseleigh Inferno asked.

"I just received it from my father." Cain mumbled. "My true father, I mean. In Kane." He looked down at it, watching the amethyst lines run up the cloudy gray steel. "Its name is Protector."

Conseleigh Inferno patted Cain's back. "Rightly named. Bond with Chantico and be Pyre's new protector. Does Guardian Eska know you have an Ether Weapon?"

Cain looked at Eirek.

"I didn't know until I met Cain up above."

"Well, this is certainly a new discovery. That leaves only..." Conseleigh Inferno closed his eyes and began counting on his fingers and mumbling under his breath. "There are three left unaccounted for."

"Three left?"

"Well, three that the Guardian does not know about. Guardian Eska has his own. And there are two others in his possession. He gave me this one before I left on my assignment." Conseleigh Inferno brandished a large warhammer with a thick square head, larger than his head. "Apprentice Mourse has one. Prince Paen has one. Cronos has one. And now you have one as well. That is good to know. Let's hope we never have to use them." Conseleigh Inferno gave a nervous chuckle and glanced at Eirek, who smiled. Not letting too much awkwardness settle in the moment, the conseleigh pushed Cain forward and nodded his approval. "It's time."

Cain approached, caution leaving his gait until the end, fifty meters from the cliff, when even he, born with blood of fire, felt the slightest bit of heat touch his skin. When the first bead of sweat dotted his forehead, he stopped and felt it. He put his fingertips to his eyes, behind his glasses that now began to fog. *Sweat?*

Rumbling shook the cavern, as if he was in the pit of some stomach. Flames flew higher into the air, eating away its lining. Cain pushed Protector into the ground and held onto it to brace himself against the tremors. Tremors became quakes, each one working its way up his body, shaking him enough that his glasses slid off his sweaty nose.

The shaking stopped.

Vision impaired, he looked up. Even without his glasses, he saw what looked back at him—Chantico. Keeping his eyes forward, he bent slowly at the knees, reaching blindly for his glasses.

The beast lurched forward, shifting its weight from the poised position in the air to the ground. As it slid, it sent fissures through the surrounding area. Behind him, anvils toppled over, creating deafening thuds. His fingers groped blindly, not wanting to remove his gaze from Chantico for even the slightest of seconds. *Where are... Found them.* Cain wiped the sweat from his face and donned his glasses. The fiery serpent slid around him, exposing to him its regal underbelly of gold and crimson scales streaked with orange. As it coiled around him, one level, then two levels, and then three, it isolated him from the others.

When it stopped, it kept its head poised to strike, eyes of fire locked on him, a long split tongue licking the air. *It is you. Again. I remember you from Vatu Volcano. Why do you return?*

Aggressive and native, her husky voice penetrated Cain's mind, causing him to take a step back. He quickly readjusted, not wanting to give in to her intimidation. He was worthy, and he would show it.

"Why did you hide underneath the volcano that day?" Cain called out to her.

*You returned to ask me that? I live in a sea of fire.* Her tongue licked the air. *Do not play coy with me.* She breathed and fire escaped from the slits of her nostril.

"And I in a sea of books. I know who you are, Chantico. My name is Prince Cain Evber. My true intention is to bond with you. You are mine!"

*I am no one's anymore. Only a son of fire can claim me. And you are not one of them.*

"I will show you that I am." Cain raised Protector in the air.

Her eyes pivoted towards the lance. Her lips pulled back, leaving her mouth slightly agape and exposing her fangs. *You mean to claim me by that?* The tongue assaulted the thick air. She lurched forward.

Upon impulse, Cain tore into his shirt, splitting it enough to expose his chest and the feather necklace that hung there.

She stopped, her head hovering only a spear's length from Cain. Flakes of yellow and red hid in the orange eyes that bore into him. She hissed, loud enough and strong enough to bring Cain to one knee. Slowly, she constricted her body around him.

As the first parts of Chantico's underbelly touched him, his forearms seared in sick, sizzling sounds. The smell of burned flesh assaulted his nose. It numbed his senses. Tighter. Tighter. The walls of her underbelly were so tight. He staggered his breaths as he struggled for air. Above him, Chantico's head swayed back and forth, a pendulum, a moment lost in time. Cain fought fatigue, fought pain. His eyes wanted to close badly, but he kept them open. His body burned; sweat enveloped him.

She opened her mouth and sprang.

Cain didn't blink. He didn't falter. "You will not intimidate me. You are mine. I know you are."

Fangs a hand away from his face, she stopped. Her tongue crawled towards him and licked him.

Upon contact, sweat dissipated from his body. As she loosened her coils, the sizzling sensation subsided. When he finally breathed again, he took in a large breath of air, pure air, that burned his nostrils, but he welcomed the change. Energy boiled in his veins, and he felt an explosion of Power, like a volcano exploding forth. He crumpled to his hands and knees; Protector fell with him. Veins popped out of his forearms like little magma streams, blood now working through his body faster and more efficiently than ever. *I did it.*

He returned to his feet, Protector in hand.

*So, you are a son of fire?*

This time, Cain spoke in his mind. *I am. I come from the lineage of Pompeii and his wife, Etna.*

*I did not think I would ever meet someone like him again. You bear his countenance, Cain Evber.* Chantico licked the air and snorted fire that stopped just short of Cain. *We are one now. When you need me, I will be by your side, fighting for you, just as I fought for him until death.*

Cain held up his arm and extended his hand. Chantico slid forward until her nose touched his hand. *You will not be lonely again, Chantico.*

*I live by your words, my King.* Chantico dove back into her magma stream.

He twisted the quill of the feather necklace in front of him. *I did it.* Beaming, Cain turned around. He pumped a fist in the air. A new man, he walked towards Eirek and Conseleigh Inferno, who had waited at a safe distance.

"Cain, you did it. You bonded with her!" Eirek called out.

"Prince Evber, you, well, I should say King Evber now. It is truly an honor." Conseleigh Inferno bowed.

"Thank..." Cain dropped to his knees and groaned. "You..." His arm went to his stomach. He suddenly felt cold. So cold. He convulsed and writhed on the ground.

"Cain!"

"He is fine, Apprentice Mourse. He is experiencing his first withdrawal."

Arms came under him, helping him to stand.

Cain's focus waned. All the energy he had felt just a moment before was depleted.

"What do you mean?" Eirek asked. To Cain, his friend's voice was very far away.

"I'll tell you when we walk back to the hovercraft."

Cain's teeth chattered incessantly as Eirek and Conseleigh Inferno helped him to the hovercraft, laying him down on the back bench. Arms hanging loose and limp at his side, Cain strained his neck to look at Conseleigh Inferno, who was flipping switches on the hovercraft. "With... with... drawal?"

The conseleigh nodded. He came back to crouch alongside Cain. The man clutched Cain's hand and put it over his heart. "What you're experiencing is normal. Chantico is no longer with you. She has retreated to the magma stream and who knows where she could be now. That is how she travels throughout the whole planet, as it is all connected. You experienced a high and energy like nothing you had ever known before, yes?"

Cain nodded weakly. "I felt as though I was as..." Cain labored for breath. "As powerful as a volcano erupting."

"It is only natural that without her, then, anything else pales in comparison to how she makes you feel. That is the feeling you are experiencing now."

"Does bonding always work this way?" Eirek asked from the front.

The conseleigh turned his head. "It does. But after the first few withdrawals, his body will become acclimated to its effects. Ard leaves will help Cain regain his strength. Or, if Chantico returns, he will regain his energy, but once she leaves him again, it will be back to this lethargy."

"Guardian Eska had me bring ard leaves with me." Eirek paused. "Shoot. I forgot them in the ship. We can go there."

"Is that okay with you, Cain?"

Cain weakly agreed.

"Then that's where we'll go. Hold on."

Conseleigh Inferno maneuvered back to the pilot's seat and finished powering on the hovercraft. As it began to move, Cain's stomach growled. His heartbeat slowed. All Cain could think about was his need for Chantico. It didn't feel right to be without her. Why did he exist?

Hours passed. At least, Cain assumed that, for the next thing he knew, he woke up to daylight. At least the end of it. Or was it the beginning? Cain couldn't tell, only able to keep his eyes open for fleeting seconds. Soon enough, he recognized voices. His eyes fluttered, more alert than before.

"...sign of him yet."

"Cain?"

"I am happy to say that, yes, he is one of the True Kings."

"Where is he?"

"Sleeping, he is tired—"

"The withdrawal?"

"Yes, Guardian Eska."

"Eirek... Conseleigh Inferno," Cain muttered.

"Guardian Eska, he is awake." The conseleigh turned to him. "How do you feel, King Evber?"

"Better," Cain muttered. He massaged his head. "Where are we?"

"Almost back to my ship, Cain. We will get you some ard leaves."

Cain collapsed again. Had they been driving through the night to get him the ard leaves? He tilted his head and looked out the hovercraft's side window, no longer paying attention. Eventually, the conversation ended.

Then, for the briefest of moments, the warmth he felt from the sun overhead faded. The light behind his eyes turned to dark. And it stayed there incessantly, like a continual shadow. Cain opened his eyes and noticed a large ship flying above them. It was close. Close enough where the sky seemed to be split in two.

Cain hoisted himself up.

"Must be heading into the spaceport in Fernis," Conseleigh Inferno yelled above the din.

But it wasn't headed for the spaceport, for as soon as the words left the conseleigh's mouth, it turned sideways. It hovered in front of them, blocking their advance towards the city. Meters above the ground, it had yet to cut its anitron source.

The hovercraft slowed.

"What is it? Can we go around it?" Eirek asked.

"We can try." Conseleigh Inferno maneuvered to the right.

The machine reversed, blocking it.

Cain furrowed his brows. *What in Abaddon's name...*

"It appears we cannot." Conseleigh Inferno looked over at Eirek. "Do you—" The conseleigh looked at Cain and then back to Eirek. He stayed silent, his thought unspoken.

"It could be a guard ship from Pyre's atmosphere? Maybe it's a routine check?"

"No, it is no ship of Pyre. I have never seen this type of ship before. Look there at its body, its cut and pieced together in ways unlike regular ships. This might be..."

Cain squinted, trying to see what both of them saw. The ship before them hovered, lights still on. Unlike most other ships, this one did not have a fish-tail end, instead it was rather rectangular. All of it looked rather rectangular, and it was one of the longest ships Cain had seen. Large guns emerged and directed their attention to the hovercraft but did not fire.

No one said anything.

"We land."

"What?" Eirek and Cain said at the same time.

"Be ready for anything. Eirek, are you ready?" Conseleigh Inferno punched the anitron button in front of him, killing hover mode.

"Now? Now? Cain isn't recovered yet."

"There is no choice, Apprentice Mourse. If this is who we think it is..."

The ship dropped, as did the one in front of them. For a moment, no one spoke. "What is going on? Who is—" Cain groaned.

"King Evber?"

"Yes?"

"I have a feeling you will want Chantico here. Please call her now and stay here, both of you, while I see what this is about." Conseleigh Inferno retracted the dome and exited the hovercraft.

*Chantico.*

*Yes, my King?*

*Can you come to our location? I need you again.*

*I will be there shortly.*

Conseleigh Inferno walked forward, hand on the throat of his Ether Hammer.

The belly of the ship opened slowly. A ramp slid out like a metal tongue. Feet. Then legs. Then arms and a body with what appeared to be sleeves of black tribal tattoos on each arm. Hand at his own side, the man walked forward, slowly exposing his countenance to the impending twilight. The shadow of the ship still shaded the man's face, but Cain didn't need to see him fully to recognize the jet-black hair. Eirek stood. Cain pushed himself up onto one arm, coughing from the exertion. He blinked and then blinked again; mind too shocked to focus. In front of them stood none other than Prince Hydro Paen of Acquava.

CHAPTER 32

# STORMING THE CASTLE

B lood sprayed Zain's face as he cut through another individual on the hill rising from the streets of Pelopon. He didn't have time to wipe it from his face—not like it mattered—it was already a canvas for the blood splatters, anyway. Since the siege began in the morning, he hadn't even had a split second to look at the castle battlement they were now storming.

The reconnaissance mission had resulted in important information—the passageway to the seaside cove was purposely collapsed. There was still room for ships to leave and enter, but the walkway that hugged the walls of the cliff had been caved in. The mission also resulted in a loss of women from Gracie's team, as two twins in their late teens had died getting out of the city. That alone was valuable to know—those that had overtaken the castle weren't just remaining inside the walls; instead, they were using guerilla tactics to ambush anyone trying to breach the castle. While the loss of life was a shame, Gabrielle reminded him that they had made their choice, they had fulfilled their purpose, and their sacrifice would not go in vain.

This information, along with what he and his uncle had discussed the previous day, spurred them into a decisive attack. They couldn't wait for reinforcements; to do so would be to tempt the enemy out of the city, where their sheer numbers would overwhelm Zain's forces. Along with the fact that those in the castle would bolster their strength, this was their only option. Zain hoped that by bringing the fight to them, they wouldn't have time to even think about making a show of hanging his mother and Lord Vangle. Instead, they would focus on the impending assault, however feeble and futile the enemy thought it might be.

His sword impaled another victim. Using his foot, he pushed the man off his blade. *Lance.* The sword changed instantaneously and skewered another man who foolishly charged at him, sword raised overhead. It was clear the man had never seen a zircha weapon before, for his eyes bulged when he realized he had just run to his own death. *Halberd.* The weapon kept the same length, but the top of the weapon now formed itself into that of an axe, wrapping around the man's back. Zain pulled him closer. *Knife.* By the time the man came eye-to-eye with Zain, his weapon had changed into a heavy knife, which he proceeded to push upward into the man's skull. The man collapsed.

Zain's slapdash coalition of Gazo's, Gracie's, Scorpions, and what remained of Lukas's forces spread throughout the city, tracking down the rogue soldiers who had thought to surprise them. When the soldiers realized this tactic wouldn't work, they retreated towards the castle fortifications. Zain's party stopped pressing after a few hundred arrows rained down upon their men, critically wounding or killing handfuls of those too eager to rush into battle. Now, the feathered shafts stuck into the ground and the carcasses served as a boundary point. To cross over would mean to leave the battle and begin the war.

As enemy soldiers retreated successfully into the castle, Zain allowed himself a moment to scan the parapets. His mother and his uncle didn't hang. *So far so good.* Breathing heavily, he said to Lukas, "Time for our plan."

Lukas shouted orders. Zain barked his own, telling those who came with him to form groups of no more than twenty men. Once successfully divided, the Power casters were assigned to the cohorts. Tacticians from Gazo's and Gracie's were selected to stay back to guide their individual party of twenty-five. Together each group would advance using a collective earthen shield to stop raining arrows and during the time the archers needed to refit an arrow to the string of their bows, they would move forward under the guidance of eyes who stayed back.

Klum Barrata joined Zain's side with two others. "Zain, it's a good idea you and I stick together. Mylow here will be one of our Power casters."

Zain didn't know Mylow, but if the headmaster himself recommended that he go with Zain, then competence wasn't an issue. "And what about Kendel?" Zain nodded to his former trainee.

"Kendel, will stay back here. He will communicate with you whenever archers have finished their barrage."

*Good.* While he wasn't Kendel's trainer anymore, Zain didn't want the young boy to have to go through what lay waiting for them inside the castle. "You understand your role, Kendel?"

"Yes, Sir Berrese."

Zain was unsure if Kendel had any lamentations not joining the troops storming the castle, but it was better this way. There were larger problems ahead of them, and they couldn't spend so much time getting situated.

"Good."

"Then it's settled," Klum Barrata said.

"Zain, my groups are assembled."

Zain nodded towards Lukas. "It's time to take back the castle."

"The falcon always watches. For Ka'Che."

"For Ka'Che."

The combined forces stormed the hill, earthen shields going up and down in sync to the drawing back of bowstrings from the archers. This tactic worked well enough until the enemy casters began vying for the spell with Zain's party. This resulted in success for some who could overpower the individual they vied against, but it also resulted in haphazard fatalities among those who were overwhelmed by their foe or foes, exerting more Power than expected. Failing in their duty to protect the others, the whole group became annihilated by arrows.

Now, at the top of the hill, the only thing that mattered was the large wooden door in front of them and the constant barrage of arrows beating down on them from above. However, they had no conceivable method of breaching the gate. They had no battering ram. No Ether Weapon. And with energy being depleted every second they were idle, Zain needed to think of something.

His telecommunicator rang again. "Kendel?"

"There are other groups with earthen shields right next to you. On your right and left. Perhaps you can join with them to make the casting easier."

"Good idea."

Mylow grunted. "Zain, I can't hold this thing forever. What do we do now?"

Zain tapped his foot. "I know, Mylow.

Kendel, tell the other telecommunicator next to you to lift the left side of their earth shield. We will lift the right."

"Okay."

Zain walked towards the right side of their earthen cave. Another Power caster was in charge of holding this wall. "Mattias, lower defenses here. Transfer Power to the top."

"That'll expose us."

"No, it won't. Trust me."

When the earthen wall lifted, Zain peered into another large chamber with men around them. It was Lukas's party. He repeated the process on the other side, seeing that the Cleaver's Scorpions were to his left. Now the three groups were combined. Together, the combined skill of the fifteen Power casters could maintain the strength of the spells with ease. It would buy Zain time as he figured out the plan to get past the door in front of them.

Underneath the earthen umbrella, Lukas strolled over to Zain. "What is being done about the door?"

"I'm thinking about it still."

Neck craned slightly, he paced the little Power-made cave. While he walked, he whisked his zircha steel, still in knife form, through the air as if he was conducting an invisible symphony. He stopped it before his eyes. *Wait a minute.* Zain took his left hand and felt the breast pocket of his academy outfit for the other knife. *That's it.*

He spun on his heels. "We can burn the door down."

"How, we have no fire, and we cannot draw from the sun as it's too far away. Not to men—"

"We don't have to draw from the sun. I can create a spark with my knives, and then we can make the flame."

"Fire creates smoke." Cleaver crossed his arms over his large belly. "This is a dome. We will suffocate ourselves."

Zain bit his lip. The man was right. Smoke inhalation could be deadly, but even more deadly were the archers on the battlements waiting for them to release the spell. Then another idea came to Zain, still as deadly because of the precision it would take, but without any other options, this was his only choice.

"That is why we lose the shield."

Lukas pointed above. "The shield is the only thing keeping us from the archers."

"And we have some of the best Power casters here in this cave. A handful of men can focus on maintaining the shield. Another handful can focus on creating a fire. Who were the casters who formed the back of the shields?" Three raised their hands. "Those three can cool the door with water once we burn it so we can enter immediately."

"How are they going to cast—" Headmaster Barrata stopped mid-thought. "You mean for them to draw upon their own water?"

Zain nodded. "These three have the most energy remaining to them."

One of the men frowned. "Just because we were in the back doesn't mean we aren't spent. We were in the back because we aren't as strong as the others to begin with."

"Then take from me. I am sweating just as much as everyone else is here. You three can have easy access to it."

Klum Barrata put a hand on Zain's shoulder. "This is ludicrous. Do you understand what—"

"I do. But this isn't their fight. This is my fight. I'll give what I need to give."

"Me as well." Lukas stepped forward. "Zain, this is *our* fight. Not just yours. I want this castle back just as much as you do. One can draw from me as well."

"And me!"

Zain cocked his head, eyebrows rising as Perrine from Gracie's Academy walked out from Cleaver's party to join Zain.

"This is my fight. You don't need to risk your safety for—"

"At Gracie's we have The Walk. I never attempted it because I was afraid I couldn't walk on water. Gabrielle made me realize that I cannot be afraid of the water. I have to face my fears. This is a start."

Zain opened his mouth and then closed it. "Thank you."

"To show you I am a man of my word, Mr. Berrese, you can take from me too," Cleaver said. "My body is bigger than yours combined. I'm sweating like a hog on a hot day. When we finish this, you help us find Zakk, and then we finish Zigarda once and for all. Deal?" Cleaver extended a massive hand to Zain.

*I'll worry about the Zakk part of that deal later. Right now, I need this.* Zain took Cleaver's hand. "Deal."

"I'll guide the others in the Power, Zain," Mylow said.

Zain nodded. "Let's do it."

Within fifteen minutes, the necessary arrangements were made. Zain, Lukas, Cleaver, and Perrine were all in front of the middle earthen shield, which was aligned with the door. Each of the Power casters stood behind them, ready to draw upon their sweat to use for water. Another five casters were spread out throughout the dome—they were responsible for opening airholes to allow the smoke to escape. The remaining six were to the side of Zain and the others in front in two groups of three. They bent forward, watching Zain intently as he stood ready with his blades. Zain closed his eyes, inhaling and exhaling, making sure he was ready for what was about to come. *This is it.*

He struck them together. A spark. A flash.

The earthen shield was retracted in front of them.

"*Palo,*" said the Power casters.

As the flames licked the wood, the fire devoured more and more of the wooden door. Zain retreated a few paces, trying to escape the heat on his face, but he couldn't. He covered his mouth but took care not to wipe his face dry. Sweat crawled out of his pores. Smoke lingered in the air, burning his nostrils.

When arrows killed two of the Power casters working on burning down the door. Zain yelled, "Mylow, you're up!"

Mylow touched Zain's body first, wiping his hand on Zain's sweat, gaining instant access the Power. The others alongside their partner did the same thing.

"*Vesi.*"

Instantly, Zain felt the heat intensify as the water began to dissipate from his body. Irritation crept across his skin, and a dryness overwhelmed his mouth and eyes, hampering his vision. He closed his eyes and focused on the sound, conserving energy. *Soon it will be over.* His throat tickled, and that sensation shot down to his rumbling stomach. His knees buckled, sending him to the ground. He gasped for air. And when he did, he realized there was no more smoke, there was no more heat on his face. He opened his eyes and saw the wood had burned down and in its place were soldiers upon soldiers. Their weapons already drawn, they were ready to meet Zain's party. And Zain didn't even have the strength to stand.

## CHAPTER 33

# MYSTERIES REVEALED

E ska was doing something he hadn't done since hiring Riagan to be his conseleigh after Ariel Schule died in his service. Out of all the applicants to take over her position as conseleigh of Pyre, Riagan had definitely been the most qualified, and Eska admired that he was young, a decade setting him apart from the other applicants. It was clear he had climbed the ladder of success swiftly. They also shared a common bonding experience, though Riagan's wasn't nearly as violent or tragic as Eska's had been. Riagan's was how Eska imagined all bondings should go. Why had his been an exception?

The only thing that had annoyed Eska about Riagan was his tendency to cling onto the pithy maxims of old. After he had been inducted as conseleigh, Riagan had mentioned to him, "Die by fire, die with honor, living in Pyre, nothing is higher." The saying brought back too many memories that Eska wanted kept locked away. So why was he standing before the painting that he had deliberately removed from every contestant's room before the start of his Trials?

The golden-framed painting with a fiery spiral stared at him. It spiraled up at him, consuming his attention. Was he drawn to it now because he knew the precarious position he was putting Riagan in? Because of the man's willingness to be used as bait? He hoped this time things would work out better and that he wouldn't have another Therian's death on his conscious.

Looking at it again made him think of Victor Zigarda. Flames had consumed him that day when they battled, and Eska had realized just how strong he had become since bonding with Vesel. To think that the man held his grudge for over two-hundred years. It confounded Eska. And he wondered what the man was doing now after waiting so long to strip Eska of his Power, nearly succeeding, but only to fail and fall short. Again.

Eska noticed how similar they were in that way. They were both puppets to the whims of fate. Victor always coming so close to succeeding, only ever to fail. And Eska not being able to fail despite everything he planned. He had thought he would have died in the face of Vesel, only to bond instead. He should have lost the Trials to Victor, but he succeeded despite how outclassed he had been compared to his rival. Despite his best efforts at electing individuals to not fulfill the prophecy, he had done just that. And even though he had changed the Trials in efforts to curb the brutality, still, people got hurt. What else would fate subject him to before he finally passed his role onto Eirek?

Eska sighed.

He stared at the painting for another handful of minutes before removing himself from the room where he stored all the paintings he had collected during his time as Guardian. The door clicked shut behind him. His shoulders slumped.

*Edwyrd.*

Eska straightened his posture. He looked around but immediately shook his head. What was wrong with him? *Tundra? Have you returned?*

*Yes. But not alone.*

*What do you mean?*

*There is something I want you to see. Come outside.*

Outside of the estate, Tundra waited for him in front of the ship, arms crossed against her chest. Its belly was already open, waiting for them to enter. While he descended the steps, she turned on her heels and stalked to the ramp, striding up, not waiting for him. Eska cocked his head at that. Either what she had for him was really important or she was mad at him for some reason. Or perhaps it was both.

Eska followed her up the ramp, meeting her in the ship's hold. Tundra stood behind two things: a Hown soldier with a large hole through the middle of his chest and the syphon bag he had commissioned with the Hown. The syphon bag moved and jerked. Someone or something was trapped inside.

"Where's Apprentice Mourse?"

"I sent him away on a mission with Cain."

"Prince Evber?"

"He could be a King."

"King? What does that mean?"

"It doesn't matter right now. Riagan will keep me updated. Who's in the bag?" Eska asked.

Frowning, Tundra clicked her tongue. "We will get to that second. I want you to examine this body first." She crouched over the carcass.

Edwyrd joined her, crouching on the balls of his feet. "His name was Claudius Morello. He came from the Talyn province in Acquava."

"Do you not see the big hole in his chest?"

"I see it, Tundra. What do you want me to do?"

"Tell me what could have made that."

Eska kept eyeing the syphon net; whatever was inside had stopped moving. Eska returned his gaze to Claudius's body. The wound was big. At least eight inches in diameter. Shot right through the heart. The neurofiber of the Hown's armor didn't appear to have offered any resistance.

"Laser. Mechanized."

"Yes. I figured that as well. But what powered it?"

"Why don't we see."

"What do you—"

Eska plucked off the golden H on the man's chest. Luckily, it still seemed completely intact, the hole in the chest missing it by two inches. Eska put the H in his palm and said, "Play last known recording of Claudius Morello." Tundra gasped, but he didn't have time to explain.

A female automated voice said, "Playing the last known recording from Hown Soldier twenty-six, Claudius Morello."

In front of Eska's palm, a yellow hologram began to play. Claudius was in a circle of men. Hydro was surrounded. Suddenly, a black net caught Hydro and pushed him to the ground. *The syphon net. Is that?* Eska's eyes glanced over to the net next to him. *No. It couldn't be.* The hologram shook. Claudius spun around. A ship hovered off the ground and then morphed into a mechanical giant with arms and wings and legs. Eska's breath hitched. He watched in horror as the machine finished morphing into something he had never seen before in his life.

From the left wing, a beam of light arced towards Claudius. He fell backward. Now only the sky could be seen. The massive android stepped over his body. Then sky and nothing else. Eska stopped the footage.

"Edwyrd, what was that thing?"

For the first time in years, Eska searched for an answer. He couldn't find one. The closest term he had in his vocabulary was a polymorphous android, but androids were only servants of the wealthy on Gar. They had yet to make mainstream waves, let alone be weaponized and constructed into something so massive.

He looked at Tundra. "I... I don't know."

"Is that... is that thing protecting Hydro? That was clearly him earlier."

"I..." Eska's mouth hung agape. "Oh no... What have I done?"

Without sparing another second, Eska reached deep into his mind and searched for Riagan.

*Riagan, are you there? Riagan!*

*Edwyrd, I'm here. What is... Why are you so flustered?*

Eska sighed. *I'm sorry. I just... I thought maybe... Maybe he had finally shown himself.*

*Not yet. We are just leaving the Forge. Cain did it.*

*He's a King?*

*He is indeed. I saw the bonding process with my own eyes.*

*And Apprentice Mourse?*

*He is well. He's with me. Cain is experiencing his first withdrawal. We are taking him back to Eirek's ship to get some ard leaves for him. It'll speed his recovery.*

*Good.*

*My Guardian...*

*Yes, Riagan?*

*Why did you reach out? You... you seemed worried.*

*I... I have reason to believe that Hydro isn't alone.*

*What do you mean?*

*I mean the ship he travels in. I haven't seen anything like it. It's... it's... it's like a zircha man-made ship.*

*A zircha ship? The amount of alloy that would take. And the skill...*

*I... I don't know either... But, listen, it can morph. And when it does, it can become a combative android.*

*How do you know all of this?*

*Tundra came back with one of the Hown bodies. His body camera recorded it.*

Silence.

*Riagan, if... if I had known what exactly we were up against, I would have never put you in the position you're in. Hydro is more than just dangerous. Be extremely cautious when approaching him. Contact me.*

*The machine is only metal, my Guardian. We have three trained individuals with Ether Weapons. And Chantico. We will be able to handle Hydro and this machine, whatever it is.*

*Please be careful.*

*I will. Die by fire, die with—*

*Don't say that. Don't say that. You will not die. Do you hear me? You will not die.*

*Very well, my Guardian. I will live to serve you another day.*

*You are dismissed.*

Eska cut the connection. His mind throbbed. Closing his eyes, he massaged his forehead. He breathed in deeply and released. Opening his eyes, he noticed the syphon net in his peripherals. He turned to Tundra.

"And there?" he asked. "What's in there?"

"Why didn't I know about these technologies?"

"Tundra, I didn't even know about a zircha ship. I can't even fathom it."

She shook her head. "The body cameras."

"Would that have mattered at all?"

Tundra stayed silent for a moment. "No." She sighed. "But this would have." She jostled the syphon net. The entity inside moved. "Something that blocks Power? How? I could have used this up north."

"I wasn't sure if it would actually work. That is why I never mentioned it. What you have there is the only one. The Hown's need for it was greater."

"But how?"

Eska raised his gloved hand. "I searched back in my reimaje's memory vault for the creation of this glove. It holds some of my Guardian's Power. It nullifies it. I figured that if I could recreate a larger version, perhaps it could nullify other types of Power as well."

"It works."

"You've tried?"

"I have. When I touch it, I cannot cast Power."

"Yes, I already know that it works in that way. It's similar to how I blessed the orbs before the second trial began. I still didn't quite know if it would have worked on Hydro, though. Based upon the last communications I had with General Satorus, I had reason to think it did, as they captured him, but they still died in the end."

"That was Doctor Cere. And I bet that machine is of his imagination as well." Tundra tsked. "It's better that man is dead."

Eska frowned. "Now the bag?"

"I believe it's the only good news that I have for you."

"Good news. What do you mean?"

"Take a look for yourself."

Using both hands, Tundra peeled back the mouth of the syphon net, letting it fall to the floor. In the center of it, hands tied together by wire cords, mouth bound and gagged, knelt a man with leathery skin and a furunculous face. As the man looked at Eska, it didn't grovel or try to get free of its bonds. In fact, he seemed to be too still. Did the man know who he looked at?

"Tundra, is this... is this a shapeshifter?"

"Yes, Edwyrd, it is."

Edwyrd crouched on the balls of his feet. "How?"

While Tundra recounted her visit to Lady Aprah, Eska stayed at eye-level with the man, inspecting him. She had digressed halfway through her story to tell that Cadmar Briggs, the real one, had successfully completed the Passage.

"That is more good news, Tundra. Truly, this is fantastic work." Eska grabbed the man underneath the chin with his gloved hand and inspected him like an intricate piece of artwork. The eyes are what allured him the most. Granite eyes with flecks of amber in them. Amber, almost the same color as the Third One's eyes. *Hmmm. I wonder.* Eska looked up at Tundra. "Is there anything else?" He switched hands, touching the man now with his ungloved skin. He removed the gag and inspected the man's gums as if he expected to find something.

"Lady Aprah says she cannot help you in the upcoming war."

Eska snapped his head in her direction. Eyes wide, he asked, "Why is that?"

"Because of this assassination attempt. If Sereya wants a war with them, then a war they will get. Edwyrd!"

Eska had kept notice of the man in his peripherals, so when he saw the man's head go back, he pulled his fingers away. The man clamped down with his teeth where his fingers had been. Eska waved his fingers in the air, hoping to play off his surprise. The man grinned.

"I was hungry, my Guardian." Then the man writhed in laughter and puss excreted from pores as well as the orifices of his nose and ears. With a large tongue, the man licked the white over the area of his mouth and laughed even more. "Tasty."

The puss sank into the man's skin. His body shook and convulsed. Within a minute, Eska stared back at a perfect replica of himself. Well, almost perfect, save for the outfit that the man wore and the lack of the reimaje on the man's head. But if Eska hadn't known better, had he not planned to get the man to do just this, he would have been shocked. But shock was what he wanted, so he let his mouth hang open and fell back from his crouch, as if he was afraid. His show only fed the shapeshifter's ego, and the laughter intensified.

"What's wrong? See something familiar?" the doppelganger asked.

The shock and disgust on Tundra's face was real. "You slimy little..." She muttered something incomprehensible. "Get out of Edwyrd's skin now!"

"So this is what it feels like to be Guardian. It feels empty." He laughed again.

Tundra withdrew her scimitar. Eska threw up his hand. "Tundra, enough."

"Edwyrd?"

Slowly, Eska got back to the balls of his feet and looked at his doppelganger. Truly, the man had become an exact replica of the Guardian himself, except for one thing. Eska smirked. "It's in the eyes."

"The... eyes?"

"I wanted him to change so that I could try to detect any difference. Now I do. The eye color doesn't change. Everything else does. I will inform the lords and ladies to watch out for this, and these trackers will be hunted down." Eska turned his attention back to the shapeshifter, whose expression mimicked the surprise Eska had shown. "What is it that your kind says, ajid volintasey fuan? Is that it?" The shapeshifter seethed. He was about to speak when Eska regagged the man. "I believe all of Gladonus will be finding you again very soon." Eska stood. "Bag him up and bring him to my chambers. No one else but us can know of this."

The man writhed, and muffled, disgruntled murmurs came through the gag, but Eska didn't care. He had extracted what information he wanted from the skinchanger, and now they had the knowledge to uncover the rest. As he went down the ramp and back out onto the Core, Guardian Eska chuckled to himself. Fate would surely be amused right now. And he was sure Victor would have been proud of his tactic. Knowledge is Power. Wasn't that his family's saying? With this mystery revealed, he would weaponize all of Gladonus with his knowledge. There would be no second Great War. Not on his watch. Not while he was still Guardian. Not while he still lived.

## CHAPTER 34

# OLD FOES AND NEW WOES

Headmaster Barrata shouted orders. Soldiers gathered in front of Zain, blocking his view from the others. As they moved inward, sunlight crept into the space where they had been, soon reaching down the back of Zain's neck. He stayed on his knees, panting.

His right shoulder lurched forward, nearly collapsing him entirely.

*Ouch.* He craned his neck upwards. A bowman restrung his bow. *I need to...*

Before he knew it, he was hoisted up and half-carried, half-dragged to where the door had burned down. The bottleneck had broken out into the courtyard, and while the battle raged on inside the castle walls now, the stragglers who needed time to recover stayed back. It was Cleaver who had carried Zain. Perrine and the casters, it seemed, had managed to make it to the cover as well.

Now within the castle threshold, Zain bent at his knees and sucked in air. "We did it. Thank you... for helping." He straightened his posture and nodded to Cleaver and Perrine. He looked around. "Where is my uncle?"

"He stormed in with the rest of the group." Cleaver moved around Zain. Snap. "We'll get the rest out of you later." Cleaver held up the broken shaft of the arrow and the fletching for Zain to see.

For being the eldest of his mother's siblings, Zain was almost surprised by his uncle's vigor, but he supposed this is why he was the Head Guard for Abraham and how he had managed to live through two large skirmishes already. Zain wondered if Lukas got adrenaline from battling the same way that Zain did during tournament fights, if this was his calling just as saving people was Zain's.

Of course he did. That was why he offered himself up to be used in the first place. He would meet his uncle inside later. What mattered now was catching up with the soldiers already fighting inside.

"We need to go." Zain rotated his shoulder blade, feeling a little discomfort, but there wasn't anything he could do now. The arrow would at least stop the blood from leaking out now, and the fight ahead of him would allow him to ignore any pain. Readying himself, he put the knife back into its pocket on his chest and transformed his zircha steel into a sword. He moved forward.

Perrine stepped in front of Zain. "We need a plan."

"The plan is to help the others." Zain pointed his sword at the battle.

"We don't have as much energy as they do. We need to be smart."

"I agree with the girl." Cleaver crossed his chest. "The archers are still shooting from atop."

Zain bit his lip. Inside, the chiming of steel and the screaming and grunting of those wielding it overpowered anything else. Arrows flew back and forth, mainly from the top. Surges of Power would crack the earth or hold someone in place. And as Zain counted the bodies lying motionless on the ground, he realized there were more of his and less of the enemy. *We're losing.*

Then he realized no one else was coming in behind them. A fraction of their men still stood on the outskirts of battle.

Zain pulled up his telecommunicator. "Kendel."

"Yes, Zain."

"We breached the door. Tell the others to come. Same method. Make sure those who can wield Power stay alive; we need them."

"Will do."

Perrine spoke up. "What are you planning?"

Zain shifted his focus to Perrine. "A surprise for them. Right now, all the arrows are going inside the courtyard. What does that tell you?"

"The archers are focusing on the immediate danger," Cleaver said.

"Exactly." Zain nodded. "Here's what we do. Once Kendel comes with reinforcements, those who can cast Power will hoist us to the top of the battlements. We will surprise the archers and storm the castle from the top."

"The others?" Cleaver asked.

"The Power casters and the others will go join the main force on the ground."

When Kendel's party arrived a few minutes later, Zain explained the plan once more. After a quick evaluation of their weapons, Zain put an axe wielder and another man with a sword to fight alongside Perrine. For himself, he took a bowman and a swordsman to accompany him. And with Cleaver, he put a man who wielded throwing knives and another man with a lance. In addition to these individuals, Zain put a Power caster in each group. In this, there was balance—a long-ranged weapon and close-quarter skill as well. This would increase their chances for success once atop of the battlements.

"Kendel, you'll stay here. Keep a lookout on—"

"I'm coming."

"Kendel, you're a scout. You should—"

"And I did my job. Now it's my turn to do more. Zain, let me fight."

Zain bit his lip but didn't have time to respond for an axe wielder named Bryan held up his axe and voiced his concerns. "This is a good plan, Zain, but with no Power casters with us on the ground, we won't be much help down below. You'll be too busy up there to protect us."

"Just stay clear of the—"

"Zain, two of the Power casters can come with me. I'll go with them. And that little one can come with us as well." Cleaver stepped forward. "Three groups on the battlements are too many. You and the little lady go. I still have enough fight in me to help with this."

Zain grunted and looked at Kendel. "You listen to him, you hear me?"

"Yes, sir." Kendel saluted.

"Cleaver, watch out for the boy. For all of them." Zain turned back to the others meant to storm the battlements with him as Cleaver and his small company pressed into the courtyard. "Okay. Let's move." Zain turned his attention to Perrine. "Do all of you women carry daggers on your legs?"

"It's the same way you men carry steel close to your hearts."

Zain smirked. On instinct, he felt for the knife in his upper-breast pocket. He pulled it out and tossed it in the air, catching it by the hilt. "You'll want to get yours out."

Perrine bent down and withdrew her own, tossing it and catching it in the air with the same fluidity as Zain. "Sure thing. I heard Gabrielle beat you using this."

"She beats everyone using that."

"Did she tell you that we used to be roommates?"

Zain shook his head. "We will talk more later. Are you ready?"

She nodded. Zain gestured to the Power casters in the groups.

"*Maa,*" the two parties said in unison.

Before Zain knew it, a small pillar formed on the ground underneath him and lifted him up and up. When the pillars of earth reached the top of the wall, Zain jumped off and onto the battlement behind one of the archers. With an assassin's fluidity, he brought his knife clean across the man's throat and pushed him off the side. By the time he turned, Zain saw another body, paces away, impaled by a sword and yet another archer on his knees, two arrows decorating his torso and chest.

"Let's go."

He gestured to the others to continue moving. As he ran along the parapets, he tried with inconsistent success to keep his focus ahead, not down and below to the courtyards. The battle had spread out from the portcullis, and Zain assumed the whole castle was a battleground: Power casters dueling in the open where they could utilize both assets and the others slinking through the halls. *Where is the—*

Blood splattered his face and his clothes. A sword appeared through the archer in front of him. Withdrawn quickly, the body crumbled. Zain held up his sword to block the impending downward strike. The man pulled back and shoved the lance forward. Zain dodged to the left. *Axe.* He dropped his throwing knife and put both hands on the throat of his axe. He swung the axe straight into the man's unprotected neck. The force made the man stumble to the left, and he fell over the battlement.

Zain went to his knees and hunched over his fallen companion. The man coughed up blood. *He's alive.*

"You need to plug this wound. Use part of your pants." Zain picked up his fallen throwing knife and cut a piece off the hem of the man's pants and handed it to him.

The man took the cloth and pressed it on his abdomen. He nodded, not having the strength to speak.

Zain turned to Perrine. "I'm going to look for someone who may be able to heal him. Stay here and guard him until I return."

Zain got up and ran, meeting the other group at a bridge that overlooked the courtyard. He explained the situation, and they agreed to take the wounded archer back to the adored in the camp.

"Make sure you look for survivors below, too."

"Will do."

The group nodded and were off, two of them tending to the wounded archer and the others going below to search for other wounded stragglers. When it was just him and Perrine, she pointed to the courtyard. "Where do we go now?"

"I need to check something first."

Perrine followed Zain down a flight of stairs and through a hallway, coincidentally meeting up with Kendel and another, dueling against three individuals. Without hesitation, Zain helped finish the skirmish quickly.

"Have you seen Headmaster Barrata?"

Kendel nodded, wiping sweat from his brow. "He made it a point to take some of his best fighters with him down the courtyard path."

"My uncle?"

Kendel shook his head. "I haven't seen him."

"Cleaver? Where's his party?"

"The big man?"

"Yeah."

"Still fighting in the main area." Kendel pointed.

Zain peered out over the banister. Mobs of men still fought down below, all of whom had donned the sigil of blood and sweat. He witnessed Cleaver sever an arm off of a man before impaling him through the gut. His eyes scoured to and fro, trying to find his headmaster or Lukas. But there was still no sight of either of them.

"Why aren't you with him?"

"He told me to take the hallways. It'd be safer than the exposed courtyard."

"Fair point. Let's go." Not waiting for the others to follow his lead, Zain turned around from the banister and made it to his mother's room, just a few doors away.

Empty. Disheveled.

Lost and dumbfounded, Zain sheathed his weapon. *Mom?* Bedsheets were sprawled about, drawers were opened, and a mirror lay cracked on the ground. There had been a struggle inside. Zain lingered in the room, maneuvering to the drawer. His eyes widened. *The vanishing sand.* It still lay in its sack, but it was clearly exposed now. Had she been trying to get to it before she was captured? He wished he remembered how to use it; it could prove invaluable during a battle like this, but his mind couldn't process that. He covered it again with clothes. He would come back to it later.

"Zain."

Zain twisted to look over his shoulder. Kendel stood at the threshold. Blood coated his armor and his face. Had that been there before? It must have been. Open air wafted through the balcony doors, carrying away any scent that may have once lingered in the room. It also brought with it steel and shouts and a sense of duty in Zain that he needed to end this fight, whatever the cost. *Mom.* Zain clenched his fist. He hurried to his mother's balcony.

There, down below, he finally saw his headmaster. Red coated his outfit, and he strode forward, alone. From atop the balcony, Zain called out to him, but he didn't respond. Almost as in a trance, he continued forward, not stopping for any of the surrounding action.

Zain pointed. "We need to get down there now." Zain turned back. Kendel stood near the balcony door. "Where are the others?"

"The men went ahead, and the lady is still coming. What do you see?"

"I need to get down below. Power is the quickest way."

"I can cast."

Zain shook his head twice. "You can? Since when? When were you going to tell me?"

"Wasn't time yet. After you left for the Trials, the Sages came and tested me."

"Can you create a slab of earth and slope it down to the ground floor?"

"Let me see." Kendel stood beside Zain. He surveyed the battlefield. "Okay. I got it. But first..."

"Zain!"

Zain turned his head. *Perrine?* Something scraped underneath his chin, connecting with the metal jaw Zain had surgery on during the Trials. A knife slid to the ground. Zain spun backwards, eyes wide open. Perrine lay on the ground, an arm outstretched, blonde hair veiling her face, blood beneath her fingertips.

"I didn't know she had any life left in her." A man snickered.

Zain withdrew his weapon. He twisted. Her fingers twitched, though, and that meant she was alive. For now. And the man... a shifter in Kendel's clothes. *No. No.*

"Definitely not like the man from before." He smirked again. "I take it you know him? Well, knew him?" The man laughed.

Zain charged. The shifter pulled out a sword and blocked Zain's first advance and then kicked out Zain's foot, causing him to buckle. A swift elbow to the face sent Zain tumbling back. The man lurched forward, sword drawn. Quickly, Zain kipped up and bypassed the sword. Shoulder into the stomach. Elbow into the jaw. The one-two combination caused the shifter to drop his sword and reel back behind the beaded curtain. Zain lunged forward, shifting to lance mid-stride. Too slow. The shapeshifter jumped to the side of the wall and grabbed hold of the beads. As Zain charged through, the shifter brought the beads around Zain's throat and squeezed. The beads snapped. The man coiled himself on Zain's back, choking him with a headlock. Zain lurched forward in pain. Zain stumbled sideways and forward, balance off-kilter. *Knife.* Zain stabbed upwards and behind him, finding something. The shifter howled in pain while still on Zain's back. He tightened his headlock. Zain was losing oxygen and focus. He stumbled to the balcony. And off.

Zain fell. Another sharp pain came to his neck. Warmth climbed up his cheek and flew into the air in front of him. A hot voice whispered in his ear, "See you in Abaddon. Ajid Voluntasey Fu—"

Thump.

CHAPTER 35

# CONFRONTATION

He walked towards a man with red hair and orange eyes. The man approached him with hands to his hip, gripping the throat of a hammer that hung off the notch. His eyes focused on the weapon. His brows furrowed. He squinted, trying to make sure of what he saw. *An Ether Weapon?*

The man stopped. "Hydro!"

He didn't quite know how to react to his shell's name. Instead, he ignored it. He had more important things to do. Nothing else mattered besides the jewels.

"It's close."

His ears twitched at the mechanical voice. He passed his gaze over the man, noticing a C on his chest. On the other hip, he noticed a satchel much like his own. *Does this man have the jewel? There is only one way to find out.*

"The jewel." He pointed.

The man covered his hip.

*He does have it.*

"I cannot allow you to have that." He brandished his Ether Hammer.

*Breaker!* Desmós's eyes widened with surprise. He snarled. *It doesn't matter. He probably doesn't know how to unlock its special ability, anyway.* Desmós withdrew Purge.

Something cawed.

A phoenix dove from the sky to land on the man's shoulder. *I will kill both of them, the man for the jewel and the phoenix who betrays its true master.* Desmós flicked his eyes to the movement behind the man with red hair. Two others exited the hovercraft.

An unexpected rumbling behind him threw him off-balance. Soon, a shadow dwarfed him. He stopped and looked back. The machine that he had been inside was transforming, arms and mounted guns sprouting from its shoulders. Wings burst from its back in a deafening screech of steel. Desmós watched the machine in awe. *What strange...* His eyes widened.

With one step, the machine lurched forward. The felsic floor shook, reverberations and aftershock numbing his shell's eardrums. When it removed its metal foot, he noticed the man and his phoenix had completely vanished. *Where did they go off—*

The man with orange hair reappeared in front of him. He swung his hammer down. Desmós jumped back. His feet slid on the smooth ground, shards of it flinging up into his face as the Ether Hammer bore down on the spot he had been just a moment before. Desmós felt the warm blood of his human shell slide down his cheek.

"Kill him!" Desmós commanded.

The machine swiped down at the orange-haired man with one arm. Ash fell upon the man from his phoenix. He vanished.

*So that's the ability...*

The man reappeared on the machine's forearm. Phoenix haloing him, he raised his hammer and swung down. Deafening tears in the metal erupted as the hammer went easily through the metallic forearm. But not quite deep enough to sever it. He threw his arm up overhead again, ready to come with another blow, when he looked over his shoulder. The other hand was coming towards him.

*Vesi!*

Desmós focused on making a sphere of water about the phoenix. It worked. The man looked up and noticed his phoenix drowning in a bubble. The man turned back and held his Ether Weapon in front of him. It didn't matter. The metallic hand was already around him, squeezing.

The phoenix popped out of existence, the water finally quelling its breath for good. At the same time, Desmós heard the final yells of the man who had just been squeezed to death in the machine's giant fist. The machine released its grip, letting the man fall to the ground, along with his weapon. The man landed with a sick thud, but the Ether Weapon made a small crater a body's length away.

Desmós stalked forward towards the dead man's carcass. *Hardly an adversary.* He smirked. On the balls of his feet, he rummaged through the man's sack at his side, the one he had protected, expecting to find the gem inside, and he did. He plucked up the rich, red gemstone that looked like a garnet cut in the shape of a triangle.

"Hydro, stop."

He looked up, jewel in his hand. Slowly, he stood, calculating this new man's worth. There was something different about him, although Desmós couldn't exactly tell what it was. He flicked his gaze to the man's side. *Another Ether Weapon.* The taller man next to him brandished one as well. *Well, isn't this—*

"We found the jewel. We must leave now."

After hearing its modulated voice, Desmós looked back at it. Could it still even fly? The left forearm that had a large crater in it, and the left hand was damaged as well.

"Hydro! Give us that jewel."

Desmós turned his attention back to the men in front of him. "What is your name?"

"You know my name."

*Hmmm...* He searched his shell's memory for any recollection of this man and came upon him almost instantly. His eyes widened. *This is the man you wanted to defeat. The Commoner.* His brows furrowed. *He does not have a Commoner face, though.* No, he had seen a similar face before. And he flicked his gaze to the taller one. *Another prince, hmmm?* He moved forward, wanting to inspect these specimens further.

Another rumble, like an earthquake ravaging the planet.

"We must leave now."

He paused but then continued towards the men, ignoring the ship's advice. He assumed it was just another one of the machine's transformations. If the ship really wanted to leave, it could kill these two individuals just as easily as the first. Desmós wondered why it hadn't. Perhaps it was only programmed to do one thing, protect the pilot and find the jewels, and since neither of these men had jewels on them, nor did they engage in combat with him yet, it couldn't act. Far too complicated for Desmós's tastes.

"I cannot allow you to take those jewels." The Commoner held up his blade, point angled toward Desmós. "You will pay for what you did to Conseleigh Inferno."

The taller man pointed his Ether Lance at him. "Hydro, why are you here? What happened to your eyes? Your body?"

Desmós inspected both of them, but immediately regarded the shorter man as more interesting. His eyes held a slight bit of purple within them. *The offspring of an Ancient. Could it be?* He raised his own blade towards the man. "You are no Commoner."

"And you are not, Hydro. What did you—"

"He wasn't the prince I needed him to be." Desmós laughed and then sheathed his sword. "Here, have a chat."

The first thing Hydro saw were Eirek and Cain, confusion marking their faces. Then he wiggled his fingers. His body felt hot. He looked up to see orange clouds and yellow ones. Behind him stood a machine and the body of Conseleigh Inferno. Next to Hydro was a crater. *An Ether Weapon? What is that doing...*

A tremor pelting the land disturbed his thoughts.

"Hydro, hand over the jewels."

He wanted to answer them, but he knew he couldn't. Not directly. He didn't know how much time he had left, and if he tried to use his sword, Desmós would regain control. Instead, he played the part the sycophant wanted him to play, hoping to show them what they needed to know.

"I cannot give you the jewels for Aiton's safety. He is depending on me. They need to be destroyed." He looked at his hands and pursed his lips. "If you want them, you will have to try and take them from *him*."

"Him?" Cain asked.

Hydro ripped his shirt open. "Des—"

A pain shot through his body. He saw no more.

Desmós smirked at both of them. "Like the prince said, if you want the jewels, you will have to come and take them from me." He withdrew his sword. While keeping his gaze on both men, he went down into the small crater and picked up the Ether Hammer with his other hand.

Now it was a fair fight.

The ground hungered for something. And this time, it didn't stop. Vibrations barraged the ground, shaking bits of tiny felsic to and fro like pebbles. Up in the distance, he saw a large, red body. His eyes widened. *Is that? Chantico? Sister?* He locked eyes with the man of fiery hair once more. "A True King? And an Ancient's offspring? Well, it seems that both of you will need to die." He turned to his machine. "Annihilate these two." He pointed his sword and hammer in their direction.

The machine moved forward. Desmós stepped to the side, letting the machine do its work. It stomped the ground in front of him, but the two had separated. It aimed its guns. A large red body with a golden underbelly slammed into it, knocking it backwards. It fired up into the air. The machine turned on its thrusters to restore its balance after the strike.

*Chantico!* His sister snapped outwards, towards the guns on its shoulders, tearing them out of its sockets, spitting each one out, shaking the ground slightly in the aftermath. *The machine! My ship!*

"Desmós, it's over."

He returned his attention to his opponents. Once again, the two men were side-by-side, weapons out. "You have no right to call me by that name." He held both of his Ether Weapons out in front of him and smirked. "And this battle has not even begun."

CHAPTER 36

# THE THRONE ROOM

Zain coughed. With a grunt, he pushed the man's forearm off of his neck. He moaned and clutched his side as he pillared himself on one arm. Feet shuffled towards him. Steel flashed. Zain rolled out of the way and swung a sword across his open legs. The man buckled. He unlatched the knife in his breast pocket and brought it across his chin. The invader keeled over. Blood sprayed the ground. Zain brought his sword and knife back over top of his chest. His stomach heaved up and down. *Can I get a break?*

Zain glanced around. Seeing no one in his vicinity, he traced the mark on his neck. His fingers felt blood. *He bit me.*

Zain heaved his torso off the ground. The two dead men lay side by side, one a shapeshifter in the clothes of Gazo's and the newcomer in green mesh armor. Zain's eyes bulged. *I killed one of our own. Why would he—*

Zain blinked and realized why the man had charged him. The shapeshifter had become him. The man lay dead, but dead in the form of Zain and in the clothing of Gazo's army. Zain also wore a Gazo's uniform, so had the man attacked? Perhaps because he had lain facedown, the academy sigil out of sight.

In time, Zain hoisted himself off the ground. He limped over to look at his lifeless self. His skin prickled. He poked his sword underneath the man's body, tempted to roll him over.

"Zain. Are you—" Headmaster Barrata stopped. He withdrew his sword. "Zain?"

"It's me. This man shifted into me." Zain pointed to the man with his steel.

"Prove it to me. I see two of you right now, one lying dead with one of our own." Headmaster Barrata inched forward.

"My mother's name is Brisine."

"You could have gotten that information elsewhere." Headmaster Barrata inched forward more.

"You sponsored Zakk to be in the Trials."

Relief flooding his expression, Headmaster Barrata stopped. "Zain." He looked down. "Then this man is a..."

"Shifter." Zain nodded. "Kendel is dead." Zain inhaled sharply as the reality of that hit him. How did Cleaver let him die? When did it occur? Zain's stomach ached for his fallen trainee. Why did he even let him come along!? He should have known better. He shouldn't have trusted anything anyone said. He should have...

Headmaster Barrata's voice dragged him from his thoughts. "Where did it happen?"

"I..." Zain shook his head. Had the shifter been him all along, or had he saved the real Kendel only to let him die in the end? "I'm not sure. I... I found him up there." Zain pointed to his mother's window. "Perrine saved me. Perrine!" Zain remembered her lying in the hallway. "We need to help her."

"I'll send others to her. You and I need to hunt down the rest of those shifters and find your mother. How many are left?"

Zain coughed. "Is that all? Kendel just died!"

"Zain, we will mourn for the dead afterwards. We don't have time for tears. Now, how many are left?"

Zain bit his lip, knowing his headmaster was right. "At least three that I know of."

"Then we have work to do."

Headmaster Barrata walked off. For the first few hundred meters, Zain followed with a limp, but the debility improved with each step as his legs reacquainted themselves to walking. On the way, Barrata ordered nearby soldiers to check the upper hallway for Perrine.

Zain caught up to the headmaster. "Have you seen my uncle?"

"He took some of his Power casters through the hallways to storm the battlements further inside. I'm to meet him in the main courtyard before the throne room. We're going to launch a two-pronged attack."

"And those from Gracie's?"

"Carla's assigned them to the corridors, scouting for survivors and those in hiding. A handful of them are also up on the battlements with her and your uncle. They'll meet us up ahead."

Zain nodded. It was a sound strategy. For the most part. The shapeshifters, however, were unknown factors. Depending on how they were utilized, their whole plan could be disrupted. "Where do you think the rest of them are?"

Headmaster Barrata scanned the area. "Anywhere. And that is the issue." His gaze flicked around the scene of chaos where people ran to and fro and the song of steel still chimed. "We will deal with that later." He stopped around a small group of Gazo's men catching their breaths. "Now we need to go meet up with your uncle and Carla and then rescue your mother and Lord Vangle. Can you take us there?"

Zain nodded. "We go straight."

"Yes, that's what I thought. Where is Gerald Starshine in all of this madness? It's surprising not to find him here yet."

"He went with me to Mendeck to see my father, but traitors in our party killed him."

Klum Barrata stared at Zain, dumbfounded. He put a hand to his side, as if he ached from some unhealed wound. "That..." He cleared his throat. "That is a shame. He was quite gifted. And unique."

"Unique?"

"Not many people make the mace their weapon of choice. To wield it to a lethal degree requires quite a bit of skill. He had that." Headmaster Barrata breathed in deeply. "Are those traitors here?"

"They are."

"Then they will receive a Traitor's Hanging. Justice here will teach them." He looked over the sword he held.

Zain gulped as he thought about such a hanging. Egregiously cruel, one hadn't been carried out for centuries. But he didn't have time to think about it more because the headmaster stalked forward, intent on dealing out justice.

As they maneuvered their way through the rest of the courtyards, they eventually got to an area where Scorpions and Spiders clashed. Cleaver fought off two men in snakesuits, but his large body was cut in multiple locations. It was a surprise to Zain the man hadn't bled out yet. He fell to his knee, stumbling slightly on a fallen body. The two men pounced at the opportunity. A soldier nearby intercepted the men, saving Cleaver from certain death, holding up his lance with both hands. After both blows were deflected, they immediately stabbed the man through the stomach, both swords lifting him up in the air in unison. His sacrifice was enough, though, and Cleaver bolted to his feet, intent on revenge. A heavy stroke decapitated one foe. Cleaver spun around and put himself behind the other man, thrusting up with his huge blade, skewering the man like he had just done to Cleaver's comrade.

"Cleaver!"

The large man grimaced. Through labored breathing, he said, "'Bout time you showed up. That boy ever find you?"

"Later."

"These soldiers are..." Cleaver coughed up blood into a fist. "Bloody fast. And strong."

"It's their armor. It's the suit, it gives them agility."

"Why didn't you say anything... before?" Cleaver grunted.

"Zain, the marquis!" Headmaster Barrata pointed.

"Those hovercrafts have been mowing us down here. Near untouchable. Got one." Cleaver pointed his sword to a flipped over hovercraft. "But those other two are more careful now. Been trying to get to him," Cleaver said.

"We have a plan in place." The headmaster looked down at the telecommunicator on his watch. "Mylow. Are you and the others in position?"

"We are almost at the rear fortifications. We've needed to clear our path of archers and casters."

"We are ready. Let us know when you're here." Headmaster Barrata didn't sever the communication but surveyed the chaotic scene in front of him. Many of the Scorpions, as well as some of Lukas's foot soldiers and those of Gazo's and Gracie's, were already battling ahead, unaware of the other plan. "Zain, who are those others with the marquis?"

"Hector, Alexyer, and Sheamus. They are the traitors."

"And the other four?"

Zain shook his head. "Just soldiers."

"Those three will receive the Hanging." Klum Barrata looked at his telecommunicator.

Mylow's voice came across. "We are here."

Zain looked up and noticed the backyard battlements had been overtaken. Archers and Power casters stood side-by-side along the back parapets. Lukas stood between Mylow and Carla Sonetta. Unlike the other two, he didn't appear to be fatigued, but his armor was just as coated with blood as the outfits of the others around him.

"Mylow, tell the others to aim for the ones in snakesuits."

The marquis saw the movement. His eyes widened as he realized the support he'd had up top had been replaced. Quickly, he barked orders to those around him. Pockets of earth erupted. The twang of arrows being fired cut through the air. Many men, including some of their own, were split in two by spires of earth or donned in arrows as a maelstrom of both overtook the field. But the tactic had resulted in one of the hovercrafts being split in two. Now it only left the marquis's convoy.

When the short barrage was over, Marquis Desmier barked orders at his men from atop of his hovercraft. Groups of Lokigh soldiers, along with snakeskin soldiers from Zigarda's company, hoisted themselves with Power to the hallways and battlements that overlooked the courtyard. The army was now spread out. From atop the battlements, Lukas took this opportunity to jump off, Mylow and Carla Sonetta alongside him, casting Power to transport them to the ground below on an elevator of earth. A few other pairs of Power casters and archers from Gracies and his uncle's vanguard also leaped off the battlements, but most remained. Those with Power fought for control with the other Power casters of the enemy army, and the archers picked off enemy soldiers.

Lukas stalked towards him. "Zain, we need to get the marquis and the others off those hovercrafts. Do you have any thoughts?"

Zain nodded. "I do."

"Make it quick. They've spotted us."

The hovercraft sped towards them. Eight men aboard slashed at soldiers on the way, a technological thoroughbred pummeling anything that got in its way.

"Mylow, we need you."

"What can I do?"

"Use earth, make a blockade in front of them just strong enough so that it takes them a moment to overtake it."

"*Maa.*" Mylow raised his free hand and up shot a pillar of earth. "Now what?"

"What beats earth?"

"Fire."

"Exactly."

"Where are we going to get—" Zain changed his sword to a knife and withdrew the other knife before Mylow could finish his sentence. "Good thinking."

Zain put his knives together in an X. "Hold onto the spell, but let them come through."

Little veins formed in the earthen shield before it burst like a windshield. The sods of earth blocked their vision, just enough for Zain to strike his knives together. Mylow pushed a ball of orange fire towards the targeted hovercraft. As predicted, all eight aboard jumped, leaving the hovercraft engulfed in flames. Each of them drew their weapons and looked down at Zain's force. This was it.

Six to their eight. It wasn't the best odds, but it would be the best they could muster here and now. And surely their skill was greater.

"I'll take the marquis. Cleaver take—"

"Where is Perrine, Mr. Berrese?"

"Injured. We talk later. We need to decide—"

"Zain!" Issac ran towards them from the corridor, alongside Garie and Nyrin. "We found you."

Zain's eyes lit up. "Nine to eight. This will be easy then. Now—"

"I'll take the Power casters," Mylow said.

"I'll fight with you." Headmaster Barrata twirled the sword in his hand.

"Leave them to me, Klum. Go with Zain to handle the marquis."

"I want Hector." Issac stepped forward.

"Me too." Nyrin stepped alongside Issac.

"Take him, but don't kill him. We need him for information." Zain furrowed his brows.

"I'll take the marquis with Zain." Lukas clenched his gauntlet.

Zain shook his head. "Go to the throne room. Headmaster Barrata and I are more than enough for him. Go free my mother and Abraham while we distract the others."

"Are you sure?"

"Yes."

"Very well."

The party dispersed. Zain and Headmaster Barrata veered off towards Marquis Desmier. Mylow and Carla Sonetta charged towards the Power casters in the group. Fissures shook the ground, but Zain had no idea whether it came from Mylow or the other side. He sidestepped the veins and cracks as he ran towards Marquis Desmier. At full speed, he tripped over a piece of earth that caught his shoe mid-stride.

Zain hit the ground. Hard.

The marquis advanced on him and lunged with his sword. Klum Barrata intercepted it with his own. Twisting his entire body, he fought back Marquis Desmier's momentum, making him stumble in the process. Zain got to his feet. He ran towards the marquis, assuming Klum would charge with him, but something stopped the headmaster from moving. Brown flashed in front of him. Zain hit a slab of earth face first. He reeled back, stunned. The earthen slab disappeared, and Marquis Desmier sprang forward.

*Shield.*

Zain held up his forearm, blocking the attack, thankful for his zircha steel. Marquis Desmier could cast Power, but at least his weapon was unexceptional.

"Are you here because you're tired of being Zigarda's puppet?" Zain circled in coordination with the man, watching for the slightest movement.

"Why else do you think I agreed to take the castle?"

The bluntness shocked Zain. He let down his guard. A boot claimed his stomach, and he stumbled backwards. The headmaster rejoined the battle, jumping and ducking, exchanging volleys with the marquis. A different soldier attacked the headmaster from behind. The sword stuck his back, splitting open the Gazo's vest. The headmaster wheeled around, swinging for his unknown assailant. Zain jumped forward, not letting the marquis take advantage of Klum Barrata's momentary distraction.

Zain exchanged blow after blow with the marquis, being wary now of the ground as well as the steel.

"*Vesi.*"

Water engulfed Zain's head, drowning him and obscuring his vision. The marquis swung at Zain. *Axe.* Trusting in his skill, Zain swung the axe head down, hoping it would connect with the sword. It did, the force of the blow carrying the marquis's body with it, freeing Zain from the water that drowned him. Zain gasped for air. *Shield.* In the blink of an eye, his axe changed to a shield, and he connected it with the marquis's jaw, pummeling him like Hydro had done to Zain during the Trials. The man rolled and collected himself. He picked up another sword. His own had fallen from his grasp during Zain's assault.

"So, Zigarda is such a bad ruler that you go across the sea to get away from him?"

Marquis Desmier massaged his jaw and stood. "Boy, you know nothing." He lunged and sliced at Zain.

Zain swatted away the sword strike. "I know weakness when I see it. You're running."

"Humph."

"I thought so. Knowledge is Power, isn't it?" Zain batted away another series of attacks. The marquis's hand flicked upward. Zain jumped.

"You learn quickly." Marquis Desmier swung sideways at Zain.

*Shield.* Zain blocked the strike that came to his face. Zain pushed the marquis's sword back and then rotated his torso. *Sword.* He came full circle and slammed his sword into the ground. "*Maa!*"

Zain didn't expect the spell to work. He had only wanted to trigger an instinctual reaction from the marquis. But a tremor of earth shot forward like an underground snake, erupting into a fist that squeezed around the marquis. Zain stood back, shocked. The spell ended. The marquis fell to the ground.

Zain snapped out of his awe. He closed the distance and grabbed the marquis by the back of his armor, putting a sword to the man's throat.

"This ends now. Drop your weapons."

Carla Sonetta stood next to a kneeling Klum Barrata and a red snakeskinned guard. A dagger came across the guard's neck, and he crumpled to the floor. Sheamus was dead, but Zain saw, with sorrow, that Garie was as well. Nyrin lay on the ground a body's length away from Hector and Issac, who were in a stalemate. The young man was getting to his feet, clutching his stomach. Hector punched Issac in the face and grabbed him from behind, threatening his life just as Zain did the marquis'.

"It looks like it isn't as over as you think it is. Release Marquis Desmier and your friend goes free."

"Zain, don't do it."

Zain held the marquis's head tightly against his blade. He looked to Headmaster Barrata, hoping for advice. His headmaster kept his eyes focused on the man that he held captive. Nyrin looked towards Zain and gestured to a knife in his hand, obscured by his leg.

Zain shook his head. The move was too risky. "Let him go and we won't give you the Traitor's Hanging."

"I don't think it works like that." Hector's gaze pivoted between the party. "Do it!" He pushed his axe closer to Issac's neck.

"Tell him to stand-down!" Zain ruffled Marquis Desmier.

The marquis stayed silent.

"Zain. It's been an honor."

"No!"

It was too late. Issac pushed against the axe and slit his own throat. Flashbacks came back to Zain of his own sacrifice that he had made so long ago. Issac crumpled to his knees, a slight smile on his lips.

Zain let go of Marquis Desmier and rushed towards Hector. Slash. Swing. Strike. Stab. Zain barraged the traitor with every combination he could think of. The onslaught and ferocity of the attacks knocked Hector's sword out of his hand. *Axe.*

"Zain!"

Zain was about to come down on Hector's sword-hand with his axe when a spire of earth erupted out of the ground in front of him. Zain was yanked back and shoved to the floor. In his place stood Klum Barrata. He held his arms in front of his body in an X. A watery shield slowed the spire of earth, before it could pierce the headmaster.

"Talk again and you die." Carla Sonetta blindfolded the marquis with one hand and held a knife to his throat with the other.

The earth retreated.

Hector took advantaged of Barrata's defensive stance to tackle the man and come down with a knife. Barrata held his knife strike at bay. Nyrin came up behind Hector and hauled him back. He interlocked his legs around the larger man's waist and then put one hand under his chin and a knife to his throat.

"Drop the knife."

Hector squirmed. "You little Niss—"

Still holding tight to Hector's jaw, Nyrin slashed a gash on Hector's cheek, then put the knife back to the man's throat. Hector stopped moving.

Zain stood and went over to Klum Barrata, pulling his instructor up to his feet. Mylow came towards them.

"Thank you, Mylow. Carla, hand the marquis over to Cleaver so he doesn't try anything."

Cleaver stepped forward and grabbed the marquis from Carla, making sure to cover the marquis's eyes first and then take him under his throat with a large forearm.

Free of the man, Carla turned to Zain, one hand on her waist and the other jabbing at Zain. "Act accordingly, Mr. Berrese. Life is a play. That is the fourth pillar. We all have our parts. That stunt you pulled almost got you and Klum killed."

Zain shivered and cowered before Carla Sonetta's haranguing.

"Carla, I'll talk with the boy. Go with Mylow to find blindfolds for these two so they can't cause any more trouble. While you're out, tell the parties to start finishing off what remains of the troops. Zain, it's time we go get your mother. Your uncle should have been back by now."

Zain looked around. Klum Barrata was right. His uncle should have returned. Unless... Zain gulped. He counted the bodies, noticing that he had yet to see Alexyer again. Where had the man gone? Zain's gaze dashed to the entrance of the throne room. Had he escaped in all the chaos? Is that why...

Zain ran to catch up to the headmaster, who walked with a slight favor towards his left side. "Headmaster, I'm—"

Without turning to acknowledge Zain, Klum Barrata said, "Zain, don't be so reckless next time. Carla is right. What you did could have gotten both of us killed."

"I—"

"Have to see each brush stroke of battle for it—"

"Determines the war's portrait," Zain finished the Headmaster's words with a sigh. "I know. Issac, he..."

"He made the bravest decision he could have, Zain."

Zain gulped. He had made that decision once himself, but he had been saved. Why had he been saved? Had his decision somehow prompted Issac to make the same choice? Zain stayed silent as they approached the double doors leading to the throne room.

"Zain, are you okay?"

Zain didn't answer.

"This is about the guilt you feel, isn't it?"

With mouth slightly agape, Zain looked at the headmaster. He nodded.

Klum Barrata put a hand on Zain's shoulder. "Death defeats us. Nothing else. Do not dwell on the past. Issac made a hard choice. A brave choice. Now let's get your mother and uncle and finish this thing once and for all." He grabbed the door handle and then released it. He looked Zain in the eye. "What if it's Zakk or Zigarda in there?"

"Zigarda's north."

"How do you know that?"

"The marquis said it last night at negotiations."

"He could have been lying."

Zain hadn't considered that. Had he been naïve to think that Zigarda wouldn't be here? That he wouldn't stay hidden as an insurance policy in case Zain actually made it this far? What if he and Zakk were here? "Then this battle truly isn't over yet."

"Do you have what it takes to confront Zakk when the time comes?" Klum Barrata studied Zain.

Zain bit his lip, wondering how he should approach the situation. Then he remembered the advice of Carla Sonetta. "*Life is a play. Act accordingly.*"

Headmaster Barrata snickered. "Get those words out of your skull, Zain. We have our own mantras, remember that."

"Only death defeats, nothing else," Zain parroted the answer he knew his headmaster wanted to hear.

"Now you are speaking like one of us. Good. Let's go."

Inside, Zain drew his weapon. Headmaster Barrata did the same. Body turned away from the throne, his uncle Lukas lay face down on the floor, a pool of blood spilling out from underneath him. Behind him and next to the throne was his mother, bound and gagged. And on the throne beside her sat Lord Vangle, bound and gagged as well. When they saw Zain, they squirmed and kicked their feet.

Inch by inch, he and the headmaster approached, backs towards one another, keeping an eye out for signs of Alexyer. How had the man overtaken his uncle? Zain recalled what Gerald had once said about how Alexyer utilized his surroundings. Had his uncle been ambushed by the man? That was the only explanation that made sense; his uncle was much more powerful. *Where could he be?*

A trail of blood leading into an adjacent room gave it away. Zain got Barrata's attention and nodded at it. The old man followed it towards the hallway. Zain continued approaching the throne, keeping his eyes peeled for anything. His mother and uncle looked at him wide-eyed, pleading muffled somethings through their gags. He didn't unbind them immediately. Instead, he turned away from them and flipped over Lukas's body. Blood covered his uncle's stern face. With one hand, Zain closed his uncle's eyes. A cut across the neck told Zain what had killed his uncle. But then something else struck him as odd. Zain noticed there was another wound in the ribs between the plates of armor. Zain leaned forward to examine it closer.

"Zain! Roll!"

On instinct, Zain rolled forward, leaping over the body of his uncle. Out of the breast pocket of his academy outfit, Zain withdrew his knife. Zain turned, saw Alexyer in his place, and threw the knife. It caught him straight in the face. The man yanked the knife out of his eye. Before he could do anything more, Zain lunged at the man and tackled him. The knife clanged to the ground, as did his sword. Fist after fist, Zain pummeled the man. Blood splattered onto Zain's face. Groans beseeched the air. Aches and pleas until the man stopped moving. Even then, Zain continued punching the man until a hand came to his shoulder.

"It's done. Zain, it's done."

Zain collapsed off of Alexyer's body. Adrenaline still pumped through him; he couldn't focus. The muffled pleas of his family turned Zain's attention. "Mom!" Zain rushed over to her, taking off her gag. "Mom, you're here. What happened?"

"That man came to free us, but... but then this one," she nodded towards Alexyer, "he came up from behind the throne like he did you and... and..." She sobbed.

"It's okay. It's okay. I'm here now."

"I know," she smiled. "Quick. Untie me."

Zain looked around for something to cut her bonds. Where had his knife gone off to? Seeing his sword behind him, he left her to pick it up. Crouched over, hand on the hilt of his sword, he noticed his uncle's body in front of him once more. It was turned away. Why? The wound on his neck had killed him, that was obvious, but what about the side wound? *That man? She knew Lukas.* Zain's eyes bulged.

Zain spun on his heels. "Barrata, don't it's a—"

He didn't have a chance to say another word. His mother tackled him, a dagger plunging into his lower abdomen. She withdrew it and raised it again. *Shield.* Zain punched his mother with his shield, sending her flying off of him and the dagger out of her grasp. She quickly recoiled, rolling with the punch and landing on her feet, fingers bracing her on the ground, ready to pounce.

Klum Barrata stumbled back into the throne room and collapsed to his knees. One hand favored a wound to his side. Blood leaked through his fingers. He needed an adored urgently. Zain tucked his headmaster's sword arm around his neck and dragged him to his feet. An arm still locked around Barrata, Zain kept his gaze fixated on the two skinchangers ahead of him.

"How did you know it was us?" The woman rejoined her comrade and picked up Alexyer's sword.

"Where is my mom?" Zain yelled.

"I'm right here. Don't you recognize me?" She laughed. A crooked smile spread out across her lips.

"You are not my—"

"Zain, wait."

Zain rushed forward, not heeding his headmaster's words. He closed in on the duo. In unison, both swung at him overhead. *Lance.* Zain's weapon changed, and he held it overhead, blocking both attacks. He spun his lance to the left, creating momentum to send his mother backwards a few paces. Zain spun on his heel, coming underneath a slice from his uncle's sword as the skinchanger tried countering Zain's movement. Zain slashed at the man's thighs, bring him to his knees.

Movement behind him caught his attention. His mother charged him. Barrata connected with her, tackling her as she lunged at Zain. Instinct took over, and he turned back towards his uncle. It was too late. His uncle launched himself at Zain and tackled him as well. He brought his sword down on Zain. Zain lurched sideways as best as he could, and the sword slid off Zain's metal side.

Next thing Zain knew, the pressure was gone. Zain groaned as his side ached. Headmaster Barrata pulled the man up by his chin. Justice cut clean across the neck of the man, decapitating him. Zain got to his feet. Headmaster Barrata was tackled from behind by his mother. Like a mad butcher, she punched him full of stab wounds.

*No!* Zain pushed himself up and found his lance. Half crawling, half pouncing, he lunged toward her, grabbing her hair and pulling her backwards with him. *Knife.* His lance changed and Zain brought the knife clean across her throat, keeping her locked on top of him as she bled out. Then, when the gurgling and struggling stopped, he released her and let her fall to his side.

*Dead. They're dead...*

Zain crawled over to Klum Barrata and turned him over. The headmaster's eyes had already closed. Zain put a finger underneath his chin but felt no pulse.

Zain sobbed. "No!"

Adrenaline still pumping in his body, he picked up Klum Barrata and carried him to the exit, but Zain couldn't hold his weight. He was too weak. The fighting, the Power, and the emotions had syphoned his resolve. He crumpled to his knees, falling down upon Klum Barrata's lifeless body.

The door opened.

Zain sucked in another big breath. He squinted, trying to see who it was. The Cleaver entered.

Zain pushed himself up, his arms weak pillars. Eyes wide, he reached out to the large man. "Help."

He collapsed, seeing no more.

## CHAPTER 37

# CONFRONTATION PART II

Every so often, Eirek's gaze would flick to the raucous fracas between the ship-turned-machine and Chantico. How long would it be until the people of Fernis, or even Lord Requart himself, would show and try to make sense of the two entangled behemoths. Luck had so far kept his own ship unscathed from the rampant raging.

For the most part, though, his eyes were focused on Desmós. He knew for certain now that the necklace had finally taken control. What that meant in terms of the fight, however, he didn't know. But he did know that Cain—with Chantico present—would put the odds in their favor.

He and Cain split off, approaching Desmós from opposite sides. Desmós looked at them from right to left, and when they flanked him, he moved forward, putting them at an angle again. Eirek gestured to Cain.

"*Palo!*"

Eirek lunged forward.

Water sprayed upward from the felsic floor, killing the stream of fire from Cain on contact. Eirek's blade found its kin in a sweet chime. Desmós blocked his attack with the sword and followed through with the hammer. Eirek jumped back, the hammer just grazing his abdomen, his efforts enough to save him from a devastating blow. A piece of his mythril armor dislodged and dropped to the ground. His stomach was now completely exposed. *This is for real.* Eirek readjusted his stance and his mindset. He was no longer sparring with Guardian Eska. This was it. This was real life. And he knew what was at stake—everything.

Cain rushed forward, lance like a spear.

Without looking away from Eirek's eyes, Desmós said, *"Maa."* A barrier of earth formed in front of Cain, halting him.

Eirek swung his sword. Desmós countered. Eirek ducked. Fire climbed over the wall of earth, disintegrating it. Cain leaped forward and brought his lance down overhead. Desmós put both weapons overhead as an X, blocking the attack and pushing it to the side. Eirek swiped at Desmós, but he swept underneath.

Pain. Eirek stepped back, flinching slightly. He looked down and noticed a slight diagonal cut along his ribs. Adrenaline told him to ignore it. Entering the fray again as Cain and Desmós continued conversing through their weapons, he slashed at Desmós. He blocked it and kicked Eirek, muttering under his breath. The attack sent Eirek soaring back more than it should have. As fast as he could, he got to his feet, feeling the heat underneath him.

An immense vibration brought all three of them to their knees. The machine had crashed. Poised to strike, Chantico lurched forward. The machine punched her head, sending her skidding into one of Fernis's city walls. She hissed.

A chorus of clangs called back his attention. Cain and Desmós dueled. Eirek ran towards them. Desmós spared him a quick glance, then held out his sword to block an overhead strike from Cain. Keeping engaged in Cain's battle, Desmós swiped at Eirek with his hammer, causing Eirek to jump back a pace toward a pool of water and electricity.

Desperate to avoid the water, he called out in mid-air, *"Maa!"* He landed on a slab of earth. Quickly, that slab of earth was overtaken by the strength of the water spell, breaking the barrier. Shocks crawled up and down his body, sending him into throes.

Through half-opened eyes, Eirek saw the machine try to stomp on Chantico. She contorted her body and slithered her way in between its legs, causing it to topple to the floor once more, bringing the fight between Cain and Desmós to a temporary halt. Eirek got to his feet and sprinted towards the stunned fighters.

By the time Eirek approached, they were deep into a series of attacks and counters. Cain jabbed his lance forward. Desmós swiped it to the side with the blade, then countered with an overhead strike using the hammer. Cain blocked as well, holding his lance above him. Eirek slashed overhead. Desmós rolled out of the way. Something brushed against his leg. He tripped and fell face first.

Instinctually, he rolled to the right. Wind rushed by his head. The floor shattered next to him, bursting into tiny shards that left cuts on his face. Eirek kicked towards the back of Desmós's legs, finding his mark. It crippled him for a split second. Eirek swung out with his sword, hitting the Ether Hammer and severing it from Desmós's grasp. Desmós stumbled. Eirek stood and wiped his face clean. Blood stained his hands, and he could feel it caking on his cheeks in the heat. *That was too close.*

Cain seized upon the opportunity, lunging forward, lance in front.

"*Salama!*" Desmós yelled.

Cain's body became a host to electric centipedes, and it shocked him in mid-air, dropping him. The lance fell from his hand.

Eirek pushed down on his quartz ring. "*Salama!*"

Cain no longer writhed as Eirek battled Desmós for control of the Power.

Desmós turned to him, eyes like polished onyxes. "How are you able to cast that?"

Eirek ignored the question. Gritting his teeth and tensing his muscles, he fought Desmós's control. When Cain recovered, they would have the upper hand again.

"Then how about this?" Desmós smirked. "*Vesi!*"

Water trapped Eirek's feet. It spread up his legs. Before it overtook him, he spread his spell over to himself. In the hierarchy, electricity beat water every time, but this water spell was more powerful, so it merely stopped its progress, rather than annihilating it all together. With his strength spread over two entities, Eirek was weakened. Cain didn't writhe anymore, but an electric coffin encompassed him.

"So the Guardian of the Core has taught you well. *Palo.*"

Where the water stopped, fire took its place, sweeping over his torso. The water controlling his legs began to boil. *What do I do?* Casting water using his own sweat would combat the fire, but he wouldn't be able to save Cain from electrocution. If he continued on his course, he might weaken too much. He needed to do something.

"*Palo.*"

*I'm sorry, Cain.* Eirek concentrated his strength, creating electricity powerful enough to fight back the water on his legs.

Cain's mouth opened in a silent scream as convulsions took him.

Desmós furrowed his brows as his spells were broken. "Don't you care about your friend? Are you that selfish?"

When he could finally move again, Eirek felt weak. His heart beat faster. Sweat slid down his body, dropping in hissing pools on the floor. "He'll live. He has her strength with him." With his sword, Eirek pointed to Chantico, who wrapped herself around the machine. One arm had already been severed. Now she constricted its left arm. She bit down on the shoulder.

Desmós frowned. "Let's see how long he can last, then. *Palo, Vesi, Maa.*" All of Power enveloped Cain's body, entombing him in black. "You better hurry."

"*Maa. Palo.*" Eirek called upon the two spells easiest to cast. He focused on slowing the progress of the black tomb and what he imagined it was doing to Cain underneath.

While focusing on combating the Power, he swung his sword towards Desmós, who backed away, avoiding the strike and then launched an offensive of his own, causing Eirek to move backwards. Parry. Parry. Duck.

A deafening screech, like steel ripping from its sockets. Crash. Thud.

Eirek looked behind Desmós. The machine's head rolled on the floor. Chantico toppled over with the rest of the mechanical body, motionless.

"*Maa.*"

Eirek stepped back and tripped, too distracted by Chantico's victory to notice the stump behind him. Desmós leaped forward, swinging the sword down. Still on his back, Eirek put his blade up, blocking the attack.

Desmós kicked. "*Voima.*"

Eirek's arm flung to the ground, sword wrenched from his grasp.

Eirek coughed and inhaled. His eyes watered. Desmós loomed in front of him, sword down. Pain came after the realization that he had been stabbed. Another gut-wrenching pain. Eirek coughed more. Blood splattered over his own chin. It caked there and pooled below. *This is it...*

There was a loud hiss.

Desmós turned around. Eirek thought he heard him say, "*Vesi!*" but he wasn't sure. He knew only the pain in his chest and his abdomen. His eyes grew heavy. His heart beat slower. Desmós vanished. Eirek blinked. Through the orange clouds above, a light shone through, almost as if welcoming him to Axiumé. *Uncle, I will see...* Eirek closed his eyes, and the world finally grew dark and cold around him.

CHAPTER 38

# PRIDE

"**I**t's been over a week now, dear. Don't turn yourself away again. I know you are stronger than this."

In a half-stupor, Luvan listened to the voice of his wife Lucine from behind the door of his study. He had locked it, as he always did when he wanted to be alone. There was no better time for that than now. What purpose did he have? None.

Guardian Eska had defended himself as well as someone could. He had cleverly brought his apprentice with him, and to Luvan's amazement, the inadequacies that the Guardian had noted in the young man hadn't shown themselves. Training with the Guardian had certainly made Eirek more competent. And perhaps that was the purpose of the Guardian of the Core. To give to others a sense of purpose and belonging, and without him, Luvan felt nothing. He wondered if Victor Zigarda or Nyom Numos felt the same. In the end, they had suffered the same fate as Luvan: subverted and deposed. In front of nearly every lord and lady, Luvan's reputation had been more than tarnished; it had been destroyed. Completely and utterly destroyed.

He thought back to the prophecy he received so many years ago from a prophetess who said his name was given for greatness. But what greatness did his name actually hold? Yet, surely it must still hold some significance, as the condition hadn't been met. Or had it?

"Luvan, honey, you can't go on like this." A gentle pounding of the oakwood door came from behind Luvan.

His wife still remained at his side, and the children were away at their boarding school. They were finishing their final years in high school. Would they have to vanish from his life in order for his name to truly be recognized? Luvan shuddered at the thought. His hand slipped to the knife on his belt.

The world spun as he swiveled in his chair, hand massaging his temple, wondering if he should let her in or not. Lucine was only trying to help, and he appreciated that, but sometimes the best help was silence. Silence and rumination. Where had he gone wrong?

He took the hunting knife from where he had placed it on the mahogany desk and pulled it from its sheath. Kicking his feet up onto the desk, he leaned back in his chair and tossed the knife up into the air. Even a little intoxicated, he still threw the knife with utmost precision and fluidity, like he had been taught by his father.

Another knock.

Again, he ignored it.

"Luvan, dear, Senator Numos is here to see you."

Luvan snapped his head in the door's direction. The change in posture caused the falling knife to slice open part of his palm. Blood trickled out of the open wound. Cursing, he stalked towards the door. He yanked the door open with his unbloodied hand, holding the other hand up; he would have his wife fetch a cloth for him.

"You? You dare to—"

"Luvan, what have you done?" Lucine asked, her eyes wide. "I'll go fetch a towel."

Nyom Numos glanced down at Luvan's hand. Instantly, he took a handkerchief from the breast pocket of his suit coat and grabbed Luvan's hand in his own. "No need for that, Lucine, I come prepared." Numos dabbed Luvan's hand. "Apply pressure."

"Well, I'll go and get the antiseptic, then. I'll be right back." Lucine put a hand on Numos's shoulder. "Help him, please."

Numos nodded. "Certainly. I will try." Numos turned his attention to Luvan, who wavered in the threshold of the doorway. He tilted his head to one side. "Luvan, you've seen better skies."

Luvan harrumphed. "What do you want, Nyom? Why are you here?"

"Are you not even going to invite me into your office?"

"No."

"Well, that isn't a very proper way to treat a guest."

"You are a guest that continually ruins my life."

Numos opened his mouth to object but then closed it. "Just because one plan doesn't work doesn't mean you give up. When plans go awry, there are always contingency plans. Change is about adapting, is it not? That's what I told you

Gladonus needed, and it still needs it, Luvan. Now, please." Numos bobbed his head, indicating he wanted to come into the study to talk privately.

Despite Luvan's contempt for the man, he spoke true words. Luvan had forgotten how to adapt. He had been too focused on his revenge that he hadn't thought about how he could pivot his position to different outcomes.

Luvan smacked his lips together. "Come in." He dragged a chair to the front of the desk he had been sitting at earlier. "Sit." He gestured for Numos to take a spot and then maneuvered back to his own position. He reached down to the floor and picked up his knife, wet with his blood, and laid it on the table in front of him, sharp edge angled towards Numos.

"Where did you learn your knife skills?" Numos asked as he settled into his seat.

"My father."

"Was he any good?"

"Very."

"Hmmm... Perhaps it's you, then."

"Don't talk, speak. I'm not in the mood to muse over your words."

Numos chuckled slightly. "Too much time away from office, perhaps?" Luvan glared at Numos. "Okay, okay. Just wanted to have a verbal joust with an equal, is all. Both times we've met like this, you managed to cut yourself with the knife."

Luvan frowned at Numos. "Maybe it's you?"

Numos laughed. "No. No. No. It most certainly couldn't be that. I am only human, after all. I only have a way with words, not with knives. I don't believe in sorcery and witchcraft."

"Yet you can cast Power quite well. A blue flame? I never took you as Blessed."

Numos fidgeted with the bifocals on his face, repositioning them to have the circular frames rest on his chubby cheeks. "Yes. Well, we all have secrets, don't we?"

Luvan nodded. "We certainly do. Like your corroboration with Victor Zigarda. Isn't that so?"

Numos didn't respond for a moment. Cane in front of him, he leaned forward and cleared his throat. He was just about to speak when the door opened behind him, and Lucine came in with some cleaning materials for the cut.

The conversation halted while Lucine tended to Luvan's wounds. When she finished, she took the cloth from Luvan and looked to Numos. "I can clean this for you if you like."

"Oh, no need. I have maids at my estate who can do that." Numos plucked the handkerchief from her hand. "Might as well put them to work. I pay them after all." He smiled.

Lucine smiled back. "Are you sure? It's no trouble at all."

"Please. It's okay."

"Well, I'll leave you two to it, then."

"Close the door when you leave, Lucine."

"Of course, dear."

When the door closed, Numos tucked the handkerchief into his breast pocket and turned his attention back to Luvan. "What brings you to that conclusion?"

"I never told Victor Zigarda about that meeting. Yet he still appeared. How?"

"Perhaps he heard about it from someone else?"

"Don't play coy with me, Nyom. I've checked call logs."

Numos furrowed his brows. "Yes, Victor and I had an arrangement. Just like you and I had an arrangement. People do these things in order to get ahead. I believe it's called synergy. We can only do so much by ourselves, after all. Imagine Eska without his conseleigh or his dragon? Powerless, wouldn't he be?"

"He would still have the Power of the Twelve, but I understand your point. Now, why are you here?"

"To create more synergy."

Luvan guffawed. "You cannot be serious?" He laughed until his stomach hurt and he coughed. "You are serious, aren't you? What would make you think I would ever help you again? You *ruined* me."

Numos shook his head. "I did no such thing. Sometimes things in life don't go as planned. Do you think I wanted to lose my position as senator? Or that Victor wanted to be deposed from being lord of Empora? No. Obviously not, my friend."

"Humph. *Friend.*" Luvan snickered. "What is Victor Zigarda doing nowadays, anyway?"

"I haven't the faintest clue. I took the opportunity to do business with him because of my luck in being afforded witness to the Trials, and I reported back to him what I saw there to build his case against the Guardian for the hearing. Now, I—"

"And what was Zigarda going to do for you?"

"He would have elevated my position."

Luvan scoffed. "To one of his conseleigh?"

"Perhaps." Numos bobbed his head. "Your place, I should think."

Luvan glared at Numos and straightened himself. Planting his forearms on the desk in front of him, he leaned forward. He picked up the knife and pointed it at Numos. "The gall on you to come in—"

Numos didn't cower in any manner. "Put that knife away. No need to be inhospitable here, *friend*." He raised an eyebrow.

Luvan eyed him curiously. Surely, Numos should have been somewhat afraid. But he wasn't. Or, at least, he didn't appear to be. Why was he so confident? He could cast Power. Blue flames, even. But were there other skills in this lard of a man that Luvan didn't know about? Luvan set the knife on the table.

When Luvan had retaken his seat, Numos continued. "Just because setbacks happen in our lives doesn't mean that we cannot continue moving forward to our goals."

"And what new goal is that for you?"

"The advancement of my career. It is..." He paused. "Well, I am sure you heard about the tragic circumstances regarding Lady Liliana, yes?"

Luvan folded his arms over his chest. He bobbed his head. Cottonmouth settled into the back of his throat. This talk was too serious and sobering for him to continue this way. Reaching towards the side of the table, he grabbed a bottle of gin and poured.

"Aahhmm." Numos cleared his throat while Luvan took a sip.

"What?"

"Are you not going to offer me any?"

"No."

"Don't be inhospitable. I am here to help you."

"Did Lucine bring you here?"

"Well, she brought me to this room, yes, but I came to your dwelling on my own volition. There are still ways we can benefit one another."

Luvan scoffed. He waved his glass in the air, clinking the ice in it. Little splashes of gin fell from the cup onto the table veneer. "Go on then. Quickly, for I have things to do."

"Like what? Intoxicate yourself even further?"

"You interrupted my meditation and now you are boring me with your uninteresting words."

"Yes, your wife has told me you haven't come out of this room for the past week."

Luvan took a sip. "Your point, *friend*."

"Right. I'll get to it. While Guardian Eska may have deposed me from my duty as a senator, it doesn't mean I cannot aim for higher ambitions. I still maintain good contacts with some of those individuals within the Hall of Voices, and

I've found out that there are changes happening in how a lord or lady is elected. Guardian Eska's dismissal of Victor Zigarda, the decapitation of Lord Grime, and Lady Liliana's unexpected death have expedited the need to change the bylaws. Democratic elections will now be held for anyone who wants to campaign for a higher office. Being lord or lady of this fine nation is no longer only open to the marquises, marchionesses, or barons of the lesser cities."

The words intrigued Luvan, but he continued looking into the drink in his hand. "And?"

"And, well, I decided that I should try for the spot, given my recent affinity for attention."

Luvan turned his attention to Numos. "You mean your recent humiliation?"

"If you'd like to call it that, sure. But what you and I did on the stage these past few weeks was truly magical, no matter how it turned out. We secured a unanimous vote from all those in power. And we nearly impeached the Guardian of the Core. One vote decided his fate. How are these not accomplishments to be proud of?"

"Because they weren't successful. And the tactic used to even bring the Guardian of the Core to the Hall of Voices was unlawful. Shapeshifters? Impersonation of someone is—"

"A serious offense. Yes." Numos smiled. "Sometimes we have to use the cards we are dealt. What we did was not successful in the way you define success. I think about it like this: If my plan with Victor had worked, then I would have lost my position as senator anyway, yes? So, what is there to be upset about? I can choose to brood over what happened, like you are doing now, or I can go out and accept what happened and move forward. Make my own sunshine despite any clouds. I already nominated myself for Lord of Mistral. I came here today to ask you for your support and public encouragement."

"You want *my* endorsement?"

Numos nodded. "I think you have much you can bring to—"

"Who else is running?"

"I was just getting to that. The senator Jamaal Berrese has been nominated, and there is also another. Tiffanie Skyswan, who is a distant relative to Liliana Voux. She is trying to use her name and her familiarity to gain votes."

"And the Berrese man? How was he nominated?"

"Well, to be honest, he is the one I am more concerned about. A fellow senator nominated him, his family does come from well-off means in Ka'Che, and his brother—"

"Won the Trials." Luvan puckered his lips. He set down his cup. He knew why Numos had come. "And you want me to cancel out that advantage, seeing as I worked with Edwyrd for a time."

"I would be lying if I told you otherwise. Yes. I think you would make a strong advocate for me, not only because of that, but also from the time we've spent together recently."

"Well, let me tell you this. I would *never* endorse you."

"Why is that? You haven't even heard what I am offering you."

"And I don't need to. You have ruined my reputation more than I could have ever done on my own."

Numos frowned. "I am sorry you feel that way, but it simply isn't the case."

"Oh? No?"

"I told you my plan at first. You laughed at me. Then *you* came and found *me. You* wanted to pursue the impeachment of the Guardian. If anyone has tarnished your name, it was you." Numos jabbed the top end of his cane towards Luvan, poking the air in front of him. He stood up and flattened the creases of his suit jacket. "But I will say that there is nothing that is done that cannot be undone. If you want to save your reputation, then go, do what you feel you need to do to get it back. Go back to Guardian Eska. Grovel. Beg. But do something. I always feel bad for individuals who can't take charge of their purpose." Numos turned on his heel. "Good day, Luvan. I hope you find yourself."

"There is no need to play with me, Nyom. Just leave. I can't imagine you ever being lord."

Numos paused at the threshold. He turned back and walked to the desk again. "And why is that?"

Luvan looked up from his drink. He took another swig.

"Well? Is it my size, perhaps?"

"Perhaps. Leaders should be role models. Charismatic. You are neither of those things, if I am being as honest as the wind blows."

"That is simply your opinion. A leader should lead. By any means necessary, he or she needs to advance the state of his or her nation."

Luvan shook his head. "And this is where you go wrong. If you do that, you will fall out of lordship like Astor Grime or Victor Zigarda. That I guarantee."

"I am Powerful. I am well-connected. And I have ambition. Purpose. That is something many don't have."

"Like who?"

"Look in your gin, Luvan. You'll see of whom I speak. Good day. Next time you see me, you will address me as your superior, as Lord of Mistral."

Luvan took a large gulp of his gin, finishing the glass. "Leave. Now."

Luvan closed his eyes and listened for Senator Numos's retreating footsteps, the most pleasant sound of the day thus far. While in his thoughts, another scurry of footsteps approached him soon afterwards.

"I thought I told you to..." Luvan opened his eyes and saw Lucine standing before him. "Lucine, sorry, I thought it was Nyom still."

"How did the talk go?"

"Pointless."

"Pointless?"

"He only wanted to use me once again to elevate his position."

"And?" Lucine held her hands together.

"I said no. I have more dignity than that. My pride dictates that I cannot work with him again. After what we did together—"

"And that is your downfall, Luvan."

"What do you—"

Lucine came closer and took Luvan's hands into her own. "Why don't you let the past be just that?"

"Lucine, I am not working with that—"

She shook her head. "No. I don't mean the senator. I mean the Guardian of the Core. Why don't you go to him and apologize? For everything. Swallow your pride and try to become his conseleigh once more."

"Lu—"

"I don't like seeing you like this. When you were his conseleigh, you had purpose. You were someone. You weren't... *this*." A tear swelled in the corner of her eye.

"But he rejected me."

"Yes. He rejected you. But did you not disobey him, too? Isn't obedience something we should strive to give our superiors? Isn't that what the Ancients always wanted? For us to be obedient to them? And yet so many chose to follow the ways of the Twelve."

Luvan sighed. He glanced at the floor, not deserving of the longing affection in his wife's eyes. Nor his wife's hold of his hands. He tried to pull away, to retreat even more into his solitude of stupor and senseless self-worth. But she wouldn't let him. She tightened her grip, squeezing his knuckles with her thumbs.

It was Luvan's turn to shed a tear. He coughed and looked at her. "Perhaps you're right."

"Say what you will of the senator, but he does have drive. He has ambition. And that's something that you are lacking right now, Luvan. I want you to find that passion again. Find that purpose."

"Lucine... How can I..."

"Promise me that you'll go."

"Go where? When?"

"The Core. Now. Take your things with you, but I will tell you this, Luvan Katore, I don't want to see you until you are the man I married once again."

She looked into his eyes with bold determination. She removed her hands from his own. Before he knew it, she placed something into the palm of his hands. It was her wedding band. Without another word, she turned around and walked out of the door, closing it behind her.

For a long moment, he stared at his palm. The closed wound and his wife's ring stared back at him. The words of the prophetess came back to him: *You will lose those closest to you.*

He clenched his hands into fists.

He knew what he must do.

CHAPTER 39

# A TRAITOR'S HANGING

Zain wished he hadn't recovered from his fatigue. If he had never recovered, then he never would have seen what remained of the body of his mother, his uncles, his family, and the mass of bodies, or what were once bodies, that lay with them. More lay dead. Many more. Most of them had been dead for a month or more, as their bodies had already started to liquify. His mother had been one of these. Her face was nearly unrecognizable now, and Zain had identified her chiefly because of the clothes she wore, defiled with multiple stab wounds. The funk that fumigated off their faces had caused a group of Gracie's women who had discovered them to drop unconscious.

Lord Vangle's family had also been found amongst a pile of deceased stacked on top of one another by the cove that had been purposely collapsed. Their skin had turned to red. Teeth and nails falling out. Zain was sure they had been left there to rot and decay as to not putrefy the entire castle. The city was awash in blood; the castle was amuck in it.

After the discovery had been made, teams of soldiers entered the cavern holding their breath and pushed the bodies as best as they could towards the cliff. Zain made it his choice to push his mother into the sea, as well as the others in his family. His mother had told him stories when he was younger about how they had come from the Krine Sea—that was why their skin was so black—and it made sense to Zain to return her to the sea once more. The stench had knocked him unconscious twice during the seaside burial. Once after he had pushed his mother into the sea. And another time when he had spent much too long debating whether to throw his cremain ring into the sea as well. In the end, he did it, deciding that his father's remains should be with his wife, not on Zain's hand. After, he pushed the rest of his family's bodies into the sea and left. Those who had died in the battle received tending from the adored who still lived. They were given the proper attention so that their bodies didn't become like those left and forgotten below the castle.

At times like this, he envied Gabrielle. She hadn't had to see any of it. Then again, she had lost women from Gracie's as well. Perrine, Zain found out, had died before reaching the adored. There were others, too, Zain was certain. So perhaps she felt the same; she just couldn't see the mass of bodies all around them. But, still, she could smell the death that overwhelmed this place, couldn't she? Perhaps it was even a blessing in disguise by the Ancients that darkness enveloped her. Perhaps they were protecting her from all the gore and death and guilt.

Why hadn't they protected Zain? He had been learning the words; he had been studying their ways; why had they abandoned him? Why had they left him here to pay with guilt? He should have been dead. Not them. It had been his fight, his family, his lies, his actions that had brought them here. Death was his price to pay. Not theirs. He had brought ruin upon them. Upon his family. All of his actions had been for nothing. His one mission he had failed. Was he destined for anything more than sorrow? Was he only destined to bring ruin upon himself?

If it hadn't been for Gabrielle's arm locked with his own, he would have faltered. He would have fallen to his knees.

"Zain, I'm sorry."

"You told me to have faith." Zain stared blankly at the headmaster's body, side-by-side with Kendel's.

"I did." Gabrielle spoke softly, barely audible.

"Then why didn't they listen?"

"It isn't for us to understand all za ways of za Ancients, Zain."

"I gave them myself. I spoke their words. I believed."

Gabrielle swallowed before she responded to him. "Did you zough?"

"What do you mean?"

"Did you truly believe? Or were you just going zrough za motions?"

Zain didn't have an answer for her. As he pulled away from her, not wanting to hear more of her righteousness, he turned to face Cleaver.

Cleaver grunted and cleared his throat. "We've taken back the castle, Zain. Now it's your turn to fulfill your part of the bargain."

"I'll get you Zigarda."

"How?"

Zain's gaze crawled from the piles of bodies of those who died in battle to the only two men that mattered: Hector and Marquis Desmier. They sat back-to-back, tied together, still blindfolded. Zain walked around the pile of dead bodies and bobbed on his feet in front of the men.

"Where is Zigarda to see how miserably you failed? We have retaken the castle."

Hector spat.

The marquis fidgeted. His voice became a crackle on the air. "This war isn't over yet."

Zain took a step forward. "Will Zigarda finally show? Is he going to come and rescue you? Where is he?"

"Jaws will clamp on you from the north and the south."

Zain furrowed his brows. "The north. Why there? What is there?"

"Our cavalry. They will come soon enough."

"Who will come?" Zain crouched and grabbed the man's jaw and put a knife to his throat.

Nothing.

"You will answer me." He pressed harder, drawing blood.

"Do it."

Zain fixated on the apple in the man's throat. He held the sharp part of the knife there for a second. Then two. And three.

"Do it!"

Zain pulled the man's head back and removed the blindfold. He wanted to see this man cower in front of him. Boring into him, he pushed deeper, the thin line of blood spreading.

"That tickles."

"Zain!"

Zain pivoted his head to Gabrielle. Forcefully and angrily, he pushed the marquis's head down, stood up, and went over to her. "What is it?" he whispered.

"No good will come from zat. Put it away." She put two hands over the knife.

"Gabrielle..."

"Let someone else handle zis. Keep your hands clean from zis."

"There is no one else! They all..." Zain couldn't finish his sentence. Head hung low, he closed his eyes, wishing to forget about all the death. Gentle hands slipped their way into his own.

"I know what zey did. But zis isn't za way. Zere are zings worse zan deaz for zese two."

Zain exhaled deeply. He knew in his heart of hearts that this wouldn't do any good. Who was he to take their life? "Yeah," Zain muttered. "Guess you're right." He slunk away.

"*Maa.*"

His ankles itched. Landlocked, a spire shot upwards. Zain pushed himself backwards and fell. Rough earth slid in between his legs, barely missing his manhood but tearing a large hole in his pants and abrading the skin. Cleaver shoved Gabrielle aside with one arm, saving Gabrielle from her own catastrophe, but t

he spire intended for Gabrielle found its way into the Cleaver's arm. He dropped to the ground, limb dangling at his side.

"*Maa!*"

The earth returned to normal. A block of earth up to their neck encased the two men sitting on the ground. The middle began to etch away at itself, constricting, as if it was an earthen snake. Zain didn't hear anyone else; the only thing he focused on was making sure these two men suffered. With sick fixation, he continued tightening his spell.

"Zain!"

A hand came to his shoulder. A band. He recognized the long, taut fingers. He looked up. "Jamaal?" Zain sputtered. The Power died. Alongside Zain's brother was Lord Vangle's receiver, Errion Vesk.

"You can cast? Since when?"

"I..." Zain shook his head. He pointed at another soldier. "Blindfold him!" Zain pointed to Marquis Desmier. Then he turned back to his brother. "What are you doing... since yesterday..." Zain stumbled over his words.

"I had been trying to get in touch with Lord Vangle for a few days now. He had left abruptly, and Errion has been trying to contact him, but he can't. What is—"

"He's dead. They're all dead."

Jamaal's eyes widened. "What do you mean?"

"Later."

"Zain!"

"I'll tell you everything later, okay? I have business to finish now."

Marquis Desmier laughed. "The cavalry is coming." The marquis repeated the words. "From the north and the south." He wiggled his feet as if trying to dance.

Zain frowned. He swept over to the two men that lay as captives. "If Zigarda shows, he will fall, just like you did." Zain turned to speak to Hector, but the marquis interrupted him.

"What if it can't fall?"

"It will. The eagle always watches."

Hector snickered at that. "It didn't watch very well this time."

"What if the eagle is blind?" Marquis Desmier taunted further.

Zain spat on the ground. "It's time I show you Justice." Zain stalked away, towards the body of his headmaster.

"Zain, what are you doing?" Gabrielle called out.

Zain picked up Barrata's sword and examined it in the dying light. "What Klum Barrata would have wanted. What my uncle would have done." Zain walked back to Gabrielle and put a hand on her shoulder. "What duty demands of me now." And then he went to Jamaal and pushed a finger into his brother's chest. "And what you should want as well."

Jamaal followed Zain's finger. Then he looked up. He spared a glance at the pile of dead bodies. Then, with a voice that Zain had never heard before, one determined and vindictive, his brother said, "Do what you need to do."

"Justice will be served."

Zain flicked his attention towards the battlements they had stormed. He stalked over to them, not needing to look to know that Gabrielle would not follow. He knew she didn't like where this road led; it wasn't *decent*, as Gracie's would say. Luckily, she wouldn't have to see the aftermath. It was a road he needed to travel now, though. These men looked up to him. These men had fought for his cause, and soldiers had died. Many soldiers. Good soldiers. Soldiers with family. Family that would now be as fractured as his own.

Klum Barrata had trusted him, instructed him, guarded him to the very end. And now he would carry out the duty that lay before him, not by obligation, but by need.

A crowd of onlookers gathered on the slight incline of the hill before the castle. Zain shifted his gaze from the blindfolded men to the parapets. Men appeared at the top, their heads and steel helms poking above the battlements. They threw a rope over. It fell. It landed.

"Get him up!" Zain pointed to Hector.

Hector was forced to his feet by a squad of three men. As his arm was being tied by the wrist, Zain talked to him. "What you will receive now is everything you deserve for what you did in Mendeck and for what you let occur here." When he didn't speak, Zain commanded, "Pull him up."

By his arm, Hector was yanked off the ground and pulled to the height of the wooden door that had, one time, helped fortify the castle.

"*Maa.*"

Nothing occurred. Why not? Had he been casting Power, or hadn't he? Surely he had. Furrowing his brows, he turned around. "Mylow, come here, please."

From the crowd, the Power caster came over to Zain. "Yes, sir?"

"I am trying to use earth. Why isn't it working?"

"Power reacts to emotions. It also reacts to your thoughts and how you imagine using it. What are you trying to do?"

"I want to bring myself up to him."

"Then command the earth to lift you. Picture it raising you to his height."

Zain extended an open hand to the ground. "*Maa.*"

Ground underneath Zain trembled and slowly it began to rise. *I'm doing it.* Zain focused on his makeshift earthen platform and brought himself face-to-face with Hector again. He dangled there. Anything but innocent. He was guilty of a crime. And it would be a crime he would pay for. With a fluid stroke, Zain came straight across Hector's arm with his sword, severing the limb from the body at the shoulder blade. Hector yelled as he fell, blood spraying the ground.

From his perch above, Zain watched the man writhe in agony. "Get him up. Tie his other arm."

Zain waited and watched as the other arm of Hector was tied. Once fitted with his noose, he was raised again to Zain's height. A height that wouldn't kill him when he landed but would hurt all the same. Blood continued gushing from Hector's arm, and it would until he died, but there would be much more suffering before that occurred.

"This one is for Gerald." Zain came clean across the other arm with his blade, sending Hector to the ground below.

The man screamed and writhed on the earth below him. It wasn't over yet.

"Tie his legs together."

The men below followed his orders, immersing themselves in the bloodbath Hector produced. He would die soon from blood loss, but before then, Zain wanted him to know pain.

Hector was lifted by his ankles. His face was contorted in agony, with no trace of the smug look of superiority he had worn before.

"This one is for my parents." Zain came across both legs with his sword, just above the knees, halfway up the thighs.

Hector screamed and fell, and Zain took on a sick fixation as he watched the man grovel on the ground before him. *The pain he feels should be real.* It wasn't over yet, though.

"Strip him naked." Zain waited until the men below finished their orders. "Now hang him by his manhood." When raised to meet Zain this time, he was unconscious, but Zain could see a tremor of a pulse in his throat. Drawing back his sword, he severed Hector's manhood. Hector landed on his head. "Is he breathing?"

Soldiers below him checked. They shook their heads.

"Good. Remove his blindfold and tie him once more around the neck." Zain turned his gaze to the parapets. "Hoist him up. Tie a knot so that his body dangles before me."

When they did as he asked, he observed the bloody carcass of the man, dismembered now just as Zain's family had been dismembered from his betrayal. *Was it worth it now?* Zain tapped his foot, still annoyed that the man's dying face had creased to a slight smile. Some men are put on this earth just to cause havoc and destruction. Was that Hector's purpose?

Zain looked back down to the ground. "Uhh, Mylow, how do I get back—"

The earthen pillar dropped. Zain fell freely through the air. *No!* Zain closed his eyes and braced for impact. Instead of landing on hard dirt, he landed on soft sand. He opened his eyes. Mylow stood, arms outstretched. He retracted his arms and let Zain sink to the ground.

"What happened?"

"If you don't focus on the spell, you lose control. Next time you want to come down from a pillar like that, think about making the pillar smaller and releasing the energy demanded to control that pillar. Does that make sense?"

Zain shook his head.

"We will work on it."

Marquis Desmier laughed. "I remember my first spell. How are you even—"

"Strip the other one and follow me." Zain walked away, not listening to the rest of the man's retort. He had just learned he could even cast Power today. How was he supposed to know the intricacies of it? Marquis Desmier's amusement annoyed Zain more than it should. When he was brought over, Zain told the men to tie him at the throat.

While they did that, Zain focused on utilizing Power once more, elevating himself to a height similar to what Hector's had been. From his perch, he scanned the field. Jamaal still watched him intently, but it seemed Gabrielle had left, along with Carla Sonetta. Had he abandoned their beliefs? Perhaps he had, but duty demanded more from him this day than did decency.

Grunts and flailing brought Zain back to the man kicking in front of him. Marquis Desmier dangled there, incapable of anything but pain and suffering as the noose squeezed the life from him. Luckily for him, he had been on Empora's side all along and therefore didn't deserve a Traitor's Hanging like Hector had. To Zain's disgust, Marquis Desmier didn't plead in his last moments alive. Rather, he taunted Zain.

"You... are surrounded... from the north... he comes... from the south..."

The man sputtered and died. His legs stopped kicking. His lips turned downward, appropriate for his death.

In the last moments of dusk, before twilight consumed Ka'Che, a raucous roar broke out from the south. Its strength sent Zain tumbling off of his earthen pillar, barely holding on with one arm. He hoisted himself back up, and while on his knees, looked south. *What was that?*

Zain pushed Justice into the ground. He watched and waited, as did those below. But after the roar there was nothing—and then chaos ensued, blanketing everyone in bedlam of an unfathomable degree. A wind hit him, carrying with it the scent of recent death. Zain turned once more to look upon Hector and Marquis Desmier. They swung, deadweight in the breeze, jesters of the afterlife, maleficent smiles etched permanently on their faces, almost as if they had known there was something truly worse than death and were glad they would not have to meet it.

CHAPTER 40

# RHAYNA

They had scaled the slopes. With every grasp of the rope guiding them, they fought the frigidity in their fingers, and with every breath taken, they inhaled the inspiration to continue something born of imagination and impossibility—a meeting with Rhayna. After the passage had become too treacherous for the horses they had taken from Marquis Desmier's stables, they walked; when the path became too steep, they climbed; and when the frost bit through the gloves of tiger fur, when the wind howled and clawed their faces, kept warm only due to the ruby rings on their fingers, when Zigarda's zeal vanished and Zakk was left to carry him on his back, what kept him going were two words: *I'm Possible.*

He didn't know why he even bothered carrying Zigarda's dead weight. Was it the sense of obligation and duty instilled in him from Gazo's? Zakk had lost whatever respect he'd once had for the man, so what drove him to this place? Why did he carry Zigarda? Why not just abandon him? Perhaps a part of him wanted to see the bond forged between Zigarda and Rhayna. What would a process like that even look like? Zain had claimed to see Rhayna once flying over the Agna Mountains, but that was right before disaster struck, leaving his former friend with a metal side, a deceased girlfriend, and scars that haunted him to this day. What would Rhayna leave him or Zigarda with?

"We're here." Zakk shook Zigarda.

Zakk couldn't say for sure, but he assumed it was true. When Zigarda's strength had worn out, Zakk had taken the feather, secured Zigarda to his back, and continued, and now the feather stood straight with only the slightest of curves at the very tip. The terrain had plateaued, and the snow that had been up to his knees had tapered to nothing more than a soft crunch beneath his feet.

Zakk shook Zigarda once more. The man didn't stir. His charcoal eyes just stared blankly up at Zakk. It was disturbing. Zakk didn't know if the man was awake and pretending to be unconscious to see what Zakk would do, if he was asleep from fatigue, or if he was dead.

Crouching next to Zigarda, he put his fingers underneath the man's chin. He felt a pulse. *So he isn't dead. There's that.* Zakk flicked open the man's robe, spotting the flask and Zigarda's life source. He also spotted the vial of blood Zigarda had kept close to his person. That was the blood of the Apprentice to the Guardian of the Core. Was there something so special about this blood that Zigarda kept it on his person at all times? Curiosity begged him to take it. Keeping an eye on Zigarda's countenance, he obliged. He swirled it around its vial, wondering its purpose. Then his intrigue turned towards the bright blue liquid Zigarda had always kept on him as well.

Brows furrowed, Zakk studied Zigarda. The man was still unconscious, features unchanged. He answered his intrigue with a slight sip. Less than a mouthful. He swished it around his mouth, feeling tingling warmth. He swallowed. Fatigue left him. His mind sharpened. *What is this stuff?*

Zigarda coughed.

Zakk went rigid. Quickly, he stuffed the vial of blood into a padded container on his belt, and then brought his hand underneath Zigarda's head to hide the movement. "Here." Zakk brought the flask to the other man's lips, being careful to make sure the liquid made its way inside his mouth.

Within moments, Zigarda's demeanor livened. He studied Zakk for a long while and then turned his gaze towards the environment.

Zakk reeled back, crouching on his heels. "We're here."

"Good." Zigarda looked back at Zakk and snatched the flask out of his hand, stuffing it in an inside pocket in his robe. He stood and straightened out his disheveled cloak as best as he could, as if he was about to meet a suitor. After he finished, he glanced back at Zakk's chest. "The feather." Zigarda held out his hand.

Zakk returned the feather necklace to Zigarda. Zigarda turned around and held it in front of him, using it like a magnet to guide his direction as he explored the summit.

Zakk didn't follow Zigarda's lead. If Rhayna were here, he would know. A large golden bird was hard to miss. Now, though, there was nothing other than a small copse of trees, a strange at such an elevation. It was as if they had found a spot where the laws of nature ceased to exist. The snow gave way to green, which died to dirt. The suns were at their zenith. In fact, they appeared so close to Zakk that he reached upwards with his hands and delighted himself in their warmth. After the brief reprieve, he deactivated his ruby ring and continued walking around the barren depression to the edge, where interspersed trees allowed light to shine through the foliage. He walked among them until he reached the cliff. Only clouds greeted him when he looked down.

"Where do you think—"

A zephyr of air pushed him to his back. He looked up, past the foliage, and saw something expand wings and blot out the suns. *Rhayna.*

She hovered there, flapping in the air, a silhouette of silence and anticipation. After a few moments, she descended. Beat. Beat. Beat. Zakk's heartrate rose to elevations it had never experienced before. With each beat of his heart, Rhayna dropped, and when she eventually touched the ground, she folded her massive wingspan into her body. He stood and maneuvered through the copse to the skirts of the small gathering of trees, wanting to get a clearer view of the Creature of Legend.

Strong and stocky, her chest stuck out with golden plumes, and freckled around the gold were feathers of red, orange and blue. The height of a small building, she stood looking down at them through electric blue eyes.

From the fringes, Zakk observed Zigarda, wondering what his first move would be. Zakk inched forward, leaving the cover of the trees. The movement caught Rhayna's attention. She studied him for a mere second until Zigarda called her back.

"Rhayna!" Zigarda shoved the feather into the air.

She cawed and hopped back. With another cautious caw, she spread her wings and flapped with a ferocity to send Zakk sprawling once more. Zigarda buckled under such might. And with each flap she gave, electricity jolted outwards. When the flapping stopped, Zakk stood and moved closer, attracting her attention. The electric-blue eyes bore into him; Zakk had never seen anything so intense. Everything about her mesmerized him.

*You wish to claim me?*

He didn't experience her voice through his ears, but rather his mind. She cut into his consciousness, and he was sure she cut into Zigarda's consciousness as well. She lulled him with her softness. Confidence. Harmony. The bird flapped her wings again. Zakk braced his body. After she finished, Zakk moved closer.

"I am the only one fit to," Zigarda said.

*You are not fit to bond with me. You are weak.* She pushed her neck forward and snapped her beak.

Zigarda jumped back. "I assure you, I am anything but weak. *Maa.*" From his left, a spire of earth rose past Rhayna's hunched height. "*Palo.*" To his right, his arm and hand were drenched in blue flames.

*And where was this strength as you ascended to my home?*

The spells died. Zigarda stayed silent. Zakk's heart beat faster.

"I am here now. My strength before you."

*Only because of his strength.* Rhayna locked eyes with Zakk. Her wings swept the ground as she walked around her home.

Zakk switched his gaze to Zigarda. Choler and criticism circulated as Zigarda inspected him. His body tensed. His hand remained open.

Zigarda withdrew his glare to focus on Rhayna. "I assure you that isn't true. What would you have me do to show you?"

*Show me your strength and courage. Let go of my feather. The first to obtain it again will be worthy.*

Zigarda let go of the feather.

Rhayna beat her massive wings, lifting herself up off the ground. The gusts of air took the feather and swirled it overhead.

More gusts of wind carried the feather farther, letting it drift gently between Zakk and Zigarda. The zephyr brought with it the song of scabbard on steel. A sound Zakk was all too familiar with. Brows furrowed, Zakk withdrew his own, matching Zigarda.

Zigarda raised an eyebrow. "You mean to betray me?"

Zakk snickered. "You pulled your sword first."

"Let me have the feather and nothing need happen to you. I owe you that. We are family, after all."

Zakk didn't respond. His eyes flicked rapidly between Zigarda and the feather, which was now halfway between them. He contemplated letting Zigarda just take it, but the feeling he had when she spoke—how his heart beat, how alive he had felt, even for the second they had connected—he wanted it. However futile it may seem.

Zakk spat on the ground. "And I know what you do with family."

Zigarda roared. A ball of blue fire propelled towards Zakk. Zakk sprinted forward and rolled under the fireball. After one rotation, he sprang from his toes, using his momentum as he felt the ground rumble underneath him. He didn't have to look back to know a spire had just erupted behind him. Even though he had never been trained in Power, Gazo's had taught him what to look for. It had taught him how to level playing fields. It had taught him that only death defeated you, nothing else. And Zigarda wasn't death.

Ten paces.

The sudden flutters in movement by both had pushed the feather back up to where Rhayna hovered, observing the battle. Gently, it fell once again.

The ground rumbled in front of him. He jumped. Not fast enough. A square block of earth caught the edge of his foot, toppling him to the ground. His sword flew from his grasp. *No!* He rolled to the left, towards his sword. A tremor of earth moved it out of his grasp. A gust of wind. Fire gushed by him, searing his leg.

The feather fell once more, gently making its way towards the cliff. It was behind Zakk now, but he couldn't bring himself to care about that. Zigarda needed to be dealt with first.

He pushed himself up. Jumping, he kicked off a spire of earth and leaped through the air. While in mid-air, he reached behind his back and pulled two knives. He flung one at Zigarda. He batted it out of the way. That was to be expected.

He landed within inches of Zigarda and thrusted forward with his other knife. Zigarda pushed his arm down. Zakk missed his mark. He passed the knife to his left hand, his dominant hand, and spun around. Bracing his left arm with his right, he managed to handle the force dealt by Zigarda's sword.

Sword versus knife. Zakk accepted it for what it was: less reach but quicker movements. He launched an offensive, not letting Zigarda think. Stab. Parry. Duck. Thrust. Two steps backward. His heart beat. A pause in the fury. He would need to get in closer to end it.

"Do you think this is my first battle, boy?"

"No. But it will be your last." Zakk panted. As much as he hated to admit it, it had been the suit so far that had allowed him to keep pace with Zigarda, given the shortcomings. Now he needed to find a way to breach his defenses.

Knife in front, he lunged forward. Zigarda batted it away and stepped back. He lunged again. Again, Zigarda batted it away. Zigarda stepped back. *Perfect.* Once more, Zakk lunged. Knife in front. He feigned an attack, but when he saw Zigarda's blade come across his torso, Zakk reined in his knife and tucked into a roll. After a rotation, he pounced from his feet and tackled Zigarda. Without hesitation, Zakk brought the knife down and twisted. Zigarda yelled and swiped at Zakk. Zakk twisted his body and held up his forearm. The blade cut through the snakeskin suit, opening up the side of his arm as well. Zakk grimaced in pain. Zigarda tried it again. This time, Zakk caught the arm at the wrist and then used his other hand to punch the bicep, causing Zigarda to drop his sword.

Quickly, he picked up Zigarda's sword, brought it up over his head, and drove it down into Zigarda's chest.

Zigarda coughed and searched Zakk's eyes. "You betrayed me."

Zakk clicked his tongue. "You betrayed yourself."

Rhayna cawed.

He looked around. The feather still floated seamlessly through the air, drifting closer and closer to the summit's edge. He stood up, removing himself from his past life. Another gust of wind twirled it, halting it for a second to carry it higher before letting it drop again once more.

Zakk sprinted. The suit allowed him to cover more distance. In a matter of moments, he was on the skirts of the copse of trees. Before it darted amongst the trees, Zakk jumped up, trying to grab it.

A wisp of wind stole it from him and pushed it through the branches, never getting caught up in the foliage, dancing up and down and this way and that so successfully it was as if the dance was preordained, coordinated by the whims of fate. From the ground, all Zakk could do was watch and follow it, darting through the limbs and boughs as it drifted closer to the cliff.

When it left the small gathering of trees, it wafted upwards. Zakk jumped for it. Felt it. But couldn't grasp it. It went beyond safety, beyond the cliff. The light breeze died. It dropped.

From the cliff's edge, he watched it float down into the unknown family of clouds gathered below it. Everything was silent and still. Everything except his heart. An electricity pumped in it, daring him to do the impossible and implausible. Zakk took a deep breath and closed his eyes. Seconds later, he exhaled and looked down. It hadn't reached the clouds yet.

*I'm possible.*

He jumped. Only the air caught him. He plummeted. Head first, air raced past his face and his braided hair, making it difficult to keep his eyes open. He put an arm over his eyes, searching for the golden feather. He would only have one chance.

*There.*

With his left hand, he reached out. Close. Closer. He reached through his fingertips. It floated right in front of him. Closer. A gust of wind pushed it sideways. Zakk's eyes bulged. He swiped at it with his left. He missed. He swiped at it with his right. He caught it and brought it to his chest. The clouds took him. A caw came from beyond. Cold wind clawed his face, but for some reason, he felt warmer than he knew he should. His body tingled as he fell like a man given new life with a shock of electricity. Blood pumped in cadence to his beating heart. *What is—*

His freefall stopped.

Clouds vanished.

Rhayna was underneath him.

*It is my Power now surging through you, Zakk Shiren.*

"You know my name?" Zakk pushed himself up and straddled the bird's back as best he could. He looked around, shocked.

*We are one now. Family. I know all of you, and soon you will know all of me.*

"I—" Zakk looked at the feather in his hand. Its radiance still struck him.

*You showed me your strength, now you have mine.* Rhayna cawed. *You showed me your courage, now I will show you mine. Hold on.*

Rhayna cut to the left like a shark through water. Snow fell, but as soon as it hit his skin, it dissipated to water, the new warmth of his body melting it. She twirled over sideways, upside down, and in-between narrow cliffs. Zakk had never felt so invigorated. So alive.

She soared upwards, past the clouds again, past the summit of her home, where Zigarda's body now lay. She brought him close to the suns, letting their warmth bathe him in newfound energy. Then she descended, touching down on the summit once more. She hunched her back and allowed him to get off.

*Gather your things.*

Zakk walked across the battlefield. He picked up his sword and his throwing knife.

A choking, wet cough slipped from Zigarda.

Zakk strolled to stand over top of him. He crouched down on the balls of his feet. Blood smeared the dying man's face, and one hand rested next to the wound in his stomach.

When Zigarda saw Zakk, he pointed to him, fingers trembling with the effort. "I was your family."

Zakk found his other dagger, still in Zigarda's stomach. He looked into the lidless charcoal eyes of Zigarda, waning in their last moments of vitality. "You were. Until I found out what you do to family." He yanked it out; Zigarda coughed up more blood. Zakk said, "As you've said before, sacrifices have to be made." He plunged the knife into Zigarda's heart and held it there until he saw the light in Zigarda's eyes vanish. *It's finished.* He yanked out the knife and wiped it on Zigarda's clothing before sheathing it.

He stayed there for a moment, straddling Zigarda. He rummaged through Zigarda's robes, finding the flask. He brought it to his ear and shook it. There was still liquid left, but he didn't need it. The energy the liquid gave him was nothing like the energy and strength Rhayna gave him. He left it on Zigarda's carcass, stood up, and turned around.

Rhayna cawed to him. *Protect me, and I will protect you.* Rhayna lowered her shoulder.

Zakk climbed on. "You have my word; I will do my best to protect you."

*Then I will never let you fall.*

"Never?" Zakk questioned.

Rhayna cawed and then craned her neck so that she could see him with her electric-blue eyes. *Never.*

"I like the sound of that. Let's leave."

Rhayna buffeted her wings and jumped in the air. She hovered there, ten feet above the ground for just a moment, and then shot skyward, twirling all the while. As he held on to Rhayna's rainbow-golden feathers, as wind darted through his braided hair, as the electricity in his heart surged, he realized one thing—he had found what he had been looking for. He had found family.

CHAPTER 41

# THE SILENCE OF BROKEN BONDS

Desmós thrust his sword down upon the Commoner. Blood came through his teeth and lips to congeal on his chin and cheeks. Desmós smirked. He delivered another blow to the chest. More blood. *Yes. That's it. Die.* The vitality in the man's eyes waned. Desmós took the Commoner's hand. *You're coming with—*

A loud hiss cut through the air.

Still on his heels, Desmós turned back. The machine he had arrived in lay asunder, demolished into unsalvageable detritus. Chantico slid over its body, undulating in his direction. His eyes widened. *I need to leave.* The hovercraft caught his eye. *That'll work. Now to buy some time.*

Desmós raised his other hand. "*Vesi!*" A watery wall barricaded Desmós from his sister. Desmós dragged the Commoner with him. *I will need you for—* "Aaahh." Desmós grunted. Pain lanced through his body.

Chantico slammed herself against the wall again and again. Each bash sent shockwaves through Desmós's shell, eventually bringing him to his knee. He grunted. He didn't want to leave the body behind, but he needed to live. Another jolt careened down his body; he was too weak in this state to handle his sister. Reluctantly, he released the other spells entombing the King, and he released his grip on the Commoner, but not without first smearing his hand with the man's blood, leaking out through the wounds in his body. He would figure out some way to use it, but right now he needed unbridled concentration and strength in hopes of overpowering his sister.

Desmós ran to the hovercraft, sparing a glance at the True King he had fought. That man lay just as motionless and silent as the Commoner. *Good.*

There was always a silence in broken bonds. In death. Death was the only true bond anyone who wasn't like him or his father could cling to.

A loud hiss.

He looked up. Chantico had broken her barrier. He pushed another button. It kicked the ship up in the air.

"*Vesi! Salama!*" He stalled her again, this time with a dual spell.

She snorted fire, but all the fire did was climb the watery wall in front of her. When she tried to go around it, he created more of it, encompassing her in a perimeter of water, so that he wouldn't have to deal with maintenance of a barrier.

Up ahead, he saw a golden ship parked outside the city walls. *That will have to do.* Desmós drove towards it. When the belly of the ship opened, a mechanical, modulated voice came over the speakers: "Welcome, Conseleigh Inferno." He didn't care who the ship greeted; it had opened for him, and that's all that mattered. He abandoned the hovercraft and walked up the ramp.

Assuming it was the same as in the last ship he'd used, he sat down at the control panel and let the muscle memory from the prince take over. The shell had served him well in the combat with the two men, and the prince's ability to use Power had given him a tremendous advantage in overcoming them. Even Desmós had his limits, and he was approaching the precipice of those battling his sister.

In front of him, water exploded. His eyes widened. *She's free!*

"*Vesi!*" He tried putting up another wall, but she charged through it.

He pushed another button. Something rumbled underneath. The ship shot straight into the air. Chantico lunged for the ship. He steered it away from her. A minor vibration rattled him from his seat, but he got to his knees and continued pushing the lever up, putting distance between him and his sister.

He kept this position until he was above the orange clouds. Until he was certain he was safe. Until he could see the stars. Then he put the ship into an auto-pilot mode, pushing a series of buttons that culminated in an automated voice saying, "You have chosen the Central Core as your destination. Thrusters damaged. Proceed to wormhole twenty-one to be taken to Hown."

Desmós widened his eyes, trying to stay awake. He was much too fatigued for this. If he was with his father, his father could just warp him there. There would be no need for these designs made by Bane, which were just a vain attempt to mimic the portals that Lyoen had given to the Common Bloods.

He went back to the control panel and typed in a new destination. After confirming the location, he selected 'auto-pilot' again, and the ship began steering itself towards wormhole twenty-three.

Oblivious of the ship's doings, Desmós scoured it for some sort of container and found one in an apothecary kit. Along with the test tubes, he had found some droppers, syringes, antiseptics, and a curious looking bag of cerise colored leaves. A quick hunt through his shell's memory told him these were ard leaves, meant to aid in recovery. Desmós gleamed. *Perfect!*

"... damaged. Travel will require more time than necessary. Forty-eight hours until destination is reached."

The proclamation throughout the ship brought him back, his vision wandering about the small ship's compartment. As long as it got him to where he needed to go, time meant nothing. Well, almost nothing. Now that he had waited so long, what were two more days, anyway? However, surely such an elongated absence from the Commoner would alert the Guardian of the Core of his death. What could he do?

Returning his attention to the bag of ard leaves, he noticed the blood on his hand. A large portion of it was still wet. His eyes widened in realization. Could he? The idea was incredulous. Ludicrous. But it was this type of desperation that might keep him alive to realize his dreams. He lowered his head to the blood, smelling it, as if inspecting something foreign. His tongue snuck out from between his lips. Then he pulled it back.

*No! I am Desmós.*

Distracting himself from what he had just tried doing, he took out the test tube and dropper. He would need more energy for this next part than he currently had, so taking his hand not coated in blood, he grabbed a handful of ard leaves and shoved them into his mouth. He chewed. The taste of ash overpowered the unbecoming smell, making him nearly want to gag. But almost instantaneously, after he swallowed them, his heart beat with more strength. It was as if the leaves had worked their way into his system immediately. Dissolved in some way by his shell's body, his muscles were no longer fatigued. Power pulsed through his veins. It reminded him slightly of what life had once been like when he and his father were bonded. When there hadn't been any silence or distance between them; when their bond wasn't broken but vibrant, teeming with Power that overflowed in abundance. With joy and happiness at being together in the blessed land of creation. In Gladima.

Alert and focused, he set down the rest of the ard leaves and put the dropper's nose to the wet parts of his hand and elbow. Gently, he squeezed the neck, extracting as much blood as he could. When finished, he examined the tube. A milliliter was there. Maybe more. What good it would do him, he didn't know. But it was easier to have taken the blood from a dead body than to try and hunt down one of the offspring. They would have proved much more formidable, even more so than that woman in the floating cave.

He glanced at the blood that remained on his hand. Much of it had already caked to his skin while on Pyre, and the wet parts that had been left was what he had deposited into the test tube. Still, the caked parts annoyed him. He didn't want to look at them, for that would acknowledge his previous attempt in desperation. But in this heightened state of awareness now with the ard leaves coursing through his veins, he couldn't stop thinking about them. The itching sensation that felt so wrong. His predicament. And the humor fate had chosen to bestow upon him in this final stretch of his journey.

He had killed the Guardian's apprentice—the offspring of Bane and Lyoen. And the other man. The one with the jewel. He must have been one of the Guardian's aides. Why else would someone have something of such great value? Had the man been sent to Pyre to draw him out? Is that why the Ancient's offspring was there as well? To truly end him?

Desmós rolled his tongue around his lips in contemplation. It would make sense. And it would be extremely clever of the Guardian to dispose of him in that manner with all the odds stacked against him. But Desmós had survived. He had overcome those odds. The Guardian's plans had gone awry. And now Desmós was on his way back to the Core with a damaged ship. If this had been a part of the Guardian's plan, he would be expecting a report. And when that report didn't come...

Desmós looked at the blood again, contemplating his next move. He knew what he *should* do, but that didn't mean he wanted to do it. Why would he lower himself to that level when he was already perfection?

Blasted ard leaves. If he hadn't taken them, he could have just passed out and not need to worry about this wicked temptation sitting in front of him. This cruel idea of irony—bond with the blood of those who wished to kill him.

Desmós stood up and went to the driver's seat, hoping to distract himself from the pressing matter. As the ship traveled through a distorted space, he tried counting the stars that surrounded him.

He gave up quickly, wondering why he had even bothered trying in the first place. *How juvenile were the gifts from Father's siblings. Lyoen gave minerals. Bane selected stars and with them, a pointless wish, as if any could actually find theirs. Only my father created something beautiful. And they will remember. Soon everyone will remember.*

He snorted and crossed his arms over his chest. Dried blood scratched his elbow. He pulled his hand back. The blood on his hand sat there, taunting him, reminding him of who he had killed and the predicament he had put himself into by doing so. Had the Guardian already tried to contact him? What would happen if he weren't even allowed to land on the Core to fight the Guardian because of his knowledge to his apprentice's demise?

Longingly, he stared at the hand. Once again, he moved closer to the hand. Then he pulled back.

*I am Desmós! I am—*

*And Desmós needs to survive! You must!*

An inner voice battled him. Desperation battled him. And he ceded to it. Without giving his pride time to rebuttal, Desmós lurched forward and bit his own hand. His tongue slathered the blood with its wetness. His teeth scraped down on his skin, gingerly peeling the blood away into his own mouth. He repeated the process, until he had completely licked his hand clean.

He swallowed. And with it, his pride.

After waiting minutes for the blood to course its way through his body, he reached inside himself. While wearing the necklace, no one could sense him, but it didn't mean that Desmós could not seek out others. His only hope was that the Commoner had bonded blood with the Guardian of the Core, and Desmós assumed that was highly likely. He searched for the Guardian's lifeforce. He found it easily. For him, nothing was difficult. He was perfection.

*My Guardian?* Desmós mimicked what he assumed the apprentice would say.

*Eirek, I was getting worried. What is the status? Is he dead?*

*It is finished.*

*Why have you not returned yet?*

*The ship was damaged in the fight.*

*The others? What about the jewels?*

*They are with me.*

*Good. I will see you when you return.*

*Yes. You will.*

*Eirek, good job today. You did a wonderful thing.*

*Yes, I did.*

Desmós cut the connection. Not wanting to talk longer. He hoped the shortness of his sentences wouldn't give much away, but he had no way of knowing if the ruse would work or not. For now, all he could do was wait, observe the monotony of the stars, and bide his time, contemplating strategies to defeat the last obstacle in his path to perfection once more. All he did know was that in less than forty-eight hours, he would return to the Core.

Eventually, Desmós looked upon what should have been his birthplace. But it wasn't. Not like he had remembered it centuries ago. There was nothing here. *Where is Gladima?* His last vision of Gladima had been of the night sky and of that man, Bane's puppeteer, Zas Banegul. He wondered if he still lived. He hoped so, so that he could repay him for what he did that evening while his father had been away, creating on the planets.

Then something strange happened that pulled him from his thoughts.

As the ship came closer, more of the planet came into view, as if it had been able to hide itself from unwanted eyes. Two rings circled the planet. They hadn't been there when he had lived here. The Gladima he knew was a perfect place that would have basked in its own narcissism. It would have never wanted to hide itself. *What has the Guardian of the Core done to you?*

The closer he got to the surface, the more disgusted he became with what he saw. There were no temples, or cliffs, or cities of bronze and silver and gold. Lush greens and the bluest rivers and lakes one could ever hope to see were gone. Instead, he saw desolation. It ravaged the land, making most of what he saw look dilapidated and lugubrious, sands drained of their color as if rain hadn't graced them forever. Instead of cities, a great estate sat in the middle, one with three levels and large columns that connected each. The place, this Core, was spotted with lakes, but all small compared to what he had flown over when he was truly alive.

At the same time, he was happy that Bane made a grave error in wanting to return justice exactly as he saw fit. For when he put Zas's daughter inside the necklace that had been made from his body, he gave Desmós a way to cling onto a fraction of mortality. Because Zas's daughter had First Blood, she would continue to live as long as no one destroyed the necklace, and her survival ensured his own survival.

As the ship descended, he examined his shell's memories for anything related to the Guardian, but found none of his battle tactics, only bits and fragments of interactions during the Trials. Through his shell's memories, he knew the Guardian was bonded to a dragon, but never had he seen them fight together. Should they coordinate an assault on him, it would make things more difficult. But he had a plan to even the playing fields, if not ensure his victory. He fingered the satchel at his side; so much Power lay within that satchel, and all of it would be syphoned away.

The ship landed without incident. That meant only one thing—his ruse had worked. The Guardian had no idea who was on board. Desmós would use that ignorance to his advantage.

With dust still swirling about the ship, Desmós pushed the button to open the ship and then retreated to its belly. He took a gem from his satchel and held it in his hand. Black eyes reflected off of it. He unsheathed Purge from its scabbard. He brought the blade to jewel and sliced the first one open. Then he did the same to another. Again and again,

he repeated the massacre. A part of him thought he heard screams as he severed each of the Twelve's lifeforce, like they were calling out to him, victims of their mortality. Only to be silenced by the other part of him that heard nothing besides the faint clattering of broken bonds onto the metal floor of the ship.

They deserved everything they received, for turning their backs on Gladima and for their role in imprisoning his brother. He held the last jewel in his hand and put the Ether Blade to the surface of the gem. He thought back to how it all started: how he had helped the prince slice off the head of Pearl. He brought the blade across, biting into the jewel's face. With ease, it split open and dropped to the floor, two halves joining their twenty other kindred. Now, there was only one jewel to go. One jewel and a Guardian. A dragon. And whoever else might try to fight against his authority.

Without another thought, he left the ship a God-Slayer, and soon, Desmós was sure he would add Guardian-Slayer to that title as well.

## CHAPTER 42

# PROMETHEUS

The sliding glass doors opened behind him.

Eska turned slightly. "Tundra, what of our guest?"

"I've put him in the apothecary and helped the adored with the necessary precautions."

"Good. I have nearly finished up here."

Tundra came to stand alongside him. "All of them?"

Eska shook his head. "Most. Lord Paen, Lady Voux, and Lord Vangle didn't answer the call. I left a message in their telecom systems. They will listen to it eventually."

"What of Empora?"

"I will head there personally after Eirek returns. It will be good for him to see the process of a newly elected lord."

"Where is he now?"

"Eirek contacted me a few days ago after he left Pyre."

"And he hasn't returned yet?"

"The ship was damaged in the confrontation with Desmós."

Tundra stepped forward and held his hands in her own. "So, it's finished?"

"Yes. It is. Eirek told me himself."

"That is truly magnificent."

"He seemed proud about the accomplishment as well."

"Did he now?"

"Yes. Slightly unusual given his nature, but I suppose he was just happy to be alive."

"The others? How is Riagan?"

"I can't seem to get ahold of him."

Tundra thumbed his knuckles. "Is that normal?"

A ding came to his mind.

*Ethen?*

*Yes, my Guardian.*

*What is it? Have you found her?*

*No, my Guardian. But I feel as though I am close.*

*Where are you?*

*Outside of Kuyan, near ta Sinking Sea. I received word in ta capital of many saying tat tey spotted a woman wit blue hair. She traveled wit a brigade of slavers. I travel wit tem to Valbeach now, on safe paths. It is Chaon's most reclusive city; I reckon she may be tere.*

*Let me know what you find, Ethen. Good work.*

*Tank you, my Guardian.*

The connection ended.

"Was that Riagan?"

"No. Ethen. He is faring well in his mission. My guess is that Riagan has just forgotten to renew the blood bond."

"That is careless of him."

"It is. But we are only human. Eirek says he and Cain are with him on the way back."

"That is good." Tundra looked to the side and then back to him.

"Are you sure about reopening it? What will that mean for the Guardians?"

Eska sighed. "It means our time is coming to an end. Eirek may be the very last Guardian Gladonus will ever see. Perhaps the dawn of the True Kings is upon us now with Cain's claim to Power." Eska grunted.

Tundra arched her eyebrow. "What?"

Eska shook his head. "Aahh, it's nothing. But it reminds me that I should have informed the lords and ladies of Cain's authority now that he is truly the King of Pyre. I need to make sure his legitimacy is not questioned."

"I will leave you to it, then."

She tried leaving, but Eska held firmly onto her hand. He smirked and brought her in and kissed her lips. Such loyalty, even to the death, is what had drawn him to her in the first place. A bleep on the monitor ended their embrace.

Eska turned his head. Behind him, on another screen in the telecommunication chamber, a notification popped up, showing that Eirek's ship exited wormhole twenty-one.

"That is Apprentice Mourse?"

Eska nodded.

"How many hours until he is back?"

"Only a few more now."

"I will let you go then." She leaned forward and kissed him on the lips once more. Eska held her by the elbows close to him, choosing once more love over vows. In between kisses, Tundra said, "Edwyrd... there is... still... much to do." She pulled back.

Eska frowned, not wanting to relinquish her touch, but then he sighed, knowing the truth of her statement. If Ethen did succeed in his mission in finding Naydeia, then Gladima would be reopened soon. And that would change everything. There was so much to tell Eirek when he arrived.

"I know."

She rubbed his shoulder and then moved her hand under his chin. "All of our work will be over soon. Then we can relax." She smiled.

Eska accepted her warmth. He leaned in and kissed her once more, not wanting anything more.

When the telecommunication door slid shut, he turned around, heart pounding. Now that he had confessed his so-called sins and had been judged innocent, a weight had been lifted off his chest when it came to his love for Tundra. He was hopeful that his apprentice could experience that as well at some point in his Guardianship. He looked again at the bleep. Having entered the sole wormhole to lead directly to the Core, it was traveling the final stretch of the voyage.

Resolved to his duty once more, Guardian Eska pushed buttons on the panel in front of him. Perhaps it was a good thing the others returned here first before they announced the big reveal. It would safeguard Cain for the moment, instead of letting him fall victim to any vindictiveness or jealousy from any of the families in power on Pyre. If Eska could gain the support of his mentor once more, then it would be easier for the others to accept Cain. Eska could then present him there as the True King, forever changing the balance of Power on Pyre.

After four rings, Garrett Omyon appeared on the screen.

"Edwyrd?"

"Mentor..." Guardian Eska nodded. "There is important news I must share."

"More than what you already mentioned?"

Eska nodded. "It might be even more important than the shifters."

"More important than capturing a shifter?" Lord Omyon rolled his eyes for a moment, musing over the idea. "And what is that? An apology perhaps?"

Eska frowned. "Apology? For what?"

"You were awfully close to impeachment, Edwyrd. And your actions against Senator Numos and Lord Zigarda... well, I can see why Luvan may have wanted to go against you in the first place. You have unbridled Power and you wield it haphazardly in some cases."

"I am Guardian of the Core. If I don't use my Power in those instances, then what is my purpose? I could not let Victor Zigarda's ruse go on any longer. Shapeshifters have the ability to cause irreversible damage."

"And that is why the Conquest was so bloody."

"And that is why my impeachment was so close."

"Would your apprentice have been ready should you have been impeached?"

"I have been training him myself day and night. He is much more capable than he was at the end of the Trials. There is always more that can be learned."

"That there is. I cannot wait to teach him myself during his year here in Nova."

"I will send him there first to round out his training in the adored arts."

"That is a wise decision."

"Thank you for your support, by the way. I wish to express my gratitude that you didn't vote against me."

"So that is what this is about?"

Eska shook his head. "No. But I wanted to tell you that, anyway. What I'm talking about is much more serious."

"And that is?" Lord Omyon raised an eyebrow and leaned in closer.

"There is finally a True King again."

"A True King? Who?"

"Cain Evber has successfully bonded with Chantico."

Eska was half-expecting Garrett Omyon to choke on words or to make some sort of face, but the old man remained as stoic as ever. His voice inclined a bit, betraying a hint of eagerness, but nothing in his face gave away the man's thoughts.

"That is certainly impressive news."

"It is."

"Who else knows?"

"Besides Riagan and my apprentice, no one. You are the first one I wanted to inform."

"Is Riagan still on the planet?"

"I believe he is with my apprentice now. They return to the Core."

"What of King Evber?"

"I believe he is with them as well. They have just destroyed Desmós once and for all."

"You are certain about this?"

"I am."

"How?"

Eska relayed the trap that had been set for Desmós on Pyre to his mentor.

"Impressive. You took good measures. So what is it that you want me to do?"

"Voice your support for his Kingship. If he has your support, then Lord Requart and Lady Scule will be less likely to work against him."

"You think them so crass? You don't trust them to do the right thing?"

"After what I saw at the hearing, I don't trust many people to do the right thing. Everyone has their own agenda and secrets."

"As do you."

Eska opened his mouth and closed it before speaking at last. "It doesn't matter. My concern is that the Third One may find him and recruit him to his side. Now that his son is gone, the Third One may start trying to recruit the other True Kings to gain some semblance of Power."

"The Third One?!" Lord Omyon exclaimed in a rushed whisper. "Edwyrd, do you have any idea how—"

"I know who he is."

"Come again?"

"I know who the Third One is. I met him."

Lord Omyon shook his head. "What do you mean you *know* who the Third One is?"

"It's Cronos."

Eska went into the story about how he and the other Guardians reached this theory after his incident at the Sage's mansion after the hearing. At the end of it all, Eska continued with, "His Ether Staff then, Foresight, it has a special ability. I know it does. But how?"

"The Smiths."

"You mean Plato?"

Garrett Omyon didn't respond for an intense minute, calculating Eska all the while.

"Is this what you had been hiding from me since my Trials?"

"Edwyrd... You already came to that conclusion yourself. You didn't need me to tell you it."

"But the Ether Weapons, they have special powers? What is Adonis's?"

"It can act as a beacon to other sources of ether."

"You mean it can detect the other Ether Weapons?"

"Not just the Ether Weapons, Edwyrd. The actual element itself. It hunts it."

"How can I use its ability?"

"Well, it would need to be activated again."

"What do you mean?"

"The Smiths did endow their weapons with abilities, but each of those weapons was tied to the Smith who endowed it. The ability was not meant to exist beyond them. One Smith blessed the swords. Another the axes. And the third one the shield, the hammer, and the spear."

"So Plato blessed all the staffs?"

"Correct."

"But he could unleash any Ether Weapon's Power if he wanted to?"

"We are waiting for the right moment."

"And that moment is now. The necklace has been destroyed. My apprentice—"

"Have you *seen* the destroyed necklace?"

Eska eyed his mentor cautiously. "Well, no, I haven't. But I have contacted my apprentice. He is alive. He told me Desmós was defeated. I can show you it when he arrives. I'm sure he's brought it with him.

And as soon as Eirek returns, we are opening the Core to—."

"You can't do that."

"We can. My conseleigh is close to tracking Naydeia."

"Naydeia?" Lord Omyon's voice quivered. He put up his hand and began speaking faster. "Edwyrd, I need you to consider the weight of your actions. You cannot—"

Edwyrd swiped his hand in the air. "Enough of your excuses! It will be better for me to open it on my terms than for the Third One to open it. If the Ancients are not restored to their former glory, then I feel as though the Third One could resurrect Desmós despite the destruction of the necklace. I have seen what he can do. I am lucky to have my life. My apprentice is lucky to be alive as well. Do you not see any of this?" He slammed the table, passion bursting in his chest.

The moment that followed was long. Tense. Drawn out. Both looked at each other, not wanting to bend to the other's will.

Lord Omyon tsked. "I suppose it cannot be avoided any longer. When your apprentice returns, come to me and I will take you to Plato. There is something you will need first before trying to bring back the Ancients."

"What do you—"

"I won't speak any more of it now. It doesn't matter. Just bring your apprentice here along with the Ether Weapons you've gathered. Let the light be with you, Edwyrd."

"And also with—"

The connection cut.

Eska slouched. He understood that his mentor wanted to keep his secrets and that he had forced him into a corner, but to be so rude at the end. Change was never an easy thing. And who knew how the system would change once Gladima was reopened. Perhaps even the whole cosmos would change.

Eska would worry about that later. He needed to finish making his follow-up calls before Eirek and Conseleigh Inferno returned. By the time everything was sorted out with Lord Omyon, Ethen should have been able to track down Naydeia, and then it was only... Well, he didn't exactly know what all went into reopening the Core, but he knew that it would reopen one way or another.

Eska contacted Lord Requart. However, to his dismay, once again it wasn't Lord Requart who picked up. It was his advisor, Stuant, this time.

"Where is Rhagoh?"

The advisor bit his lip. "He is rather... preoccupied at the moment, my Guardian." He bowed and smiled.

"With what? He has been busy now for days."

"And a lot has happened here in the past few days."

"Yes, Cole mentioned that to me last time. Why is the lord ignoring me?"

"My Guardian, he isn't ignoring you. He is merely just tending to a—"

"Large mess outside Fernis. Yes, Cole explained that to me as well. Is everything okay?"

"My Guardian, it isn't my place to say..."

"Then get Rhagoh and let him tell me. What kind of mess is going on there in Fernis? Do I need to go there myself and help?"

Stuant waved his hand in front of the screen. "No. No. No. My Guardian. That isn't necessary. I will tell Lord Requart to call you as soon as he is available."

"I am expecting his call."

He cut communication and tried his luck with Lady Scule of Lurid. As hoped for, she answered. After Eska explained to her what happened with the bonding of Chantico, she surprised by revealing that she already knew.

"What? How?"

"Our Luridian hovercrafts come installed with cameras. I merely looked at the footage of what occurred when the ship was returned to me."

"That is—"

"Quite clever, I know. I appreciate the call, though, my Guardian. It is a comforting hearing it come from you. It gives my eyes credibility. So what happens now?"

"Cain should have a proper inauguration ceremony. I expect all of the families in power to accept him."

Lady Scule said nothing.

"Farah, you will swear your fealty to the King."

"The others will?"

"Yes. Both have agreed to," Eska lied.

She sighed. "Very well, then, my Guardian. I will. Truly a momentous event has occurred."

After the connection cut, he lingered for a moment, contemplating everything that he had learned from his mentor. The Ether Weapons did have special functions. Why hadn't he told Eska before? He removed Adonis from its sheath and looked at it, catching himself in the cloudy amethyst storm clouds. He reflected on all the events that had occurred just within the last year. Tumultuous is the only word he could find to describe it. *Could I have done anything differently?* He sighed. He knew he couldn't have. He had always been a subject to fate. Fit for fate, as Zeph had told him time and time again.

Dragging himself out of the chair, he exited the telecommunication chamber. Much to his surprise, a breeze hit him. *Are the doorways in the lobby open?* He went to the lobby. One door flapped back and forth, blown inward. Dominic tended to the door.

"Were you doing work outside?"

"No, my Guardian. I've just been polishing the statues." As the servant started closing it, a strong wind pushed him back, denying his efforts.

Eska widened his eyes. He knew what that meant. Sauntering forward, he placed his hand on the door. "It's okay, Dominic. I need to get some fresh air. I can close it behind me."

Outside, a strong wind pulled him by his cape towards the cliffs, nearly yanking him off his feet. *She isn't giving me a choice this time. What else had happened since her disappearance from the floating cave?* Eska used Power to carry him towards Gamrol Cliffs, these questions at the forefront of his mind.

Inside the cavern was a vacuum. It choked Eska. Quickly, he steadied his breathing to acclimate himself to the change. Zeph stood before him, translucent, not physically, but through her Power of the windies in the cavern, she manifested herself. Blue curls fell past her shoulders, defying her true age. As usual, her blue lips looked lush and her physique slender, covered with a transparent nightgown. But that nightgown had been severed, and below the cut, there was a gash in her midsection. Eska's eyes widened as he saw the wound. *So it was her blood I saw.*

"He stole the jewel from me, Edwyrd."

He bit his lower lip. "Was it from a man with black hair?"

Zeph blinked, dumbfounded. "Yes. It... it was... How?"

"It doesn't matter. The threat has been neutralized."

"Neutralized? How? The man carried an Ether Blade with him. And—"

"And we have taken care of him."

"How? He was strong. Did you not—"

"My apprentice has told me he is dead."

"Have you seen the body?"

"No. But it will be on the Core within the hour. Why do you not believe me?"

"He could counter the wind, Edwyrd. The wind."

Eska shifted his posture a little and heard a stammer in his voice when he spoke. "But... how is that possible?"

"When I battled him, he formed a sphere around me, putting me into a vacuum, like space."

"Well, it is a good thing that he has already been taken care of then by my conseleigh, apprentice and a True King."

"True King?"

"Yes. One has been found again. The dawn of a new era starts."

"Or a dawn of corruption."

"What do you mean?"

"If Desmós is truly dead as you claim, the Third One will—"

"He *is* dead. Why is it so hard for you to believe?"

"After all the things I have seen in this lifetime, Edwyrd, the only way to believe something is to see it."

The words chilled Eska. Doubts now crawled in his mind surrounding the actual death of Desmós. Should he try reaching out to Eirek again to confirm? No, that would be silly. He would be here within the hour and Eska would be able to see the body himself. He had to have faith, despite what Zeph claimed otherwise.

Changing topics to not erode his faith further, he asked. "Anyway, where are you now?"

"I..." Zeph moved her body here and there, looking at something he couldn't see. "I went to Chaon."

"How do you know?"

"I see Mount Klaff."

*Then it definitely is Chaon. It also means Chaon has a drop-off point. Interesting.* Eska knew that each planet had an access point and a drop-off point, but their exact locations had remained a mystery to him.

"Where are you on Chaon?"

"It seems like I am in a city by the sea."

"Which side is the sea on?"

"The east."

"You are in Valor, then." Eska bit his lip.

While unfortunate that she was wounded, at least she was living. Furthermore, it seemed truly fortuitous that she stumbled through Myoli's portal and wound up in Chaon. Perhaps there was an opportunity to make the most of this and salvage the situation. Eska furrowed his brows.

"What are you thinking about?"

"One of my conseleigh is currently tracking down your daughter. She will be helping my apprentice reopen Gladima."

Zeph's eyes widened. "You will do it yourself, then?"

"Better to do it while in our hands than in the hands of the Third One, is it not?"

Zeph nodded. "Where is your conseleigh headed?"

"To Valbeach. He is traveling across the Sinking Sea now."

"Naydeia isn't in Valbeach. She is in the Sinking Sea."

Guardian Eska put a hand to his chin. "You are certain of this?"

"I am."

"How do you know?"

"After my near-death experience, she felt my life force shudder and contacted me. I was going to make my way there myself to see her."

"There is no need to do that now. I will tell Ethen. Can you make your way to Kuyan? It's the capital in the eastern part of the nation. Past Slaver's Forest."

"I will find a way there."

"Then I will tell Ethen to bring Naydeia there when he finds her."

"Even if he has the authority of conseleigh, my daughter will not listen—"

"I gave him your necklace."

Zeph coughed. She put a tiny fist over her mouth. "You did what?"

"To convince Naydeia and, if necessary, take her by force. She cannot resist the wind. Hardly anyone can."

"How do you know that?"

"Because I've used it on the Third One myself. And if it stopped Him, it would stop her, am I right?"

Zeph nodded. "Yes. And if he uses it, I will be able to sense it, but..."

Eska searched her eyes when her voice tapered off. "But what?"

"That leaves you weaker on the Core."

"There is no threat anymore. I have told you—"

"Be that as it may," Zeph cut him off. "I will allow you to control my windies there."

"You do not think that I could defeat him by myself should he still be alive?"

"Not even I can see how the whims of fate would play out in that battle, Edwyrd."

Eska pushed his lips to one side. The reservation in her voice raised the hair on his arms. His muscles twitched. Unease in his stomach threatened to disrupt his bravado.

"Berol."

The wind formation of Zeph's body broke slightly in an almost imperceptible way. Right before Eska hovered a small fairy-like creature, not even the length of a fingernail.

"Yes, Mistress."

"You will obey the Guardian's command."

"As sure as the wind blows."

"As sure as the wind blows," Zeph repeated.

Eska sighed. "Thank you. For your gift. Despite how unnecessary it is. We will speak again after Naydeia is found. Farewell."

Eska turned away and left, hearing the howl of the retreating whirlwind and feeling its vivacity on his neck and ears. When he went outside again, it was almost dusk. The day had been unusually busy, and not in a good way. Still, it wasn't over.

He pinged Ethen. Regardless of anything else, it was imperative that his conseleigh find Naydeia. The Core had to be reopened one way or another.

When he found his conseleigh, he told him of the plan that he and Zeph had drafted. Ethen agreed to change course and convince his traveling companions to guide him through the other parts of the Sinking Sea.

Upon finishing his talk with Ethen, he saw what he needed more than ever to see—Eirek's ship descending. Was it his lack of faith that made him so anxious about the ship? Was his instincts trying to tell him something? Or was he just being irrational due to the conversations he had before?

"Berol."

The wind lifted him off the ground and rushed him back towards the estate. He would greet his apprentice, and the others at the door. And, once and for all, he would lay eyes upon Desmós's dead body. As he was being carried back to the estate, he watched the ship intently. It finally touched down when he was within walking distance to the estate, dust veiling it for a little while.

A sharp pain jolted his body. Then another. He tumbled out of his wind cloud and fell to the ground.

"*Maa*," Edwyrd said, softening his landing to a cushion of sand instead of hard ground.

Grains of sand stuck to his skin. Some had crawled down his throat, choking him. He coughed and pushed himself up. The ship had landed. Another sharp pain ripped through his body. It was as if he was having repetitive heart attacks. The sand reverted back to dirt as he lost control on the Power.

*Tundra.*

*Vesel.*

*I need you.*

Another sharp pain tore through him.

Off in the distance, Vesel roared. His vision blurred. Tinnitus struck him, dizzying him. His breathing shortened. *What is—*

Another jolt. Not wanting to expend more energy than necessary, he crawled forward, closer to the estate. Another. He collapsed, kissing the dirt. Another. He shook in throes on the ground. Strength and warmth left his body, syphoned by... *Who?* With blurry vision, he watched as the dust settled. No one was visible in the cockpit.

Steps on the porch alerted him of Tundra's presence. A raucous roar told him Vesel's proximity. Knowing the other two were close gave him strength to get to one knee. His breathing still heavy, he looked onward.

"Edwyrd, what is going on?"

"It's—"

Eska collapsed upon himself again as an eighth jolt ripped through him. He contorted in constant spasms.

"Edwyrd!" Tundra knelt by his side. One hand cradled his head, and the other held his hand. "What is..."

Another jolt caused him to jerk violently, his weight sending Tundra backwards.

Soon enough, she was back at his side, caring for him once more. "What is happening? Talk to me." Her voice quivered.

"The... Twelve... je... jewels." Sweat beaded his face. "He is..."

A large thump shook the ground. Hot air spread over Eska. He tilted his head back and saw Vesel. Looking into the dragon's eyes, he saw his sister. *Alicia.* Vesel roared, spewing silver flames. It offered momentary relief. Eska pushed himself back into a sitting position. He leaned back. He inhaled deeply, not taking his breaths for granted any longer.

The ship began to open.

A tenth jolt sent Eska backwards, the back of his head crashing onto the ground. Writhing in spasms, he felt mortality shift back into his body. Confidence left him just as Power had. Shivers controlled him now, and the ringing in his ears awarded him no time for thinking. He blinked, finally feeling the weight of his own eyelashes.

"Edwyrd. Talk to me." She held his hand. "Breathe. In and out. Breathe."

For the first time in a while, he felt her tears fall down upon his face. "Hydro... Desmós."

"Stay with me. Breathe. We need you. Breathe. I need you. Be strong."

"I..." He closed his eyes.

He kept them closed, trying to regain his strength. In the distance, Tundra shouted. Vesel roared. Steel and ice clanged together. Tremors shook the surrounding area. Light flashed in front of his eyelids, warming his face. The cacophony of it all stung Eska's senses. *I must get...* A shriek. He pushed himself to open his eyes. He sat up. He blinked. *Tundra!*

She had been knocked to the ground. *Vesel, where is Vesel?* His dragon was caged in a sphere of water, drowning. *No!* Tundra held her sword up to block one of Desmós's attacks. She lashed out with her whip and wrapped it around his ankle, then yanked, causing him to topple backwards, but he gracefully rolled back to his feet in the same time it took Tundra to get to her own.

Eska pushed himself to stand. "Tundra!"

She looked back. "Edwyrd! Hydro!"

Eska grimaced. It wasn't Zigarda who fought him. Nor Hydro. No. Neither would have ever been able to tax him in such a way. This was Desmós. Hydro had been lost.

"*Vesi!*" Eska focused his Power on freeing Vesel from his cage. "*Maa!*" He focused another spell in trapping Desmós, but he fought back. *Good. Split your Power.* He looked back at Vesel. His spell was working. The water level was lowering. Soon enough, it came below Vesel's chest, and he breathed fire towards Desmós. The silver flames were met with a water wall as Desmós engaged in battle with Tundra.

Eska concentrated harder, using his dragon's diversion to his advantage and exploiting Desmós's weakened concentration on three fronts. A little lower and Vesel would be able to escape the spell himself by using his wings. He must free Vesel. It was the only way to match Desmós's control of Power. Eska pushed.

Desmós's eyes glowed a sickly obsidian color. "I expected more from a Guardian." He scoffed. "Today you will die."

With an anguished cry, Tundra unleashed a series of strikes.

Desmós blocked the assault with a mocking grin. He punched Tundra, sending her toppling to the ground behind her, then jumped forward, ready for the kill.

"Berol."

A gust of wind rushed by Eska, and the prince was stopped mid-air. Tundra choked. Desmós choked. Only Eska was acclimated to the conditions he created. Desmós flicked his attention towards Eska, eyeing him with newfound interest.

"You have no business here on the Core." Eska undid his reimaje and threw it in front of him. He thought of the stars above. Soon enough, the reimaje reflected his thoughts. "I will show you true strength! Berol!" The cyclone that spun around Desmós, keeping him locked in place, formed itself into a hand and dragged him towards the reimaje. "Now you will die. Cold and alone and forgotten, just like your master."

Desmós's brows furrowed. He moved his lips in a rapid but silent motion.

On the ground, Tundra choked and panted. *Hold on, my love. This will only take a moment.*

A pillar of dirt erupted in front of and behind Eska until it entombed him. Water filled the tomb, and then fire joined the water in harmony, and soon enough electricity crawled throughout the space as well. Blackness enveloped him. Pure blackness. It syphoned his strength, bringing him to one knee. *What kind of Power is...* A roar ripped through the air. Then a batting of wings. A scream. The darkness collapsed around him, fading from view.

Tundra panted. She gulped in air. Above, Vesel flew with Desmós in the sky, the talons on his feet dug into Desmós's back. Suddenly, Vesel dropped Desmós. Yellow and blue crawled over his silver frame. *Electricity!* Eska's eyes widened as his dragon went limp and plummeted with Desmós to the earth below. *No!*

While in freefall, Desmós raised a pillar of earth to meet him.

"Berol!" Eska commanded the windies to knock Desmós off his perch and crash him to the ground. To his dismay, the prince held on with one hand. He withdrew Adonis. *Time to finish this.* As fast as he could, Eska ran towards the fight.

Vesel fell past Desmós. The prince kicked off the pillar of earth, sword raised, and descended upon Vesel's underbelly.

"Berol!" Eska caught Desmós in mid-air. *I will end you.*

Desmós's lips moved. Again, a block of earth encompassed Eska. Then water. Then electricity. Before the process could be completed, Eska moved his control of the wind to destroy the elements encroaching his body. *This is what Zeph warned me about.* The earthen barrier crumbled before him. His lips moved to one side. *Time to—*

A sharp pain struck through Eska's core, shaking him worse than any of the previous jolts that had ruptured his body. It brought him to his knees. He yelled. Through sweat-filled eyes, he saw a streak of fire. There was a roar. And then a yell. Eska blinked. Desmós fell towards the ground from the pillar of earth. The same pillar that Vesel had landed upon after being electrocuted while in midair. The pillar of earth collapsed, returning to the Core. Eska tried standing. His dragon fell, landing with a deafening thud. Eska collapsed to the ground, the same as Vesel. His back arched. He coughed and wiped blood from his mouth.

"Edwyrd! Edwyrd!" Tundra came to his side. "What is wrong? Speak to me."

"Ves..." He couldn't finish his sentence. "Protect..." He coughed.

"You're bleeding. Where?" Her fingers scoured his body, trying to find the source of the wound.

Eska shook his head and pointed his finger. "Vesel..." Vesel struggled to stand.

Tundra left his side.

Eska took a long moment to regain his sense of place. Soon enough, the song of weapons came back to him, and he knew he needed to join the chorus. There were shouts. Vies for Power. His head danced to the same beat as his heart. In and out of consciousness, he blinked. He thought he saw another ship descending from the atmosphere above. *Who is that?*

Eska pushed himself onto his elbows. Then to his knees. Taking a deep breath, he staggered towards the fight that Tundra was trying to remain in. She had caught Desmós's wrist with her wristlace and now fought in close-quarters with him, blade to blade. Ducking one of her horizontal slashes, Desmós swept her feet out from underneath of her. She fell backwards. Desmós attempted to pounce on top of her, but she kicked him away. Desmós's weight yanked the wristlace from Tundra's grasp.

Eska limped forward. The reimaje was only a few feet in front of him on the ground. *If only...*

"*Salama!*"

The spell wasn't directed at him, but at his dragon. Vesel shook in spasms. As he did so, Eska did as well, once again crumpling to his knees. He coughed. Blood splattered the earth and made his dry lips wet. When the dragon went still, Eska regained his composure. Tundra's eyes glowed. She still had fight left in her, and that is why he loved her. There was no pleasantry in the north; cold and death and winter were all she knew, and she would live to see those things greet Desmós or die and meet them herself. She was as stubborn as ice in winter.

Vesel rolled to his feet and sprang towards Desmós, spewing flames of silver. As he flew, blood trailed from him onto the barren terrain. Before contact, Desmós put up a watery shield. Within moments of reaching the watery wall, the dragon pulled back, shot upward, and, tucking his wings inward, somersaulted, then shot down using the momentum.

Eska bent down and grabbed the reimaje. *Vesel, throw him to me. I will lock him in space.* Eska threw the reimaje in the air and held it with control of the wind.

Vesel chomped down towards Desmós, trying to bite as much as he could. Desmós held the sword above his head. Teeth met sword in a vicious stalemate that made Desmós drop to one knee. Silver fire glowed in Vesel's mouth. It washed over Desmós.

At least, it should have.

Desmós rolled out of the way, exposing only his back to the shower of flames and rolling underneath a swipe from the dragon's talons. The man then jumped up and brought the sword clean through Vesel's neck, decapitating the dragon.

The reimaje dropped. Eska collapsed. Tremors seized him. Controlled him. His mind couldn't process a thought. With a heavy breath, he blinked, looking up to the sky. The other ship was closer now. *Vesel is gone. Alicia is gone. Vesel is gone. Alicia is gone.*

A scream. Vibration to his right. He turned his head to see Tundra fall, a large gash deep in her side. She bled out beside him on the barren ground. Their eyes met. Hand extended. Red painted over the natural blueness of her lips. She coughed, and then gave herself to the ground she rested upon. She turned to him and mouthed: *I'm sorry.*

*Tundra!*

Eska felt nothing. Her eyes were pale. Open. But pale.

*It will not end like this.*

A thud sounded off in the distance.

He started undoing the glove on his left hand. Footsteps approached him. Eska gulped. He struggled to keep his eyes open. His eyelids were so heavy.

Desmós appeared before him. Purge clutched in his hand, the sword stained with the blood of Eska's dragon and love. He panted. Beads of sweat lined his face, black and marked with tattoos. The eyes were a sickly obsidian, devoid of any humanity.

"This is where you die. Just like your dragon, just like your apprentice, and just like your conseleigh." He spat on Eska's face and held Purge out in front of him.

Eska blinked. "How?" Eska groaned, hoping to buy time as he began removing the glove on his hand.

"You above all people should know the power of blood." Desmós smirked.

Eska didn't allow himself to be distracted by the pettiness. Instead, he finished removing the glove on his hand.

"This is from my father. *Ajid Voluntasey Fuan.*" Desmós brought the sword down.

Eska turned over his ungloved hand, exposing the mark of the Guardian. In a last-ditch effort, he said, "*Loiste!*"

A light shot out of his hand, spearing Desmós in the chest. It spread around the man, blinding him. Eska raised his body, clenching his fist on the way up. He punched forward, drawing from any Power still left within his crippled body. The hit connected with Desmós's stomach. When it did, he said, "*Voima.*" The man flew backwards and disappeared from view. A few seconds later, he heard a thud.

Eska collapsed and closed his eyes. He breathed, listening to nothing but the peace he created and his own ragged breaths. For now, that was all that mattered. He wasn't sure if the last spell was enough to kill Desmós. In truth, he didn't think it was, for much of his strength had already been syphoned.

Footsteps soon encroached.

"Edwyrd. Edwyrd!"

The shaking of his shoulders forced him to open his eyes. "Lu... Luvan."

"What happened here?" He looked to his left. "Tundra!"

Eska looked on as well. Tundra lay motionless in a pool of her own blood. *Gone. Everyone is gone. Gone. Gone. Gone.* He tilted his head back up to the sky; the stars were out. *If Gladima is reopened, and the Third One and Desmós take form, then only the Ancients can stop him. But they're sealed. Only...* Squinting, he searched.

"Edwyrd, what happened?"

"They are gone. All of them."

"Who?"

"Everyone is dead. I failed... Desmós ... Leave... before..."

"Leave? This was not how it was supposed to happen. This is not what she said would happen."

Eska couldn't understand his babble, but he did know that Luvan needed to leave should Desmós return. He needed to take the reimaje so Desmós couldn't add its Power to his repertoire.

"Luvan... Luvan... listen to me closely..." Eska coughed, spitting up blood onto Luvan's face. "Take my reimaje. Take Adonis. Escape to Chaon through the reimaje."

"How... how... but... but... you?"

"Do not worry about me. There is still one thing I need to do. Ethen is there. He is finding Naydeia. Go to him, help him bring her here. Tell them what has happened. Only she—"

"I... No... It wasn't supposed to go like this..."

"Fate is rather funny, isn't it?" Guardian Eska coughed, choking on his blood. He had to turn himself to the side and spit. "Go! Leave me here!"

"But..."

"Go!" Eska yelled, using what little energy he had left to push Luvan away.

He crashed back down on the Core. Even though it was only a fraction of inches, the effort it consumed rippled through his body. It shook his very self. *Where are you? Where are you?* With each breath, vivacity slipped away from him. He thought he heard a faint *goodbye*, but he wasn't sure. He wasn't sure of anything anymore. Anything besides his star. Now he needed it more than ever.

*There*. Eska inhaled deeply. Finally, it was time. *I am ready. I want to make my wish.*

*Then tell me what it is you desire, Prometheus.*

*Prometheus.* If things had been different, he would have contemplated this name longer. He would have contemplated the female voice that spoke to him. But he couldn't. Instead, he told her what he desired.

*That will require a great price.*

*Take what is left of me.*

*Very well.*

Eska watched as his star flickered and faded away. In the moments before he closed his eyes, he saw the sky go dark as one of its brightest faded from view. It had lost many bright stars that night. But it wasn't so black. Another light attempted to balance his own that slowly diminished. As he closed his eyes for the last time, he reached blindly for Tundra's hand. He found it and clutched it. Finally, ice had gotten the better of her. *Alicia. Vesel. Tundra.* Each broken bond had resulted in overwhelming silence. Soon he would be with them. Forever. It brought a weak smile to his cracked lips. *The rest is up to...*

# EPILOGUE

Naydeia sat at a wooden table in the dining area of a small shack that was supposed to be reclusive but had been anything but within the last hour. Arms crossed over her chest, she looked at a copper-skinned man who intrigued her, but not for the obvious reasons. It wasn't the man's oblong beard, nor the golden C pinned to his dark green tunic and the introduction of himself as Conseleigh Ethen Rorum, one of Guardian Eska's aides, that intrigued her. The Ether Axe that he laid on the table would have left many others lost for words as well, but not her. She already had her own Ether Weapon, and Vigor was nothing compared to Insight. And it wasn't even the fact that he had found her here, in the middle of the Sinking Sea that had kept her silent and calculating since the man barged in here, beating Nivarre with a display of weapon skill that one only earned with years of experience. What truly humbled her and occupied her thoughts was what this man had set down on the table between them.

It was a small gray orb attached to a strand of gossamer. When she had picked it up, noting the small storm clouds within the necklace, which gave it its gray hue, she thought she could even see flecks of shakti hidden within those clouds. The celadon flecks gave away that this was the handiwork of her mother. It also revealed how this man actually tracked her down. Her mother and Guardian Eska had always been close. Why? She didn't know. Perhaps she wanted to build rapport with the Guardian so that she could play the puppeteer to the whims of fate, always trying to find some way to go back to Gladima so that she could see her husband again. If it weren't for their relationship by blood, she would have disavowed her mother for being so short-sighted.

Reopening Gladima now with her husband gone, the Twelve syphoned away, and the Other and Desmós on the loose and tracking her down was a recipe for a disaster. Her mother needed her and, more importantly, the ring on her finger that contained a fragment of her husband's blood, to reopen Gladima. When she had felt her mother's life force flicker near the brink of death, she had reached out to her through telepathy, and they had exchanged words again. The man that had come to track her down in the jungle had done the same to her mother, stolen a jewel from her, and, most surprising of all, had *lived* to tell the tale.

How he had been so fortunate was beyond her. She already had berated herself in not taking further action against Prince Paen when she had the opportunity. But when she saw Anne Banegul that day, right alongside the Prince, she froze. Then when she had regained her senses, he was already gone and running, and she tried caging the Prince through Power, but it was as if she was being blocked by its hierarchy. As if electricity suddenly sprung up out of nowhere and quelled her cages of earth.

After ruminating on that encounter, Naydeia realized that Desmós had truly taken a bite into the Prince's soul. And that whatever she saw hadn't been real but a ploy of Desmós to appear more innocent. The truest type of insidious sycophant, camouflaging himself long enough to seep to the depths of the Prince's mind and enthrall him, consume him, and use him as his vessel. And it could only be that lost Power was how he had escaped the meeting with her and her mother alive. But should Naydeia ever met that Prince again, she would kill him.

To help her accomplish this goal, she needed to know more about Desmós and how to beat him. That is why she was here, trying to utilize the skills her husband had taught her so that she could fix Zas, who had become nothing more than a blabbering shell of his former self since his exile from Gladima. She wanted him. Needed him. He had overcome Desmós once before, and together they could overcome Desmós again. She needed to know how he had done it before the Other and he could be reunited. If that were to happen, the whole system would fall into chaos.

Naydeia had wanted the conseleigh to speak first, so she busied herself with examining the necklace in her hand over and over again, although she had already gleaned its attributes and handiwork. The only recurring sound in the silent standoff between the two was Zas who rocked back and forth in his chair blabbering random memories he still had left. However, after interminable minutes of this prolonged silence, she grew tired of the games. She laid the necklace on the table and smiled coyly at the conseleigh.

"So, Conseleigh Rorum, the Guardian of the Core has sent you to track me down?"

The conseleigh straightened, bringing his forearms to rest just behind the throat of the Ether Axe. "Yes. And we must leave here and go to the Core."

She smirked inside. *Such a show of intimidation. Does he not know those things do not work on me?* "How do you know I am who you are looking for?" She arched an eyebrow.

"Would I 'ave received such an," the man paused, choosing his words carefully, "*inviting* welcome if you were not?" When she smiled, he continued. "The staff, leaning in the corner in the other room, it's an Ether Weapon, which is probably why you seem so disinterested in mine. Your 'air is blue, like the description I 'ave been given by Guardian Eska, and since talking wit you I can tell you 'ave a way wit words. It seems you certainly are exactly who I am looking for."

She forced a smile, then stood and walked past Nivarre and into another room, where a group of natives watched the scene unfold. She grabbed her Ether Weapon and came back into the room. "You are quite observant. I suppose I will not need to be hiding this any longer."

"I don't tink you were hiding it at all."

"No?"

The man shook his head. "It's a test. You know tat ta chances of me taking you against your will are next to none, but you also want some way to establish credibility to anyone who is even lucky enough to sit 'ere wit you. Isn't that correct, Naydeia?"

Naydeia's smile turned sour. *So he is more clever than he looks.* She laughed off her annoyance and tucked a strand of hair behind her ear. "What's in a name?"

"Many tings, if you ask the Guardian."

"And if I ask you?"

"It doesn't matter what your name is, what matters is 'ow you define tat name. I am 'ere to 'elp you make your name what it used to be."

"And what did it used to be?" Naydeia scrunched her face.

"More tan a legend. Or a myth. Tere was a time when you didn't need to hide, or feel it necessary to block communication wit your own mother."

Naydeia pretended to wipe dust off the table, seemingly disinterested in his babble. If this man knew what her mother wanted to do, then he would understand why it was necessary to block communication with her.

"Tere was a time when you were more. Tat time is now. It is 'ere. We must go."

Naydeia slammed her Ether Staff into the ground.

*Mother, why did you tell this man where I lived?*

As if her mother had been expecting her, she telepathically communicated with Naydeia. *Because Guardian Eska has a plan to open the Core. A plan that will work.*

*It will not work, Mother. Not while there is still a chance at the Third One regaining his might. He has Foresight. He sees our moves.*

*And that is why we must plan ahead of even that.*

*What do you mean?*

*We must act now while Desmós is still weakened. While the Other is still weakened. While—*

"Levia. Anne. Desmós. Power. Power. Power. Pain. Pain. Pain." Zas's babblings and spasms distracted Naydeia from the conversation with her mother.

Naydeia turned her attention to Conseleigh Rorum. "You don't know anything about us."

"No. I don't. But Guardian Eska does. He knows much about you and your family. Tis necklace on te table he received from Zeph, your mother, isn't tat so?"

Naydeia's neck tensed. She brushed bangs out of her eyes in an attempt to hide her discomfort.

"He knows about your husband, Galan, and how he recently perished. He knows about ta legacy tat you have strive to uphold through lineage upon lineage of descendants now dead by their own accord or Pirini Lilapa. And he knows tat one of tose descendants is now his apprentice."

"Eirek..."

Naydeia let his name fall from her lips. She covered her mouth immediately and looked at the conseleigh. She wanted to ask about him, but she had taken a vow with her husband to see to her daughter's child from afar. To cut ties with him so that he could discover his bloodline for himself, so that he wouldn't be seduced by the Power that came with his Ancient Blood, whatever faint trace was left in him. Speaking about him made her want to ping his blood, check and see how he fared. She closed her eyes, on the precipice of contacting Eirek and finding his energy when Zas interrupted her concentration again.

"Pain leads to Power. Power leads to pain. Levia. Levia. Anne." Zas rocked back and forth. "All roads lead to home. Home is where the heart is."

"What—"

"Excuse him, he doesn't usually talk this much."

"What is he saying?"

"He is remembering. He no longer thinks, he just remembers and recites what he used to know." Naydeia stood and went behind the man and placed her hands on his shoulders. She massaged them. He had been awfully talkative today. What did that mean? In her months of living with him, the only other time she had seen him this talkative was during Pirini Lilapa, but that was to be expected by anyone with First Blood whose life and energy revolved around Gladima.

She looked towards someone in the other area and nodded. A woman with rings around her neck and raw cloth that covered only a minority of her entered the room carrying a clay teapot. She set a clay cup down on the table and poured. She then retreated, and Naydeia proffered the liquid to Zas's lips. Within moments of drinking it, the shaking decreased, and the murmurs stopped, but he still just sat there, lost.

"My father did him a very cruel injustice to appease my husband's mother. Since that day, he has never been the same."

"You are talking about the creation of the necklace?"

"Hmmm... I am. You are well-versed in the stories of Gladonus."

"Guardian Eska makes sure each of his conseleigh are privy to this sort of information."

"Yes, and what other information are you privy to?"

"We don't have nearly enough time for tat. We must meet your mother in Kuyan, and from tere she will guide us back to te Core. Ten we can reopen Gladima wit your blood."

"Why would I want to see Gladima reopened? My husband and I separated so that it could not be reopened."

"I do not believe you."

"Oh?"

"If you truly didn't want to 'ave it reopened, you wouldn't 'ave kept your lineage alive. I tink tat down inside you, you want to return tere, for yourself and tose people around you." Conseleigh Rorum paused. "Like your mother." With his head, he motioned to his right. "For this man here." He looked her deep in the eyes, then continued. "And for te last of your lineage, for Apprentice Mourse. I think you've gotten so good at seeing the insides of others, Naydeia, tat you 'ave forgotten what it is tat you truly want."

"What do you know of my seeing inside others?"

"You did tat to my friend, Luvan Katore, did you not?"

She frowned. "How do you know that?"

"His wife mentioned something to me, and you just confirmed it."

"I... Insight has told me that he will be one of the ones responsible for opening Gladima, not you." Naydeia massaged the upper portion of her staff.

"How do you know I have no small part to play as well? You 'ave never used your staff on me."

"Let us see that right—"

The light drifting in from outside stopped for a brief moment, as if clouds blocked the suns. In that exact moment, a roar shook the shack. Sand from the roof shimmied its way down into the room, creating a stint of sandy rain. Those in the other room retreated, no longer caring about the meeting taking place. Nivarre went to the window.

"In the west, there is a light."

Naydeia bolted to her feet. Prickles crawled up her skin. She blinked. "No. No. No," she rasped. Her mouth had become dry.

Zas started babbling again, rocking back and forth. "No. No. No. Power leads to Pain. Pain leads to Power. All leads to home. Home. Home. Levia. Levia. Anne."

Naydeia ignored them and hurried past both. "It can't be."

"What is it?" the conseleigh asked.

She ignored him.

Pushing open the door, she stepped outside. A gust of arid wind mauled her face. A large light shone on the horizon, past what was left of the backdrop of Mount Klaff. Her heart beat. Sweat lined her brow, but not from the heat that was overtaking her body. In the sandy area around the shack, she paced. She rubbed her hands together, wanting some kind of explanation.

"It can't be. It can't be." She dropped to her knees. "No. No. No."

She was picked up and turned around. Conseleigh Rorum shook her slightly and stared into her eyes. "Naydeia, what is it?"

Another boisterous roar bellowed out from the distance. She threw her forearms over her head and braced herself. Sand swirled around them, scratching her exposed skin with grainy, unforgiving claws. Never had she felt something so maleficent. Not since Desmós. Not since the Great War. Pure evil overtook the air around her, making her shudder. Fear seeped into her. Now, there was nothing certain in this system. Now, there would be only chaos.

Conseleigh Rorum shook her and yelled. "Naydeia, what is 'appening? Tell me!"

Vigor drained from her face as well as hope, and Naydeia looked at him. "Deimos is free."

# MAPS

The following pages are the maps of each of the domains the characters travel throughout the book. These are to guide you in understanding their journey and to bring to life more of this stellar system that is Gladonus.

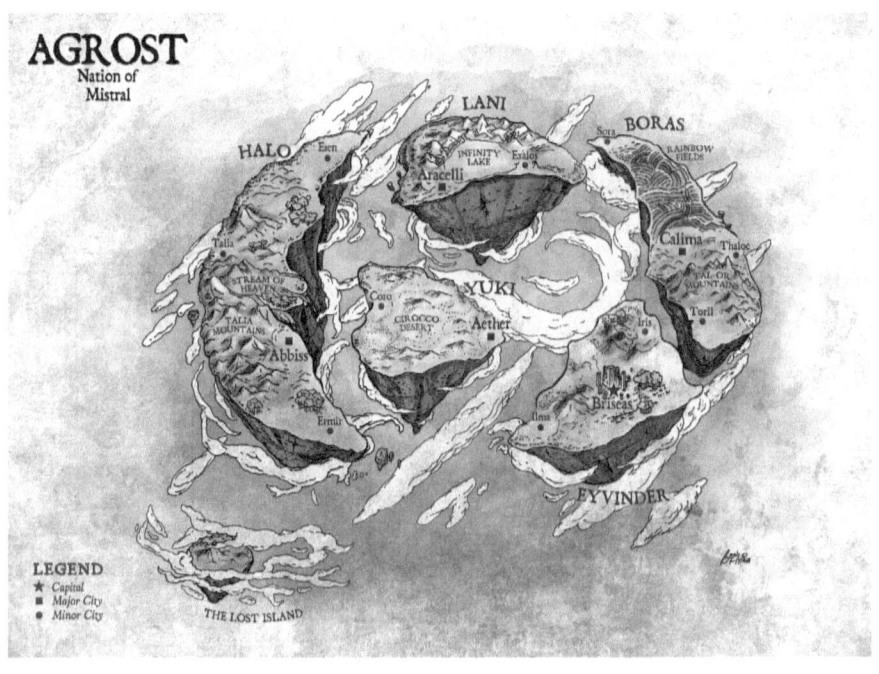

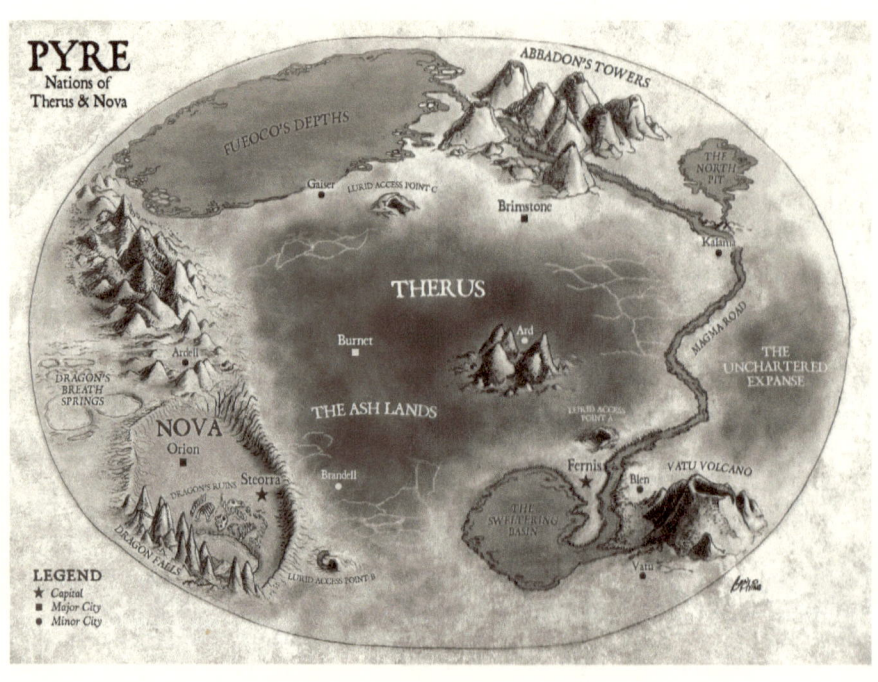

PYRE
Nations of
Therus & Nova

ABBADON'S TOWERS

FUEOCO'S DEPTHS

THE NORTH PIT

Gaiser    LURID ACCESS POINT C

Brimstone

Kaiana

THERUS

Burnet    Ard

MAGMA ROAD

Ardell

THE UNCHARTERED EXPANSE

DRAGON'S BREATH SPRINGS

THE ASH LANDS

LURID ACCESS POINT A

NOVA

Orion

Brandell

Fernis    VATU VOLCANO

DRAGON'S RUINS    Steorra

Blen

THE SWELTERING BASIN

DRAGON FALLS

Vatu

LURID ACCESS POINT B

LEGEND
★ Capital
■ Major City
● Minor City

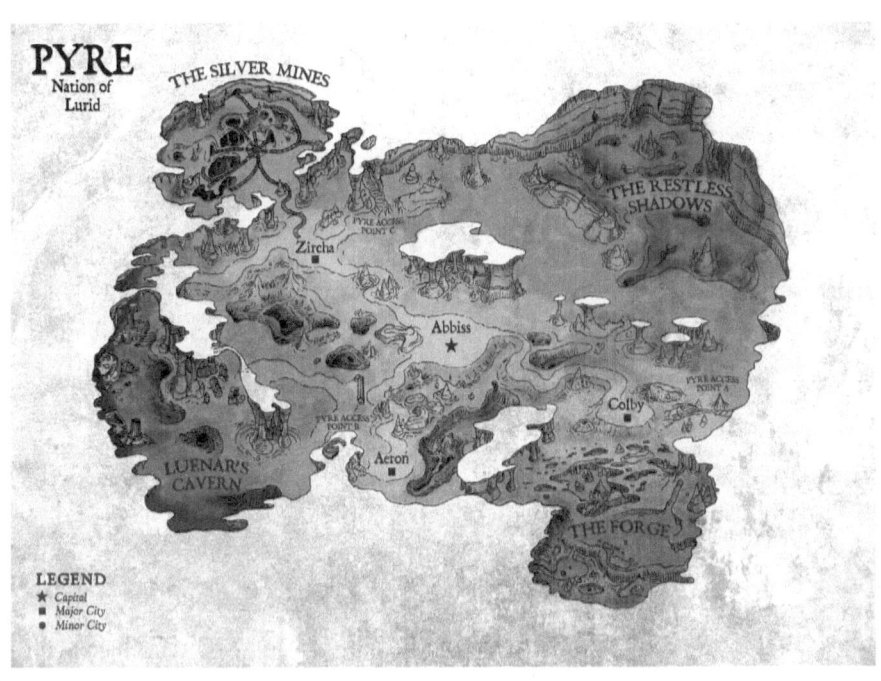

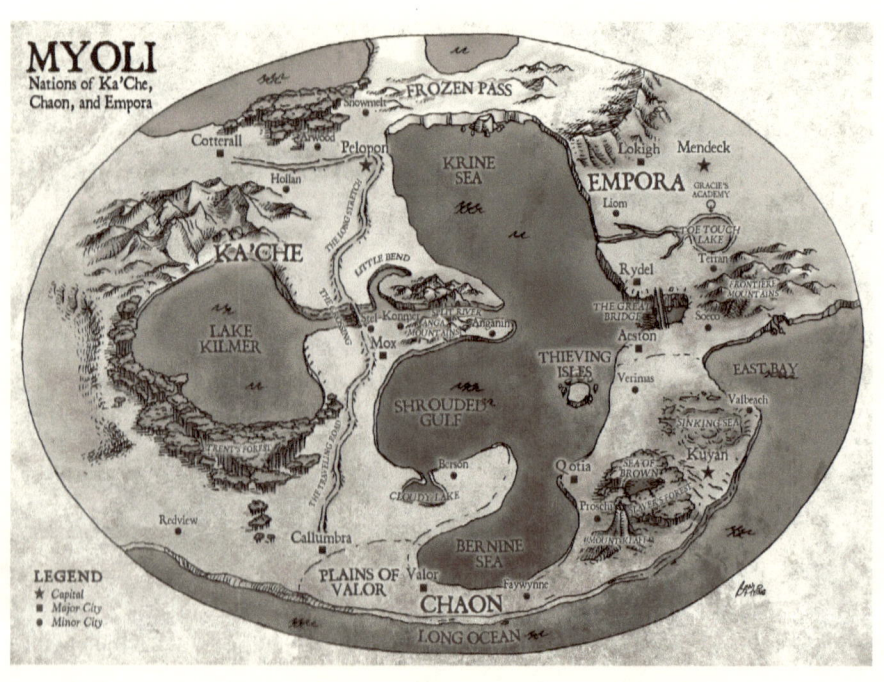

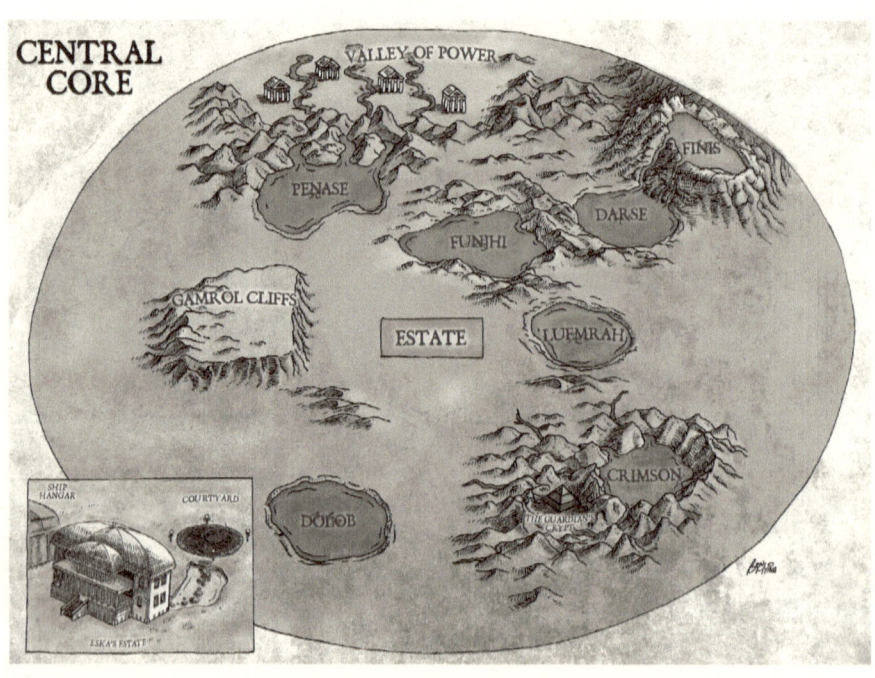

# CHARACTER TREES

This section of the novel is designed to give readers a sense of reference for the characters in the novel. Each nation will be displayed along with the ruling house and their sigil. Those who make up that house will be noted below. In certain cases, some characters in the story will not be directly related to the house, in that instance, their relationship to the house will be explained on the page. It's important to note that I only listed the houses that are pertinent to this novel so as not to overwhelm you more than necessary.

After making your way through the nations of importance and the families in power, a few pages will be taken to detail the two prominent academies in the story and those who attend them, along with a few of their sayings and beliefs. Finally, a brief history on how the Twelve came to be and a list of their attributes will be shown at the end.

Thank you for reading and I hope this helps you as you make your way through the book.

# THE CENTRAL CORE

G UARDIAN EDWYRD ESKA, Guardian of the Core for 185 years. Bonded to a dragon named, VESEL. Has one sister, ALICIA, deceased. Was sponsored to participate in his own Trials by LORD GARRETT OMYON from Nova. Has four respective aides called his conseleigh:

- TUNDRA IYCEL, conseleigh of the planet Onkh. Before being an aide for Guardian Eska, she was Lady of Sereya. He has been in Eska's service for thirty-five years.

- LUVAN KATORE, conseleigh of the planet Agrost. Before being an aide for Guardian Eska, he was a politician for the nation of Mistral. He has been in Eska's service for thirty years. He is now currently dismissed from his duties for disobeying the Guardian's orders.

- ETHEN RORUM, conseleigh of the planet Myoli. Before being an aide for Guardian Eska, he was a weapons' instructor and trainer for the Lord of Chaon, Zalos Kapache. He has been in Eska's service for fourteen years.

- RIAGAN INFERNO, conseleigh of the planet Pyre. Before being an aide for Guardian Eska, he was Lord of Therus. He has been in Eska's service for eight years.

- CRONOS, one of the four Sages, and is the only one who speaks. Is of First Blood and helps train the apprentice after Coronation. Very versed in the language of Power.

- COLIN, the oldest, most respected and trusted servant for Guardian Eska.

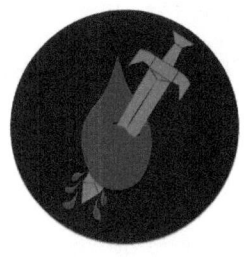

# Nation of Acquava

A ITON PAEN, Lord of Acquava. Son to HYDRO PAEN THE FIRST and ATESIA, both of whom are deceased. Has two siblings:

- HYDRO THE SECOND, heir to Acquavan throne and also a contestant to partake in Guardian Eska's Trials.

- ANYA, deceased.

**Figures of Import:**
- DARIEN DORNELL, receiver to Lord Paen.

- LEN POSAIR, advisor to Lord Paen.

- ELIAS WARD, lead adored to Lord Paen.

- KORTH CENTELL, head acqua guard, from the Hart Isles.

- YUNVA YIGYR, one of Lord Paen's acqua guards.

- KENT POIL, one of Lord Paen's aqua guards.

- CASSIUS FRAUSTER, one of Lord Paen's acqua guards, from Gar, deceased.

- HOLDEN HAUGHTER, one of Lord Paen's acqua guards.

- PROFESSOR IGNIS HARUKO, private Power instructor for the Paen family.

**Marquises of the Lesser Houses in Acquava:**

- ROY TITYLE, marquis of the Katarh province.

- MARQISS PUWL, marquis of the Rhemu province.

- HEKTER SIGURD, marquis of the Roil province.

- ALYN BLOCTER, marquis of the Summer Isles.

- CADELL PERIWINKLE, marquis of the Hart Isles.

- SETH AXYEL, marquis of the Talyn province.

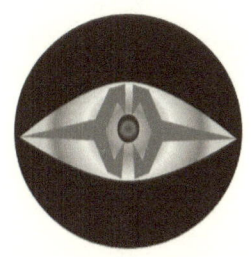

# Nation of Gar

O LIVIA APRAH, Lady of Gar. Only daughter of the deceased VISIS and AUTUMN APRAH.

**Figures of Import:**
- HORM DUBHALEN, head elite for Lady Aprah

- CORRIGAN BRIGGS, second in command to Lady Aprah's Father of CADMAR BRIGGS, a contestant who participated in Guardian Eska's Trials currently completing The Passage.

- Jöðurr ELDREDGE, advisor to Lady Aprah.

- Gøti LANAM, receiver to Lady Aprah.

**Marquises of the Lesser Houses in Gar:**
- ROWAN BERNAL, marquis of the major city of Nore.

- WILLIAM CREAZON, marquis of the major city of Brockstun.

- ROGER LUTEN, baron of the minor city of Roan.

# NATION OF SEREYA

A STOR GRIME, deceased. Had two wives, both deceased. First wife was named NEVA gave birth to WHITTIKER, currently a weapons instructor at the academy of Storm Academy. Second wife, WYNTER gave birth to CANICE, currently studying the Adored Arts on Pyre. These sons are now currently the rulers of Sereya.

**Figures of Import:**

- KALEN KATARH, advisor to Lord Grime.

- JEL PARON, receiver to Lord Grime.

**Marquises of the Lesser Houses in Sereya:**

- NICHOLAS COLDEN, marquis of Eurador

- CONNER ERTICH, baron of the minor city of Soya.

# Nation of Cresica

LINN CLAYSE, Lady of Cresica. Lives in the capital, Syf. Single. Her father is RYBERT. Mother, LYNDA, deceased.

**Figures of Import:**

- AERYN SHIREWOOD, advisor to Lady Clayse.

- EMBRY KNOSSOL, receiver to Lady Clayse.

- ROLAND, personal guard.

**Marchionesses of the Lesser Houses in Cresica:**

- ALBONY EVENGALE, marchioness of the major city, Stynt. Has two children OSWYN (older) and EZRA (younger), now deceased.

- MARA SURG, marchioness of the major city, Lisyn.

- TIPHANE TALHEND, marchioness of the major city, Cruxe.

- MELODON SHEER, marchioness of the Triangle Islands.

# Nation of Epoch

D AVEN EVBER, Lord of Epoch. Lives in Castle Thoth, in city it was named after, Thoth. Married to DAWN. Has one son, CAIN, who participated in Guardian Eska's Trials.

**Figures of Import:**

- NATHAN ALAOIS, advisor to Lord Evber.

- FINNIAN LUGUS, receiver to Lord Evber.

- CASTOR LEELAN, head of the owl guards.

**Marquises of Lesser Houses in Epoch:**

# Nation of Ka'Che

A BRAHAM VANGLE, Lord of Ka'Che. Son of TYON. Lives in Pelopon, the capital. Married to SHAYNA. Has four children:

**Abraham has three other siblings:**
- LUKAS, an older brother who is Denied.

- ELORINE SESSO who is married to RAMSEY.

- BRISINE BERRESE, the youngest, married to LARON. Have two children and one adopted child:

  ○ JAMAAL, oldest son. Married to REINE. Has two children, AMAYA, four years old, and KALANI, six years old.

  ○ ZAIN, a student at Gazo's Academy. Also, a contestant who participated in Guardian Eska's Trials.

  ○ ZAKK SHIREN, adopted son of Brisine and Laron. Family murdered at the age of six. Taken in at the age of twelve. Another contestant who was to participate in Guardian Eska's Trials but never ended up participating.

**Figures of Import:**
- ERRION VESK, advisor to Lord Vangle. Nicknamed ERIE and the LORD'S EAR.

- OWLEN MANSEN, receiver to Lord Vangle.

- AENEAS KHRÉOS, captain of the *Sea's Commander*.

- BERN DENARDI, first captain of the *Sea's Commander*.

- GERALD STARSHINE, a royal guard in service to Lord Vangle, deceased.

**Marquises of Lesser Houses of Ka'Che:**
- RAMSEY SESSO, marquis of the major city, Cotterall.

- BRYNN ROPIS, marquis of the major city, Callumbra.

- DARAN MOXXIE, marquis of the major city, Mox.

- AARON NOR, baron of minor city, Snowmelt

- CRAIG STONMER, baron of minor city, Hollan

- DEREK WORMWOOD, baron of minor city, Arwood

# NATION OF EMPORA

V ICTOR ZIGARDA, Lord of Empora. Lives in Mendeck. Never married. Had one younger brother, RENAUL, now deceased. Renaul's legacy was carried on by three children:

- HAYDEN

- SELBY

- MEADE

**Figures of Import:**
- EDWYN LYZE, advisor to Zigarda.

- YUAN SHIMES, receiver to Zigarda.

- DR. GENUS CERE, lead scientist for Zigarda.

- ZAKK SHIREN, lead bodyguard for Zigarda.

**Marquises of Lesser Houses in Empora:**
- PILLIAN DESMIER, marquis of the major city, Lokigh.

- SHEAMOUS STRONGHAND, marquis of the major city, Soeco.

- MYCKEL CRUNE, marquis of the major city, Rydel.

# THE TWELVE

The gestalt that is the Twelve are the warriors who survived the Great War and managed to escape before Gladima sealed itself away. Born on Gladima and endowed with First Blood, the Twelve used their Power and authority of birthright to claim home to the other planets as their home had now vanished. By showcasing their strength and ability, many citizens view them with awe and wonder and have surmised that they are deities sent to rule over Gladonus in the absence of the Ancients. Those belonging to the Heavol Tribe were created by Ancient Lyoen. Those belonging to the Evolic Tribe were created by Ancient Bane.

Rivals towards one another, and tensions still high after the Great War, a constant feud ended with them needing to quell the events of the first Pirini Lilapa (year 150 AGW) together. What's more, a prophecy floated upon the air that spoke of the Twelve's loss of Power. The considerable effort it took to stop Pirini Lilapa and the vulnerability that it exposed them to, along with their heightened sense of paranoia due to the prophecy, made them realize they would need to create a role to handle such an occurrence if it should happen again. The first Guardian of the Core, Jorey Raule, fulfilled that role in the year 165 AGW (After Great War).

**The Heavol Tribe**
Fueoco = God of heat and fire.
Orekus = God of underworld.
Myethos = God of the suns and day.
Saeluste = Goddess of mental health, wisdom, and intelligence.
Trema = Goddess of the lands and harvest.
Lucine = Goddess of birth and peace.

**The Evolic Tribe**
Pearl = Goddess of water, seas, and oceans.
Anemie = Goddess of the sky, lightning, and Axiumé.
Luenar = God of the moons, night.
Theothe = God of physical health and beauty.

Crestal = Goddess of cold winds and winter seasons.
Tomahawke = God of war and death and suffering.

# ABOUT THE AUTHOR

    Michael E. Thies currently is an English educator living in Suzhou, China. He completed a master's degree in Digital Strategy from the University of Florida. An aficionado of gym, cooking, and eating well, he is also a certified Holistic Health Coach through the Institute of Integrative Nutrition (IIN). To keep up-to-date more with him make sure to visit his website www.michael ethies.com

# ALSO BY